THE BANK

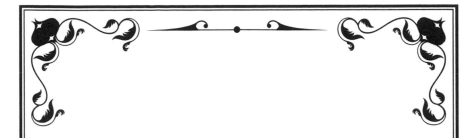

THE
BANK

BENTLEY LITTLE

Cemetery Dance Publications
Baltimore
2020

Cemetery Dance Publications
132-B Industry Lane, Unit #7
Forest Hill, MD 21050
http://www.cemeterydance.com

The characters and events in this book are fictitious.
Any similarity to real persons, living or dead,
is coincidental and not intended by the author.

First Trade Hardcover Edition Printing

ISBN: 978-1-58767-740-3

Cover Artwork and Design © 2020 by Elderlemon Design
Interior Design © 2020 by Desert Isle Design, LLC

PROLOGUE

1932

THEO SAT NEXT to his dad on a hard seat in the bank president's office. He had never been inside the bank before, and the surroundings were intimidating. The walls of the high-ceilinged room were paneled in dark expensive-looking wood, and the space was larger than their entire house. The president's desk before them seemed the size of a small boat, and the man himself was big and fat and didn't look as though he'd ever had a hungry day in his life.

The president gave a cursory glance to the papers Theo's dad had given him, then dropped them on top of his desk as though he found their touch greasy and unappealing. "I'm not sure what you want me to do here, Mr. Gianopuolos. My loan officer thoroughly examined your case and provided you with the reasons why he didn't think it feasible for our bank to lend you the money you requested." He spread out his hands expansively. "I'm not sure what you expect me to do here."

"Overturn his decision." Theo's dad leaned forward in his chair. "This is a good idea, Mr. Jones."

"Times are tough, Mr. Gianopuolos, as I'm sure you know. The bank is not in a position to take irresponsible risks."

Theo could hear the frustration in his dad's voice. "This is hardly irresponsible. And it's barely even a risk. Yes, times are tough. But that's exactly why this sort of business has such potential. The location I've chosen is down the block from the movie palace, on the same side of the street as the First Baptist Church, the biggest church in town. People will be walking by the restaurant constantly. And, as I explained in my interview with Mr. Thompson, I plan to leave the front of the restaurant open, no wall, like a grocer's. That's the way they do it in Europe, although they have tables on the sidewalk. They call them cafés."

"As I indicated, there's really nothing I can do here. If I start overruling the determinations of my staff, they'll lose confidence in their ability to make decisions, and our entire system will cease to work. I have to trust my employees to do their jobs, a sentiment I'm sure you can understand, since if you had your own business, you would have to trust and believe in your employees as well."

"But this is a good investment!"

"Be that as it may..."

His dad took a deep breath. "I understand that you might not believe in this idea, but if I could just show you—"

"Oh, we believe in the idea, Mr. Gianopuolos." The president leaned forward. "We don't believe in *you*."

His dad was taken aback. "What?"

"That name. *Gianopuolos.* What is it? Greek? People aren't going to want to buy food from a Greek. Not in this town. We want real food here. American food. Now, while the bank could not support an establishment that had tables on the sidewalk which would impede pedestrian traffic, your idea of a restaurant with an open front is intriguing, and if the right man came along, we might see fit to invest..."

Theo tuned out the president. Next to him, his dad had slumped in his chair, and when Theo hazarded a glance in that direction, he saw a look of humiliated defeat on his father's reddening face. He wished his dad would jump up and punch that fat banker right in the nose. But his father was not that kind of man, and such an action would only get them kicked out of the bank, possibly arrested. As he'd learned already, even at age eight, rich people had power and poor people didn't, and if you didn't stay in your place there would be trouble.

So his dad had to sit there and take it, and afterward he shook the bank president's hand, thanked him for his time, took back his papers, and he and Theo left the office. They walked, defeated, through the lobby toward the front door. Were the tellers smiling? Were people laughing at them behind their backs? It sure felt like it, and Theo wished that someone would rob the bank and take all of its money.

His dad must have misinterpreted his anger as disappointment. He put an arm around Theo's shoulder. "It's all right, son. We'll be fine. Maybe not as rich as we could have been, but we'll be fine." He wanted Theo to believe that—*he* wanted to believe it—but Theo sensed a change in his father, a retreat from hope, a withdrawal into himself. It was a difference that showed in his voice, even in his walk, and Theo was afraid that change in his dad would be permanent, a fear that was to prove not unfounded.

They walked out of the double doors onto the sidewalk.

When *he* grew up, Theo vowed, nothing like this would *ever* happen to him.

He would make sure of it.

ONE

I

DENNIS WHITTAKER, THE Montgomery High School principal, a thin, stressed-looking man in an unfashionable brown suit, frowned as he looked from Kyle to Anita. "I don't know what we're going to do about your boy."

Kyle glanced at Nick, sitting between them and staring at his shoes.

"If you'd tell us what he's done," Anita said crisply, "it might help."

The principal picked up a stapled sheaf of papers from his desk, leaning forward and handing it to her. "This is your son's play," he said. "Just look at the title."

Kyle leaned over to see the cover sheet. *"I'm Taking a Shit* By Nicholas Decker."

"The play consists of a young man sitting upon a toilet for an hour and a half, staring at the audience, repeating the title over and over again."

Kyle took the pages from his wife and flipped through them. Sure enough, the directions and dialogue on every page were the same:

KENNY
(Grunting)

Uhhh, I'm taking a shit. Uhhh, I'm taking a shit.

"You know we can't have this in our school. I don't care how avant garde Nick thinks he is, this is just not proper subject matter for Montgomery High."

"Mrs. Nelson said we could write whatever we wanted!"

The principal fixed the boy with a stare that brooked no argument. "This is not what she meant and you know it, young man."

"We'll take care of this," Kyle said, standing. "Thank you for bringing it to our attention."

Whittaker sighed. "I'm afraid it's not as easy as that. With the graffiti on the gym last week and the paper doing that series on cyber-bullying, the board's under a lot of pressure to crack down on troublemakers. And if they're under pressure, I'm under pressure. I can't afford to be lenient here. We're talking a minimum two-day suspension."

"For writing a *play*?" Anita said.

"For writing *that* play, yes."

Kyle tried to calm the waters. Knowing Anita, this could escalate quickly. "Couldn't you just call it probation and let him stay? It's honestly more of a punishment to keep him in school than to let him stay home."

"I'm sorry."

"Let me get this straight," Anita said. "My son is being suspended from school for completing an assignment in a way that you do not like, while students who did not complete the assignment at *all* face zero punishment."

"Those students will receive failing grades. And it has nothing to do with what I like: Nick here used profanity."

"So what sort of grade will Nick be receiving? Or is he to be punished twice by being suspended *and* receiving a failing grade?"

"That will be up to the teacher."

Anita stood, and Kyle and Nick followed suit. "This is a slap-on-the-wrist offense, Dennis, and you know it. Drinking at school? Taking drugs? Stealing? Fighting? Those are suspension crimes. Using a bad word? Slap on the wrist, Dennis, slap on the wrist."

Nick seemed surprised to hear his mother address the principal by his first name, and Kyle realized that his son was probably not aware of the fact that the two of them had dated back in high school.

In a small town, the past was never past.

Without another word, Anita marched out of the principal's office, Kyle and Nick following. The three of them walked past the counselors' doors and past the attendance desk into the school's main hallway. "Get what you need out of your locker," Kyle told his son. "We'll wait here."

Nick hurried away, stopping before a bank of lockers halfway down the corridor.

"Dennis." Kyle shook his head. "Did you notice how he said '*upon* a toilet' instead of 'on?'"

She nodded, smiling despite her annoyance.

"Still trying to impress you."

She hit his shoulder. "Knock it off."

He watched Nick open his locker and take out a book, putting it in his backpack. He lowered his voice. "I know we need to take this seriously, be sober concerned parents and all. But...*Taking a Shit*?" Kyle chuckled. "That was pretty damn funny."

"It was hard not to laugh," Anita admitted, smiling.

Nick had slung the backpack over his shoulder and was already returning. "Okay, so you need to take him home," Kyle told Anita as he approached. "I have to get back to the store."

"I have to go back to work, too."

"I know, but Gary's out today. There's just me, and I'm already half an hour late opening. These days, I need all the customers I can get. Someone stops by and sees that the store's closed, they're likely to go online or—"

Anita nodded. "I get it. I'll take Nick."

"Take me where?" he asked, walking up.

"Home," Anita said sternly. "Where you will remain and do your schoolwork."

Nick nodded. "So how long's my suspension? He said it's a

'minimum two-day suspension,' but he didn't give a maximum, and kind of left it open, it seemed like."

"Shit," Anita said. "Wait here." And she strode back to the principal's office.

Neither Kyle nor Nick commented on the fact that she had just uttered the same curse that had gotten Nick suspended, and a moment later she emerged into the hallway. "Two days."

Kyle nodded. "Two days." They walked outside, where he pinched Nick's shoulder and gave Anita a peck on the cheek. "See you guys at home."

He headed across the faculty parking lot to where he'd pulled his Ram truck in between two teachers' cars, and Anita and Nick made their way toward the field, where Anita had parked her Kia in the visitor's lot.

2

ON his way downtown, Kyle had allowed himself the fantasy that when he got to the shop, there would be two or three people waiting patiently in line for it to open. But of course the sidewalk was empty, and behind the name "Brave New World" painted on the front window, the bookstore was dark.

He pulled around the alley in back, his oversized pickup taking up two of the three spaces behind the building. Entering through the rear door, he switched on the lights as he walked in. From the safe beneath the bottom shelf of the small storage space next to the bathroom, he counted out money for the register before going up to the front of the store, unlocking the glass door and flipping the sign from Closed to Open. He popped a Mozart CD into the player behind the counter, and music issued from the speakers he'd mounted in the corners of the room.

What he hadn't told Anita was that Gary was out today because he was interviewing for another job, at the Costco in Sirena.

Gary was not stupid. He knew that the store was struggling, and he knew that it might be only a matter of time before Kyle had to let him go. Sirena was forty miles away, but the starting salary at Costco was more than Gary was making now, after five years, and the benefits were far beyond anything Kyle could offer.

Which was why Kyle had given Gary his blessing.

Bookstores had been dying on the vine since the advent of Amazon, and while independent and used bookstores had hung on a bit longer than most of the chains, they were falling by the wayside as well. For awhile, *Harry Potter*, *Twilight* and other blockbuster young adult books that appealed to all ages had guaranteed at least minimum foot traffic. And children's books had been consistent sellers no matter what the state of the economy. But phones and their game apps continued to significantly chip away at people's reading time, and Brave New World was having a difficult go of it, especially since the junior college bookstore had expanded its inventory to include not only textbooks but general fiction and nonfiction.

Some of the surviving chains now included Starbucks or Starbucks-like cafés in their stores, trying to encourage patrons to hang out and (hopefully) buy more, and in his most ambitious moments, Kyle had considered doing such a thing himself. His shop was adjacent to a narrow empty retail space that could easily be converted into a coffee bar/bakery with a wifi hotspot, but unless he won the lottery or received an inheritance from an unknown rich relative, there was no way he could afford to buy, rent or renovate anything.

And even if he did, there was no guarantee it would work out.

He could end up even more deeply in debt.

Thank God Anita had a traditional job with an assured income. They couldn't really survive on her salary, but if he could continue to limp along the way he had been, they should be able to get by. And, who could tell, maybe eventually things would turn around.

Although that seemed less and less likely by the day.

Kyle sat behind the counter and switched on his computer to check his emails. Spam mostly. Ads from publishers for upcoming releases. Offers from distributors that he would like to be able to take advantage of but could not afford.

The bell above the door jingled, and he looked up expectantly, hoping to see a customer, but it was just the mailman. "Kind of early today, aren't you, Gil?"

"Doing the route backward. Thought I'd mix things up a bit." The mailman handed Kyle a stack of envelopes and catalogs held together with a rubber band. "How's business?"

"Slow."

"Downtown ain't what it used to be," Gil agreed. "Hell, the postal service ain't what it used to be. Thank God for junk mail, or I'd be out of a job." He nodded as he opened the door and stepped back onto the sidewalk. "See you tomorrow."

Kyle waved goodbye and watched through the front window as the mailman continued up the street. Sorting through the envelopes in his hand, he came across an official-looking one from the bank and tore it open, frowning. According to the statement inside, he had not made last month's mortgage payment on the store and now owed the payment amount plus a hundred dollar late charge.

He specifically remembered writing that check. Now he was going to have to spend half the day on the phone trying to get this mess straightened out. "Morons," he said aloud, as his first customer of the day walked into the store.

"You talkin' about the gov'ment?" Durl Meadows grinned as he approached the counter. Durl had been one of his very first customers when he'd opened Brave New World, special ordering a copy of *The Anarchist's Cookbook*. He and Kyle saw eye-to-eye on almost nothing, but theirs was a friendly, almost playful opposition, and Durl had turned out to be one of the store's most loyal customers, continuing to order self-published right-wing conspiracy books as well as, incongruously, romance novels. "For my wife," he always said, although Kyle suspected that was not the case.

Kyle sighed. "No, not the government. The bank."

Durl shrugged, still grinning. "Same diff'rence."

"They say I didn't make my mortgage payment."

"And you did."

Kyle nodded.

"Now you have to call India to get it all untangled."

"Probably."

"Well, have fun with that." Laughing, Durl headed over to the stand of new releases facing the front window. He scanned the titles but obviously found nothing there to interest him. Motioning toward the alcove at the left rear corner of the store, he said, "Looks like you're expanding your used section."

Kyle nodded. "I've been getting a lot of trade-ins lately. Mystery and romance readers go through books quickly. People like you—"

"My wife."

"That's what I was going to say. People like your wife speed through books. Makes sense to offer them a place where they can trade old books in for ones they haven't read yet."

"Or they could trade with each other an' skip the middleman."

Kyle nodded sagely. "Sure. They could do that. If they don't believe in the free market and want to live in some hippie Communist world where no one owns anything and no one needs money and everyone just shares what they have, man."

Durl chuckled. "Y' got me."

"I haven't had time to put them on the shelf yet, but you might take a look in that box on the floor. Rene Wallace brought them in, and there's quite a few Nora Roberts in there. Maybe there's some Delia hasn't read yet."

"Maybe so," Durl said, walking back toward the corner. "Thanks."

Kyle picked up the mortgage statement from the bank, found the toll-free customer service number below the bank's corporate address in the upper left corner. "If you need any help, let me know!" he called out to Durl.

"Will do!"

Prepared for a long wait, he picked up his phone and called the bank.

3

DRIVING Nick home, Anita passed by not only the optometrist's office where she worked, but also the nursery, where Steven was visible behind the chainlink fence, watering a table of perennials. She tried not to let her expression change, maintaining her focus on the road ahead, though her face felt hot and she could sense a sudden increase in her pulse rate. They were scheduled to meet today at lunch—not at the nursery this time, but at his place. She was not sure that was such a good idea. They'd been spending a lot of lunches together, and everything so far had been leading in one direction, but flirting was different than...what came after flirting, and maybe it would be smarter for her to use Nick's suspension as an excuse to cancel. She could back away from the precipice, get things back on a friendship footing.

But was that what she really wanted?

She thought of the way it had felt last week when he had taken her hand in his, his thumb gently rubbing the knuckles on her—

"Mom! Pay attention!"

Anita slammed on her brakes, barely avoiding hitting the car in front of her, which, for some reason, had come to a stop in the middle of the street.

"Were you daydreaming? It's like you didn't even see that guy stop!"

"I'm all right," she said. "I was just...distracted for a moment."

A skinny, boyish woman threw open the passenger door of the car and bolted out, running toward the Shell station. The car swerved to the right, across the other lane, following her.

"What's that about?" Nick wondered.

"None of our business."

Nick looked out of his window behind them as they moved forward again. "You think she was kidnapped and trying to escape?"

"No, but maybe you should put that imagination to use and write about something like that next time instead of...what you did."

They drove the rest of the way home in silence. When they arrived, Anita quickly unlocked and opened the front door before stepping aside. "I'm already late for work. Close and lock the door behind you. And stay here. I don't want you leaving the house."

"I thought it was a slap-on-the-wrist offense."

"It is. But you're still suspended, buddy. And if that little stunt showed anything, it showed poor judgment. Did you really think that was an acceptable thing to turn in as your writing assignment? To Mrs. Nelson? At Montgomery High?"

"No," he admitted.

"All right, then."

"But I can go on the internet, right? Or watch TV?"

"After you get your homework done."

He grinned. "I only went to first period. So I only have one assignment."

"Then you email your teachers and get your work for the next two days. This isn't a vacation." She glanced at her watch. "I need to go. But I'm checking up on you. I'm calling the house phone. Randomly. Throughout the day. And if you're not there to answer it..."

"What if I'm in the bathroom?"

"You heard me."

Nick laughed. "Don't worry. I'm not going anywhere."

Anita did the I'm-watching-you hand gesture, using two fingers to point at her eyes then one to point at Nick, before getting back into the car and making a U-turn in the street. He was a good kid and she trusted him, but as this incident showed, he was a bit of a smartass and a little too full of himself for his own good.

She was hoping that this would be one of those rare days when Dr. Wilson was late to the office, but no such luck. Immediately after pulling in, she saw the optometrist's Mercedes parked in the small lot on the side of the building. Pulling next to it, she quickly got out, grabbed her purse and hurried through the side door, where Dr. Wilson, striding down the short hallway, turned to see her walking in.

"Sorry," she apologized. "Family emergency."

The optometrist was frowning, but as that was his natural expression, she wasn't sure if he had any reaction at all to her excuse. She chose to believe he did not, and made her way to the front counter, stashing her purse beneath the desk. The office had only been open for a half-hour, and as yet there were no patients, but the optometrist was strict about employees showing up on time, and she mentally kicked herself for not calling in to explain that she was going to be late. It would have made her seem less...flaky.

Dr. Wilson hated flakes.

The optometrist had already gone back into his personal office and closed the door, and Anita waved hello to Jen, the other assistant, who was rearranging a display of designer frames.

"*You're* late?" Jen said, walking over. "That's a first."

"Happens to the best of us."

"What was it?"

"Nick got suspended."

"Really?" The other assistant dropped her voice. "Was it drugs? My nephew Tommy got caught with marijuana a couple years ago. Never recovered. He's still a screwup."

Anita shook her head. "No. Nothing like that. The principal called us in because Nick wrote a play with the word 'shit' in it."

"That's all? Well...shit."

They both laughed.

The buzzer rang as the front door opened and a patient walked in. After that, there was a mini-rush, and all three of them were suddenly busy as two new patients came in for eye exams and three older patients either ordered or picked up glasses.

Everyone was gone by eleven, and with the office empty and no appointments until one-fifteen, Dr. Wilson told Anita and Jen they could take an early lunch. The two of them paused outside the office. "Are you...going over to the nursery?" Jen asked carefully.

"Why?" Anita responded, suddenly defensive.

"No...I...Sorry. No reason."

Was it that obvious?

The situation with Steven was clearly spiraling out of control. She needed to nip this in the bud, to use a gardening term, to stop things before they went any further and did some real damage. The best idea would be to stand Steven up, not show and not tell him and let him figure things out from there.

Standing him up would only make him more interested.

She knew that.

Was that why she was doing it?

She thought of his hands touching hers, the way it felt when he stood next to her.

"No. I have no plans," Anita told Jen. "Want to grab some lunch?"

"I'll get my purse."

Anita walked outside and waited next to the door, staring numbly out at the three cars in the small parking lot. What was wrong with her? She had a good life, a nice family. Was she so self-destructive that she just had to sabotage things when they were going well? It's what her parents had said when she'd dropped out of ASU her sophomore year, and she was beginning to think that maybe they were right.

Wasn't Nick doing exactly the same thing with his *Taking a Shit* play?

Maybe it ran in the family.

Kyle was the stable one, the rock, and he didn't deserve any of this. He was a good father, a good husband, and deep down she loved him. The last thing she wanted to do was hurt him.

So why was she allowing this to happen?

Jen opened the back door and emerged outside. "Ready to go?"

Taking Jen's car, they drove over to Juan Wang's, the new Asian fusion fast food joint that had opened up in what had previously been the Lottaburger. The tables were all outside, but it was a nice day and they had the place to themselves. After ordering, they waited until their names were called, and then carried their trays from the pickup window to their table.

Anita unwrapped a straw and stuck it through the hole in the top of her cup of iced green tea. "So what's going on with your loan?" she asked. "Find out if you qualify yet?"

Jen sighed. "We actually don't. But with my parents co-signing... maybe." She took a bite of eggroll burrito. "Do you realize how humiliating it is to be thirty-five years old and still have to have your parents vouch for you? My twenty-year high school reunion's coming up in three years. You'd think I'd be enough of an adult by now to be able to buy a house with my husband. But no…"

"What's your credit score?"

"Pretty good. Both of us are responsible, always pay on time. It's the income. We don't make enough, even together, for the bank to think we can handle the payments on a house. Trailer, yes. House, no."

"What are you going to do if they turn you down?"

Jen shook her head. "Lane thinks we should try one of those online lenders. But I don't know. I've heard a lot of sketchy things about those places. I read the other day about one company that went under and sold all its debts to another lender who demanded immediate full payment from everyone who'd taken out loans."

Anita nodded. "It's the wild west out there on the internet. And I'm not sure how well-regulated some of those companies are. I think you're much safer with a real bank."

"Me, too. But it all depends on whether we're accepted or not." Jen held up her eggroll burrito. "This thing is really good. I didn't think I was going to like it, but it's amazing."

Anita speared a fiesta wonton with her fork. "Mine's good, too."

"I should probably go back to bringing my own lunch to work, though. Try to save a few bucks." Jen sighed. "Then maybe I wouldn't have to keep relying on my parents."

4

SEVENTEEN years old, and he still didn't like staying in the house by himself.

The minute his mom drove off, Nick turned on the TV in the living room and the light in the hallway, needing to hear some noise and wanting make sure there were no parts of the house that were dark—even though it was mid-morning on a particularly bright day. Such fears were childish, he knew, but he couldn't help how he felt. He wondered if things would change once he became an adult, but the truth was, he didn't really see that happening. He'd be eighteen in less than a year, and it was hard to imagine any radical changes in personality taking place in that time.

He wasn't exactly sure why he still got scared being home alone. The house wasn't that old. It wasn't as if they lived in some historic mansion where a rich madman had murdered his wife in the 1800s. Theirs was just a regular home on a regular street with a bunch of others that looked just like it.

But he'd always had a vivid imagination, one that had inevitably turned toward darkness. As a little kid, he remembered seeing a movie on television about an escaped lunatic who lived between the walls of an ordinary family's home, and for years afterward, every stray noise Nick heard in the house made him think that someone was hiding in the walls or the attic or the crawlspace.

His phone buzzed, and Nick picked it up to see a text from a number he did not recognize.

It was some bank, offering him his own credit card.

That was weird.

He automatically deleted the text. It was probably just some scam. How could he be eligible for a credit card? He didn't even have a job. Someone was just fishing for personal information to use in order to create a fake account or…get a credit card.

Maybe he *was* eligible.

The idea appealed to him. Last summer, he'd wanted to upgrade his phone and had asked his dad for a loan, only to be told that the embarrassing antique he carted around was perfectly fine. If he'd had his own credit card, he could have charged it.

His phone buzzed again, but there was no text this time, no call. Apparently, the phone was ringing for no reason.

Was he being hacked?

Suddenly filled with panic, he flipped his phone over, pulled off the cover, slid open the back and yanked out the battery. He had no idea how sophisticated hacking operations were these days, but since phones could be tracked even when they were turned off, it made sense that they could be hacked that way, too.

The one thing in his favor was the fact that he almost never put correct personal information about himself online. His Google account was connected to a fake name with a fake address. For anything requiring a birthdate, he typed in random numbers.

Although…

The phone bill was paid by his dad, so it was probably linked to a credit card.

Should he call his father and let him know? If he did, his dad would just give him a lecture about *allowing* himself to be hacked. Besides, there was no guarantee that that was what was going on.

Maybe it would be better if he just waited to see what happened.

He decided to keep the battery out of the phone for the rest of the day and then put it back in before his parents came home.

Leaving everything where it was, Nick walked into the kitchen and got a water bottle out of the refrigerator. Twisting off the top, he took a long drink as he looked out at the back yard through the window over the sink. If it wasn't a hack, what could have made his phone ring like that? he wondered. Was there something wrong with the device itself? Some sort of technical glitch?

Maybe it was a ghost.

The idea was absurd, and he knew it was absurd, but once in his mind, the notion was impossible to shake. He glanced back at the doorway. He was suddenly afraid to go into the living room and even *look* at his phone, certain for some reason that he would see something on the no-longer-dead screen, a picture, the face of a little boy, an overly serious little boy with obsidian-black hair and hard piercing eyes, looking out at him.

This, Nick understood, was one reason he continued to scare himself even though he was almost an adult: the specificity of his fears. He was never afraid he was going to see some generic ghost or amorphous blob. It was always an old lady with no teeth hiding in the closet, or a gibbering monkey-faced man crawling down the hallway.

Or an overly serious little boy peeking out at him through his phone.

He had no idea where these ideas came from or why they occurred to him, but from the second his brain conjured such an image, he was consumed with nothing else until he could prove to himself that it was not real.

Forcing himself to be brave, steeling himself for whatever he might see, Nick returned to the living room and picked up his phone.

Nothing.

A black screen.

Relief flooded through him, and he put the battery back in, turning on the phone, reassured that he saw nothing unusual on the screen as it came to life. He probably had a touch of OCD, since the stress and worry he'd felt disappeared as quickly as it had come, replaced by a sense of calm.

The phone rang, and he jumped, nearly dropping it.

Before he could yank out the battery again—his first reaction—he saw from the number that the call was from was his friend Victor. A glance at the time told him that at school they were on break.

"Hey," he said, picking up.

"Where are you, man? What happened?"

"Suspended," Nick said, and felt a little proud. That was not something that had ever happened to either of them.

Victor's voice dropped conspiratorially. "What did you do?"

"Nothing. It was that play I wrote for Nelson's class."

"They suspended you for *that*?"

"Yeah."

"It's cuz it had the word 'shit' in it, right?"

"Which, right now, you are saying freely in the hallowed halls of Montgomery High," Nick said drily.

"How long are you suspended for?"

"Two days."

"What are me and Aaron supposed to do at lunch?"

"You'll figure something out."

The school bell rang in the background. "Gotta go," Victor said. "Later."

Nick clicked off. After talking to his friend, the house suddenly seemed quiet—*too* quiet—and he started to feel a little creeped out again. He checked to see if there'd been any messages sent in the minutes his phone had been off. There hadn't. And while he was glad there was no photo of a serious little boy, he was a little disappointed that there was no credit card offer.

Maybe he shouldn't have deleted that first text.

It would be nice to have his own credit card.

TWO

1

"**THE BANK CALLED.** Another foreclosure. They're faxing over the forms now."

"Goddamn it." Sheriff Brad Neth picked up his coffee cup, took a sip, then spit the coffee back into the cup, grimacing. There was nothing he hated more than cold coffee.

Unless it was enforcing a foreclosure eviction.

"Who is it?" he asked his deputy. "Anyone we know?"

Hank Dillman shrugged in that bony-shouldered way that Brad always found irritating. "She didn't say. Want me to check the fax?"

The sheriff waved him off.

Foreclosures were down from the peak of the recession, but this was still the second one in as many weeks, and Brad always got a queasy feeling in the pit of his stomach when he had to kick people out of their homes. Especially families. It didn't sit well with him, and while it was legal, it didn't feel right. He'd gone into law enforcement to catch bad guys, not to make life more difficult for good people who were down on their luck, and it seemed like a violation of his oath to conduct evictions on behalf of a private company. He was a *public* servant, damn it, and it was his job to uphold and enforce the law in order to protect the citizens of Montgomery.

"Carol!" he called. "Who's available this morning?"

There was a beat, then the receptionist called back, "Mitch is off, Hildy and Clint are taking nights this week, Vern and Issac are out on that domestic call, and Norris, Paul and both Bills are on patrol. I think it's just you and Hank."

Damn.

"Okay, thanks!"

The usual policy was to carry out an eviction as soon as the paperwork came in, but he didn't work for the bank. It wasn't his job to be at their beck and call. He was the sheriff. It was his decision when to send someone out, and he was going to do it when it was convenient for the department. Which meant when two of the others came back.

Hank poked his head in the door. "It's Carl Yates," he reported.

"Oh, crap."

There went his plan.

"You sure it's Carl? Not Chet?"

"It's Carl."

The sheriff pushed himself out of his seat. "That foundation's shaky to begin with. You put this kind of stress on it..." He grabbed his hat from the top of his file cabinet. "Come on. Let's see if we can talk him down before we kick him out."

The only car left in the lot was the SUV with the bald back tires, but Hank had driven his motorcycle, and Brad wasn't about to let the deputy into his own car, so he tossed Hank the SUV keys and said, "You drive."

They were nearly blasted out of their seats when the ignition was turned, all four speakers blaring a scratchy, static-y hard rock station out of Flagstaff. "Damn it," Brad said, turning off the radio.

"Issac."

"I told that asshole..." Brad picked up the paperwork that Hank had lain on the seat between them. "Where is it? Over on Juniper?"

"Yeah." Hank backed out of the parking space, swung around and pulled out of the lot onto the street. "So how are we going to handle this? You want me to let you do the talking?"

"Unless you have some insight that I don't."

"It's all yours, Sheriff."

Brad dropped the paperwork on the seat. "Thanks."

"Maybe we'll be lucky and he won't be at home. We can just post the notice, padlock the door—"

"He'll be home. They're always home."

Sure enough, Carl's pickup was in the carport, and the black space behind the shabby house's torn screen indicated that the door behind it was open. Picking up the stapled eviction pages, Brad and Hank got out of the vehicle. This was going to be a tricky one. Carl Yates was about as stable as a bowling alley built on quicksand. He might come out drunk and weeping, or he might barricade himself inside the home, hiding behind boxes of those reconstituted ink cartridges he sold.

Or he might allow himself to be evicted with no problem.

It was impossible to tell.

Brad approached the house warily, announcing his presence as he walked up the path to the front door. "Carl!" he called. "I'm here with Hank! Got a foreclosure order!" He thought he detected movement behind the screen door. "You hear me, Carl? Bank's taking back the house! You need to get your stuff together and get out!"

The screen opened just as Brad reached the porch step.

Carl, naked and holding a handgun, grinned at him. "How goes, it, Sheriff?"

"Damn it!" Brad dropped the papers as he fumbled for his own weapon. Behind him, he could hear Hank doing the same.

"We don't want no trouble, Carl," the deputy said.

"That's right," Brad assured him. "Your beef is with the bank, not us. We're just doing our job. So put the gun down, we'll forget this ever happened, and you get yourself a good lawyer and settle things with the bank." He had gotten into the stance and was aiming his weapon at the man on the porch, whose own gun was pointed downward, loosely grasped in his dangling hand.

Carl's smile suddenly disappeared, replaced by an expression of rage. "Get a lawyer?" he screamed. "Get a lawyer? I can't even make the monthly payments on this shithole!" With one swift movement, his hand was raised, the gun pointed at his temple.

"No!" Brad shouted.

And Carl pulled the trigger.

2

WHEN Coy Stinson was ten, his parents took him and his full piggy bank to the Valley National Bank, where a nice old lady helped him count all of his pennies, nickels, dimes and quarters. He had been entranced by the way each type of coin was carefully packed into a brown paper tube, all of them making hard solid rolls when they were filled: four groups of different-sized cylinders lined up in a neat row on top of the teller's countertop. He had then been given his very own passbook to keep track of his money, and a free calculator just for opening an account.

If it had been up to him, he would have gone back to the bank each time he found a penny on the ground or a dime in the coin return of a vending machine, handing his passbook to the teller so she could stamp the date and write in the amount he had deposited. But his parents had frowned on that idea and made him wait until his piggy bank was full.

The bank, to him, had seemed a wonderful place. Calm, quiet, warm in the winter and cool in the summer, the people nice and polite, adults addressing him as "sir."

The view from the inside was not as rosy.

He had worked at the Montgomery Community Bank since graduating from high school. Supplementing his work experience with classes taken at the community college, Coy had risen to the rank of loan officer and then senior loan officer. He liked being able to help people realize their dreams and improve their lives: get that new car, buy that new house, build that addition, purchase that adjacent lot. What he didn't like was turning people down, shattering their dreams, condemning them to the hardscrabble lives they were already living.

Foreclosures were the worst.

But that, luckily, was not his department. He *issued* loans. What happened after that was the responsibility of Cal and Maggie, who processed the payments. Theoretically, he had the hopeful, positive end of the transaction, the most optimistic part of the process, particularly since the bank had such a generous lending policy. But Montgomery Community was small, and when his clients went under, he knew about it, even though he wasn't directly involved, and a lot of times it broke his heart. Coy remembered a newlywed couple whom he'd helped to buy a condo in that new development on the east end of town. The husband had just been hired as a salesman by Apache Toyota-Chevrolet, and the wife worked part-time as a pharmacist's assistant at Walgreen's. Every time he'd see them at the grocery store, he'd always ask how they were doing, and they'd always gush about how they loved living in Montgomery and how they loved their home. Unfortunately, the recession hit, the man lost his job and, unable to keep up with the payments using just the wife's part-time salary, they walked away from the condo, leaving town without telling anyone where they were going.

Now there was Carl Yates.

How had that gone so terribly wrong?

Coy sighed. The financial world was like those stores in old western movies: a nice impressively respectable false front hiding the small squalid building behind it. He glanced over at Maggie, on the phone with a client who was obviously underwater and obviously pleading for leniency in making some sort of payment. Maggie, as usual, was bending over backwards to be accommodating, but rules were rules and there was only so much she could do. Just from hearing her side of the conversation, he could tell that this story would not end well.

Rumor had it that the bank was in trouble. Too many bad investments. He wasn't privy to the details—none of them were—but they'd all been exposed to a little piece of the puzzle, and when they got together at break or lunch to compare notes, all of the arrows seemed to point in one direction.

For the past year, Coy had been dating Florine Jacobs from Evergreen Title, and it was Florine who'd first hinted to him that everything at the bank might not be hunky dory. She told him that word had come down from the corporate office that an auditor was looking into Escrow accounts associated with Montgomery Community. The expression on his face must have given away the shock he felt because she immediately said, "Don't tell anyone I told you!" Her voice was panicked. "You can't say a word about this to anyone!"

"I won't," he promised. And he hadn't. But he had kept his ears and eyes open, had expressed his doubts about the future to coworkers who expressed their own doubts, and he worried that the day might come when he was forced to look for a new job.

The very thought of changing employers depressed him. He'd spent his entire working life at Montgomery Community. He liked it here. He liked the work, liked most of the people. He even liked the building. The only other bank in town, aside from the small Federal Employees' Credit Union next to Wal-Mart, was a Bank of America, and the B of A was not only fully staffed, but the last time a position opened up, they transferred someone from the Prescott branch instead of hiring locally. It was going to be next to impossible for him to find a banking job here in town. He'd either have to apply somewhere besides a bank or move to another, bigger city.

It was a slow afternoon, not only for the loan officers but for the tellers as well. Between one and three, a few calls came in, a couple of old ladies stopped by to make withdrawals, but that was it, and Coy saw Maggie and Cal exchange worried looks. It was not unusual for there to be slow periods in banking, but those slow periods were not only becoming more frequent, they were lasting much longer. It was part of a pattern, a pattern that did not bode well for the future.

As low man on the totem pole, Jimmy Collins, the newest teller, took his lunch break last, and when he returned to the bank shortly after two, he was so excited he was nearly out of breath. "Have you heard the news?" he asked, addressing them all. "The Bank of America! It's closed!"

"There *is* a God," Cal said, grinning.

"B of A's closing? Why?" Coy wondered aloud.

"Not closing. *Closed.* And why? I have no idea. Not enough foot traffic would be my guess."

Maggie nodded. "Most of their customers just use ATMs."

"Or bank online," Jimmy offered.

Cal grinned. "Which means we're the only game in town."

Thank God, Coy thought. Maybe the worst of it was over. Maybe things would start picking up now that their competition had called it quits. He glanced around the familiar room, his gaze settling finally on his desktop, on his engraved wood nameplate, on the little *Pirates of the Caribbean* coffee cup Florine had brought back for him from a trip to Disneyland. He smiled, feeling happy, feeling, for the first time in a long time, safe.

3

BURNING butterflies gave off a smell that was completely unique.

He didn't exactly *like* the smell. But he didn't *hate* it, either. He found it…interesting.

V.J. touched the flame of the lighter to the wings of the final butterfly. Like the other two he'd caught, it had been immobilized by a pin to its midsection, although, unlike the others, its wings were still fluttering.

That ended quickly, though, and once fire had consumed the bug's body, V.J. pressed his right index finger into the ashes. They were warm but not too hot—*pleasant*—and he held the finger in front of his face, looking at it, seeing some of the glitter from the colorful wings in the gray ash that coated his skin. Placing his finger on the blank three-by-five card next to the burnt butterflies, he rolled it from left to right until a clear fingerprint was visible. Carefully cutting off a length of scotch tape—*one inch long; it had to be one inch long*—he placed the tape over the fingerprint to protect it, then opened a small metal filing box and added the card to the others he'd made.

He put the box back into its niche on the shelf above his desk, then went into the kitchen, pouring himself exactly ten ounces of orange juice, drinking it in three complete swallows in less than twelve seconds. Immediately afterward, he went into the bathroom, closed and locked the door, pulled his pants down, sat on the toilet and defecated.

There was a moment of concern when he looked into the toilet afterward, but he took out his measuring tape and determined the length of the stool. He was okay. It was five inches exactly. More than three and less than six.

He sighed with relief.

All was right with the world.

4

WHEN Brad got home, the girls were fighting again, and Patty was on the phone with her sister in Texas. He broke up the fight—apparently Sue had tried to play with one of Jillian's dolls after Jillian had specifically told her sister that she could only touch her toys if she paid her a quarter or let her punch her arm ten times—and told both girls to apologize to each other and *share* their toys or neither of them would be playing with any toys for two days.

Patty hung up the phone when she saw him. "I heard what happened," she said, coming over and giving him a hug. "I can't believe it."

He shrugged, not wanting to talk, especially where the girls could hear. "Yeah, well…"

"What'd Carl do? I heard he robbed a bank."

"*What?*" Brad looked into her face. "Where did you hear that?"

"It's all around town."

"Jesus." He shook his head. "That's not what happened. We were just serving an eviction notice. Bank was foreclosing."

"He didn't—?"

"No!"

"Well, at least they got the bank part right."

"Who starts these rumors? Shit."

"So he....?"

"Yeah. Right in his front door."

"How'd Chet take it?"

"I don't know," Brad admitted. "I let Hank inform the family."

"Hank?" She frowned. "You think that was a good idea?"

"I guess we'll find out tonight."

Chet Yates, Carl's brother, had the midnight-to-three slot on the Montgomery radio station, where he ranted about various conspiracy theories cooked up in the crazier corners of the internet. For years, he had been urging people to ditch their cell phones, convinced that the federal government not only used the devices to track individuals' whereabouts but that the phones emitted targeted radiation specifically designed to cancel out certain genes in order to create future generations of designer citizens. He also believed that the Montgomery town council, in league with unspecified dark forces, was passing laws and ordinances whose sole purpose was to make the community more receptive to a military invasion.

Yet he'd always been considered the stable one in the family.

Patty took his hand. "My bet is you'll get the blame. He'll go after you *and* the department."

Brad sighed. "Yeah."

"And you'd better be careful. He's going to rile up his listeners, who, let's face it, aren't exactly the most levelheaded bunch on the planet. Remember when the fire chief got a raise and he told his listeners to set more fires to make sure the chief earned his salary?"

"Don't worry," he told her. "I can handle Chet Yates." He walked over to the refrigerator and got himself a Heineken. "So how was your day?"

"Looks like I'm going to sell that fixer-upper over on Williams, although the couple who want to buy it, the girl from APS and her husband, what's his name, are going with an internet lender to finance it."

"Are they sure that's a good idea? I mean the reason that housing crisis—"

She patted his arm. "Honey, honey, honey. I know what I'm doing. I told you a thousand times, don't worry about it. I'm not out to cheat anyone."

"Yeah, well we don't want another Carl Yates on our hands." He shook his head, sighing. "At least I sure as hell don't."

"Oh, I stopped by the bookstore today at lunch. Got myself a Dean Koontz and you that Ladies' Detective Agency book you don't have."

Brad smiled for the first time since he'd come home. He loved those Alexander McCall Smith novels. It wasn't something he'd ever admit to Hank, Issac or, really, any of his men, but he found it soothing and relaxing to read about an African lady detective.

"When I got back to the office, Tom saw the books and I guess it jogged his memory because he told me that the empty storefront next to Kyle's place is going to be a new bank." She sounded huffy. "I didn't know anything about it. I'm only Montgomery's top seller five years running, but apparently this 'bank' decided to lease through Evangeline at Century 21."

"They did have the listing," Brad pointed out.

"And look how long it took them to get even a nibble. I told that moron Jeffords two years ago that I could have it leased within six months. Even offered him a no-commission deal if I couldn't deliver. But he stuck with 21."

"Maybe he's friends with them."

"Maybe Evangeline will blow anything in pants in order to get a commish."

"Blow what in pants?"

They turned to see Sue standing in the doorway, a quizzical look on her face.

"Never you mind," Patty said. "Are you getting hungry? Are you ready for dinner?"

"What are we having?"

"I defrosted some ground beef. So tacos or burgers. Your call."

"Burgers!" Sue shouted.

"Burgers it is," Patty said, as Sue ran off to tell her sister that *she'd* gotten to choose what they were going to have for dinner.

"Any mail today?" Brad asked.

"Junk," Patty told him as she started washing her hands in the sink. "It's on the coffee table if you want to look at it."

He went into the family room, turned on the TV and sat down on the couch. He picked up the small pile of envelopes atop today's *Arizona Republic*. An ad from AT&T asking him to become a customer—even though he'd been one for twenty years. Another ad from Big O Tires announcing an upcoming sale. An "offer" to help him refinance his mortgage.

A postcard with his name on the cover.

And his photo.

What the hell? The photo was old. He was wearing his uniform, but he was at least ten to fifteen pounds lighter. It was impossible to tell where the shot had been taken, because his head and upper torso had been cut out of the original picture and placed against a black background. Above his photo, in yellow against the black: **BRAD NETH!**

Frowning, he turned over the postcard.

"We know who you are! Can your current bank say that? Our guess is no. But we make it a point to know your needs, and pride ourselves on providing unparalleled service to all of our customers. Including BRAD NETH!

We're looking forward to banking with YOU!"

He read the words again, then turned the postcard over. It was clearly an ad for a bank, but there was no mention of the bank's name and no return address. Strange. He didn't like the fact that the company behind this not only knew his name and address but had access to an old picture of him. Ordinarily, he would have dumped the postcard, along with the other junk mail, into the trash, but it occurred to him that this might be part of some scam, and he set it aside. He'd take it into work tomorrow and ask around, see if anybody else got one of these.

"It's kind of quiet!" Patty called from the kitchen. "Can you check on the girls, make sure they're okay?"

That brought a round of giggling from the girls' bedroom, and Brad smiled, standing up. "I'll see what's going on!" he said, loud enough for all of them to hear.

There were squeals, then silence, and he stomped loudly as he headed down the hallway. "Ready or not, here I come!"

THREE

1

I T WAS A customer who told him.

As always, Kyle had parked this morning next to the metal trash bins in back of the store and had not gone outside since opening up. But when Rollie Brown came to trade in a bunch of Michael Connolly books for store credit, he happened to mention that the vacant space next to Brave New World was going to be home to a new bank.

Kyle frowned. "A bank? Are you sure? Seems kind of small for a bank."

Rollie shrugged. "That's what it says."

Sure enough, when he went outside with Rollie to look, leaving Gary in the store, the adjacent space was no longer for lease. Not only was the Century 21 sign gone, but a new sign had gone up in its place, a square notice on the inside sill, leaning against the window, stating that this was to be "The Future Home of The First People's Bank."

"See?" Rollie said.

The First People's Bank.

An interesting name, Kyle thought. Was it really the *first* people's bank? Because he would be willing to bet there'd been others, if not in Arizona then in other states. And what exactly constituted a "people's bank?" Or was it actually the *first people's* bank? Which brought up the question: who were the "first people?" Native Americans? Was it owned by some tribe? Or were the first people some lost race that had been on Earth long before the rise of man?

This was why he never got anything done, he realized. He wasted his time on things like speculating about the etymology of names that had no meaning beyond commercial viability.

Kyle peered through the dusty glass. The single room inside was long and narrow, more suited to an ice cream parlor than a bank. Against the side wall opposite his own store, a built-in wooden counter ran most of the length of the space, and in the center of the floor lay a jumble of chairs and broken tables, along with a couple of empty cardboard boxes. It was the counter that had given him the idea of turning the place into a coffee bar, and he noted with regret that if the space was to become a bank, the counter would have to be demolished.

"You're right," Rollie said. "It is kind of small for a bank."

Kyle nodded. "Yeah."

Unfortunately, there went his hopes for expansion.

It had been a pipe dream, of course, particularly with the way things were going financially, but the death of any dream was hard to accept, and he walked back next door feeling oddly bereft.

Gary looked up from the counter, where he'd been tabulating the trade-in price for Rollie's books. "Is it really going to be a bank?"

"Looks that way."

"Where are they going to keep the money? There's not even enough room for a safe." He shook his head. "It doesn't make sense."

Kyle shrugged. "I guess we'll find out."

"Oh, and the books?" Gary told Rollie. "Two dollars cash, six dollars in-store credit."

"I'll take the credit," Rollie said.

"You want us to write you a credit slip," Kyle asked, "or do you—?"

"I'll pick out something right now."

Nodding, Kyle left him to it, while Gary wrote the price of each book inside the front cover in pencil before shelving all of them in the Mystery/Suspense section.

Kyle put on a CD of Celtic music he'd bought at the Renaissance Faire in Phoenix back when he and Anita were dating, and the gentle sound of pipes and mandolin filled the store. He loved this music. Half of the songs were traditional, the other half originals, and the musicians were uniformly wonderful. He probably put on this CD at least once a month. Listening to it now, he wondered if the group had ever recorded another. Or if they even still performed together. The line between musicians who became successful, he thought, and those who didn't was completely arbitrary. It had nothing to do with talent or technical ability and everything to do with luck. For his money, these guys were every bit as good as Mumford and Sons, but they'd been in the wrong place at the wrong time, and for all he knew they now spent their weekends watching football or shopping at Home Depot rather than playing music.

The thought depressed him.

It was much the same with literature. Some of his favorite books were by one-hit wonders, authors who'd had a single novel published and then dropped from sight. What happened to artistic drive when the talent behind it was not nurtured? he wondered. What were those authors doing now? Were they still writing, still trying to get published, or had they given up entirely?

The loss of the empty space next door had put him in a weird mood, and he was grateful when Rollie brought his purchases to the counter. In his usual meticulous way, Rollie had calculated the price of the two books he had chosen down to the last cent, even adding the tax, and when all was said and done, they owed him a nickel, which Kyle gave him rather than writing out a store credit slip.

The store was dead for the rest of the morning, until Walter Peters, the Baptist minister, stopped by shortly before lunch. He was the only clergyman in town who was a regular reader—or at least who bought his books locally rather than online—but the minister's taste ran to nonfiction books on sports and Las Vegas, and the store hadn't gotten anything new in either of those areas for some time.

The minister browsed the stacks for ten minutes or so, although he still left without making a purchase.

The last CD had ended some time ago, but Kyle hadn't put on any more music. Sometimes he enjoyed the silence, though he knew that drove Gary crazy. Gary would rather listen to country music than work in silence—and he hated country music. Gary was going home for lunch, however, and for the next hour Kyle would have the place to himself.

"You want me to bring you anything?" Gary asked before he left.

Kyle shook his head. "I'm good. Got a sandwich and an apple in the fridge."

"You sure?"

"I'm fine."

"See you in a while."

Gary walked back through the store and out the back door to where he'd parked his car.

Behind the register, Kyle sat down in the used office chair he'd bought at auction when Mandy Clegg's travel agency had gone out of business two years ago. He stared out at the street, saw few cars and fewer pedestrians—*no* pedestrians, in fact—and wondered how much longer he was going to be able to last, how much longer *any* of the old downtown businesses were going to last. All of the action was at the other end of town by Wal-Mart and Safeway. If Brave New World were located in the Safeway center, he might have a chance at survival, but the rent was so high for those spaces that half of them were empty.

He picked up the Charles Williams book he'd been reading. One of the advantages of owning your own store. Hopefully, the lunch hour would bring in a few customers, but until then...

The quiet was conducive to concentration, and within minutes he was completely enveloped in Williams' world of small town crime.

The stillness of the store was shattered not only by the ringing of the bell above the door but by the muttering of the man who stepped through it. Dirty, heavily bearded, wearing what looked like

Aqualung's coat and smelling of long-layered sweat, the man parked himself in front of the counter and stared unblinkingly at Kyle. "Did you eat it?" he asked in a gruff rumble.

Montgomery didn't really have a homeless problem, and the few displaced individuals who resided in the area were generally well-known to local residents and, in a weird way, part of the community. But Kyle had dealt with this guy before, and he was no quirky eccentric. He was mentally ill and genuinely menacing.

"You need to leave," Kyle said, politely but firmly.

The man grinned, his remaining teeth stained brown. "You need to eat it."

He wasn't about to get sucked into a conversation by asking, "Eat what?" He'd made that mistake last time, engaging in a dialog with the man, who had proceeded to start yelling before throwing a shelf full of books to the floor and running out.

"If you don't leave," Kyle said, "I'm calling the sheriff."

"*I'm* the sheriff!" the man shouted, spittle flying from his mouth. "The other police are pansies!"

Kyle picked up the phone, dialed 911.

"You have to eat it!" the man insisted.

And then he was gone.

Kyle hung up the phone before it was answered. The bell above the door rang as the homeless man shoved it open and staggered across the sidewalk into the street, where a too-fast pickup truck honked and swerved around him.

"Fuck you!" the man yelled at the departing pickup.

Kyle watched him knock on the front window of a store across the street, then stumble down the sidewalk out of sight. Sitting back down, he attempted to return to his book, but the mood was gone, and he couldn't get into the story. Luckily, a customer came in, a woman he didn't recognize. He smiled at her, asked if she needed any help, and when she said, no, she was just browsing, he nodded and then put on some music.

2

ANITA went to the nursery at lunch.

She hadn't intended to go back at all, at least not by herself, but the text Steven had sent her had been a little too *Fatal Attraction* for her taste, and she felt the need to meet in person and put a definitive end to all of this. It was her own fault for not doing so earlier. At every juncture, she'd either continued onward or left things ambivalent. Even yesterday, standing him up, she hadn't clearly put on the brakes.

Mostly because she hadn't wanted to.

She wanted to now, though. She wasn't sure when the epiphany had come, but this morning, helping Iris Jensen pick out a new pair of glasses, Iris Jensen who had been her eleventh grade biology teacher, Iris Jensen who had been married to Coach Thomas for over thirty years, Anita realized that she couldn't lose what she had, that she was lucky to have the life she had with Kyle, with Nick, and it would be crazy for her to throw it all away. What had she been thinking? How had she ever let it get this far? Maybe, between financial problems with the store and the tribulations of raising a teenager, they had let the romance gradually slip away, but that was no reason to start something with someone else. Kyle wasn't hitting on young women buying used copies of *Fifty Shades of Grey*. Why had she succumbed to Steven's flirtations?

No matter. She was stopping it now, before things went too far, before what happened could not be forgiven. She loved Kyle, and if their life together wasn't a passionfest, that was on her as well as him. It was a cliché trotted out by every fake-credentialed relationship adviser on every daytime talk show, but the two of them needed to talk. They needed to communicate.

There were no other cars in the nursery parking lot when Anita arrived, and that gave her pause. She'd been hoping to talk to him when others were around, wanting the safety of witnesses, and she almost decided to drive away and come back later, but at the last minute, she parked in the gravel next to the open gate and shut off the engine. She waited, hoping he might come out, hoping she wouldn't have to leave the car, but when he didn't emerge after several minutes, she grabbed her purse, got out, and walked into the nursery. The register was unattended, and the potting shed behind it was empty.

"Steven!" she called. She looked around, not seeing him among the vegetables, bedding plants, shrubs or fruit trees.

"In here!"

Her eyes looked toward the greenhouse where the nursery grew exotic and indoor plants. She hesitated, thinking it might be better if he came out, but then dismissed her concerns as paranoia, and walked over to the small building.

Steven was misting some orchids at the far end of the room. He put down the mister as she approached. "Hey," he said.

"I told you, I don't want you texting me," she told him.

Steven smiled, held up his hands. "Sorry," he said. "Didn't mean to overstep my bounds. The loving hubby didn't see it, did he?"

"And I want you to stop calling him 'the loving hubby.'"

Steven frowned. "Hey, hey, hey. What's going on here? I'm getting kind of a vibe."

Anita took a deep breath, hoping this would go well but afraid that it wouldn't. "I think we need to stop," she said.

"Stop? Stop what?"

"This," she said, indicating the air between them. "Whatever is going on here."

The frown deepened. "What's going on here..." He waved his hands in a mockery of her motion. "...is a mutual—"

"*Was* a mutual—"

He nodded, smiling tightly. "I get it. I know what's happening. You've come by to end it."

"There's nothing to end."

"That's not what you said at lunch the other day."

Anita reddened. "Okay. You're right. But I'm ending it now. It's gone far enough."

"Is it the text? I admit, maybe I was a little forward, or a little too enthusiastic, but you've got to admit, we've had some pretty—"

"It's not the text. Or not just the text." Once again, she breathed deeply. "I made a mistake, okay? It's my fault. But now I'm correcting that mistake."

"That's what you think we were? A mistake?"

He walked out from behind the orchid table, and she gasped. He had undone his pants, unbuckling, unzipping and spreading open the front of his jeans, and his penis was sticking out, completely erect. A week ago—two days ago, even—she might have been amused or even aroused by such a gesture, but now there seemed something threatening about it, and she took an involuntary step backward.

"A lot of things grow in here," he said. There was an insistence in his smile that caused her to gauge how far it was to the exit. "Come on. You know you want it."

Any thought she had of being strong and standing her ground fled, and without another word, Anita turned tail and ran. She sped out of the greenhouse, past the potting shed and the register counter, into the parking lot, where she scrambled into her car and started the engine. Filled with panic, she dared not even glance toward the nursery, but kept her eyes on the rearview mirror as she swung the car around then determinedly faced forward as she drove out of the parking lot onto the street.

Her heart was pounding so hard she could feel the pulse in her wrists, hear the blood thumping in her head. Farther down the street, she saw Nick's friend Victor walking his dog. *Wasn't he supposed to be in school?* He looked over at her as if he didn't recognize her, then turned his attention to the sidewalk in front of him.

He knows! was her first thought. It didn't make any sense, but it was easy for her to imagine that he'd walked his dog over to the nursery and had been about to come in when he saw Steven with his exposed erection.

Oh God, Anita thought. *What if he tells Nick? Or Kyle? Or his parents? Or anyone?*

But that was the guilt talking. He couldn't have seen anything. The event had happened in the greenhouse, away from the street. He would have had to come into the building in order to see anything—and he hadn't.

Still, she remained nervous and jumpy, and she found herself driving up Airport Road and then back to the downtown along Frontier Street, next to the creek, in order to calm herself down. She still had nearly a half hour to spare, and though she'd brought her lunch today, she'd left it back at the office. Not yet ready to face people, she went through the drive-thru at Burger King and ate in the car in the Safeway parking lot before heading back to work.

Her phone rang when she was halfway between her car and the office door. After checking to make sure it wasn't Steven, she picked up. "Hello?"

A woman's voice with a Southern accent: "Am I speaking to Anita Decker?"

"Yes," she said suspiciously.

"This is Marjorie with Citibank. We are detecting attempted activity on your Visa account at—" There was a second's hesitation. "—the Best Buy at 7400 Brookpark Road in Cleveland, Ohio."

"*What?*"

"The purchase location triggered an automatic warning, which is why we are contacting you. Would you like us to put a stop to this transaction and place a hold on your card?"

"Yes!" she said frantically.

Another short pause. "The transaction has been denied and the account placed on hold. We are alerting local authorities of an incident of attempted credit card fraud and providing them with the location."

Holding the phone between her neck and shoulder, Anita rummaged through her purse, where she found her Visa card. "How can they be using my card?" she asked. "I have it right here."

"Thieves engaging in identity theft often make their own cards—"

"Is there anything else I need to do?" she interrupted. In her mind, high-tech thieves were simultaneously making online purchases, cleaning out her bank account and opening new lines of exploitable credit using her identity.

"In the event of an identity breach, we suggest that you immediately call the credit monitoring companies Experian, Equifax..."

She stood in the center of the small parking lot, listening to the litany of steps she needed to take to ensure that this attempted identity theft intruded no further into her life, stunned that such a thing could happen.

First Steven, then this...

Could things fall apart any more completely? What was next? Was their house going to be robbed this afternoon? Was the bookstore going to burn down? Was Dr. Wilson going to fire her?

She glanced down at her watch. Her lunch ended in two minutes, and the optometrist was not the most sympathetic person when it came to excuses for being tardy. She hurried inside the building. There was a whole host of things she needed to do in order to protect her financial security. Dr. Wilson glanced at her when he saw her, then glanced up at the clock and then without a word walked down the short hallway to his private office, shutting the door.

There were no patients yet, and Anita commandeered one of the computers, then thought the better of it and used her phone to access the Experian site, then thought the better of *that* and got a phone number from the website so she could call the credit monitoring company directly. She didn't trust the security of anything at this point, but she needed to do what the woman had told her and get control of her personal information, not to mention freeze all of her accounts.

"What's going on?" Jen asked, walking in and putting her purse under the counter. "You look kind of frazzled."

Anita shook her head. "You won't believe it."

"What?"

"Credit card fraud. Someone pretended they were me and tried to charge something. I got a call about it five minutes ago, when I was walking in."

"Jesus!"

"It was happening right then. *Live!* As they were talking to me on the phone! Some guy in a Best Buy in Ohio was trying to use my card to buy...I don't even know! I forgot to ask! How stupid can I get?"

Jen put a hand on her arm. "Calm down. It's not your fault. You're not stupid. You're just upset."

"Wouldn't you be?"

"Of course! Something like that? I'd feel so...violated."

Violated

An image flashed in her mind: Steven with his erect penis.

You know you want it

She pushed the thought away. "I need to get this taken care of. Cover for me, will you? I'm going to go in the bathroom and make some calls."

"You don't have to hide in the bathroom. He'll understand."

Anita glanced toward the optometrist's closed door. "You didn't see the look he gave me when I came in. Because I was *almost* late. Cover for me?"

"Sure."

In the bathroom, she sat down on the closed lid of the toilet. She tried to call Kyle, but he'd set his phone to voicemail, and when she called the store, the line was busy. So she spent the next ten minutes talking first to a computer, then to a man with a thick Southern accent who elicited the information needed to secure her credit line. She was about to call Equifax when Jen came in and said, "Better wrap it up. Mrs. Wheeler's here for her appointment. He'll be out in a minute."

"Thanks," Anita said, shutting off her phone.

It was a busy afternoon.

She didn't have time to call Kyle until it was almost time to go home.

3

ONLY one day to go and his suspension was over.

If this was one of those 1980s teen movies his parents always forced him to watch when they came on TV, he'd return a hero, his street cred boosted by his battle with The Man. But things didn't work that way anymore—if they ever had. What was actually going to happen was that he would go back to school to find that no one had even noticed he'd been gone.

Nick finished watching the last of the morning's *Parks and Recreation* reruns on FX, then turned off the TV and reluctantly switched on his laptop. His teachers had not only emailed his homework assignments, they'd tacked on *extra* work, apparently to punish him for getting suspended. As if that weren't bad enough, his dad was making him help out at the bookstore this afternoon. So after he finished his schoolwork and after he ate his lunch, he was supposed to show up at Brave New World to shelve books or straighten books or do something equally useless.

Feeling depressed, he checked his email, scrolling down. The spam he received was getting much more adult. Not porno-adult but business-adult. There were offers to enroll in real estate seminars, ads for automobiles, lists of job opportunities and several recommendations for various financial institutions. He tried to remember if one of his fake profiles had him recently turning eighteen. That could explain this sudden influx of commercial announcements.

His attention was caught by the tagline of the last email: *Nicholas Decker! Are you bored, suspended from school and in need of money? Just click...*

Suspended from school?

That was pretty specific.

He knew enough not to click on spam from unknown senders, but the fact that the description was tailored so directly to his own situation intrigued him. He deleted it along with the rest of the spam and, seconds later, another email popped up: *Nick! Need some easy money? Before you go to the bathroom and pop some Pringles, click on this!*

That was not just specific, it was downright creepy.

He *did* have to go to the bathroom. And he *had* been planning to grab some Pringles before starting on his homework.

He deleted the unopened message and quickly exited his email account. It had to be a coincidence. Still, it was more than a little unnerving, and he forgot about going to the bathroom, skipped the

Pringles and got to work on his algebra. It was after ten and the day was bright, but the inside of the house seemed dark, and after the third math problem, he got up and turned on not only the light in the dining room, where he was working, but in the kitchen and the living room as well. It suddenly seemed quiet, too, and he turned the television back on, lowering the volume until he could hear a murmur of voices loud enough to make it seem as though he was not alone, but not loud enough to be distracting. Feeling better, he worked on his homework until he was finished, then made some macaroni and cheese for lunch.

He was done eating by twelve forty-five, but the *Twilight Zone* episode he was watching was a good one, so he waited until it was over before heading to the bookstore. Taking his bike out of the garage, Nick thought about how far it was to Brave New World, and how, even if he took the shortcut, he would have to pedal up the high hill on Bluff Road.

He needed his own car.

But his parents were adamant that he was not going to get one until he graduated from high school—and then only if he maintained a 3.5 average his senior year.

He rode his bike out of their neighborhood, onto the highway and toward downtown, staying as close to the shoulder as possible. The high school's lunch period was over, but in a small redneck burg like Montgomery, teenagers weren't the only ones who liked to swerve their pickups in order to scare bicyclists.

The afternoon was warm, and Nick was sweating by the time he approached the center of town. Frowning, he looked to his left. Was that his mom's car in front of the nursery? She was a plant lover with an impressive yardful of flowers that had been a stop on the Montgomery Garden Tour last year, so there was nothing inherently unusual about her spending her lunch hour looking at plants. But the sight of her Kia parked in the gravel lot gave him an uneasy feeling. He couldn't say why, or what about it felt wrong, but something sure did, and he found himself pedaling faster in order to get away from the nursery before she came out and saw him.

He turned onto Main.

Ordinarily, he would have ridden his bike through the alley to the back of the store, but the last time he'd done that, he'd gotten a nail in his tire. Not wanting to risk another flat, he got off his bike at the gas station and walked it along the sidewalk the rest of the way down the block.

There was a big white sign in the dingy window of the empty storefront next to Brave New World, and he stopped to check it out. The sign stated that the space was to be the new home of The First People's Bank. Nick was surprised. A bank in a narrow, crappy little spot like this? That made no sense. There was movement behind the window, a furtive shifting from one side of the room to the other, though the darkness and dirty glass would not let him see the figure clearly.

He purposely turned away, not *wanting* to see it.

As pathetic as it was, and as impossible as it might seem to be frightened in the middle of the day on a public street, he *was* frightened. Something about the figure's quick jerky moves reminded him of a nightmare he'd had, and Nick pushed his bike forward, opening the door of the bookshop and pulling the cycle in behind him.

His dad was already grinning. "Ready for work?"

"Can I at least put my bike away first?"

"Against the wall by the bathroom."

"I know. I've done it a million times."

"You're going to have a fun afternoon!"

He did not have a fun afternoon. There were no customers, and after about an hour, he ran out of things to do, so he spent the rest of the day browsing shelves he knew by heart while his dad and Gary chatted by the front counter.

Even school was preferable to this. He didn't understand how his dad could spend all day every day cooped up in here, and Nick vowed that as soon as he graduated he would put Montgomery in his rearview mirror and move somewhere cool. Los Angeles, New York or, heck, even Austin.

Of course, he would need to *get* a rearview mirror first.

He definitely needed that car. And then he'd need to win a scholarship to a decent college in a decent city, because unless they hit the lottery, the only thing his parents could afford to send him to was Montgomery JC. The problem was, he wouldn't be able to get a scholarship without teacher recommendations. Which were going to be pretty tough to come by unless his situation at school started changing pretty quickly.

Life was getting complicated.

"You okay back there?" his dad called.

"Fine!" he called back.

He put the horror movie book he'd been perusing back on the shelf. Hearing an unexpected noise behind him, he turned, startled. There came a quiet knocking from the other side of the wall.

It was mid-afternoon, and his dad and Gary were ten feet away, but the sound still gave him goosebumps. He thought of that vague dark figure moving behind the window next door and imagined it positioned on the other side of the wall, tapping with a claw-like finger in an effort to get his attention.

"Hey, Dad!" he called. "Come here!"

He'd hailed his father out of panic, but it occurred to him even before his dad came over that since there was going to be a new bank on the other side of the wall, they were probably just starting construction.

Still, he found the noise unsettling, and when his dad heard it and wondered what was going on, the two of them and Gary walked outside and peered through the dirty windows of the nascent bank.

The space was empty, no one there.

"Rats?" Gary suggested.

"Too regular for rats," his dad said. "It sounded like someone tapping on the wall, maybe looking for a stud or a beam."

Nick popped back into the bookstore. The noise was still audible. He hurried outside to tell Gary and his father.

"It has to be something in the walls," his dad acknowledged.

"Better hope it's not termites," Gary said as they walked back into the shop.

It wasn't termites, Nick knew. He didn't know *what* it was, but his dad was right. It sounded like builders. The fact that they could all hear the tapping while none of them could see anything did not sit well with him, and rather than stay by himself in one of the aisles, Nick hung out with his dad and Gary by the register.

Victor stopped by after school let out. His friend already had a car—a Jeep his dad had picked up for two hundred bucks at the county sheriff's auction last year. The transmission could not be put into reverse—which made for some awkward and complicated parking arrangements—but other than that, the vehicle ran fine, and when Victor asked if Nick could cruise with him over to Sonic and hang out, his dad let him go.

"Punishment's over," he said. "Have fun."

They didn't actually go to Sonic. They went over to the high school, where Victor pulled around to the parking lot next to the field so they could watch the cheerleaders practice. He had a crush on Stacey Wilder, who wouldn't give him the time of day at school but who had said hi to him during the summer when he'd seen her at the movie theater. He seemed to be laboring under the delusion that if he put himself in close proximity to her, she would somehow succumb to his charms.

Victor got out of the car and Nick followed suit, both of them leaning against the side of the Jeep, facing the field.

"Rumor has it," Victor said, "that your mom's getting boned by the gardener."

Nick felt the heat rush to his face. "Who said that? We don't even have a gardener." But an image flashed in his mind of his mom's car parked in front of the nursery.

Victor shrugged.

"You can't just tell me something like that and then pussy out when I ask who said it. Who said it?"

"Mrs. Nelson."

"Asshole."

"I don't know, dude. It's a rumor going around. Who gives a shit? Just enjoy the view."

They were silent for a moment, watching the cheerleaders perform a routine.

"You really think this is going to impress Stacey? Stalking her?"

"I'm not stalking her."

"We're spying on her cheerleader practice. It's creepy. Chicks don't like that."

"Is there an ounce of testosterone in your body? You have no idea what chicks like."

They'd been ranking on each other, half-joking, the way they usually did, but a touch of anger had entered Victor's voice, and the look on his face was serious.

Nick backed off, backed down.

Montgomery?

He wouldn't mind putting his *friends* in the rearview mirror.

Silently, he turned his attention to the cheerleaders.

4

V.J. killed the dog out in the open, and it felt glorious. Rather than dispatching it in the garage or storage shed, the way he usually did, he took the animal to the park and slaughtered it on the tennis court. There were little kids and their parents in the playground, and a few joggers on the paths, but the basketball and tennis courts were all empty, so he had this section of the park to himself.

There was something exciting about doing it where he could possibly get caught, and even as he entered the park with the stolen pet, leading it on a leash, there was a bounce in his step. The terrier barked at another dog—a setter being walked by a hot woman in tight exercise pants—and he and the woman nodded at each other and smiled, sharing the camaraderie of fellow dog walkers.

He passed a homeless old fuck digging through a garbage can by the side of the path and muttering to himself. V.J. ignored the shambling man and strode up to the tennis court, opening the chain-link gate and shepherding in the terrier. From the other side of the park, he heard the familiar sounds of children playing, and, from the street, the noise of passing cars. Tying the dog's leash to one of the low poles that held up what was left of the net bisecting the center of the court, V.J. withdrew the sacrificial knife from the sheath attached to his belt. Before the animal could sense anything amiss, he knelt down, petted the dog's head with his left hand and with his right hand shoved the knife deep into the terrier's heart. There was a gush of blood, a single bark and then the dog was still.

V.J. glanced about to make sure he hadn't been seen. He could still hear the children playing, and far away saw a woman jogging, but no one was in this part of the park—except that homeless fuck, staring at him from the other side of the fence.

His heart lurched in his chest when he saw the ragged figure. But the bum was crazy and even if he told people what he'd seen, no one would believe him.

V.J. stood, raising the bloody knife, intending to scare the man off, but to his surprise, the bum nodded his approval and smiled.

Respect.

The man was giving him respect, and V.J. was filled with a satisfied sense of pride. He nodded back his acknowledgment, and the derelict wandered off, carrying a bag of recyclable cans and bottles over his shoulder

V.J. got back to work.

The dog had four legs, so after amputating the last one, V.J. took out the compact mirror he carried in his pocket and carefully pulled out four of his eyelashes, two from the left lid, two from the right. Aloud, he said, "One, two, three four, that's all there is and there ain't no more." Then he put the eyelashes in his mouth and swallowed.

Placing one dog leg in each of the tennis court's four corners, he left the limbless body at the foot of the net, equidistant from each side, and then walked around the net four times, stomping his left foot at the completion of each circuit.

It was freeing to perform such an expansive version of the ritual and to do it outdoors, exhilarating to kill the animal in such close proximity to other people. He felt invincible, and as a special treat to himself, he pulled down his pants, pissed on the corpse, then pulled his pants up again and ran all the way home.

FOUR

1

HIS PARENTS WERE still fighting when he woke up. Nick could hear the low drone of angry voices from the kitchen, and he debated whether he should sneak up quietly so he could hear what was going on, or make enough noise in his approach to silence them. He opted for the former, and the muffled sound separated into individual words as he tiptoed carefully down the hall.

"...freeze the account."

"You didn't think it might be important to call me first so *my* information wouldn't be compromised, too?"

"I explained that."

"Four hours? Come on!"

"You should've answered your phone! Besides, nothing happened, did it?"

"That's not the point! It could have! Maybe it still will!"

"How many times do I have to say I'm sorry?"

Nick walked around the corner into the kitchen, and his parents moved away from each other, his mom to the stove, his dad to the refrigerator. Neither of them spoke. Nick reached around his dad's side and grabbed the carton of orange juice, then took two slices of bread from the open package atop the counter and popped them into the toaster. He wasn't usually very talkative first thing in the morning, so his silence wasn't that unusual, but theirs was, and Nick decided to wait it out and see who broke down first.

He'd poured himself the orange juice, spread butter and peanut butter on the toast, and was halfway through his breakfast when his mom sat down next to him with a cup of coffee. His dad had gone outside to see if the newspaper had been delivered.

"Got all your schoolwork done?" she asked.

He nodded.

"Do I need to write you a note for this?"

"No," he said. "I wasn't sick. I was suspended."

"Still, maybe you should check in at the office to make sure you don't have to fill something out with the registrar. You can call me if I need to sign anything."

"Okay," he told her, though his plan was just to go to first period like he normally did.

"Oh, I forgot to tell you. I saw Victor walking his dog yesterday."

Nick shook his head. "I don't think so, Mom. He doesn't have a dog."

"Not a little gray-brown mutt?"

"Barky? That was in elementary school. Barky's been dead since junior high."

"Well, whatever. I saw your friend, and it was in the middle of the day. I think he was ditching school."

Your mom's getting boned by the gardener.

Nick shrugged. "I wasn't there."

"You don't ditch school, do you?"

By this time, he'd finished his toast. "No, Mom." Downing the last of his orange juice, he glanced over at his dad, who was entering the kitchen reading the paper. "I'd better get dressed." He favored his dad with a big fake smile. "I go back to school today."

"Yes you do, David Mamet. And I expect you to behave."

"Yes sir, sir!"

"That's what I'm talking about."

"Leave him alone," his mom said. "He's nervous."

"I'm not..." he began, but let the sentence trail off. It wasn't worth it. He didn't want to get into a fight with his parents and didn't want to rekindle the fight they were having with each other. "I gotta get ready." Heading to the bathroom to brush his teeth, Nick realized that maybe he *was* a bit nervous. Especially about going back to Mrs. Nelson's class. How awkward was that going to be?

He brushed his teeth, washed the acne cream off his face and checked to make sure he didn't need to shave today (not yet). Having forgotten to pick up some clean clothes from his bedroom, he opened the bathroom door, started to walk out...

And stopped.

Something was wrong.

A chill raced down his spine. Nick knew what he'd see without looking, and when he *did* look, forcing himself to glance down the hall in both directions, it confirmed what he'd already suspected.

Heart pounding, he ducked back into the bathroom and quickly closed the door. What he wanted to do was call out "Mom! Dad!" until one or both of his parents came to his rescue. But he was seventeen, too old to exhibit such childish fear, and he knew he was going to have to get through this himself.

He stared at the closed door, thinking about what lay on the other side of it.

The shadow.

For several weeks now, there'd been a shadow in the hall that he didn't like. It was only there sometimes, but there didn't seem to be anything consistent about when it appeared. It wasn't a certain time of day or night, had nothing to do with the light in the hall, or illumination from any of the bedroom doorways or the living room. It just...appeared every so often. There was no rhyme or reason to it, and what really freaked him out was that it didn't seem to correspond to any tangible object. Every time he saw the shadow, he attempted to identify its source, only to be confronted with the fact that there was nothing inside or outside the house even vaguely similar to its shape.

For its contours changed. It was still identifiably the same shadow, but sometimes it appeared more humanoid in shape, other times more amorphously bloblike. Always it was faint, barely perceptible, as though it were attempting to hide in plain sight. And always there was about it a palpable sense of *wrongness*, that same disturbing impression he had gotten upon opening the bathroom door, a feeling that something nearby was not as it should be.

Nick looked at himself in the mirror, waited a few seconds, then, gathering his courage, opened the door again and peeked out.

There it was, hovering on the wall next to his parents' bedroom door, an elongated form with what appeared to be three arms, unmoving but possessing a strange quivering aspect.

Something about the shadow reminded him of that figure he'd seen through the window of what was going to be the new bank, and he immediately shut the door again. Too embarrassed to admit he was afraid but not too embarrassed to do something about it, he pressed his shoulder against the door again. "Mom!" he called.

No response.

The shadow had killed her.

"MOM!"

"What?" she called back from the kitchen.

"Come here!"

Footsteps, and then her voice. "What is it?"

He opened the bathroom door a crack and poked his head out. "Could you get my jeans and that *Star Wars* t-shirt from the top of the hamper in my room? I forgot."

She was already turning back toward the kitchen. "You called me over for that? Get them yourself. What do you think I am, your servant?"

But her presence had done its job. The shadow was gone, and he was safely able to dash into his bedroom, where he changed out of his pajamas and into his clothes.

Although he usually rode his bike or his mom dropped him off at school, his dad took him today, and Nick had the feeling that his parents had planned that in order to have his father give him a lecture. Sure enough, before they pulled to a stop across the street from Montgomery High, his dad said, "We're not going to have any more of *that* this year, are we?"

"What?" he asked innocently.

"Nick..."

"I'll be good. I promise. I'm turning over a new leaf."

"Being sarcastic isn't—"

His fingers were on the door handle, but he didn't pull it yet. "I'm not being sarcastic. Okay, I am. Sort of. But I'm really not. I actually did do some thinking while I was out, and I realized that if I'm going to get any scholarships—which, let's face it, is the only way I'm going to a decent college—I'm going to need to..."

"Straighten up and fly right?"

"Yeah." Nick laughed. "I'm also going to need good grades and teacher recommendations. If that's going to happen, I need to start toeing the party line."

His dad nodded. "Lecture over. I'm impressed. Have a good day."

Nick opened the car door.

"How are you going to get home? Want me to pick you up?"

"I'll call you," Nick said.

He waved goodbye as he dashed through a break in the drop-off traffic.

Inside, he met up with Victor. Their lockers were in the same row, and his friend was just taking out his textbook for first period when Nick walked up.

"Hey."

"Hey."

He'd seen several kids from his classes on his way in, but, as he'd anticipated, none of them had asked about his suspension. He doubted if most of them had even noticed. So it was somewhat gratifying when Sue Romsberg stepped up to her locker between them, and Victor said loudly, "So what'd you do while you were suspended?"

"Robbed a bank, raped a kitten. The usual."

Sue wrinkled her nose in disgust, quickly grabbed a book out of her locker and hurried away.

Victor laughed. "That'll get them talking."

The first bell rang, and the pace of movement in the hallway sped up as students began rushing to get to class on time.

"Douche at twelve o'clock," Victor muttered, head lowered.

Nick looked up to see Mr. Whittaker walking down the hallway toward them. The principal offered Nick an insincere smile as he passed. "Glad to have you back, Nicholas."

Glad to have me back? Nick thought. *I wasn't on vacation. You suspended me.* But he nodded, offered his own insincere smile and hurried off to his homeroom, where Mrs. Nelson shot him an unreadable look. Was she trying to tell him that she had won their little skirmish? Was she attempting to let him know she was not happy he was back? It was impossible to tell, and Nick looked away from her, glancing out the window, thinking that yesterday at this time he had been lounging around on the couch watching TV.

The final bell rang, and Mrs. Nelson stood in front of the whiteboard, smiling at them as she scanned the class. "Before we get started today, I thought I'd give you a little heads up on your next assignment. It's not due until next week, but I want to give you a little time to think about it. As we're going to be discussing gender perspectives in this unit, I'm going to have you revise your plays, switching the gender of the protagonists." Her gaze rested finally on Nick, her smile broadening. "For some of you, of course, this will involve extensive rewriting…"

2

PASTOR Walter Peters looked out the window of his church office to make sure one of the auxiliary ladies was not on her way up the drive, then toggled from the sermon he was writing back to the website FreshBets, to see if odds had changed for the game tonight.

He gambled sometimes. And the Lord did not always smile on the choices he made. Like last week when the Suns lost and he was out over a hundred. But it wasn't a big deal. Only pious old biddies like Norma Crenshaw would think it was.

Which was why he had to be so careful.

Life would be so much easier if everyone could just be honest. Norma and her ilk were always so *certain* about what God thought, which actions He approved of and which would send a person straight to hell, but the truth was that their actual knowledge of the Bible was spotty at best. They only used the Good Book to reinforce their own prudish beliefs. He'd often thought about building a sermon or two around verses that would set them straight. They would be shocked, no doubt, to discover that it was worse to be a glutton than an abortionist. Because, according to Deuteronomy, if your child was a glutton, you were to take him to the edge of town where the men of the community would stone him to death. While Exodus said that if you caused a woman to miscarry, you were merely to pay a fine.

Sermonizing about that might shut them up.

But no one really followed the Bible. Rich people did not give everything they had to the poor in order to get into heaven, as Jesus explicitly said. Worshippers proudly displayed their faith on bumperstickers and t-shirts, rather than keeping their beliefs to themselves and praying in private as proscribed in Matthew. Most of his parishioners—true believers all—had not even bothered to read the first few pages of Genesis, where a curiously human-sized God, apparently speaking to other gods as He walked through the Garden, decided to expel Adam and Eve not because they disobeyed him and He wanted to teach them a lesson, not because they had become tainted with sin, as commonly believed, but because He was afraid they were about to become gods, too.

*"The man has become like one of **us**, knowing good and evil, and now, lest he put forth his hand and take also of the tree of life, and eat, and live for ever..."*

It was fear of man's potential for godhood that had caused the Lord to banish humans from paradise, but Walter doubted that a single one of his most judgmental parishioners was aware of that fact.

Although he would bet that, to a person, they'd condemn his immorality and call for his resignation if they ever got wind that he gambled on sporting events.

Hypocrites.

The phone rang, and he hurriedly toggled back to his sermon before answering, just in case someone walked in while he was on the horn. It turned out to be a robocall, and he almost hung up, but the hook grabbed him: *"Does your bank offer no-interest gambling loans? We do."*

Walter's grip tightened on the receiver.

"Signature loans of up to three thousand dollars are available to pay off existing gambling debts or to use as a stake in future wagers. Press one if you would like to learn more—"

There was the familiar sound of the front door opening and then closing in the chapel, and Walter quickly hung up the phone. His hands were sweaty, and he wiped them on the towel he kept nearby just for that purpose before walking into the next room. He hoped it wasn't someone with a serious problem—he was not in the mood for that right now—but he needn't have worried: the chapel was empty.

Walter frowned. That was strange. He knew intimately all the sounds of his church, and he had definitely heard the loud squeak of hinges and even louder clack of the closing front door.

"Hello?" he said to the empty room. There was no response, but he said it again. One could never be too careful these days. It wasn't out of the realm of possibility that some unbalanced person with a grudge against God, the church or himself might decide to come in with a weapon and start shooting.

No one answered, however, and he saw no sign that anyone was in the chapel. On the off chance that someone was hiding behind or beneath one of the pews, he walked down the aisle, looking down each row. When he came to the door, he opened it to see if the person who'd come in had somehow gotten out without him hearing or seeing it, but the church grounds were empty, as was the road.

He must have simply imagined that someone had come into the church.

Guilt?

It wasn't beyond the realm of possibility. He'd been looking at the betting site, and while he didn't consider gambling to be wrong or immoral, he knew parishioners like Norma did, and perhaps that had subliminally affected him. Closing the door, he walked back to his office to finish working on his sermon.

But his sermon was not on the screen of his computer. Instead, he was looking at FreshBets. And not just the odds page but a betting page. Somehow, within the past few minutes, a new account had been created under his name, and he had bet over five hundred dollars on the outcome of a hockey game.

He knew nothing about hockey, had no interest in hockey and would never bet on the sport.

How had this happened? Who had done this?

He looked around the small empty office and found himself saying softly, "Hello?"

3

THE fat man's body lay at the bottom of the ditch, naked, bloody and unrecognizable. Hank Dillman turned away, feeling slightly nauseous. The smell alone was enough to make him gag, and while he wasn't an expert in these things, it seemed pretty obvious that the corpse had been here for at least a couple of days. Jasper Brooks, who'd discovered the body and called it in, stood watching him with distaste, completely unaffected. Jasper had been in Vietnam, and, as he never tired of telling anyone who would listen, he'd seen horrors. He had no respect for law enforcement officers or the veterans of subsequent wars, none of whom, in his view, would have survived a week in a *real* war zone.

The paramedics, who'd arrived seconds after Hank, had pronounced the man dead but were waiting for the sheriff and the M.E. to arrive before transporting the body.

Where the hell were Brad and the other deputies? Hank had called for backup the instant he'd arrived on the scene, and the rest of them should have been here by now. The last killing to have happened in Montgomery was an unintentional shooting six months ago: Petey Lawson showing off his father's Glock to his friend Chris

Frietag and accidentally pulling the trigger. The last actual murder was a year before that: a domestic dispute where a wife had stabbed her drunken husband after he beat her and attacked their son.

But he had never seen anything like this before.

He hazarded another look at the body. He had no idea who it was, but the violence that had been perpetrated upon it was so brutal that he doubted if the victim's own mother could make a positive ID. Where a face used to be there was only a black sinkhole, since the front of the skull had been bashed in and had collapsed in on itself, filling with blood that had long since congealed and was now covered with flies. The chest and abdomen were perforated in dozens of places, seemingly at random, the entire body covered in a dried coat of reddish brown.

Hank turned away. He might have been able to handle the sight if it hadn't been accompanied by the most putrid stench he had ever experienced. It was like a dirty toilet bowl full of vomit had been blended with carburetor cleaner and then poured over a pile of shit. He walked over to the ambulance, where the two paramedics leaned against the side of the vehicle, smoking. He breathed in the second-hand smoke in an effort to erase the smell of the body.

"Who do you think killed him?" Rich, the older paramedic, asked as he exhaled.

"We don't even know who he is yet. Either of you have any ideas?"

They both shook their heads.

"I guess we'll have to wait for fingerprints. I don't even see any clothes around. Maybe he was killed somewhere else and dropped off here."

There was the sound of approaching engines, and Hank walked around to the back of the ambulance where he saw two department cars approaching, lights and sirens off.

Thank God.

"What took you so long?" he asked Brad as the sheriff and Issac got out of the first vehicle. Mitch and Bill F. were emerging from the car directly behind them.

"Issac forgot the camera. We had to go back for it."

"I thought I could just use my phone—"

"No, you didn't. You know the protocol. You forgot." There was a tone in the sheriff's voice that kept the deputy from responding. "So where's the body?"

"Over here!" Jasper called out.

"It's bad," Hank warned, though he'd told that to Brad over the radio.

"No ID yet?"

"No clue."

Brad walked to the edge of the ditch and looked down. "Jesus," he breathed.

"I think we can safely call this a homicide," Issac said as he started taking photos.

"No one's touched the body yet?"

Hank shook his head.

"You?" Brad asked, looking over at Jasper.

"Haven't touched a thing."

"So how did you find him?" The sheriff glanced around. The ditch ran alongside the edge of the forest, several yards away from the dirt road on which they'd all parked, a control road running between the highway and the refuse transfer station. "This seems a little out of the way."

"I was out for a walk."

Brad eyed him suspiciously. "A walk?"

"It's a free country."

Hank, Brad and the other deputies shared a look. They all knew that there'd been complaints from residents living on the outskirts of town about shots being fired on some of the side roads.

"You sure you weren't out here for a little off-season hunting or unlawful target practice?"

Jasper held up his hands. "I'm unarmed. *Sir.*"

The sheriff turned his attention back to the body. "Let's canvas the area and look for a weapon. Issac, finish up those photos. Bill, go to the back of the car and get some tape to cordon off the scene." He addressed the paramedics. "When the M.E. gets here, give me a shout. I need to talk to him."

Hank felt relieved. In quieter moments, he sometimes day-dreamed about being sheriff, but the truth was that he was much more suited to following orders than giving them, and he was glad that Brad had arrived to take over. He could handle the small every-day stuff, but all the training in the world could not prepare him to deal with something like this. He faced away from the body, took a deep breath of fresh air.

Jasper snorted derisively.

"You have something to say to me?" Hank demanded.

Jasper grinned. "No, sir, officer. Nothing at all."

JASPER Brooks was being an asshole, as usual, mocking Hank and behaving as though he was a part of the investigation. So Brad found it especially gratifying to send the old coot on his merry way. Jasper was the first to have come across the body and it was obvious that he felt proprietary about his discovery and wanted to see this through to the end, but the sheriff pulled rank, informed him that this was a crime scene and that he needed to go. They would contact him later for an official statement.

Brad had never dealt with anything like this before, and despite the outward calm he attempted to project, the brutality of the mur-der and urgency of the situation felt overwhelming. Theirs was a small town sheriff's office. They weren't really equipped to deal with something of this magnitude, but unfortunately there was no other law enforcement agency to which they could legitimately pass off responsibility. This case was all theirs.

Brad looked down again at the fat man's corpse leaning against the dirt side of the ditch.

Nothing was left of the victim's face, but there was something familiar about his hairline, and while Brad couldn't immediately iden-tify the man, he knew he knew him. He just didn't know from where.

Brad, Hank, Mitch and Bill F. started their search. They found nothing on the road or in the ditch, but in the trees and brush beyond were ample areas where a weapon could have been tossed, and they spread outward from the crime scene. Between two scrawny pines, he came across a rough path and saw, in the center of the hardened dirt, a dark spot the size of a baseball that could easily be dried blood.

"Here!" he called out.

With much trampling of weeds and snapping of twigs, the others hurried over. It occurred to him that they should have treaded more carefully, that they might have destroyed evidence. Although most of them were hunters and familiar with the outdoors, none of them had ever worked on anything like this. They should probably be a little more circumspect in their movements.

Mitch crouched down next to the spot, looked at it carefully. "Blood," he confirmed.

"All right," Brad said. "Proceed slowly." He remained in the lead, moving with caution down the primitive trail. It seemed to be angling toward the refuse transfer station, though that was still a good half-mile away. The terrain at this elevation was high chaparral, and the path wound between copses of juniper, holly and overgrown manzanita. He saw no other evidence of blood on the dirt, and was about to stop and suggest that they return to the head of the trail and concentrate their search efforts in the brush around that area, when the path passed over a small rise and ended on the edge of a flat clearing.

He halted, shocked, completely unprepared for the sight that greeted him.

For it was not a weapon that he had stumbled upon but a massacre.

Bodies—he counted twelve, but the wildflowers grew high and there could conceivably be more—lay staggered along the south end of the small meadow. Unlike the man in the ditch, they were fully dressed, the men in white shirts and suits, the women in blouses and skirts. There was no path through the weeds and wildflowers, none of the grasses had been trampled, and he ordered the deputies to walk behind him single-file so as to disturb the site as little as possible.

"Go back and get those paramedics," he told Mitch, who was bringing up the rear. "Tell them what we have here. I count twelve so far, which means we're probably going to need more ambulances."

Mitch hurried off, talking into his shoulder radio as he ran, and the rest of them moved forward slowly. Maybe it wasn't a massacre, Brad conceded. He saw no blood. But the bodies definitely looked dead. He thought he should make sure and called out, "Gila County Sheriff's Department!"

No response. No sign of movement.

Kneeling next to the first body, that of a man, Brad placed a finger on the neck. The skin was cold and there was no pulse. He looked back at Hank and Bill F. and shook his head.

The man and the woman next to him he recognized as Mike Gamell and Juana Rodriguez, two former tellers from Bank of America. Standing up to look at the other bodies, he was pretty sure they had worked at the bank as well.

Brad knew who the fat man in the ditch was now: Bank of America's former manager. Glen something. Teagan? Teague? Taylor? It definitely started with a T.

"Glen Taggart," Bill F. said, as though reading his thoughts.

"And that's Cissy Platter," Hank said, pointing. "She signed my car loan."

If he had felt overwhelmed at the sight of the manager's body, Brad now felt completely out of his depth. Ignoring the crackle of his shoulder radio, though he heard Issac addressing him by name, he walked slowly past the prone corpses, seeing no wounds, no sign of injury, though there'd been blood on the trail here. Why had this happened? How had it happened? Was it some sort of suicide pact, a murder-suicide or just plain murder? The manager's killing could have conceivably happened on the day the Bank of America closed, since it was obvious that he'd been dead for a few days. But it was odd that no one had reported him missing. Was he married? Did he have family? Brad would have to have someone look that up.

It was the other deaths that really concerned him, however. They had obviously died more recently. No one had yet reported any of them missing—it was quite likely that their loved ones still did not know—and yet for some reason all of them, every employee of the bank, three days after the bank's closing, had either committed suicide or had been executed out here on the way to the transfer station.

Executed.

That was the word he'd been looking for. There were still no signs of violence readily apparent, but the manner in which the bank employees had been laid out on the ground reminded him of nothing so much as an execution.

"Sheriff!"

Issac was practically shouting through the com device now, and Brad pressed the talk button at his shoulder. "Neth here."

"You found more bodies and Mitch says they're all B of A employees?"

"As far as we can tell."

"Jesus. I thought maybe he got it screwed up and..." There was a lengthy crackle of static.

"I found two more over here!" Hank called out, pointing into the brush near the spot where he was standing.

Issac came back on the line. *"...many of them?"*

"Sorry," Brad said. "You faded out there for a minute. Say it again."

"I said, maybe we should contact the other employees and see if they know anything. How many of the bank's staff do you think you have out there?"

"Another one!" Bill F. called out.

Brad closed his eyes. "All of them," he said.

4

THE bank had turned them down.

Jen had not gotten the word over the phone, in person or through a formal letter. She'd gotten a text. Lane had gotten the same text, and she had called him only seconds before he'd been about to call her. Such a means of notification seemed far too casual for such an important decision, and she'd wondered aloud to Lane if such a move was legal. It certainly didn't seem ethical, and she'd said that maybe they should report the bank to the Better Business Bureau.

"It won't make us any more eligible," he'd told her.

"Why *aren't* we eligible? Even with my parents co-signing, we're still too big a risk?"

"I guess so."

A feeling of dejection had settled over her. "So we're permanent renters. For the rest of our lives."

The real estate agent had had another idea, though. She'd texted both of them moments later and said she was working on alternative financing. She wanted to meet at the house to talk to them about it rather than at her office, which made Jen suspect it might not be completely on the up and up, but it cost nothing to hear her out, and at this point what did they have to lose?

Lane had instantly called Jen back. "We're still in!"

"Let's hear what it is first. I'll meet you at the diner after work. We need to go together and show up at the same time so she doesn't have a chance to lobby one of us alone."

"You want to call her and set it up?"

"Okay. See you at five?"

"I'll be there, babe."

The diner was B.B.'s Roadside Diner on the south end of town. Montgomery actually had two diners, as well as a Denny's, but B.B.'s was the one they preferred, and they ate there at least once a week, on days she was too tired to cook.

Jen got off a few minutes early and waited for him in the booth closest to the door, attempting to drink Coke through a paper straw that had flattened with the very first suck and that she was unsuccessfully trying to pinch back into shape. At the next booth over, an overly made-up middle-aged woman was snuggling next to a sleazy looking older man, both of them engaging in an embarrassingly exaggerated display of affection.

In movies, when women sensuously sucked on men's fingers, it seemed arousing and provocative because it brought to mind oral sex. But she'd tried it once with Lane, and his finger had been rough and unappealing, the skin tasting of old onion and barbecue sauce from the hamburger he'd eaten for lunch. The whole thing had been disagreeable, and after that she had sworn off getting sex tips from films.

Not so the floozy in the next booth. She was holding the man's right wrist with both hands, two of his outstretched fingers in her mouth, her eyes closed in a sad parody of sexual arousal.

Rose, the waitress, stopped by to ask if she wanted a refill.

"Just another straw," Jen said.

Reaching into the pocket of her blue apron, Rose pulled one out. "Here you go, hon."

Jen nodded toward the oversexed older couple. "Can you get them to tone it down? It's a little…gross."

Rose gave her head a small, barely perceptible shake. "New owner," she whispered, and quickly moved to seat three highway workers who had just walked in.

B.B. didn't own B.B.'s Roadside Diner anymore? When had that happened? Jen hadn't even known the place was for sale. She glanced over at the next booth. And one of *them* was the new owner? What had happened, she wondered. Why had B.B. wanted to sell? The diner was almost always busy; it was hard to believe it wasn't making money.

Maybe he was sick or had some family emergency. Maybe his wife or his parents were sick.

She hoped the new owner—or owners—were smart enough to leave things as they were and not make any changes. The diner was a Montgomery institution.

Through the window, she saw Lane's pickup truck pull around the side of the building, and a moment later, he walked into the diner and sat down in the seat opposite her. "Sorry. We had a last minute delivery, and I couldn't get away." He picked up her glass, took out the straw and downed the last of her Coke, chewing on the ice. "Evangeline seems kind of hush-hush. Any idea what her plan is?"

Jen shook her head. "I have no clue. And the fact that she wants to meet at the house instead of her office seems kind of suspicious to me. I hope this is all on the level."

He nodded. "I was thinking the same thing. I mean, we want this house, of course. But I'm not getting involved with anything risky."

"Or illegal."

"I don't know if she'd go that far."

Jen shrugged. "She has kind of a reputation."

"Well, we'll hear her out."

"Yeah, but if it turns out it's some kind of internet scam or some friend of hers or whatever, we're not doing it."

"That's okay. We'll just keep renting and wait." He put a hand on hers. "Don't worry. We'll get there."

"Yeah," Jen said unconvincingly. She raised her hand. "Rose? Check?"

The house they were looking to buy was located behind the downtown in a neighborhood of modest wooden homes that had been built in the 1950s or 60s. They were ten minutes late, so the Realtor should have already been there, but her Lexus was neither in the driveway nor on the street outside. Lane parked his pickup in front of the house while Jen pulled her Accord into the carport. After getting out, she pointed to the FOR SALE sign in the middle of the brown lawn. "That'd be a SOLD sign if it wasn't for that stupid bank."

"I know." They walked out to the sidewalk, scanning the street for any sign of Evangeline. "Speaking of banks, did you hear about all those people from B of A?"

"I know! I can't believe it," she said.

"John's brother's one of the deputies who found them. They were all laid out in the field Jim Jones style."

Jen shivered. "Let's not talk about it." The sun was starting to go down, and the shadow of the house had almost taken over the lawn. The street was quiet, and while that had seemed like a selling point for the neighborhood up to now, at the moment she would have preferred to hear a car go by, kids playing, even a lawnmower or a teenager's stereo.

Lane must have read her mood. "Should we check and see if it's unlocked?" he asked.

"I don't think it is, but sure."

Together they walked up to the front door. There was a lockbox attached to the handle, but it was open, the key easily accessible to anyone who happened by. Lane took it out. "Shall we?" Without waiting for a response, he unlocked the door.

Jen stepped inside behind Lane, who had reached around the edge of the doorframe and flipped on the light. With no curtains on the windows, the dusk outside looked like night, and without furniture, the rooms stretching out before them looked bigger than the exterior of the building seemed able to hold.

She wandered into the remodeled kitchen, admiring the recently installed countertop grill and the greenhouse window over the sink that looked out at a surprisingly big back yard. Of course, the yard was in darkness right now, with only the faintest hint of orange sunset showing through the trees. It was odd being here as evening fell, and it gave the house a distinctly different vibe. She moved through the small dining room, and she and Lane both walked down the hallway, past the single bathroom and what she was already calling the guest room, to the master bedroom.

Since her first tour of the house, she had been certain that this was the place for them—they both had—but now something seemed off. The bedroom had only one window, and while that had never bothered her before, those three windowless walls made her think of a prison cell. Above the spot where, in her mind, she'd put their bed, she noticed a recessed square in the ceiling: the entrance to an attic. It had to be a small attic, she reasoned, probably little more than a crawlspace, but she still didn't like the fact that its entrance would be right over their bed.

"Hello!"

The Realtor's unexpected greeting made her jump, and Lane laughed as he took Jen's hand and led her back out to the living room.

"Sorry I'm late," Evangeline told them. "I was getting everything together for you."

She was carrying an iPad, and she turned it on, swiping and tapping before showing them the screen. "So what's happening is there's a new bank opening a branch in Montgomery, and they're reaching out to local business leaders like *moi*, who work with the banking community on a consistent basis. In an attempt to get a foothold in this town, they're offering us what they're calling *introductory* loans. Basically, to show their good faith, to let everyone know that they're invested in Montgomery and here to stay, and not some fly-by-night operation, they're providing a limited number of loans to families and couples who might have been turned down by traditional lenders, but who local movers and shakers, again like *moi*, believe deserve a second chance." She smiled brightly. "And of course I immediately thought of you!"

Jen looked at Lane, met his gaze. Maybe this wasn't such a bad idea.

"What's the interest rate?" Lane asked. "And points and fees and all that?"

Evangeline was all business. "Points vary, depending on whether you go fixed or adjustable, fifteen-year or thirty-year. The rate's actually a quarter of a percentage point lower than we were looking at with Montgomery Community." She held up the iPad, showing them the numbers. "It's a good deal, but it's not one that's going to last. We either take it or we don't, because this is like those cheap car prices auto dealers offer to get you onto the lot. It's a lure. So what I need from you is authorization to start the paperwork."

Jen looked at the blackness on the other side of the living room windows, thought of that attic entrance in the bedroom, and wasn't sure she still—

"Do it," Lane said, making the decision unilaterally.

She stared at him, thinking they needed to talk this over, thinking there should be a discussion, but when Evangeline looked quizzically over to solicit her opinion, Jen found herself nodding in agreement as though she had no will of her own. "Okay," she said. "Go ahead."

FIVE

1

IT ARRIVED OVERNIGHT, fully formed.

Kyle drove to work the way he always did, but before he even reached the curve that led into downtown, he spied a string of red balloons trailing upward into the sky above the pine and cottonwood trees that shielded the old business district from the newer retailers on the highway. Once around the curve, he saw vehicles parked on both sides of the street and a crowd of people lined up in front of... the bookstore?

No.

The bank.

He slowed the pickup as he drove by. This was impossible. When he'd closed up last night, the space next to Brave New World had been vacant. But now a tasteful conservative sign mounted above the freshly spotless windows identified the newly open business as The First People's Bank. Numerous balloons drew attention to a Grand Opening banner strung on a wire above the sidewalk. Through the windows, he could see well-dressed men and women seated at desks.

So overnight, someone had come in and completely cleaned and refurbished the dusty, abandoned formerly empty store? It didn't make sense, but the evidence was right in front of his eyes.

The bank was…there.

He reached the end of the block, turned right, then turned right again into the alley.

Maybe the bank would bring increased foot traffic to the downtown. As the shop next door, Brave New World would definitely be in a position to take advantage of people cashing paychecks and withdrawing money. And if even half of those former Bank of America customers switched to The First People's Bank, there'd be dozens of individuals downtown each day who ordinarily would not be in that part of Montgomery, some of whom might not even know Brave New World even existed. As far as he was concerned, this was a prime opportunity to gain new customers and turn around the store's fortunes.

It still seemed a strange location for a bank, not least because there was parking only on the street. There was no adjacent lot or parking structure, not even enough spaces for employees in the back. The entire thing seemed poorly planned out, and Kyle wondered how such a thing had ever gotten approval from the planning commission or the town council, both of which had become by-the-book sticklers about making sure renovations and new developments provided adequate parking after condos built near the golf course ten years ago turned out not to have enough parking spaces available for the number of units constructed.

Where was the bank going to keep its money? he wondered. As Gary had said, there wasn't enough room for the type of walk-in safe that most banks had. The former retail space was almost exactly the same size as Brave New World. Its boundaries were defined by the flat walls it shared with his store on one side and Trixie Johnson's consignment shop on the other.

He pulled into his parking spot and got out of the truck, locking it.

The whole situation seemed more than a little off.

Walking past the twin blue dumpsters shared by the business tenants in this block of buildings, Kyle was surprised to find the rear entrance to the bookstore locked. Opening up, he walked in, turning on the lights. Where was Gary? He was supposed to have opened this morning. True, it was only ten minutes after nine, but his clerk was seldom, if ever, late. If he was going to be tardy, he always called, texted or, in the case of a doctor's appointment, talked to Kyle in person and made arrangements ahead of time.

It occurred to him that Gary might be next door, applying for a job. Kyle supported his friend's efforts to find a new place to work and didn't begrudge him applying at the bank, but if that was the case, it would have been nice if he'd been informed so he could have shown up a little earlier.

In the storage space, Kyle got money out of the safe for the register. He was going to miss Gary when he was gone. The two of them had been through a lot together. On the other hand, it would be convenient having his friend work at the bank next door, if that's where he ended up finding employment. He might even open up a business account there and start making daily deposits rather than using his little safe.

Kyle counted out bills and placed the money in the register before putting on one of his "morning" CDs (*Solid Colors* by Liz Story, who at one point had lived over in Prescott, although he had no idea where she made her home now). He unlocked the front door. Outside, there was a small crowd on the sidewalk. Odd to have people lined up for a bank opening, he thought, but when he talked to Julie Hopper, who was standing at the end of the line in front of the bookstore's window, he found out the bank was not only offering free food and beverages as part of its grand opening, but was giving out tote bags to anyone who showed up and an assortment of gift cards to those who opened new accounts.

Still wondering about Gary, he called the other man's cell phone and then his house, reaching voicemail on both and leaving messages for Gary to call him back as soon as possible. *Could* he be next door? There were no customers yet, so Kyle locked the door behind him and walked over to the bank, bypassing the line since he had no interest in getting a tote bag.

What they had done with the place was amazing. Soft recessed ceiling lights illuminated dark wood walls hung with western art. On the carpeted left side of the long room were desks and chairs and potted palms. On the right half was a marble floor, a line of teller windows and two dark wood tables filled with pastries, donuts and miniature bottles of orange juice and water. There was indeed a walk-in safe in the back and, visible inside, a wall of safety deposit boxes.

Before heading for the food, the others attending the grand opening were collecting pamphlets and blue tote bags imprinted with the bank's name from employees standing next to boxes filled with the items just inside the door.

One of those employees was Gary.

Kyle was stunned. Gary was *already* working here? They'd *already* hired him?

When had that happened? It must have been this morning, because Gary sure as hell hadn't given any hint about this yesterday when they were closing. Although, if it *had* been this morning, Gary would have had to be interviewed and accepted hours ago in order to give him time to go out and buy that suit, because Kyle knew for a fact that his friend didn't own anything that nice.

Where could he have bought a new suit in Montgomery at eight o'clock in the morning?

Everything about this seemed wrong, and Kyle bypassed the line, walked behind a smiling Stepford woman passing out pamphlets and tapped Gary on the shoulder. "Hey."

"Hello, sir."

Gary didn't recognize him.

Kyle took a step back. How was this possible? He frowned. "What's going on here?"

"Our bank offers a range of services—"

"What the hell, Gary?" It occurred to him that maybe the bank *wanted* its employees to pretend not to know its customers out of some misguided sense that detachment implied objectivity.

But, no, the expression on his friend's face revealed no hint of familiarity, no indication that Gary had ever seen him before.

The cold that settled over him had nothing to do with the ultra-efficient air conditioning that had been installed overnight.

Gary offered him a bland smile.

"Would you like a tote bag, sir?"

2

AS soon as Coy arrived at work, Ben Shanley called him into his office.

"Close the door," he said.

Coy did so, then sat down in the proffered chair. The bank manager stood up from his own seat and started pacing, saying nothing for several moments, as though trying to gather his thoughts.

"We have competition," the manager said finally.

Coy frowned. "What?"

"There's going to be a new bank in town. It's opening up on Main Street next to the bookstore."

"I did hear a rumor about that."

"It's more than a rumor. I want you to do some research. Find out who owns this bank, where it comes from, when it's opening, the whole shebang. No doubt they know the name and background of every member of our board, of the president, of me, of you, hell, of everybody who works here. We're going to need some hard data in hand if we're going to compete on a level playing field." He shook his head. "This new deregulation push is opening up banking to every Tom's Hairy Dick that comes down the pike. Half of these halfwits probably have no idea what they're doing and'll quickly go under, but they could still screw things up for established institutions like ours." Shanley sighed. "And just when I thought we were getting a break with that Bank of America thing."

A break? Coy studied the manager's face. Was he aware that the Bank of America employees had been killed? It was hard to tell, but Coy didn't want to be the one to broach the subject so he simply nodded in agreement.

The truth was that the rest of them were freaked out about it. Rumor had it that the killings were related to the branch closing, that one of the employees had not taken it well and had killed himself and all of his co-workers (the smart money was on Tim Takamura, who had always seemed highly strung and just this side of unstable). But there was also the distinct possibility that some serial killer was targeting bank workers. In which case they could all be in danger.

Coy cleared his throat. "So you want me to..."

"Find out everything you can. Strengths, weaknesses, anything we can use against them, anything that'll help us retain our customers. Information is power, as they say, and I want as much information at my fingertips as you can find. And if you dig up any dirt..." He shrugged. "All's fair in love and business."

Coy nodded. The parameters were vague, and he still wasn't sure exactly what he was supposed to do, but he pretended that he did. "When do you need this by?"

"As soon as you can get it. I want all of your attention on this. If there's anything else that's outstanding or under deadline, pawn it off on Cal. Maggie can pick up his slack if need be. Got it?"

"Got it," Coy said and rose to go.

"We're fighting for our lives here," Shanley said. "Don't let me down."

He walked back to his desk, and the first thing he did was call Florine. If another bank was attempting to encroach on their territory, the agents at Evergreen Title would know. But when he asked what she knew about the bank that was supposed to be opening in Montgomery, she pled ignorance.

"I haven't heard anything about it," Florine told him.

He didn't believe her.

That was a first. And either way, whether she really *was* lying to him or whether he just *thought* she was lying to him, it marked a distressing milestone in what had been, until now, a pretty harmonious relationship.

"It's supposed to be opening in an existing space in the old downtown," he pressed. "Next to a bookstore. You sure you haven't heard anything?"

"No," she said.

There it was again.

She was lying, and when he tried to think of reasons why she wouldn't be honest with him, the one his mind kept coming back to was that Evergreen Title was planning to deal exclusively with the new bank. He thought about her previous warnings that Montgomery Community was being audited.

Should he say anything to Shanley?

Not yet. He needed more intel before he started formulating theories and making accusations. Heck, he didn't even know the *name* of the bank, which was the minimum information required if he was going to conduct any sort of research. Coy talked to Cal and Maggie, the tellers, even the security guard, but no one seemed to know anything, although Maggie said she was pretty sure there was a "Coming Soon" sign in the window that spelled out some of the details.

So his first order of business was to check that out. He let the manager know he was going, then drove down Frontier to Main, to the location where their rival would be opening.

Opening?

It was already open, and Coy was surprised to see a line of people on the sidewalk, waiting to get in. Driving by, he looked at the crowd. It had to be social media. There was a whole new world of below-the-radar advertising that passed him by and he knew Shanley was going to be upset that half the town knew about the bank's debut before they did.

Circling the block at the end of the street, Coy drove slowly back up Main, searching for a parking spot. He finally found one on the side street next to Ray's Photo and walked down the sidewalk to the new bank.

The First People's Bank it was called, and Coy mentally took off points for the generic name. *Montgomery Community.* Now there was a name for a bank. It connoted stability *and* local involvement.

Still, now that he had the name, he could start looking into the bank's background. As a loan officer, it was his job to dig into the financial histories of those who were applying for loans, and if he did say so himself, he was good at it. Successive Republican congresses had made it easier for companies to hide their financial shenanigans, but the information was there if you knew where to look, and he did.

But that applied to the greater institution. Shanley also wanted him to learn what he could about this specific branch, their immediate rival, and Coy walked inside to collect names and business cards, get the lay of the land.

There was a line of people waiting to get blue cloth bags and pick up pamphlets that were being passed out, and another line of people in front of tables stacked with food and drinks. He recognized some of them as—

former?

—Montgomery Community customers, but many others were unfamiliar to him. He wanted to get his hands on those pamphlets, but he decided to forgo the line and pick them up on his way out. Instead, he snooped around the tellers' windows, peeking at the area behind the partition.

"What are *you* doing here?"

Coy turned to see Florine walking toward him from where she'd been speaking to two men in dark business suits. He almost did a double take, unsure for a second if it was really her. Hadn't he just called Florine at work? How could she be here? It was possible that she'd had her calls forwarded from Evergreen Title to her cell. But why had she denied any knowledge of the new bank when here she was, apparently meeting with some of its executives? Confused, he started to ask her what was going on, but she cut him off.

"I said, what are you doing here?"

"I—"

She slapped him. Hard. Her knee drove deep into his groin, and he went down in an explosion of pain.

Strong hands grabbed him and carried him through the lobby. He hadn't noticed any security guards when he'd walked in, but every bank had at least one, and he was pretty sure that's who was silently removing him from the building. He saw some of his—

former

—customers glance at him, then look quickly away, and then the glass door opened before him and the two men who had been carrying him placed him butt-down on the sidewalk. The pain was still excruciating, and he leaned back against the building, waiting for it to subside.

What the hell was going on?

Something far outside the normal bounds of business, that was certain.

Experimentally, Coy attempted to stand. There was a brief slash of agony that flared from his testicles to his stomach as pressure was put on the muscles that met at his crotch. The pain receded slightly as he balanced on two feet, enough at least for him to walk, and he hobbled past two men heading into the bank.

He definitely had something to report to Shanley, but what it meant he had no clue.

Slowly, he made his way up the block to where he'd parked, hoping all the way to feel a tap on his shoulder or an arm around his midsection as Florine came after him to apologize. But she didn't try to catch up to him, and when he reached the end of the block and looked back down the sidewalk before turning, there was no sign of her.

3

ANITA went over to the bookstore at lunch. She showed up without warning, bearing food from Juan Wang's, which Kyle had said earlier in the week that he wanted to try. She couldn't remember the last time she'd done something like this, couldn't remember the last time *either* of them had acted so spontaneously, and she realized that maybe if she'd been more consistent in putting this sort of effort into the marriage, the situation with Steven never would have happened.

It *hadn't* happened, though. That was the point. It had *almost* happened, but she'd come to her senses and realized what she would be losing if she went down that path.

She remembered when she and Kyle had first started dating. It wasn't until their senior year in high school, but they'd already known each other forever. He'd sat behind her in second grade, and she could still recall the way he would kick the back of her chair when he was bored, swinging his legs until she turned around and told him to knock it off. In junior high, they'd run with entirely different crowds (not that boys and girls intermingled much at that stage anyway). Her lunchtimes had been taken up with nearly every club imaginable, while he could usually be found hanging out with his weird friend Roger in the library. But in high school, they'd been thrown together in AP English and History, and she'd discovered that she...kind of...*liked* him.

She'd been the one to make the first move. If it had been left up to him, it never would have happened. They'd been spending a lot of time together preparing for a debate in history, since they were the only two reliable members of their team, and one afternoon as they were preparing to leave school, she'd asked him if he wanted to stop by Lottaburger with her on the way home and get something to drink. A Coke, maybe. At that point, she'd sort of been dating Dennis Whittaker, but there was nothing really serious between them yet and all they'd done was kiss, so she didn't feel guilty about asking out Kyle, and she was more excited than she had ever been in her life when he acquiesced and said yes.

By the next week they were dating, and they had remained together ever since.

So how had it come to the point where she was flirting with the guy who owned the nursery?

They'd gotten off track somehow. Maybe it was *because* they'd been together for so long, and neither of them had ever seriously gone with anyone else. Who knew? But she'd almost made a huge mistake, had caught herself just in time, and was now committed to making sure their marriage stayed strong, if not for their own sakes then for Nick.

"Lunch is served!" Anita announced as she walked into the store, the bell above the door jingling.

Kyle, caught by surprise, looked up from the book he'd been reading. "Hey!" he said. His face brightened when he saw her, which made her feel guilty.

She handed him the white Juan Wang's sack. "I got you an egg-roll burrito. You said you wanted to try one."

"Thanks," he said, genuinely grateful. He opened the sack and looked in. "You want to trade for the leftover chicken sandwich I was going to eat?"

Smiling, she shook her head. "You can have that, too. By the way, what's all the commotion next door?"

"The new bank's open."

"Already?"

"Oh yeah." He reached under the counter and pulled out a blue canvas bag. "Check it out," he said drily. "They're giving these away free. Even if you don't open up a new account."

"For their grand opening?"

"Yep." There was a weird pause. "Oh, and Gary's working there now."

She frowned, confused. "What?"

He shrugged, tried to smile, but she could sense his uneasiness beneath the gesture. "I don't understand it, but when I got here this morning, the store was closed—Gary was supposed to open—and when I went to check out the bank, there he was, all dressed up in a brand new suit, greeting customers and handing out these." He raised the bag. "You know he's been applying at different places because of our... financial situation. With my blessing. He even put in an application at the Costco in Sirena. I've been hoping he'd catch on somewhere—there's not really enough work for two here right now, and it'd be a load off my shoulders if I knew he had a steady job—but he didn't tell me anything about the bank. Hell, just yesterday we were both wondering how many *weeks* or *months* it would be until it even opened."

There was another weird pause.

"What is it?" Anita asked. "What aren't you telling me?"

"He didn't seem to recognize me. When I went over there. He gave me my bag." Kyle held it up again. "But he didn't know who I was."

"What do you mean, he didn't know who you were?"

"He didn't know who I was."

"How is that possible?"

"I don't know. I'm just telling you what happened. It was the damnedest thing."

"Are you sure he wasn't just trying to act professional?"

"I'm not sure of anything." He pulled his wrapped eggroll burrito out of the bag.

"I'm going to see for myself."

"Go right ahead. I'll just be here eating my lunch." He took a bite and made a satisfied face. "Mmmm. You're right. These things are good."

"Told you." Giving him a quick wave, Anita walked outside and headed next door. *The First People's Bank*. That was the name? It seemed like they were opening themselves up for false advertising charges right off the bat. Out of all the banks in the country, could this really be the *first* people's bank?

She opened the glass door and stepped inside. Cool air greeted her, cool air and a pleasant soft scent that reminded her of something she'd smelled in childhood, something she'd liked. The new bank was tastefully decorated and free from the generic formality of most financial institutions. It seemed welcoming, comfortable.

A friendly well-dressed young woman she didn't recognize met her just inside the door and offered her a tote bag as well as some informational pamphlets. Anita looked around, trying to find Gary, but saw no sign of him. Another man approached her, however, emerging from a small group of potential customers gathered around a snack table at the opposite end of the lobby. He was clearly management level, and he directed the actions of a few other employees by hand motions as he walked.

"Hello," he said when he reached her. He took her right hand in both of his and gave it a squeeze. "I'm Mr. Worthington, the manager. Welcome to our bank."

Undeniably attractive, the man exuded confidence and competence, and his casual manner put her instantly at ease. "Thank you," she said.

He smiled. "I know you're not a First People's customer—yet. But I'm hoping you'll let me talk to you about the services we offer, and that you'll give us a chance to show you what we can do for you."

Anita smiled back. "Sure," she said.

"All right, then." Placing a light hand on her back, he smoothly guided her to an unoccupied desk. His hand slid away as he moved around to the other side of the desk, gently brushing her hip, and she felt an electric thrill pass through her.

For the next ten minutes, he made a convincing case as to why she should move her checking and savings accounts from Montgomery Community to The First People's Bank, touting the myriad benefits offered free to customers as well as the personal attention provided by the friendly professional staff. Anita listened politely. She'd had no intention of switching banks, but after hearing Mr. Worthington's spiel, she found herself wondering if it might not be prudent to talk to Kyle. The man's presentation was very effective, very persuasive. Sensing, perhaps, that she had become more amenable, he backed off, giving her room. "So here's my card. You have our literature. Talk it over with your husband. We're a great little bank, and we'd love to have your business." He grasped her hand again, and it was as though he'd pressed one of those secret acupressure points, one that went directly from her palm to her...

She reddened, pulled away. "Thank you," she said. "I'll certainly think about it."

"Call or stop by if you have any questions." He flashed her his winning smile. "Anytime."

"Did you see Gary?" Kyle asked when she returned to the bookstore.

"No," she told him, lifting her tote bag by its straps. "But I did get one of these."

That night, in bed, she imagined it was the banker on top of her rather than Kyle, and when she came, she cried out loudly and involuntarily in a way that she had not done for a long, long time.

4

A bird wasn't the same as a pet, but he'd caught it and sacrificed it, so it still counted, and after cutting off the wings and feet and placing them in the corners of the foursquare court, V.J. said, "One, two, three four, that's all there is and there ain't no more," then pulled out four eyelashes, put them in his mouth and swallowed.

He had completed the ritual at the park again (he was starting to like the park!) and was in the process of recording the particulars in his notebook, when he sensed movement nearby and off to his right. Looking up from his work, he saw two men standing on the walkway next to the foursquare court, watching him.

Startled, his first thought was that he'd been caught, and his initial impulse was to run, hoping that he would not be followed or recognized. But he ascertained almost immediately that the two men had no interest in confronting him about what he'd done. On the contrary, they seemed pleased with what they'd witnessed.

It wouldn't pay to be too accommodating, however, and there was no guarantee that he was reading this situation right, so he faced the men and demanded, "What are you looking at?"

The one on the right stepped forward, hand extended. He had short neatly combed hair, a pleasant open face, and was wearing a dark blue suit with white shirt and red tie. He smiled as he introduced himself. "Julius Pickering. You can call me Jay." Seeing that V.J. had no intention of shaking his hand, he let his arm fall, though the movement seemed smooth and natural rather than awkward.

V.J. closed his notebook. "That's great," he said. "But I gotta go."

"My associate and I would like a word with you first."

The man with him had stepped forward as well. He, too, was clean shaven and wearing a business suit, but there was a slovenly air about him, and something familiar in the way he stood.

V.J. squinted.

Was it that homeless guy?

"I would like to offer you a job," Pickering said. "You'll be working with Mr. Heywood here."

"I'm Mr. Heywood," the other man muttered.

V.J. recognized the voice. It *was* the homeless guy.

What's going on here?

"The two of you will be processing loans for The First People's Bank."

"Processing loans? I'm not qualified—"

"You're plenty qualified." Pickering motioned toward the bird legs and wings in the corners of the foursquare court.

This didn't seem right. But it was as though he was in a trance or under some sort of spell, his brain unable to connect the dots and determine why this was not normal.

"What would I be doing?"

The man smiled, and something about that smile both frightened and attracted him.

"What would you be doing? Many things," he said softly. "Many things."

SIX

1

"**S**0 WHAT DO we do?"

The question hung in the air, and Brad had no idea how to answer it. The final results from the autopsies had come in, and according to the M.E. the men and women they'd found in the meadow had not died from poisoning, as they'd assumed, but had died of natural causes.

All of them.

At the same time.

He did not know where to go from here. How were they supposed to investigate something like this? It was clearly not a natural event—the victims were all dressed up, for God's sake, all former B of A employees, all lying together in a field—but getting to the bottom of what had happened was going to involve far more than the ordinary law enforcement techniques and procedures with which he was familiar.

Glen Taggart, the Bank of America manager, had most definitely *not* died of natural causes, not with all those stab wounds and that caved-in face. He had been murdered. The report on Taggart showed that two weapons had been used in the assault: one with a sharp blade, most likely some type of knife, the other a heavy blunt object, possibly a baseball bat. This, at least, was something they could sink their teeth into, and Brad told the assembled deputies that they were going to focus their efforts on finding the bank manager's killer or killers as quickly as possible, which, hopefully, would lead to a solution to the deaths of the other bank employees. They would be going over Taggart's house and the homes of the others with a fine-toothed comb, as well as interviewing friends, relatives and neighbors. He ordered both Bills to survey security cam footage from the gas station and Circle K on the north end of town, as well as any other businesses or residences that might have footage of the road that led toward the refuse transfer station, and told Mitch to rustle up a posse and start looking for weapons in the underbrush near the site.

"We're going to get this bastard," he promised.

But that was easier said than done. Their manpower was stretched so thin because of this that if the mayor had murdered his mother on Main Street that afternoon, there wouldn't have been an officer available to arrest him, yet by the end of the afternoon, not a single lead had turned up. Brad spent the day not only coordinating the efforts of his various teams, but consulting with both the M.E. and, via videoconference, a profiler from Phoenix, and by the time he knocked off at six, after instructing Vern to call him at home if anything turned up afterhours, the only thing he had to show for it was a headache.

Grateful not to have heard a peep from either the radio in his car or his cell phone on the short ride over, he unlocked the front door and wearily entered the house. "I'm home!" he announced. Jillian and Sue were both seated on the living room floor in front of the television, and they jumped up at the sound of his voice. "Daddy!"

When the expected sound of Patty's voice did not immediately call out to him from the kitchen, he glanced in that direction, suddenly noticing that aside from the girls and the television, the house was silent. Brad frowned. "Where's Mommy?"

"She had to go out."

"And she left you here by yourselves?" Brad was incredulous. This was not only completely unlike Patty but was completely unacceptable, and anger built within him. Yes, the door to the house had been locked when he'd arrived home, but he'd just come back from investigating the deaths of fifteen people, including the most brutal murder in Montgomery history, and he didn't think this was the time to be leaving little girls alone. It wasn't the 1940s for God's sake, when people let their kids run wild, blithely talk to strangers and come home when the sun went down. This was *now*. What the hell could she have been thinking?

Outside a car door slammed. Patty was home. A moment later, the front door opened. "I'm back!" she announced, but the chipper tone of her voice was undercut by wariness. She had seen the car in the driveway, knew he was here, and knew he would not be happy.

She got *that* right, Brad thought.

He confronted her the second she stepped into the living room. "What were you thinking?" he said accusingly. "Leaving the girls by themselves? I come home and you're nowhere to be found and they're in here all alone watching TV?"

"I'm sorry," she said contritely.

"You're sorry? I can't believe this! Do you know what I spent my day doing? Looking for whoever slaughtered Glen Taggart and laid out all those bodies in that field!"

"I *am* sorry," Patty said, and there was true remorse in her voice. "But I was gone for less than twenty minutes, and this was an opportunity too good to pass up. It's that big house near the golf course. You know those acre lots they were trying to sell for awhile but only that one house was built? It's listing for a million plus. A million plus! That's the biggest residential sale ever in this town, and the owners wanted *me* to sell it for them! How could I turn that down?"

"You didn't have to abandon your children!"

"Mommy didn't abandon us," Jillian said defensively.

"Go in your room," Brad said. "Mommy and Daddy need to talk."

With furtive looks toward each of their parents, the girls slunk out of the living room.

"I didn't call you," Patty said, "because I knew you were too busy to get away. And, all right, maybe I should have brought them with me. But some of these clients are temperamental and don't like kids, and I didn't want to lose the listing. It was just a quick trip to the office, ten minutes or so, and I made sure the girls were locked in here and wouldn't open the door."

"What if there was a fire? Or a gas leak? Would they have been able to get out or would I have come home to find their charred corpses?"

"That's a terrible thing to say!"

"Things happen. And it's our job as parents to make sure they don't happen to *our* daughters. I thought you understood that."

"I do. Of course, I do."

But his faith in her had been shaken, and the anger and fear he felt was nearly overwhelming. He would never be able to put out of his mind what he had seen out by the control road, and while he usually wasn't one to bring his work home with him, this was different, and the fact that Patty had been willing to leave Sue and Jillian all alone in order to secure a listing while such a psycho was on the loose left him feeling off balance, as though he'd just discovered after all these years that she was someone he didn't really know.

She reached for his arm. "I made a mistake. A mistake I will never make again."

He looked into her eyes. "But why did you make it in the first place? It's not as if you're a new mother and aren't used to having children. This isn't something that just came up. You've been taking care of Sue and Jillian for years. I always thought you were a good mother, but now—"

She pushed him away. "That's not fair!"

"I'm sorry, but that's—"

"I'm as good a mother as you are a father, and I spend more time with them than you do. Just because I left them for fifteen minutes—"

"I thought you said it was twenty."

She glared at him. "Did you know that Natalie Bloom, that perfect mother, left Hannah in the car one time when she went in to the bank when Hannah was a baby? Because she *forgot*? In the summer? And do you know that Dottie's daughter Livia answered the phone the other day when I called because Dottie had fallen asleep in front of her computer, and Livia was in the kitchen next to the phone because she was trying to make macaroni and cheese even though she's too young to use the stove? Plus, I don't think there's a day that goes by that I don't see that little boy down the block, what's-his-name, wandering out into the street with his parents nowhere in sight. So before you start accusing *me* of being a bad parent, I suggest you look around and do a little comparison shopping."

Neither of them were going to budge on their positions, but the girls were already frightened by the fighting, and Patty *had* promised not to do it again, so even though he was still angry, Brad forced himself to calm down and nod. "Okay," he said.

"Okay what?"

"You made a mistake, you learned from it, and you're not going to do it again."

"Oh, I *learned* from it?"

He shot her a look, and she stopped herself, glancing toward the hallway and the girls' bedroom beyond. "Fine," she said.

He took her hand. "I'm only making a big deal of it because there are fifteen people dead—*fifteen!*—and that bank manager..." He shook his head. "You didn't see what happened to him."

"I know. And I'll be careful."

"Okay."

They hugged and made up, and both of them went back to get the girls and tell them everything was okay.

2

NICK met up with Aaron at lunch, the two of them sitting on the low brick wall in front of the band room. Once again, Victor was MIA.

"Where is he?" Aaron wondered, unwrapping his sandwich. "He's been out for three days now."

"Maybe he has mono."

Aaron snorted. "Victor? Right. Who'd he be kissing?"

"Well...Stacey could have spit on him."

Aaron laughed. Nick chuckled at the thought, too, but the truth was that he was worried. He'd tried to call his friend several times, had even gone by his house yesterday after school, but there'd been no one home. That was odd. Victor had always been something of a latchkey kid, but he took advantage of that, and when his parents were out, he was usually in, acting as though he were lord of the manor. But he was not at school, not at home, not answering his phone...so where was he?

As much as Nick dreaded the idea, he was thinking he might tell his parents and have them call Victor's parents to find out what was going on.

"So are you rewriting your play?" Aaron asked.

Nick nodded. "Sure. It's now called *Diarrhea Jones Goes to the White House*, and it's about a man with irritable bowel syndrome who's invited by the president to spend a weekend at the White House. Hijinks ensue."

"Seriously, bruh, Nelson'll have your ass if you don't do something more...normal. Maybe something without shit in it?"

He chuckled. "I know. But I still haven't come up with anything. Although I'm thinking of making a YouTube video of me reading my new poem, *Mrs. Nelson is a Bitch*."

Aaron's eyes widened. "Are you serious?"

Nick laughed. "No. But it'd be cool, right?"

"It'd be awesome!"

"Maybe this summer we'll do something like that. Post it anonymously."

Greg Holloway and three of his jock friends walked by, and one of them threw a half-empty Coke can that missed Aaron but splashed soda on his backpack. The four boys continued on, laughing and high-fiving each other.

"Assholes," Aaron muttered.

"Someone's going to have to change the oil in our cars when we're rich and famous." Nick smiled. "High school doesn't last forever."

"Thank God."

They ate for a moment in silence.

"So, hey," Aaron asked, "do you have a bank account?"

"What?"

"Did your parents ever open up a bank account for you, where you, like, save your money?"

"What does that have to do with the price of poon in Thailand?"

"I was just wondering. I always had this sort of piggy bank in my room where I kept all my cash. It's like a Thomas the Tank Engine I got when I was a little kid, but it didn't make any difference because I never had much money. I mean, my grandma would give me twenty bucks for my birthday, and my parents paid me a measly allowance, but that usually went pretty fast. Now, though, all of a sudden, my dad's on my ass about opening up a bank account." Aaron paused. "It's kind of weird."

"Yeah," Nick admitted. "I have a savings account. I never touch it and don't even know how much is in it, but I think my parents deposit money in there periodically."

"He's really hyped up about this new bank, too. That's where he wants me to open my account." Nick snorted. "Did I say *wants*? I meant *insists*." He shook his head. "Fuckin' weird, man."

"That bank's next to my dad's store."

"Yeah?"

"Yeah. And the guy who used to work for him works there now, only there's something…I don't know, *strange* about it. He and my dad were friends, but it's like now they're not. I don't know the details—my dad doesn't exactly *share* things—but the whole thing seems kind of…off."

"Well then that's where I want to keep *my* money," Aaron said in a sarcastically chipper voice.

Finished with his lunch, Nick balled up the brown paper sack he'd brought it in and tossed it at a nearby trash barrel, missing by at least a foot. Mrs. Nelson walked past just at that moment, and she frowned at him. "Pick it up," she ordered. "We'll have none of that here."

He'd intended to pick it up, but there was no way she was going to believe that, so he didn't even try to argue the point. Dutifully, he hopped off the wall and deposited the wadded up sack in the trash can. The teacher continued on.

"Mrs. Nelson *is* a bitch," Aaron said under his breath, and they both laughed as Aaron dropped his trash into the barrel before the two of them headed toward the library for the rest of the lunch period.

ON the way home, Nick decided to stop by Victor's house again. After school, he'd tried calling both his friend's house and cell, with no luck, so he thought he'd check in person, see if anyone was home. Even if Victor was gone, maybe his mom or dad was there, and he could ask one of them what was going on.

Because something definitely wasn't right.

Victor's Jeep was not in the driveway, as expected, but to his surprise, Nick saw the family's beat-up Explorer parked in front of the garage. That meant that either his mom or dad were home, although why no one had answered the phone was a mystery.

Maybe they'd just arrived and hadn't been there when he called.

Feeling a little better, Nick stepped onto the porch and rang the bell. He hoped Mrs. Clark answered the door. His friend's mom was definitely easier to talk to than his dad.

A minute passed.

He rang the bell again, then knocked on the door, even though he'd heard the bell's three-toned chime sound inside the house.

Maybe whoever was home was in the bathroom. Or maybe Victor's parents were having sex. Maybe they'd come home for a quickie—which would explain why neither of them had answered the phone.

Nick smiled to himself. Maybe *Victor's* mom was getting boned by the gardener.

But when no one came to the door, and when he realized that he could hear no noise at all coming from inside the house, Nick began feeling slightly unsettled. It was the Explorer in the driveway that concerned him. If it wasn't for that, he would have assumed no one was home, but with the SUV here and no one answering either the phone or the door, he couldn't help wondering if something had happened to Victor's mom. Or dad. Or both.

His cellphone rang, and Nick jumped, startled.

He pressed the Talk button. "Hello?"

"Nicholas Decker? This is Mr. Worthington from The First People's Bank. How are you this afternoon?"

"Uh, fine," Nick said warily.

"Great! Great! I'm calling because we're reaching out to younger people in Montgomery, people like yourself, in order to let them know about all the services we provide. For instance, do you currently have free checking?"

"I'm...I'm not really interested," Nick replied.

He was about to end the call, when the man said forcefully, "Don't hang up."

It was an order not a request, and though Nick's first instinct was to say something rude and sarcastic before defiantly clicking off, he found himself suddenly afraid to terminate the conversation.

"Now listen to me carefully." The man's voice was low, deadly serious and brooked no argument. "Get off Victor Clark's porch, leave his yard, stay off his property and stop snooping. Do I make myself clear?"

How did the man know he was here? Even as Nick looked in vain for signs of a security camera, he was thinking, *Why would the* bank *be monitoring Victor's house?*

"Do you understand me? Leave. Now."

Nick did end the call, turning his phone off completely, but he also hurried off the porch and back to his bike, pedaling away as fast as he could.

What the hell was going on?

He wasn't sure. But with Gary defecting from the bookstore to the bank, and Aaron's dad pressuring Aaron to open a bank account, and the bank spying on Victor's house and ordering him to stay away, *something* was up, and it definitely had to do with First People's.

Frightened and feeling cold, Nick pedaled hard all the way home, letting himself into the house and locking the door behind him.

And when the telephone rang, he did not answer it.

3

PRAISE Jesus!

His bets had come in. All of them. And they'd come in big.

Walter could not stop smiling. The small group of worshippers who attended Wednesday's Bible Study were already in the meeting room, waiting, but the pastor could not seem to tear himself away from the FreshBets results page on his computer, where a bright green box was displaying the flashing number **$2,000.**

Two thousand dollars!

There were college games coming up this weekend, and one of them, as far as he was concerned, was a sure thing. He was definitely going to bet on it—he just wasn't sure how much of his winnings he was going to roll over into that action.

Of course, the first thing he was going to do was put some of his winnings toward the church's renovation fund. They'd been raising money for over a year to add new pews, re-roof the building and build a larger rec room for youth outreach. Five hundred dollars was a big chunk of change and would help a lot in reaching their goal. Norma Crenshaw and her crowd might refuse those ill-gotten gains if they knew where the money came from, but as far as he was concerned, it was like what happened in *Guys and Dolls* when Sky Masterson rolled the gamblers in the sewer for money against their attendance at the Salvation Army mission meeting. Using the wages of sin for a higher purpose, fighting fire with fire, as the Salvation Army general said. That's what he was doing.

Although…

Maybe he shouldn't give the church half. Maybe he should hold back a little bit more in order to…reinvest. If he could turn a hundred or two of that five into another thousand, that would be even better, and would help the church far more in the long run.

Walter could sense from the tenor of voices in the meeting room that his Bible study group was getting restless, so he took a last look at the proof of his winnings—

$2,000!

—before lifting the Bible from his desk and picking up his sheaf of notes about today's topic. He opened the door to the meeting room, smiling broadly. "Good morning!" he said. "What a glorious day God has blessed us with!"

AFTER the meeting, Doug Coats, who, appropriately enough for a man with his last name, owned both the dry cleaners in the Safeway center and the laundromat at the trailer park, hung back while the rest of the group said their goodbyes. When everyone had gone, he approached Walter, still standing in the doorway. "Pastor? Do you have a minute? There's something I'd like to discuss with you."

Walter had been yearning to get back to FreshBets, but Doug was a good guy, as well as one of the church's top fundraisers, and this *was* his job, so he smiled in the most pastorly way he knew how and said, "Sure, Doug. What's on your mind?"

"Tourists."

"Tourists?"

"Yes. Tourists. I've been talking with some other local business-men, and we were discussing how, for a town this size and this type of area, Montgomery has very few visitors. As you know, a lot of businesses are dependent on foot traffic, and while the people here are great, they don't get out much. They go to work, go home—" He gestured around him. "—go to church, but their routines are pretty well set. Shops like Henry Davies', for instance, are usually found in areas with a lot of tourists. Those businesses are not doing well. You follow what I'm saying?"

Walter nodded, though he had no idea where this was going.

"Well, we were thinking that Montgomery could use some sort of...attraction, maybe an arboretum, like Boyce-Tompkins in

Superior, something impressive enough to put us on the map and attract visitors here. There's that big plot of land on the south side of town that backs up to national forest. We were thinking that if someone bought that, developed it into an arboretum with native southwest plants, put some promotional muscle behind it, we might be able to drum up some tourist business for Montgomery. And once the word started spreading..." He opened his arms in an expansive gesture. "Maybe we'd have new shops, new restaurants, even a hotel here. Who knows?

"Now Henry and everyone don't have any money to do something like that. They're barely surviving. My businesses are doing well, but the investment would be substantial, and the bank doesn't seem to want to back me. For something like this, I'm carrying too much debt. I don't look good on paper. So I was wondering if maybe you could vouch for me with the bank. Or even set me up with other investors who might want in. Your word carries weight in this town, and I think if you supported me, it might help a lot."

"To start an arboretum."

"That's right."

Walter sighed. "I'm not sure it's such a good idea," he admitted. "For one thing, it sounds risky to me—"

"The *bank* thinks it's a good idea. And if it's so risky, why are they putting up the money for it?"

"I thought you said—"

"That was a test, Pastor. The loan officer at the bank said that it was a waste of money for me—or anyone—to donate money to the church because you don't know the first thing about finance. I defended you—I always liked you, Pastor. I always believed in you— but then he asked where all that money you collect goes, why there haven't been any improvements to the church like there's supposed to be. He's the one who suggested I test you about money matters."

The elation he'd felt since learning about his winnings fled, and Walter felt himself sinking into gloom. "The church's money is in the church's account," he said in an effort to defend himself. "Nothing's been done with it yet because we haven't reached our goal. And we won't reach our goal," he added, "without the generous support of worshipers like yourself."

Doug shook his head. "Sorry, Pastor. I want to use my money to do something *real* for this town." He nodded goodbye. "I'll still see you in church on Sunday, though."

Walter watched him go, then shut the door, walking dejectedly back to his office. He stared out the window for a moment, looking at the church's empty parking lot, before sitting down in front of the computer on his desk. A screen saver showing Jesus ascending to Heaven was exhibited on the monitor, and he pressed the spacebar to clear the display. *BET NOW!* flashed red against a blue background, accompanied by a triumphant fanfare of simulated horns.

If Doug Coats really was going to stop contributing to the church, Walter thought, then he was going to have to raise quite a bit of money to make up the difference. Which meant that instead of putting half of his winnings toward the renovation fund and reinvesting the other half, perhaps he should bet the *whole* thing in order to receive a higher yield.

BET NOW!

He clicked on the flashing words, and from the displayed list of weekend sporting events, chose the game this Saturday that he knew was a sure thing.

The odds were three to one!

He put in the whole two thousand.

And topped it off with a hundred more.

4

ANITA had purposely been avoiding the new bank, had made a special effort to stay away from the entire downtown, even Brave New World, ever since…that night. She had tried her damnedest to push the entire incident from her mind and had almost succeeded in convincing herself that it hadn't happened, but when the bank manager arrived at the office for a meeting with Dr. Wilson, it all came back in a rush.

There were no patients in the office, and Jen was talking to her about how they were still waiting to hear from Evangeline about financing through First People's, when the waiting room door opened and Mr. Worthington walked in. Jen immediately sat down in front of the window, trying to look professional and responsible in front of the bank manager, while Anita, overcome by a sudden panic, rushed off to the restroom, locking the door behind her.

She sat on the closed lid of the toilet, practically shaking.

What had happened with Steven—

almost happened

—was one thing, a complicated combination of unique personal circumstances. But she wasn't a cartoon character—the horny dissatisfied wife looking for new meat—and what she'd experienced at the bank and afterward, that night, in bed with Kyle, had left her feeling decidedly uneasy. Going over it in her mind, as she had many, *many* times since, she could not help but feel that it had not been a natural response, that something had...happened, that Worthington or some unknown element within the bank had influenced her, impelling her to react as she had, manipulating her thoughts and emotions. It was a crazy theory and made no sense, but while she had not shared it with Kyle, she could not automatically discount it.

Primarily because of Gary.

Kyle was still confused about what had happened with his friend, Anita knew, and she had to admit that Gary's behavior was not only completely out of character but downright bizarre. Futile attempts to contact his former employee had left Kyle feeling frustrated—apparently he was never at home anymore, even when the bank was closed—and reports from friends and acquaintances seemed to confirm that he was not himself these days. Durl Meadows had told Kyle that Gary had been his teller when he'd cashed his paycheck, and not only had Gary not recognized him, but he had barely recognized Gary, who for some reason had shaved his head. And according to Rollie Brown, who lived on Gary's street, even when Gary was home at night, his house remained dark, all of the lights off.

Something was definitely up with that bank.

Through the thin wall, Anita could hear the muffled sounds of the two men talking. Her intention had been to wait them out, to stay hidden until Worthington left, but as the minutes dragged on and he showed no sign of leaving, she realized reluctantly that she was going to have to leave the bathroom and start work. If she remembered correctly, Zak Patel was coming in this morning for an eye exam, and Zak did *not* get along with Jen, which meant that she would have to deal with the old bastard.

She flushed the toilet to make her visit to the restroom seem legit, then washed her hands and went out. Zak Patel was stepping into the waiting room as she approached the window, and Jen shot her a grateful look, vacating the chair to allow Anita to sign him in. After checking his insurance, taking his co-payment and printing out a receipt, Anita told Zak to have a seat, the doctor would be with him shortly.

Moments later, Dr. Watson emerged from his office looking pleased. Mr. Worthington followed, shifting his briefcase from his left hand to his right. He smiled at Anita, an open, white-toothed smile that automatically caused her to smile back. Instantly, she regretted doing so, because his smile widened, shifted, and suddenly there was something lascivious in it, something that made her realize he was thinking about her in a way that was decidedly not professional. She recalled a scene from *Gone With the Wind*, where Scarlett, reacting to a visual appraisal by Rhett Butler, says, "He looks as if he knows what I look like without my shimmy." That was how Anita felt, and while she had to admit there was an attraction on her part, it was a *forced* attraction, not something she sought or wanted, but something that was *pulled* from her.

How?

She had no idea, but the same thing had occurred at the bank, and it frightened her. She watched Worthington exit through the waiting room. Before walking outside, he waved goodbye to her.

"What's up?" Jen asked, seeing her face.

"Nothing." Anita tried to shrug it off.

But Jen had known her long enough to be able to read her

moods, and after more prodding, Anita admitted that the man from the bank made her uncomfortable, that she'd encountered him before at First People's grand opening and there'd been kind of a weird incident.

Jen responded with a sympathetic nod.

Anita suddenly thought of something. "That's not who you're dealing with for your loan is it?"

"I don't know. Maybe. I told you, we haven't met with the bank yet. Evangeline's still setting that up."

Dr. Watson indicated to them that he was ready for a patient, and Anita called Zak Patel and led him back to the exam room.

Things got a little busy after that, and it wasn't until almost noon that Anita finally had a chance to check her email. Where she found fifteen messages from The First People's Bank, each titled: *BANK WITH US!*

She deleted the entire group without reading any of them.

After getting off work at five, Anita stopped by Safeway to pick up some groceries for dinner, but halfway to the register, her cart filled with milk, orange juice, pasta, spaghetti sauce, tortillas and cans of refried beans, she realized that she'd forgotten to get money from the bank. She had still not received a replacement Visa card, and with no way of paying for the groceries, she tried calling and then texting Kyle. He did not pick up his phone and, though she waited several minutes, did not reply to her text, so, feeling conspicuous and embarrassed, she put everything back and drove home. *He* could pick up something for dinner, she thought, and, sitting in the driveway, she texted him exactly that.

Neither Kyle nor Nick was home yet, and she wasn't sure if she was worried by Nick's absence or angry at him. School ended at three, and he should have been back long before this. Following the suspension, he was supposed to keep them informed of his whereabouts, and the fact that he was not where he should be left her feeling both irritated and concerned. She stepped out of the car and was about to call his cell, when he cruised into the driveway on his bike, braking next to her.

"Where have you been?" she asked. Now that he was here and safe, anger had superseded worry. "You're supposed to tell us if you're going to be late."

"Dad wanted me to stop by the store. He was having computer problems and needed technical assistance."

"From you?"

"Well, Gary's gone, and in comparison..." He left the sentence unfinished. They both knew Kyle was not very tech savvy.

Anita locked the car door. "What was the problem?"

"Nothing. He just forgot his password and ID for ordering books from a distributor. He kept trying to use his sign-on. I helped him create a new password. After that, he asked me to stay and keep an eye on things while he caught up on stuff." Nick opened the garage door and brought in his bike. "Oh, by the way, he's going to be a little late. Hey, what's for dinner?"

"That remains to be seen," she said.

Walking up to the front of the house, Anita found a blue placard hanging from the doorknob. "SORRY WE MISSED YOU!" read the white calligraphic message at the top of the navy rectangle. Below that was an ad for a Visa card offered by The First People's Bank. Beneath the ad, scrawled in Sharpie on a blank line, was a note— "CALL ME!"—and a signature: *Mr. Worthington.*

She glanced across the street at the Riveras' house and the Swartwoods' but saw nothing hanging from either of their front doorknobs.

He'd only come to her house.

A sliver of cold slid down the back of her neck. The idea that he had been to her home creeped her out, as did the fact that he seemed to be aware of her credit card troubles. Or maybe that was a coincidence. She didn't know and wasn't sure she wanted to know, and when Nick closed the garage and walked around the corner, she folded up the doorhanger and shoved it into her purse before unlocking the door and following him inside.

5

PLACING her wrinkled lips around the sad fibrous old penis, Helene Coppick reflected that this was not the way she'd wanted to spend her Golden Years. Mr. McAfee must have sensed her hesitation, because his bony fingers pressed down on the top of her head to prompt her, and, steeling herself, she dutifully got to work. She tried every technique she knew, with no response, but finally, after twenty minutes of sustained tongue action, a thin salty trickle leaked out from his semi-erect organ, and he was done.

Taking out a handkerchief, she expelled into the cloth what she'd been holding in her mouth, then stood. Like the majority of units at the assisted living center, Mr. McAfee's room was small. Never having had a family, his was even more depressing than most, as there were no photos displayed, nothing hanging on the walls, and the only pieces of furniture were the bed, television and dresser that came with the unit.

After finishing, he always seemed disgusted by her, and he gestured toward the billfold on top of the dresser. "Get yourself a ten," he told her. "I'll see you next week."

Knowing he didn't like her to talk, she nodded, extracted the money and left his room. Her own room was just down the hall, and she walked past two women in wheelchairs parked along the side of the corridor and an attendant carrying a tray of medications before unlocking and opening her door, stepping inside.

Heading immediately into the bathroom, she rinsed out for a full two minutes with Listerine, then brushed her teeth and gargled with the mouthwash one more time. Taking out the soiled handkerchief, Helene scrubbed it with soap in the sink, hanging it on the towel rack to dry. She looked at herself in the mirror before turning away, unable to meet her own eyes.

She placed the ten dollar bill in the pocketbook in her purse.

Her own unit was homey, filled with furniture and decorations from her old house, and she settled into her flowered couch, turning on the television, trying not to think about what had just transpired.

On the end table next to her was a framed photo of her and Orville, her late husband, standing in front of a redwood tree. It was her favorite picture of the two of them, taken by a nice young woman to whom Orville had passed their camera. She'd been fifty and he'd been fifty-five, and as far as she was concerned, neither of them had ever looked better.

She refused to look at the picture now, too ashamed to subject herself to Orville's Kodak-frozen gaze.

Helene closed her eyes, overcome as always by a feeling of sadness as she thought about the series of events that had led her here to Senior Acres.

Orville's death had been the beginning of the end. He had died too young, and when his pension had been gutted a few years later and she'd found out how little she'd be getting from Social Security, she'd lost the house. The two of them had never had kids, and she herself had been an only child, so there was no one to take care of her or take her in, and she'd ended up living in a cheap apartment, before a fall on the cement outside the building and a subsequent trip to the hospital had caused her doctors to conspire with social services and the insurance company to put her here. Where she would live out her remaining days until she died.

The despair she felt was nearly overwhelming, and Helene forced herself to concentrate on the television, though in truth she had no interest in the case being "tried" by the TV judge and no clue as to what was happening on the program.

Moments later, there was a knock at her door, a jaunty shave-and-a-haircut rap on the wood. Who could it be? She wasn't expecting any visitors, and it was far too early for dinner or her medicine delivery. Curious, Helene got up from the couch, walked over and opened the door.

Standing in the corridor was a young well-dressed man who looked like a...

"Banker," he said, offering her his hand to shake. "Name's Pickering. Julius Pickering. And I'm with The First People's Bank. May I come in?" He didn't wait for an answer but pushed the door open all the way and gently pressed past her. "Nice place you have here."

She didn't like having strangers in her room. It made her feel uncomfortable, and she left the door open, hoping he would take the hint and leave.

The man bent down to look at the photo on the end table. "Is this Orville? Good looking man, wasn't he?"

How did he know her husband's name?

"What do you want?" Helene asked.

He straightened, turning to face her. "To the point. I like that." The man smiled, and his teeth were as white as those of men in commercials. "How would you like a job with us, with the bank?"

"A job?" she repeated.

"A job." He leaned closer. "A job a hell of a lot better than sucking old men's shriveled dicks." He laughed heartily. "Come on, Helene. Do you honestly *want* to service Clement Barnes today at four o'clock? Is that really the way you'd like to spend your tea time?"

How could he know about that?

She was filled with a deep humiliating shame, but beneath the shame was a profound uneasiness. Who was this man? Where had he found out all this information about her, and why was he here? To offer her a job at his bank? Could he possibly think that a 75-year-old former housewife was the best qualified person for *any* position?

Nothing about this added up, and as he continued to snoop around her living space, examining the pictures on her walls and the knickknacks on her shelves, checking out her bed, Helene's uneasiness graduated to agitation. She wanted him out of here. She wanted him gone.

He picked up a small figurine then put it down. "So what do you say? Would you like to work at the bank?"

She shook her head. "I don't know anything about banking and I'm too old to learn."

"You're never too old to learn."

"I'm too old to work, though. I'm here because I fall sometimes, and I'm not well. Besides, I can't go out. I don't even think they'd let me leave."

"Oh, that's taken care of," Mr. Pickering said easily. "I talked to the administrators. They're fine with it."

Again, stronger, that feeling of apprehension. He had come here specifically looking for her and had gone to the effort to get pre-approval for her to work at his bank? How and why had he chosen her, and what made her different than all of the other residents in the home? For that matter, what made her different than all of the men and women in town who were actually looking for a job?

He was staring at her as if he knew exactly what she was thinking. "You are unique," he said. "And you have exactly what we're looking for." He sat down on the couch and patted the cushion next to him, indicating that she should sit down. After a moment's hesitation, she did so. "Staffing a business is like putting together a jigsaw puzzle," he told her. "The right piece has to fit in the right spot in order for everything to work. That's what I'm doing now: looking for the right pieces. And one of them is you."

Against her will, Helene felt herself drawn in.

"What would I have to do?"

"Just come with me," he said. That ultra-white smile was back. "We'll get you set up."

6

THE doorbell rang at midnight.

Coy was jerked out of a sound slumber, the immersive dream in which he'd been a James Bond-type spy winking out of existence. Suddenly, he was looking not at a beautiful woman inside a secret underground lair but up at the ceiling in his cold dark bedroom as the doorbell chimed. He always slept in his underwear, so he hopped out of bed and grabbed his robe from the hook on the closet door before hurrying toward the front of the house.

"Hold your horses!" he called as he tied the robe's sash, the bell continuing to ring.

It was only as he unlocked the door that it occurred to him that he should have first checked to see who was out there. It was midnight—not exactly the time for visitors—and all those B of A employees had recently been murdered by God-knew-who. Maybe someone with a grudge was killing off *everyone* in Montgomery who worked for a bank.

Then he was opening the door.

It was Florine.

Coy stood there confused, not sure why she was here at this hour or why she was here at all. Her face betrayed no emotion, and his first hopeful thought that she'd come to apologize and make up died before it had even fully registered.

"Florine," he said numbly.

She was carrying a briefcase, and she pushed past him, into the living room. Opening the briefcase, she dumped its contents onto the floor. The room was suddenly filled with the disgusting odor of human waste, and he looked at the falling papers and saw that they were all defaced with streaks of brown.

Coy put a hand over his nose and mouth, realizing what he was looking at, what she had done.

"Your loans are shit," she said flatly. "Evergreen Title is no longer going to process your escrow accounts or work with Montgomery Community Bank in any capacity. From here on in, we will be working exclusively with First People's Bank."

He couldn't get past the excrement-encrusted papers littering his living room carpet. He wanted to pick up and throw away the documents but wasn't sure he'd be able to do so without vomiting. At the same time, he wanted to grab Florine and order her to tell him what the hell was going on. None of this made any sense, not the shit-stained paperwork or the midnight visit or even her earlier attack on him at the bank. It was as if she'd become possessed or was on drugs. She wasn't acting like herself, at least not like the Florine he knew, and he had no idea what had happened or what to do about it.

Coy took a step forward, deciding to make an effort. "Can we just...talk?" he said.

He'd been hoping to seem concerned and reasonable, but the disdainful look she gave him made him realize that he'd come off as simpering and ineffectual.

His attitude hardened. This was his house, and it was the middle of the goddamn night. If this was the way she wanted to play it…

"Get out," he ordered. "And take this shit with you. I'm calling your boss in the morning. I don't think Evergreen Title—"

She kicked him.

He'd half-expected it and sort of saw it coming, so he was able to move out of the way enough that her foot missed his crotch, but her shoe slammed into his right knee, causing him to cry out in pain and sending him flailing backward. The easy chair broke his fall, and he collapsed into it, his leg blazing with agony.

"Bitch!" he yelled. It was her least favorite word, and he said it to hurt her, but there was no acknowledgment that she'd even heard it. Instead, she closed her now empty briefcase and started for the door.

He staggered to his feet. He wanted nothing more than to push her down and watch her fall face-first onto one of the shit-stained documents, but he knew that was wrong and restrained himself. How had they come to this? They'd talked about moving in together. They'd both used the word "love."

She opened the door, then turned to face him, her face distorted with fury. He had never seen such an expression on a woman, and the intensity of it took him aback. "I don't want to see you again, I don't want to hear your voice, and once Montgomery Community is out of business, I want you to move to another state or die."

He couldn't help himself. "Florine…"

She whirled away from him and strode out of the house toward her car, parked on the street. There were no lights, only a dim half-moon in the sky, but he had the impression that there was someone in the car waiting for her, a suspicion confirmed when she opened the passenger door and got in. The shadowy figure was laughing, and she started laughing, then the car door slammed shut and the vehicle drove away.

Coy stood there in his doorway, in his bathrobe, looking out at the night, the stench of feces in the living room behind him, confused and frightened, wondering what was happening and where all this was going.

SEVEN

1

SITTING ON THE dais at the front of the council chambers, Mayor Derrick Montoya looked out at a room far more crowded than it should have been. In addition to Alice Deming, the annoying gadfly who was at *every* meeting, and the usual handful of people with specific business before the council, the seats were filled with shopowners from the old downtown, as well as an incongruous group of old ladies and young hippies from the preservation society. Derrick was not looking forward to this meeting. He was no dummy; his day job was lawyer, and he knew exactly why these people had shown up and what kind of trouble they could cause the town.

The mayor glanced over at his fellow councilmembers. Roy Freeman, as always, was on his phone, texting something to somebody. Lacy Rogers and Shelley Sue Porter, the two women on the council, were chatting cattily with their heads together. Al Moore, the oldest councilman, who Derrick was pretty sure suffered from Alzheimer's, stared blankly out at the middle distance.

None of them knew what they were in for tonight.

But hell had no fury like a business owner who hadn't been treated fairly.

Glancing up at the clock, Derrick waited four more minutes, until it was exactly seven, before calling the meeting to order. They all stood for the flag salute, Pastor Peters said a prayer, the council ran through some old business, spent about an hour on new agenda items, and then the floor was opened to the public.

The line of speakers that formed immediately after the announcement went straight down the center aisle and curved along the wall at the back of the chambers, emptying most of the seats in the room.

Here it comes, Derrick thought.

Trixie Johnson, owner of the consignment store next to the new bank, stepped up to the podium. "I have a question about the new bank in the old downtown."

A noise emerged from the crowd, collective grunts of agreement that coalesced into a single expression of support.

"State your name and occupation for the record," Derrick said, trying to maintain the illusion that he was in control.

"You know who I am, Derrick."

"For the record."

The woman sighed. "My name is Trixie Johnson. I'm the owner and operator of It's New to You, and like most of the downtown business owners, I'd like to know how a *bank* became my new neighbor."

A cheer went up from the crowd.

"I mean, they have to have a business license, don't they? I want to know who approved this and when? Because I sure as hell didn't hear anything about it. All of a sudden, I went to open my shop one morning and they were there."

"Time," said Lacy Rogers, who was responsible for making sure speakers did not go over their limit.

"I'm just getting started!"

Voices in support: "Yeah!" "Let her talk!"

"You can speak again once everyone has had a chance to express their opinions," Derrick told her. "Just go back to the end of the line."

Fred Winters, the barber, lightly touched her shoulder. "Don't worry. I got this."

Trixie stepped aside and Fred moved into her place. "Fred Winters, owner of The Hair Force. I also want to know how this was approved. Aren't businesses supposed to provide adequate parking? The town had to do a traffic impact report when I wanted to expand my shop from three chairs to five. And I was turned down because there supposedly wasn't enough available parking, even though I wasn't bringing in any new customers, I was just hiring an extra barber so we could cut the customers we do have faster. How did these guys skate by? Was there a report done? Because, if so, I want to see it."

Nods of agreement, expressions of "Yeah!"

"Time," Lacy said.

Derrick sat there listening as speaker after speaker expressed the same concern: how had the bank been granted a business license so quickly, without a public hearing or community input? The problem was, neither he nor anyone else on the council could explain why or how such a thing had occurred. The Planning Commission had recommended approval of the new business, as it often did. The council had rubberstamped the recommendation of the Planning Commission, as it often did.

Only...

The council's approval had been given in a closed special session, a rare move that quite possibly wasn't legal. And the Planning Commission had made its determination in an unannounced meeting without hearing from anyone other than the applicant, which was definitely illegal.

And, astonishingly, it had all happened only last week.

Derrick should have known at the time that this wasn't proper, but for some reason neither he nor anyone else involved noticed anything inappropriate in their actions, and none of them had made any effort to follow the correct and usual procedures.

It was coming back to haunt them now. The established businesses in town were outraged by what they considered to be favoritism shown to The First People's Bank, and he had to admit that they had a point. No other enterprise or individual, to his knowledge, had had such an easy time of it.

Trixie was back at the podium again for a second round, once more stating her name and occupation for the record, her voice filled with scorn as she did so. "I guess what I want to know, what we all want to know, is if this is the new normal. Can we *all* expect such a hands-off approach from the town? If we want to change or expand, are we going to be able to do so without jumping through hoops? Are we going to be able to do whatever we want, regardless of the effect on other properties or businesses? Because that's the precedent you've set with this new bank. I don't know which one of you they paid off to get such treatment, but clearly something underhanded is going on, because none of us have ever gotten this kind of treatment."

Derrick had had just about enough of this. He banged his gavel on the dais. "Listen here..."

The door at the back of the council chambers opened.

He'd been about to go on a tirade, lecturing Trixie—and all of them—about the importance of civility, but when he saw the man passing through the doorway, the reprimand died on his lips. Something about the lone figure left him feeling intimidated. Dressed all in black, wearing a suit so expensive that Derrick doubted anyone present had ever seen its like, the man strode into the council chambers with confident purpose, ignoring the gathered speakers and pushing through their ranks toward the front of the room.

While Derrick did not know who the man was, he was pretty sure he knew where he was from.

The First People's Bank.

He wasn't sure why he thought that, but the certainty was strong within him. When the council had okayed the new business, there'd been no representative from the bank present—another oddity—and they'd simply acted based on the report put in front of them. But something told him that if the councilmembers *had* met with anyone from the bank, this was who they would have seen.

A hush fell over the room as the man in black stepped up to the podium.

Trixie had moved aside, as had Fred Winters, who'd again been planning to follow her.

The Bank

The man stood there for a moment, standing tall, staring straight ahead. His voice when he finally spoke was so low that Derrick had to strain to hear him. "You petty, petty people." The man looked around the room. He still had not introduced himself, but neither Derrick nor any of the others were about to take him to task for that. They were all daunted by his presence, and the entire room was hushed as they waited to hear what he had to say. "You came here tonight to speak out against the bank? How many of you have taken out bank loans to start or support your businesses? The majority of you, I'll bet. And all of you have what little money you've managed to accrue tucked safely away in savings accounts or CDs or checking accounts, from which you withdraw funds to make the payments that keep your lives running on an even keel: gas, water, electricity, groceries, mortgages, rent. Banks are the bedrock of all of your lives. Without banks, you would be burying your money in coffee cans in the back yard or stuffing it under your mattresses." His voice rose. "Do you know the importance of the financial sector to the total economy? There would *be* no economy without banks! Not in this country, not in this world!

"And yet here you are, gathered together in an effort to prevent our bank from conducting its lawful business, all of you supposedly capitalist shopowners and entrepreneurs." His voice dropped again as he glanced around the room. "You petty, petty people."

Without another word, he turned, leaving the chambers the same way he'd come in, the people lined up to speak against the bank's approval parting before him as he made his way out the door.

Everyone seemed to be stunned into silence, and Derrick took advantage of the unexpected stillness to declare an end to public discussion and make a motion that the meeting be adjourned. It was seconded, approved, and with a single tap of his gavel, the night was done.

But people did not exit the council chambers immediately. They milled about, talking low amongst themselves, and he realized that they were afraid to leave, afraid of encountering the man in black.

Derrick and the rest of the council remained behind as well.

Because they were afraid of the man, too.

2

KYLE finished tabulating receipts and was surprised to discover that there'd been a slight uptick in sales from the week prior. Combined with the fact that Gary was no longer here, which meant that he no longer had to pay an extra salary, the bookstore was actually ahead of where he'd projected it would be. Not in the black, of course, but definitely in a pinker part of red for the month.

It had to be the increased downtown foot traffic.

Because of the bank.

There were even two customers here right now, in what was ordinarily an off-hour. One of them, Jason Ling, found an old James Blaylock paperback on the sci-fi shelf and brought it up to the counter for purchase. "So tell me," he said, "why did they call these books 'steampunk?' I never understood that."

Kyle didn't either. From what he could remember, "punk" referred to a DIY ethos in late-1970s rock that ran counter to more polished, technically accomplished music, and instead celebrated roughness, simplicity and a sort of willful amateurishness. How that corresponded in any way to the futuristically complicated Victorian machinery featured in steampunk novels he had no idea. "You got me," he admitted. "I think they were just putting the word 'punk' on everything in those days to make it seem cool and hip. Cyberpunk, splatterpunk, steampunk…"

"Maybe so." Jason handed Kyle the book and took out his wallet. "Hey, I heard Gary's working at the bank next door now."

Kyle nodded noncommittally.

"Heard he's been acting kind of squirrelly."

"Yeah?"

"It's not my bank, but my brother Jim goes there now, and he said Gary's talking in a weird accent, like he's British or something."

My brother Jim goes there now.

Like attending a church, Kyle thought, like belonging to a specific denomination…

He chided himself for getting distracted and going off track. The vagaries of syntax weren't the point here. Gary's British accent was the thing to focus on.

Gary's British accent.

He had not heard about that before, and the information left him confused. As far as he knew, Gary didn't even have the ability to do accents. Even if he did, why in the world *would* he?

Kyle gave Jason his change, then looked down at the stack of receipts he'd been tabulating. Originally, he'd thought about opening up a business account next door. It would definitely be more convenient than driving all the way across town to Montgomery Community. But he'd quickly soured on that idea. Part of it was definitely Gary, but part of it was just what he'd heard from other downtown shopowners. Word had it that the bank was financing a consignment store over on Manzanita Street that would be direct competition for Trixie. And supposedly it had turned down Tony Antonucci, one of the very first people in town to open up an account there, for refinancing, while lending that sleaze Gordon Turner enough money to buy into a partnership at Larry Price's law office.

Kyle shook his head. At one point, he had even considered getting a safety deposit box so he could—

He blinked. Something had been bothering him about the layout of the bank since he'd first gone inside. He'd been unable to pinpoint its origin, but the irritation had been subtly gnawing at him, and he suddenly realized what it was.

The interior was larger than the space available.

Yes. That was it. Like the Tardis, the bank was bigger on the inside, though there was no physical way for that to be possible.

It had to be an optical illusion.

It wasn't, though

No. He didn't think it was. Kyle glanced at their shared wall, trying to estimate what exactly was behind it at that location. One of the desks next to the potted plants? He'd only been in there the one time, but he recalled pretty well the layout of the place.

Jason had left and when, a few moments later, his other customer did the same, Kyle found himself looking at the wall again. Slowly, he walked around the counter and across the shop. He recalled the noises he and Nick had heard through the wall before the bank had moved in, and, on impulse, put his ear to the plaster. Through the barrier between the businesses, faint but clear, came the sound of low laughter, an eerie noise, like something out of a horror movie. And then...

His name, whispered.

"Kyle."

The phone rang, and he jumped, hitting his head on the edge of a shelf. Rubbing the spot to make sure no bump was forming, he hurried over to the front counter and picked up the phone on the third ring. "Hello?"

"Come on over," a man's voice said. "You don't have to spy on us through the wall."

A chill passed through Kyle as he heard the words, and he instinctively glanced toward the spot where his ear had been against the plaster.

"We're waiting for you, Carl."

"My name's Kyle not Carl," he started to say, the fact that he had to correct the caller giving him confidence. But there was already a dial tone, and he hung up the phone without finishing his sentence.

There *was* no one waiting for him when he walked over moments later. There were a few customers—a middle-aged man seated across the desk from a loan officer, an elderly woman being led back to the safety deposit boxes, a young woman speaking with a teller—but other than that, he saw only bank employees going about their regular duties. There was no one he could identify as the person who had called him. Glancing over at the wall he shared with the bank, he attempted to identify the location at which he had been listening, but the dimensions truly were off in here, and the nearest he could figure, he had been opposite an empty section of wall between a water cooler and an unoccupied desk.

Where had the laughter come from?

Who had whispered his name?

Kyle stood in place. There was no sign of Gary, and none of the employees were individuals he recognized.

"May I help you sir?"

He was startled to find a cleancut man in a gray business suit standing to his right. "No," Kyle said, shaking his head.

"Very well. Please let me know if I can be of any assistance."

Kyle walked forward, further into the bank. How could this place be so much bigger than his store when the original space had been smaller? He passed one teller window. And another. And another. If he'd taken this many steps toward the rear of Brave New World, he'd already be in the alley.

Suddenly, there did seem to be an employee Kyle recognized. He was not sure where he knew him from, but the man emerging from a side office—

Had there been *a side office before?* Could *there be a side office?*

—looked familiar. The man approached him, and in a sudden flash, Kyle understood who he was.

The mentally ill homeless guy he'd kicked out of the bookstore.

His hair might be cut and combed, and he was wearing a white shirt and tie, but Kyle recognized him by the expression on his face. "Did you eat it?" the man asked, the familiar crazy words spoken in a calm, matter-of-fact manner. "You need to eat it." The man smiled, and missing teeth revealed the real person under the civilized veneer. "Are you going to call the sheriff? *I'm* the sheriff. The other police are pansies."

It was a replay of their last interaction, and the fact that it was taking place here, in this professional business environment, left Kyle feeling off balance. How had this lunatic gotten hired, and what could his job possibly be? Hadn't the person who hired him noticed yet that there was something wrong with him? Hadn't his co-workers?

He was surprised that the man wasn't yelling at him, shouting incoherent threats.

Suddenly, Kyle regretted coming over to the bank. It had been in response to the phone call and the weird noises he'd heard through the wall, but whatever he had hoped to find was not here, and he did not even know what that could possibly be. He was also not sure he'd locked the door to his store before walking over.

"You have to eat it," the man before him said in a calm, rational manner, and Kyle turned away and left the bank the way he'd come in.

He had *not* locked the door—

How was that *possible?*

—but a quick check showed him that the register was untouched, and it didn't seem as though anyone had come in during the short time he'd been gone.

Kyle looked from the back door of the shop to the front window. The space was measurably smaller than that of the adjoining bank, and more than any vague feelings or intuitive impressions he might have, it was the concrete reality of this demonstrable fact that left him feeling troubled. This kind of thing was supposed to happen on the pages of the novels that he stocked, not in real life, next to his store in downtown Montgomery in the middle of a workday.

The bell over the door rang as Gil walked in, sorting through a handful of envelopes before presenting a small stack to Kyle. "How're things?" the mailman asked.

"The new bank," Kyle said. "Do you deliver there before me or after?"

"Depends on the week," Gil told him. "I like to vary the route." He tapped his forehead with the remaining envelopes in his hand. "Keeps the mind sharp. Staves off Alzheimer's."

"You get any vibes off the place? Notice anything weird?"

"It's bigger than it should be."

Kyle pointed at the mailman. "Exactly!"

"Optical illusion, I assume. You know, my wife and I were on vacation one time and stopped by this place called the Mystery Shack. It was built on a slant, and things rolled uphill, and all the measurements inside there were wrong. They had a room that was bigger than it was supposed to be."

"But this isn't some tourist trap trick. It's a bank."

"I know, but same theory, I presume."

Kyle shook his head. "I don't like it."

"Isn't that your bank?"

"Me? No."

"Well, I moved my account there, and let me tell you, they know how to treat a customer right. And you have to admit, it's kind of revitalized the downtown."

Kyle nodded distractedly, noncommittally, and Gil waved the mail in his hand in a goodbye gesture. "See you tomorrow."

"See you." He watched the mailman pass in front of his window, heading toward the bank. He had always liked Gil, had always enjoyed talking to him, but he'd cut off today's conversation as soon as he learned that the mailman had an account with First People's. It made no sense, but he had to admit that he thought a little bit less of Gil than he had before—and perhaps did not like him quite as much. Was this a harbinger of the future? he wondered. Was the town going to start squaring off: people who supported the bank against people who didn't?

The thought did not seem as ridiculous as it should have, and as a young couple he didn't recognize walked into the bookstore, Kyle looked at the wall opposite him and wondered, if he put his ear to the plaster, would he still hear that low creepy laughter? Would someone whisper his name?

3

"DID you hear Chet Yates last night?" Hank was looking even more worried than usual when Brad walked into the office.

The sheriff sighed, pouring himself some coffee. "I don't stay up that late."

"Maybe you should. He's calling you out, saying you're not just responsible for his brother's death but for the Bank of America massacre. That's what he's calling it: the Bank of America Massacre. Carol's already taken calls from some of his army, saying that you should resign."

"His army?"

"That's what his fans call themselves."

Brad looked over at the receptionist. "That true, Carol?"

"I think they do call themselves an army—"

"I mean about the phone calls."

"Oh yeah. Four so far. They talk tough, but they're too afraid to leave their names." Carol grinned. "But I have their numbers."

Brad chuckled. "Good girl. I think I'll return their calls. Put the fear of God in them."

"Woman," the receptionist said.

Brad frowned. "What?"

"You said 'good *girl*.' I'm not a girl, I'm a woman."

"Oh. Sorry. Didn't mean—"

"I know you didn't. But..."

"I'll remember next time."

"Thanks."

Hank rolled his eyes, but Brad didn't respond, hoping Carol hadn't seen the deputy's expression. The 21st century was filtering very slowly into small towns like Montgomery, but it was definitely making inroads, and some people—like Hank—were having a difficult time adapting.

Brad changed the subject before his deputy said something stupid and he ended up having to referee a fight between his employees. "So where are we on the murder? Anything new?"

"Actually, maybe. The M.E. said the lab's still sorting through all the DNA even though there's probably nothing we can use. But remember those footprints Mitch found? One's clear and usable, and it's not one of ours, it's not Jasper's and it's not Taggart's. The chances of some random innocent guy shuffling around out there at that spot..." He shrugged. "Pretty slim."

"I guess that's something."

"Oh, it's more than something. Norris has been looking into it, and he says that footwear's pretty unique. Pointy-toed but not boots. If our guy bought 'em online or from a catalog we're out of luck, but if they're from someplace in town..."

Brad smiled. "You've been busy little bees this morning. Let's hear it for good old-fashioned police work. Make copies of the print photo and send the Bills out to see what they can find. I want an answer before noon."

Hank nodded. "You got it." He hurried down the hall.

"Carol," he said, "get Chet Yates on the phone for me, will you? I want to talk to him."

"He's probably still asleep."

"Good. Wake him up. I'll take it in my office." He walked past her desk and through the doorway, gulping down his lukewarm coffee and tossing the cup in the wastebasket next to his desk. Moments later, Carol called out that Chet was on the line. Brad picked up the phone. "Hey, Chet. How's it going? I thought we should talk."

"I know why you're calling me at this hour! You can't intimidate me! You can't shut me up!"

Brad sighed. "I'm not trying to shut you up or intimidate you, Chet. I'm calling to talk some common sense."

"You murdered Carl, and I'll have your job for it! I'm already consulting lawyers!"

Even though his brother had killed himself and Chet probably wasn't really talking to lawyers, Brad knew enough to leave the subject of Carl alone. But he wasn't about to have this blowhard spread conspiracy theories about the B of A deaths on his radio show. The situation was weird enough that those theories might actually stick, and more than ever before, clear-headedness was needed on behalf of both the department and the public. They couldn't afford to let this thing get out of hand and start a panic.

"I'm actually calling about the murder of Glen Taggart and the bodies we found in that meadow out by the transfer station. I heard you were discussing them on your program last night."

Chet wasn't about to let his brother's suicide go.

"I know you're claiming he shot himself—"

"He did, Chet. I was there. I saw it. I tried to stop him."

"Even if he did, it wouldn't have happened if you and your thugs hadn't staged your Waco raid! You know, there's a new bank in town, Neth, and they're not going to be hiring you to do their dirty business. The Gestapo hold you and Montgomery Community have on this town is over!"

"Chet..."

"And I don't have to talk to you, either! I know my rights, and I will not be badgered by you or your jackbooted minions!"

There was a sudden dial tone, and Brad replaced the receiver in its cradle. He was pretty sure that Chet had not merely hung up but had slammed down his phone. Rather than smooth the waters, his call had made things worse, and he had no doubt that the radio show tonight would consist of an exhortation for Chet's "army" to resist any and all efforts by the sheriff's department to solicit cooperation in catching Taggart's killer.

There was a knock on his doorframe, and Brad looked up to see Carol standing there.

"I saw that you were off the line."

"And?" he prodded.

She motioned for him to follow her, and he stood, walking out to her desk, where she gestured toward her computer. "I got this email."

Leaning over, he read the message: *These days, too many banks are DYING and unable to meet your needs or lessen your KILLING financial burdens.*" The words "dying" and "killing" were not only in all capital letters but were highlighted in red. "*No worries!*" the text continued. "*THE FIRST PEOPLE'S BANK is now in Montgomery and Open For Business! No longer will you need to pay $15 for a box of checks or make a $32.50 minimum payment on your Visa balance of $379.92. Our banking services are provided free of charge to all of our valuable customers. Most importantly, we'll make sure that your Money is always SAFE!*" The word "money" was in green, the all caps "safe" in red. Behind the message, instead of a white background, was a photo of the meadow where the bodies of the Bank of America employees had been found.

"They're exploiting the murders to get customers," Carol said. "That's not right."

Brad straightened. "No, it's not right. But it is legal."

"I know. That's not what I brought you here to see." She pointed at the sentence which referenced the Visa bill. "That's the exact minimum amount I pay and my exact balance. How do they know that? That's personal information. I don't have an account with this bank, I've never even been there, yet somehow they were able to find out how much I owe on my credit card and how much I pay each month?"

The truth was, with all of the data mining and information sharing that went on between companies these days, he wasn't sure what information was legally private and what wasn't. It was the wild west out there in cyberspace, and he wasn't in a position to enforce any rules or regulations that applied to such things. He was just a small-town sheriff. This was the purview of the feds, the responsibility of acronymed bureaus and agencies he knew nothing about. But he thought about that bank ad he'd received, that postcard with a photo of a younger skinnier him, and he felt a faint stirring of apprehension at how close to invasion of privacy these banks were skating.

Carol took a deep breath. "I know we're all busy right now, but I was wondering, if I have some free time, if I could look into this and see if it's legal. I've heard things about this new bank from friends of mine, and I'm not sure it's all on the up and up."

"Of course," Brad said. "And if you find anything, let me know." He pointed to the screen. "You're right, that's wrong. Make sure you save it, and print it out just in case. Same thing with anything else you get. When I get a chance, I'll ask around and see what I can find. I know the downtown merchants are up in arms about this bank. And if they're concerned, I'm concerned. So, yeah, see what you can dig up."

Carol smiled. "Thanks."

The morning was busy. In addition to the murder investigation, an angry husband took a baseball bat to the car windshield of a man he suspected was sleeping with his wife, and a daytime drunk driver crashed his pickup truck into the fence on the side of the Unitarian church. It was shortly before noon when Bill F. called in and announced that he actually had a lead: a clerk at Shoe Barn remembered selling a pair of pointy-toed shoes during the store's Presidents' Day sale. He recalled the transaction not only because the shoes were of a type that had been on the shelf forever and had never before sold, but because the man who bought them was an odd duck.

"Odd how?" Brad asked.

"You want the description? He was clean-shaven with medium-length brown hair parted on the side. He was also nearly seven feet tall, extraordinarily thin and dressed in what the clerk called 'old-timey clothes.' He had a, quote, 'girl's voice.'"

Disappointment accompanied Bill F.'s depiction. Brad could not recall ever seeing anyone even remotely matching that description in Montgomery, and while he certainly didn't know everyone in town, a man like that would have stood out in almost any crowd. Which meant that he probably wasn't a local.

Could he have been someone hired for this job?

That was an ominous possibility, and Brad didn't even want to think about that. Not yet, at least.

"It's been awhile since President's Day," Brad said, "but canvas other nearby businesses and find out if anyone else remembers this guy. I'll have whoever's available talk to the families of the victims, see if that description rings a bell with any of them."

"Will do," the deputy said.

Brad didn't have much faith that they'd find the guy (and who knew if he was really involved? A footprint was a pretty inexact clue), but he allowed himself to hope that *someone* would know *something* about him. And if they were lucky, that might lead to more concrete information. Both he and the department were way out of their depth here, and when he tried to look ahead, every scenario he imagined ended in failure.

To his surprise, however, the unique description of the man rang several bells among those contacted, and within two hours, they had not only a name but a location. Leaving Carol and a one-man skeleton crew consisting of Clint, who'd been called in even though he was scheduled for night shift, Brad led the rest of his team to an apartment building on the east side of town. Ostensibly, they were only going to question the man—one Leroy Fritz—but with the possibility that this guy was the murderer, Brad was taking no chances. He and Hank were going to talk to Mr. Fritz, while the other deputies would be stationed around the street, ready to act if things went south.

Fortunately, the apartment building was on a cul de sac. Out of sightline of the apartment, Brad had two cars blocking the road should an escape by vehicle be attempted. Three men were on the sidewalk in front of the building in case he attempted to flee on foot.

As usual, the editor of the *Montgomery Gazette*, who seemed to have his radio scanner on twenty-four hours a day, arrived shortly after they did, setting up a position with his camera where he could get a view of the perp walking out of the house but still be far enough away to avoid any fireworks.

Was he a perp?

That they still didn't know, and Brad and Hank walked up to the ground floor apartment and knocked on the door. "Sheriff!" Brad announced.

Fritz gave up without protest, without struggle, and it seemed almost as though he'd been waiting for them. He stepped aside after opening the door, allowing them to walk in, where they saw a series of knives coated with dried blood lying on a coffeetable whose top was covered by blood-stained newspaper. The confession he readily offered seemed pre-written, pre-rehearsed, and despite all of the evidence before them, Brad could not help thinking that this was a set-up, that it had all been staged for their benefit and that the man they were arresting was less perpetrator than pawn.

As they'd been warned, Leroy Fritz was a very odd man. Wearing a vest with a pocket watch and so tall that he had to duck to get through the doorway, he did indeed have a high girlish voice. His mannerisms, too, were quite feminine. *Gentle*, Brad thought, and that did not seem to match the harsh brutality of Taggart's killing. People snapped, though, and kind men and demure women committed murders all the time, their friends and neighbors inevitably expressing shock that the individuals they knew could do something like that.

Except Leroy Fritz seemed like *exactly* the type of person who would do something like that. It was only Brad's gut instinct telling him that the picture was framed a little too clearly.

Back at the department, the sheriff decided to talk to Fritz before booking him, though he was well aware that they had more than enough cause to lock him up immediately. Hank had been left behind and was leading a team to canvas the houses on Fritz's street and get whatever information or opinions his neighbors might have.

On TV, at least, people were always confessing to crimes they didn't commit, and Brad sat across from Fritz in the interrogation room, with Mitch working the camera to record the interview, trying to elicit details of the murder that only the killer would know. The suspect had waived his right to counsel and said he was willing to answer any question, so Brad went through everything, step-by-step. Fritz knew everything, even specifics they had kept out of the paper and not discussed with the public. His descriptions and time-line matched perfectly with what they knew, and although it shed no light on the bodies found in the meadow, it wrapped up Taggart's killing in such an air-tight manner that even Brad conceded that the weirdo had to have done it.

There was no time to go out and get lunch, but Carol brought him back a burger from B.B.'s when she went out, and he ate it gratefully as his deputies booked the man and placed him in a cell.

He had just gotten off the phone with the coroner, keeping him up to speed on the morning's events, letting him know that he could send someone out to get a DNA sample from the suspect, when Patty stopped by.

"Can you pick up Sue and Jillian after school," she asked, "and watch them for a few hours? Those new clients who are buying that house near the golf course, that house for *a million five,* have asked me to be there for the inspection, and obviously I can't bring the girls along."

"This is not a good time."

"They'll just stay in your office and do homework."

"Not a good time," he repeated. "Too much is going on, and I don't want them around it. Can't you ask one of their friends' moms if they can come over?"

Patty nodded. "Okay, but can you pick them up on your way home?"

"I may be later than you."

"We'll play it by ear, then. I'll make some calls and let you know." She gave him a quick kiss, offered a short wave and was gone.

The afternoon sped by, but he got a lot done. Once the arraignment tomorrow made everything official, they would be able to put the Taggart murder aside and concentrate on the bodies in the meadow and the ordinary crimes that continued unabated as long as the earth kept spinning. He didn't want to look a gift horse in the mouth, but Fritz's identification and capture had been easy, almost too easy, and he thought again that the entire thing seemed as though it had been staged.

Because he was able to get so much work accomplished, Brad called Patty and told her that he'd be able to pick the kids up at six if she wasn't finished yet with her clients. She was indeed tied up, she whispered, and was going to be home later than she originally thought, her tone of voice letting him know that she was not going to have an easy time with this couple and that there might be other late nights.

"Don't worry," he told her. "The girls and I'll pick up a pizza. We'll save you a few slices."

"No pepperoni," she admonished. "You have that cholesterol test coming up."

"Can't hear you," he joked. "Your phone's cutting out."

"Gotta go," she whispered, her voice dropping. "Bye."

"Bye."

Jillian and Sue were at their friend Shannon's house, so Brad drove home, parked in the driveway and walked down the block to pick them up. "Sorry for the inconvenience," he said to Shannon's mom when she greeted him at the door. "Patty and I really appreciate this."

She waved away his apology. "No problem."

"I hope they weren't too much trouble."

"Those two? They're little angels." She looked back over her shoulder. "Grab your stuff, girls!" she called. "Your father's here!"

A moment later, they emerged wearing their school backpacks and carrying little pink plastic pigs. "Daddy!" they cried in unison.

"What are those?" he asked, pointing to the pigs.

"We got 'em at the bank," Sue said. "Shannon's mom took her there to put her money in, and the man said that if we came back later and did that, too, he'd give us a piggy bank." She held it up for his inspection. "It already has a penny in it!"

"I opened a savings account for Shannon," her mom explained. "I thought it might be fun for your girls if they came along, too."

"We have to go back and open an account," Jillian said seriously. "If we don't, it's stealing. Because they already gave us our piggy banks."

"We'll see," he said.

"We have to!" the girls shouted in unison.

Shannon's mom shot him an apologetic look over their heads.

"Yeah, thanks for that," he told her dryly. "We'll talk about it on the way home," he said to the girls. "Come on. If you hurry up, we'll have time to get a pizza before Mommy gets back."

"Pizza!" The piggy banks forgotten, they ran past him outside. "Bye, Shannon!" "See you tomorrow! "Thank you, Mrs. Carrell!" "Yeah, thanks!"

"We really appreciate your help," he said. "Again, sorry to impose. I promise we won't make a habit of it."

"Glad to do it," she told him honestly.

Jillian and Sue were speeding down the sidewalk and already halfway home. He could see the pink pigs in their hands bobbing up and down as they ran, and he grew angry at the thought that someone at the bank had tried to both bribe and bully his daughters into opening accounts there.

When he had a chance, he was going to have to go down there, find that asshole and give him a piece of his mind.

Brad sighed as he hurried to catch up to the girls, wondering why every problem in his life lately seemed to involve banks.

4

THE gym was silent, and Nick could not recall ever experiencing such a thing at an assembly. Even if students *tried* to be quiet, low conversations and muttered comments inevitably echoed off the wooden floor of the cavernous room, and in a crowd this size, there were always smartasses who made the kids around them laugh at rude jokes mocking whatever was being said.

But today you could hear a pin drop, and when some kid near the top of the bleachers coughed, it sounded like a lion's roar in the stillness.

It had not started out this way. When they first heard about the assembly over the morning announcements, a cheer went up in Nick's biology class, which was supposed to be taking a test today. All the way down the hall and into the gym, the jostling students were loud and boisterous, and as they stomped up the wooden steps onto the bleachers, they laughingly celebrated their unexpected good fortune. *All* of the classes entered the gym excitedly and enthusiastically, and when Principal Whittaker, standing before the lone microphone in the center of the basketball court, made a plea for silence, very few people even heard him.

But the volume of the PA system was turned up, the more forceful Vice Principal Bollinger ordered everyone to be quiet, and the clamor gradually subsided enough for the principal to again address the students and inform them that the assembly today had been called in order to introduce them to an important aspect of adult life that they would all soon have to deal with: finances.

"So let me introduce," he said, "from The First People's Bank, the bank manager, Mr. Worthington!"

Mr. Worthington. That was the name of the man who had warned him away from Victor's house, and when the representative of the bank spoke, Nick immediately recognized his voice. A chill passed through him, and he wondered exactly how this assembly had come about. It certainly wasn't typical. Ordinarily, assemblies were scheduled far in advance and were very school-centric: pep rallies, award ceremonies, band concerts, student performances. He could not remember one ever structured around an outside speaker. Especially a speaker representing a private business.

This wasn't an assembly. It was a free commercial.

Mr. Worthington was explaining the history of the American banking system. Very few people were paying attention. Nick wasn't really listening to what the man was saying, but just hearing that voice again made him feel scared, intimidated, and put him directly back on Victor's front porch. He recalled the exact wording of the threat Mr. Worthington had made over the phone. *"Get off Victor Clark's porch, leave his yard, stay off his property and stop snooping. Do I make myself clear?"*

Why had Mr. Worthington been so closely monitoring the Clarks' house?

And where *was* Victor?

His friend had still not shown up for school, and staring down at the man from the bank, Nick could not help thinking that he had something to do with Victor's absence. In the back of his mind lurked the idea that the Clarks' house was as empty now as it had been the day he'd stopped by, that the entire family had somehow just...disappeared.

Mr. Worthington appeared to be looking directly at him—and smiling—and Nick stiffened, suddenly paying attention to the speech.

"Now, as a gift to you from the bank, in appreciation for allowing me to come here today and explain a little bit about how our financial system works, college saver accounts have been opened in all of your names, with the bank providing each of you with an initial twenty dollar deposit."

A murmur of excitement passed through the assembled students.

"You may add to this amount at any time, earning even more interest on your investment, and of course, as education accounts, the earnings you receive from them will remain tax free."

Nick frowned. This wasn't right. Hadn't some bank been fined millions of dollars for illegally creating accounts for people without their permission? The same thing seemed to be going on here, with a twenty dollar bribe thrown in to cover their tracks. Nick glanced at Aaron, sitting next to him. "What if you don't want an account?" he whispered.

"What's that?" Mr. Worthington was looking straight at him. "Did I hear a question up there?"

Nick shook his head, his mouth dry.

"I didn't think so. Now listen," Mr. Worthington said conspiratorially, as though he were talking to the students directly and did not want the faculty to hear. "We at the bank know that most of you will not be going to college. Even with your new accounts, who can afford that, right? But Pam and Ned, if you put in two dollars a week, by the end of the school year, you'll have enough saved for a night at the El Rancho Motor Lodge out on the highway. A night of bliss, if you know what I'm saying." He grinned lewdly at the couple in the front row.

"And Hanson Berg! " He pointed to the long-haired senior at the top of the bleachers. "You'll have enough to rebuild the engine on that old Mustang your dad left you."

He continued picking out students in the audience, not only knowing their names, but bringing up the things each of them wanted, the specific things they could buy or do with money earned from their new savings accounts. The gym gradually grew quieter, until eventually it was completely silent, everyone finally aware that there was something definitely amiss.

Principal Whittaker looked pale and ill, but he made no effort to cut off the banker or stop his intimate suggestions as to how they could use the money from their accounts.

Mr. Worthington finished his list of examples with Nick. "Nicholas Decker," he said, pointing. "Maybe you *can* use your college saver account for college." He paused cryptically. "Or maybe not."

Smiling, he went on to explain that in order for students to access their accounts, they would have to go into the bank with a valid ID and fill out some paperwork. But the accounts were all there, under their names, linked to their Social Security numbers.

How was that *possible?* Nick wondered. But he knew enough not to open his mouth and ask aloud.

Things seemed weird at home that night, too. Both of his parents were quiet, his dad distracted and in his own head, his mom preoccupied by thoughts she obviously had no intention of sharing.

Your mom's getting boned by the gardener.

He pushed that thought out of his mind.

Thankful for once to have homework, Nick went straight to his room after dinner, closing the door and putting on his headphones so as not to hear whatever conversation his parents might be having. Before turning on his laptop, he checked his phone on the off-chance that Victor had responded to the message he'd left after the strange day at school.

He'd received fifty texts.

All from The First People's Bank.

Heart pounding, he quickly scrolled through them. The first few were generic come-ons, trying to get him to open a new account—

hadn't he already been assigned a college saver account?

—or apply for a credit card. But the rest were the same message over and over again, at first all lowercased then gradually shifting to all caps: "the shadow is in the hall...The Shadow is in the Hall... The Shadow Is In The Hall...The SHADOW Is In The HALL... THE SHADOW Is In THE HALL...THE SHADOW IS IN THE HALL..."

Forty-five times the message was repeated, the increased capitalization implying a growing sense of urgency. The fact that someone from the bank knew about the shadow, something he had not shared with anyone, was frightening enough, but the obsessive repetition, the *warning*, filled him with genuine dread. Maybe Mr. Worthington had somehow discovered his secret fear and was using it to intimidate him, but Nick was suddenly afraid to leave his room, and he took his headphones off, grateful to hear his parents' voices from the front of the house. He looked over at the closed bedroom door, half-expecting to see a creeping darkness seep onto his floor from underneath it.

Recognizable footsteps passed by—his mom walking to the bathroom—and he immediately took advantage of her presence, lurching out of his chair and pulling open his door.

Just as the door to the bathroom closed.

Leaving him to face the shadow.

It was in the hallway, exactly as the bank's texts had warned, hovering somehow in the narrow space between his doorway and the wall opposite, wavering in the open air in an extremely unnerving manner, its unsteady motion emphasizing the fact that it was not a real shadow, that it was...something else.

A ghost.

He immediately ducked back into his bedroom, shutting the door. The phone in his hand buzzed, and he quickly shut it off, putting it face down on his dresser in case it continued ringing the way it had that time before. His heart was pounding crazily, and he was about to call for his dad to save him—

What if the shadow killed his dad?

—when he heard the toilet flush and the sink run and the bathroom door open. He yanked open his own door, and there was no shadow, only his mom, startled by his abrupt action.

"What's going on?" she asked.

"Nothing," he told her.

She looked at him askance but continued walking, and, grateful for her protection, he walked with her back to the front of the house.

5

JEN didn't like the bank manager.

Come to think of it, she didn't like Evangeline much either. But she was stuck alone here with both of them because Lane, as usual, was late.

The bank manager's office was silent save for the buzzing of a fly that had somehow gotten in and was speeding about the room. She watched as the insect bumped into the window and kept flying, wondering why it didn't sustain brain damage from repeatedly slamming its head so hard into various surfaces.

She and Evangeline had engaged in some polite chitchat upon first arriving, but the bank manager showed no interest in any sort of conversation that did not involve the matter at hand, and he remained stoically seated behind his desk, staring at them blankly, saying nothing. Now they were all sitting silently, waiting, and Jen mentally cursed Lane for being late, deciding that if there had to be any more such meetings, the two of them were going to arrive together.

The fly hit the window again with a tiny audible thwack.

She couldn't take much more of this.

"Sorry I'm late," Lane apologized, hurrying into the office. "Got caught up at work." He sat down on the chair next to Jen. "So where are we at?"

Evangeline walked over and placed a manila folder on the desk before them, opening it to reveal a stack of documents at least an inch thick. "A few more papers to sign and then we're in business." She handed each of them a pen. A series of yellow tabs marked the pages where a signature was required, and she turned to the first, pointing. "Sign here. Both of you."

"What are we signing?" Jen asked. Lane was already halfway through his signature.

"This just agrees to the release of the escrow funds."

There were eight more lines where they needed to sign, and the Realtor explained the reason for each as she turned to the appropriate document. She moved to the other side of the desk, and went through the same procedure with the bank manager, closing the folder when he was through.

The manager opened his own folder, lying on the desktop in front of him. "Before we complete the sale, the bank has a few stipulations. This is a three-bedroom house; am I correct?"

"Yes," Evangeline said. Jen nodded.

"We would like you to set one of those bedrooms aside for a purpose to be determined at a later date."

What? Jen thought.

"Sure," Lane agreed.

Not only did he announce the decision unilaterally, without any discussion, but he did not spare even a token glance in her direction. Jen looked at him, feeling as though she were in an Ira Levin novel: *Rosemary's Baby* or *The Stepford Wives,* where the husband plots and conspires with other neighbors behind his wife's back. She'd read both books within the past month, as part of a recent horror kick, and had been surprised by how relevant they were in these post #MeToo days. This was the second time Lane had sidelined her with Evangeline, and while it had seemed unexpectedly out of character at first, she was starting to think that maybe he didn't believe the balance of power in their relationship should be as equal as she did.

"Wait a minute," Jen said. "This is *our* house."

"Yes, and we're giving you a very good deal on it. A *very* good deal. I don't think the granting of this small concession is too much to ask." The banker pushed the folder across the desk toward them. "As you can see, I have already signed for the bank. All we need is your signatures."

"This is all part of the agreement," Evangeline assured her. "I thought I explained that to you."

She hadn't, and they both knew she hadn't, but Jen ignored her and focused her attention on Lane. "We need to talk about this."

"What's there to talk about?"

"This!"

"What do you want to do? Not buy the house? Just because we have to let the bank use one of our rooms, an extra room we don't even need?"

The Realtor and the bank manager were both watching the exchange dispassionately. Jen didn't like fighting in front of them, but there seemed no alternative. "We've gone through so much to get this house because we want a place that's *ours*. We can't just set aside part of it for someone else."

He reached for her hand. "Look, a lot of people who buy their first house and are trying to make ends meet rent out a room to a college student or something to help with the mortgage payment. That's all we'd be doing here. Except instead of another person living in our house, it would just be an empty room where the bank...I don't know, stores stuff. Is that so bad?" He turned toward the bank manager. "And we can renegotiate later, right? If for some reason we need the other room, if we have a child, say, we can amend the contract and change the terms or the rate or whatever, right?"

"Everything's negotiable," the manager said agreeably.

"See?"

It was the first time Lane had mentioned having a child, and Jen felt herself soften. He was right. It would help them make the payments and letting the bank use a room was better than having a stranger living with them. Reluctantly, she nodded her assent.

"Perfect," the bank manager said, pushing the agreement across the desk for them to sign.

They each affixed their signatures to the document, and Evangeline collected it. She spent the next several minutes at a side table, sorting through pages and using a quartet of stamps to imprint required seals on the appropriate documents, while Jen and Lane sat in silence and the bank manager stared at them expressionlessly. His gaze made Jen very uncomfortable, and she tried her best not to look in his direction.

There was a series of electronic hums and swooping repetitive click-clacks as Evangeline made copies of the documents on a Xerox machine in the corner of the office. Placing the pages in a slick double-pouch folder emblazoned with the name and logo of her real estate office, she placed the folder on the desk in front of them, giving the bank manager a nod.

He opened a drawer. "Here's the key, then. It's all yours."

Jen and Lane looked at each other, surprised. "That's it?" Lane asked. "That paperwork doesn't need to be sent somewhere and processed? We don't have to wait for official approval or some kind of formal...thing? That's it? It's ours?"

Evangeline laughed. "It's all yours. You can move in tonight if you want."

Relieved and happy. That was how Jen felt as she took the keys from the Realtor's fingers a second before Lane could grab them. The unease she'd felt only moments prior had disappeared, and, spontaneously, she leaned over to give her husband a kiss. The house was theirs! They were officially homeowners, and even if they had to roll out sleeping bags on a bare floor, she decided that she *did* want to spend tonight in their new home.

As quickly as they could, she and Lane took their leave and sped over to the house. Leaving her car parked on the street in front of the bank, they took Lane's truck, and she called her parents on the way to tell them the good news.

Lane pulled the pickup into the driveway—*their* driveway!—and they both got out. Now that the home was theirs, Jen saw its potential in a way she had not before. She walked across the small yard, thinking that she could plant some flowers in front, to brighten the place up. It would also be nice to have a fruit tree or two, maybe in the back yard. Apples, perhaps. Or peaches.

"Hey!" Lane called from the stoop. "You have the keys. Open up."

The interior of the house had not changed since their last visit. She walked slowly through the empty living room, thinking how much bigger it was than the one in their apartment, visualizing where their furniture would go and how she would decorate each area. A refrigerator and electric stove had been left behind in the kitchen, apparently too big for the previous owners to take with them, and she opened the door of the refrigerator to make sure it was on, then turned the knob controlling one of the burners on the stove to verify that it was working. Both appeared to be functioning properly.

She stepped into the hallway. It was darker than it should have been, and Jen immediately saw why.

The door across from the bathroom was closed.

She reached for the knob, tried to turn it.

"This door's locked," she said, frowning.

"That must be the room they were talking about, the one they said we have to set aside."

Her excitement faded as she confronted the physical reality of a barricaded segment of their new house. Was there really going to be a part of their own home that would be off limits to them, that they would not be allowed to enter? The thought left her dispirited. She tried to remember what the room looked like but for some reason couldn't seem to recall. On a whim, she walked back outside and around the east side of the house, intending to look in the window. The drapes were closed, however, and there was not even a crack through which she could peek.

Lane had not followed her, and when she returned, she found him in what was going to be their bedroom.

"I don't want to sleep here tonight," she told him.

"The first night in our new house and you don't want to stay here?"

"No."

"I thought we'd put a mattress on the floor, get a bottle of champagne...It'd be romantic."

"Romantic? With that boarded-up room ten feet away?"

"It's not boarded up."

"It might as well be." She glanced down the darkened hall. "It's creepy, Lane. It's like those rooms in horror movies where the deformed son is tied up or grandma's stuffed body is in a chair by the window."

"Come on."

"What do you mean, 'come on?' This is *our* house..."

"Yeah, but like they said, we got a great deal, and it's better than renting out a room to some loser."

"Is it?" She took a deep breath. "I'm happy we have our house. I am. Really." She stepped into the hallway, and he followed her. "But this..." She rattled the knob on the locked door. "Having a forbidden room right in the middle of our home? It's creepy, Lane. You know it is."

"It's not ideal," he admitted.

"We should've asked for more details. *What* are they going to use the room for? Can they access it anytime they want? Can they show up at three in the morning and order us to let them in? Or do they have a key to the front door so they can come in anytime they want, whether we're here or not?"

Lane was silent for a moment. "You're right." He grasped the knob himself, tried to turn it. Kneeling down, he peered at the keyhole. "You know, I might be able to pick this lock..."

Panic rose within her. "No!"

He stood, turning, surprised by her outburst.

"Don't open it."

"Okay," he said, and there was something in his acquiescence that led her to believe he was starting to become as wary of the room as she was. He hugged her. "But it's nice to have our own house, isn't it? Instead of an apartment? It's good to have our own place."

"Yes," she said, and thought of that *Twilight Zone* episode about the boy who sent people into the cornfield. "It's good."

EIGHT

1

ON FRIDAY NIGHT, he lost it all.

And more.

Walter sat alone in the office, his entire body covered with a thin sheen of sweat, though the night was cool, as was the temperature inside the church. He stared at the betting site, realizing that not only were his winnings gone, and his initial stake, but he had foolishly and inexplicably wagered additional money—church money!—in a sure thing that had turned out to be not sure at all.

Now what was he going to do?

The same base impulse that compelled him to gamble was urging him to disappear, to take off under cover of darkness and never show his face in this town again, while the higher nature that had led to his life in the church was telling him to do the right thing, turn himself in and face the consequences of his deeds. Walter didn't know which course of action to take, and while in days past he might have prayed to God for guidance, he was afraid this time that he had fallen too far, and he sat there dejected and bewildered, frightened and despairing.

The lights in the church flickered, though the screen before him remained unaffected, and he glanced up, frowning.

The lights flickered again, and a shadowed form appeared in the doorway.

The person must have walked up during that fluttering second of darkness, but the timing of the effect made it seem as though he'd simply *appeared*.

"May I help you?" The pastor stood. His pulse was racing, an involuntary reaction to the individual's sudden appearance, but he was still a minister—for the moment—and still in God's House, and if this was a lost soul seeking guidance, it was his duty to provide what aid and comfort he could.

"May I help *you*?" The figure stepped forward, into the room. It was a man, a cleancut pleasant-looking man dressed formally in a dark blue suit. "My name's Pickering," he said. "Julius Pickering. I'm with The First People's Bank."

"Yes? May I help you?" Walter repeated.

"May I help *you*?" the man said again. "I understand that you've found yourself in some precarious financial straits."

Walter's face felt hot. "No," he said, keeping his voice neutral.

"Yes," Pickering countered. "In fact, I believe you lost nearly eighteen thousand dollars to a wagering website on a series of, may I say, *very* foolish bets. The site is owned by our bank," he clarified.

Walter was stunned. "That can't be legal."

"Well, it *wasn't*," Pickering admitted. "For a brief period of time. But most of those overly stringent rules enacted after the recession have been..." He waved a fluttering hand in the air. "...relaxed. Congress came to realize, after some well-timed donations from the lobbying arm of our industry, that, in today's complicated and interconnected world, financial institutions require diverse investment streams. And thus..." He gestured toward the computer.

Walter was confused. "Have you come to...collect?"

Pickering laughed. "Is that what you're worried about? No. I haven't come to collect. In fact, I've come to propose a deal. We both know that you don't have the money to cover your losses. Not without 'borrowing' from the church coffers. Am I right? Of course

I am," he answered himself without pause. "And what I'm here to offer you is…a way out. Our bank is invested in this community, and we want the community to invest with us." He chuckled. "Financial humor. Anyway, we don't want one of Montgomery's most respected and influential citizens to slink away under the cover of night. No. Mistakes might have been made, but nothing that can't be ameliorated, and as the owners of FreshBets, we are in a unique position to provide you with a solution to your dilemma. Simply stated, we will issue you a loan and use that loan to settle your obligation.

"You will still need to pay back the debt, of course, but a fair payment schedule can be arranged, and in lieu of interest, the bank will merely ask you to perform a few favors on its behalf. If this arrangement sounds satisfactory to you, merely nod your head, and we will consider that an agreement of stated terms."

The cleancut man in the dark blue suit stared at him, an unnervingly unwavering smile on his face. The silence extended to a length that became uncomfortable, and under the man's unblinking gaze, Walter found himself nodding acquiescence.

"Thank you," Pickering said.

The lights flickered again.

And the man was gone.

Walter blinked, facing the empty doorway. Had the banker been here at all, he wondered, or had he, in his despair, imagined a savior come to solve his problems?

No. The man had been here. The details of the encounter were too specific, the offer the man had made unambiguous. So did that mean…?

Walter sat down again and refreshed the screen on his computer.

His debt had been erased; his FreshBets balance was at zero.

Favors, he thought. What exactly did that mean?

He wasn't sure, but he had no doubt that he would soon find out.

SUNDAY morning.

Walter looked out at his congregation, his eyes misting over. Even the sight of Norma Crenshaw and her widowed minions sitting in the front row, their pinched judgmental faces looking up at him in the pulpit, left him feeling grateful. How fortunate it was that he had not heeded his initial impulse and abandoned his flock. The thought that he'd almost lost it all due to his own weakness filled him with shame, but the fact that he'd been rescued from his transgressions by the benevolent grace of The First People's Bank made him marvel and wonder at the amazing intricacies of life.

The Lord worked in mysterious ways.

Walter cleared his throat. "We will, as always, begin with a hymn, 'Bringing in the Sheaves,' page 34 in your hymnals. But first, we will hear from Mr. Worthington, manager of The First People's Bank, who has a few thoughts he would like to share with us all. Mr. Worthington?"

From behind him stepped the manager, who proceeded to provide his institution with a free ad, pointing out members of the congregation who had already started banking with First People's, and comparing the benefits they would be receiving with those of parishioners who had made a different choice.

Walter stood to the side, watching. Wasn't there something in the Bible about Jesus throwing the moneylenders out of the temple? It seemed to him that there was, but his thoughts remained fuzzy, his brain unable to focus, and while he knew on some level that that was one of the most famous stories in the New Testament, one of those with which even nonbelievers were familiar, he could not for the life of him recall any specifics.

How was that possible?

He didn't know, but he stood there patiently, as he had promised he would do, until Mr. Worthington had finished his spiel, whereupon he thanked the man before again telling everyone to turn to page 34 in their hymn books.

After his final sermon of the morning, after the last parishioners had gone home, Walter retired to his office, feeling weary and drained. If before his mind had been fuzzy, now he was merely exhausted. Outside, a monsoon was brewing, thunderheads gradually overtaking the eastern half of the sky, an increasing humidity making up for the drop in temperature that resulted from dark clouds now blocking the sun.

Walter turned on his office lights, sat down in his chair.

And the lights flickered.

His pulse quickened as he glanced around the room. Sure enough, a figure was standing in the doorway.

Pickering.

If he hadn't known better, he would have thought that the man had *appeared* just as the lights sputtered.

Did he know better?

"What can I do for you?" Walter asked.

The man stepped into the room. "Another favor."

Walter looked at him, resigned. "What is it?"

"One of your parishioners. Ms. Leslie Patrick."

"What about her?"

"We understand that she is attempting to adopt the foster child she has been caring for, and that you have generously offered to act as a reference on her behalf in order to prove that she is fit to be a parent."

"Yes."

"Well, we need you to tell her that you are withdrawing your recommendation—"

"I can't do that!" he said, shocked.

Mr. Pickering held up his hand. "—withdrawing your recommendation and support of the adoption unless she places a thousand dollars into a CD at the bank. Three-month, six-month, twelve-month. Doesn't matter."

"Leslie doesn't have a thousand dollars!"

"Oh, but she does. She keeps it in a makeshift safe—a metal file box, really—at the back of her linen closet in case of emergencies." He gave Walter a tolerant smile. "You have to admit that that is not the most secure method of saving money."

How can he possibly know that? Walter wondered. But he had no doubt that it was true. Mr. Pickering stated it as though it were a fact, and the pastor believed him utterly. Still, the question remained: how had he obtained such personal, *secret*, information?

"If she places her money in a certificate in our bank, her funds will not only be safer, but they will be earning interest. A win-win!"

"But if she's keeping her money in a box, maybe she doesn't want to—"

Mr. Pickering's face clouded over. "Then she should not be allowed to adopt a child. She's neither mature nor reliable enough to care for another person."

"I—"

"—will be happy to do a favor for the bank that saved your sorry ass," Pickering finished for him. He looked into Walter's eyes, and what the pastor saw there made him turn away.

"Okay," he said softly.

Mr. Pickering was all smiles. "That wasn't so hard, was it? Once again, The First People's Bank thanks you for your assistance.

The lights flickered again, and when Walter looked, the man was no longer in front of him.

Had he walked out during those few seconds when Walter had been briefly distracted and glanced up at the ceiling lights?

Maybe, maybe not.

Either way, he was gone.

2

THIS couldn't be right.

Sitting at his desk on his lunch hour, Dr. Wilson frowned as he looked down at the bank statement in his hand and mentally tallied the numbers in front of him. He'd only made one withdrawal of a hundred dollars from his checking account since switching banks last week, but according to these figures,

(*wasn't it a little soon to be receiving a bank statement?*)

not only was his checking account down a hundred, but so were his savings and money market accounts. What should have been a simple withdrawal from a single account had metastasized, some incompetent clerk pressing a wrong computer key and taking two hundred extra dollars from him.

Why was everyone so stupid these days?

Checking his schedule, Dr. Wilson saw that the next patient wasn't due in until one-thirty, and he told Anita and Jen that he would be back soon, before angrily exiting the office through the back door.

Driving to the old downtown, he reflected that the location of this new bank was a lot more inconvenient than Montgomery Community. Not to mention the fact that it didn't have a parking lot.

What kind of bank didn't have a parking lot?

He found a spot up the block in front of the sewing store and pulled his Mercedes next to the curb behind a filthy dented pickup, leaving extra space between the two vehicles just in case. Walking back down the sidewalk to the bank with his statement in his hand, it occurred to him that he should have brought along his receipt from the withdrawal. He didn't know exactly where it was—it was probably at home on his dresser or mixed in with the pile of bills on his desk—and he hoped he wouldn't have to go back and get it to show the truth of his original transaction.

Even though it was the lunch hour, there were no other customers in the bank, and Dr. Wilson strode directly up to the first teller, who appeared to be looking down at his phone and texting rather than preparing to assist patrons. Upon reaching the window, however, he saw that the young man was not on his phone but was using a finger to move a group of dead insects on the counter in front of him so that they were lined up in order from biggest to smallest.

What the hell?

He should have moved to the next window and conducted his business with another teller, but the young man's bizarre activity irritated him, and he cleared his throat loudly. "Excuse me!" he said in the most disdainful and authoritative voice he possessed.

The teller—*V.J.*, according to his nametag—looked up from his row of bugs, glaring. "What's your problem?" He was not merely rude but aggressively hostile, and Dr. Wilson was taken aback by the intensity of the young man's antagonism.

The optometrist slammed his statement down on the faux wood surface between them in an effort to regain the upper hand. "I withdrew a hundred dollars from my checking account, and, according to this, you also deducted a hundred from my savings and another hundred from my money market. I want those mistakes corrected and that money credited back to my accounts."

"And I want you to shut your mouth."

He was shocked by the response, though by this point perhaps he should not have been. Anger quickly followed shock, and he immediately pulled rank on the little pissant. "Get me your supervisor. Now!"

"No."

Dr. Wilson could feel the heat rushing to his face. "What do you mean, 'No?' I demand to see your supervisor!" He shook his head, frustrated. "You know what? I'm closing my accounts. And I'm going to tell your supervisor or manager or whatever-the-hell-he-is exactly *why* I'm not banking here anymore." He glanced around the room, searching for someone who looked like he might be in charge. In the quiet of the bank, the other employees had to have heard this loud exchange, but none of them were looking over, all focusing, or pretending to focus, on their work. Even the other tellers were counting money, writing on slips of paper or otherwise engaged.

His teller—V.J.—met his eyes, his gaze hard. "We're confiscating your car."

"What?" he exploded.

The teller leaned forward. "Do I stutter?"

"You can't do that!"

"Guess again." The teller fixed him with a look of scorn. "Did you even bother reading your terms and conditions? Because if you had, you would know that, should you threaten to terminate any contract or arrangement with The First People's Bank before the agreed-upon date, which in your case is death, we have the right to impound your assets."

Dr. Wilson moved over to the next teller window. "Excuse me," he said to the woman behind the counter.

Without so much as a glance in his direction, she pushed a small placard toward him: *Window Closed*.

He glanced to his right. *His* teller—V.J.—had somehow stepped out from behind the counter and was standing there in a fighter's stance, legs spread, hands balled into fists.

"We're taking your car. Give me the keys or I'll kick you in the nuts right here, right now."

It seemed impossible that any employee of any bank would ever say such a thing, but Dr. Wilson had no doubt that the young man in front of him was willing to carry out that threat. Could he take the teller? Probably. But he was outnumbered here, and engaging in a physical altercation would deny him the high road. With the crazy way this situation was spiraling out of control, he needed to think long-term, to play the long game rather than succumbing to immediate gratification.

"Where's your supervisor?" he tried one last time.

The teller held out his right hand, palm up. "Keys."

Other bank employees had stood up from their desks or emerged from behind their teller windows. A man in a well-tailored suit stood in the open doorway of a side office, watching.

"Keys!" the teller demanded.

"I drove here. How am I supposed to get back to my office?"

"Walk, you over-privileged fuck."

Stunned, Dr. Wilson removed his car key from his key ring and dropped it onto the young man's palm, striding past him, through the bank and out the door.

He'd walk, all right. He'd walk straight to a lawyer's office and sue those sons of bitches. This wasn't legal. It couldn't be.

But as he marched up the sidewalk, a small voice in his head wondered if perhaps it was.

3

"NICE wheels," Brian said admiringly as he walked up to his friend's new car in the bowling alley parking lot. He hadn't seen Oscar all week, had half-assumed that he'd blown town, and it was definitely a surprise to find out that he was not only still here but driving a brand new Sentra rather than that old auction-bought Jeep he'd had ever since Brian had known him. "But how can *you* afford a ride like that?"

"That new bank," Oscar said. "Got me a car loan."

"No shit?"

"No shit."

"How's that possible?"

"Competition, man. These guys're new and they're trying to horn in on territory that's already sewn up, so they have to think outside the box. Which is why they're trusting me with a car loan and giving Jimmy G. a checking account."

"Jimmy G.?"

"Jimmy G."

The thought was so incongruous that Brian laughed.

"Dude. They don't turn anyone down. For anything. You understand what I'm saying? It's not like a normal bank where you have to have...I don't know, references and a plan and shit. They just take you at your word, and as long as you can pay it back, everything's fine."

"So?"

"*So?* So you can get a loan. Remember what we were talking about at Rachel's? Your idea? They'll front you the money for that."

"Bullshit."

"I'm serious! And once you sell enough, you pay them back and you're on your way. Easy breezy."

Brian looked at him skeptically. "They're going to lend me money to buy pot."

"That's what I'm telling you, man. They don't care."

"That makes no sense. They're a bank. A *real* bank."

"They're different. With them, it's strictly business. Like I said, they give you the money and don't care *what* you do with it so long as you pay it back."

It seemed crazy, and definitely too good to be true, and Brian wondered if Oscar was fucking with him, or was maybe drunk. Or high. But his friend seemed not only serious but totally grounded. And he *did* have a new car...

"So..." Brian took a deep breath. "...what would I do? How would I go about it?"

"Nothing to it. Just go over to the bank, ask for a loan officer, tell them what you need—" Oscar must have read the skepticism on his face. "I'll go with you if you want," he offered.

"Okay."

They shot the shit for awhile longer before making plans to meet at the bank at ten o'clock the next morning.

Brian slept in and almost missed the meeting, but the sun shone through a gap caused by a bent slat in his bedroom shades, hitting his closed eyes and waking him up just in time. He wasn't able to eat breakfast or take a shower, but he put on his best clothes, combed his hair and gelled it into place, then hooked up with Oscar in front of the book shop next door to the bank.

"Okay," Oscar said. "The guy you need to talk to is named Worthington. He looks like a straight-up, middle-aged banker dude, but he's actually pretty chill, and he will get you your money."

"So I should let you do all the talking?"

"No, I'll just introduce you. After that, you're on your own. But it'll go well. I promise."

"I don't know..."

"Come on." Oscar pressed a hand against his back, and suddenly the two of them were no longer in front of the book shop but were walking past the front window of the bank toward the door. Oscar opened it, walked in, and Brian followed. They passed by a line of teller windows on the right, and maneuvered around a couple of desks on the left until they were standing before the desk of a man who looked like a network news anchor and whose nameplate identified him as: *Mr. Worthington. Manager.*

"Good morning, Mr. Worthington," Oscar said. "This is my friend Brian. He's interested in a small business loan."

A look passed between them, but Brian didn't have a chance to think about what that might mean because the manager was reaching across the desk to shake his hand, while telling Oscar, "Thank you. Would it be all right if I spoke to your friend in private? You can wait by the water cooler. We also have some complimentary coffee."

"That's okay," Oscar said. "I have some things I have to do. Talk to you later," he told Brian.

"Sit down," Mr. Worthington urged.

Brian did so, in a comfortable office chair across the desk from the bank manager. He felt awkward and ill-at-ease in such a formal environment, and he wished Oscar had given him a few tips on what to say. If he'd known his friend was going to bail, he would have practiced his pitch ahead of time. As it was, he had no concrete proposal to present, only a nebulous idea for a blatantly illegal operation, and Oscar's vague assurances that the bank was willing to loan him money for whatever scheme he devised.

"So you want to apply for a small business loan," Mr. Worthington said. He favored Brian with a supportive smile. "Tell us what you have in mind."

Brian stumbled his way through a necessarily ill-defined explanation of what he wanted to do, a description of mobile sales that declined to identify the product being sold. He finished with a lame, "And that's my plan."

"You want my honest opinion?" Mr. Worthington fixed him with a level gaze. "Your idea seems a little half-baked."

If he hadn't been so intimidated, he would have said, *It's completely baked.* But something about the banker discouraged any attempt at humor. Brian stood. "That's what I thought."

"Sit down."

It was an order not a suggestion, and Brian dropped back into the chair.

"I didn't say we wouldn't give you the money. I was just stating the fact that you don't seem to have thought this through. Now you want this money to buy marijuana—"

Brian felt the panic rise within him. "I didn't say that!"

"Calm down; the bank doesn't care about anything except ensuring that its customers make sound investments."

"But I didn't—"

"You didn't have to. It's our job to know our customers. Now what I'm suggesting is that perhaps marijuana is not such a promising venture. States' decisions to legalize and decriminalize pot are leading to lower prices and lower profit margins nationwide. But this opioid epidemic seems ripe for exploitation. Not only does law enforcement's aggressive stance keep prices high, but addiction ensures repeat business. And, as luck would have it, the most recent statistics indicate that street opioids have overtaken prescription opioids as the leading cause of drug deaths. So, this, we feel, is where the money is, and I'm sure if you invested in this type of merchandise, you would quickly and easily get an impressive return on your initial outlay."

Brian couldn't believe what he was hearing. Was this a trap? Was the room bugged? How could the man have possibly known that his plan was to deal weed? Had Oscar told him?

He needed to get out of here as quickly as possible.

Mr. Worthington smiled. "Calm down," he said, and it was as though he could read Brian's mind. "We're on your side. Because if you make money, we make money. Now what I'm suggesting is that we can hook you up with some of our other customers who are already involved in the supply end of this business. I assume distribution is your specialty?"

Brian nodded dumbly.

"So you would find customers, the supplier would provide you with access to product, selling it to you at a markup above wholesale..." He leaned forward, smiling tolerantly. "...as suppliers are wont to do, and you would then market it at street value, which should net you a hefty profit. Does this sound satisfactory to you?"

Brian said nothing, unsure of how to respond.

"You're wondering about specifics. Well, we're trying to help you get this enterprise off the ground, so we're talking easy terms. Right off the bat, we'd start at one percent annually. Of course, once your business is established, we would probably renegotiate. We reserve that right, since it's what allows us to fund no-collateral start-ups like yourself."

Could this possibly be true?

The banker smiled. "So we're agreed, right? Opioids it is. And once all the papers are signed, the t's crossed and the i's dotted, we'll put you in touch with two suppliers, one from California, one from Utah. That should allow you to meet your demand, even if you're able to expand your base beyond the bank's current estimates. If all goes well, by this time next week you should be in business."

Mr. Worthington held out his hand out across the desk. "Deal?"

Brian looked into the man's eyes, trying to gauge whether he could trust him.

"Deal," he said, shaking the banker's hand.

4

CHET Yates walked into The First People's Bank cap in hand. Well, not literally, maybe—his fading red MAGA hat was still pulled on tight, covering his bald spot—but certainly in a figurative sense. Upon opening the glass door and stepping inside, he glanced nervously around, trying to figure out who he needed to talk with about getting a loan. This was his last hope, and if things didn't go well here today, it was podcast time, and who knew how much of his army would follow him online?

Who knew how many of his listeners even had internet access?

It was his own fault, really. Chet was well aware of the fact that his show had devolved into a nightly single-issue rant, but the sheriff had killed his brother, and there was no way he was going to let that slide. He might go down for it, but he would go down swinging.

He was looking for a sign that said *Loans* or *Loan Department*, but before he could pin down a location, a bank employee stepped up to him and asked, "May I help you?" Although wearing a white shirt and tie, he looked kind of like a mentally ill homeless guy who'd accosted Chet outside the station a couple of times.

That wasn't possible, though.

Was it?

"I need to talk to someone about getting a loan," Chet said.

The bank employee smiled, revealing several missing teeth.

It was.

"Follow me," the man said.

Despite Chet's uneasiness, he did so, and was ushered past a row of tellers' windows to an office. The office was larger than seemed possible for its location and filled with heavy wooden furniture that made him think of the bank in *Mary Poppins*. The employee who'd led him here was suddenly nowhere to be found, and a distinguished-looking older gentleman stood up from behind a massive desk and beckoned him in. The man was dressed in an expensive three-piece suit, and Chet removed his hat as he stepped forward, suddenly self-conscious about his appearance. He should have dressed better, he thought, more appropriately for the circumstances. It was probably a strike against him already.

"Mr. Yates," the banker said. "Have a seat." He gestured toward a high-backed leather-upholstered chair directly opposite his own.

Chet sat down.

The man smiled. All of his teeth were white and perfectly even. "To what do we owe the pleasure? I understand that you're looking to secure a loan?"

Chet nodded.

"Would this be business? Personal?"

"Both, I guess." Chet shifted uncomfortably in his seat, the leather squeaking as he did so. "I need a loan because...well, I'm a radio broadcaster—"

"We know who you are, Mr. Yates."

"—and I currently don't have any advertisers. Without advertisers, the station will not be able to support my show."

"I thought Big O Tires and Discount Furniture bought time on your program."

"They pulled out...recently." He was starting to sweat. The banker was getting close to asking him *why* both Big O and Discount Furniture had quit the show, and Chet did not want to go into that. He had come up with a convincing lie as to why he had been dropped by his sponsors but, now that he was here, in the belly of the beast, he was not sure he'd be able to sell it. Besides, if the bank performed any kind of due diligence, they'd quickly find out the truth.

"Is this because you suggested that Sheriff Brad Neth should be shot?"

Obviously they'd *already* done their research.

But how was that possible? Had they anticipated that he would come in here to ask for a loan? As farfetched as that might seem, he could think of no other explanation, and, realizing that it would do him no good to lie, he nodded dejectedly. "Yeah. That's why."

"Well, it seems to us that your sponsors not only acted hastily but disloyally. We're new to town and of course don't take any stands on local politics—we're here to serve *all* the people—but who's to say? Maybe you're right. Maybe Sheriff Neth does deserve to be shot." He leaned forward. "We're not advocating violence, you understand. But this political correctness has gone too far. It's even affecting your livelihood. We at the bank are firm supporters of free speech. There's no political correctness here, just good old-fashioned honesty." He smiled knowingly. "We're willing to call a spade a spade."

Did that mean what he thought it meant? Chet looked into the blue-gray eyes of the banker and saw what he hoped to see.

"Words never hurt anyone, and if Sheriff Neth ends up getting his head blown off, it's not because you suggested it, it's because someone did it. And no matter what your lily-livered advertisers might think, that's not your fault."

"So..."

The banker leaned back in his chair. "So we're willing to support you. Papers need to be drawn up, and I'll talk to one of our loan advisers about that, but I can safely say that we will be offering you the business loan or personal loan that will most suit your needs. And because of the unique circumstances of your situation, we're prepared to provide the loan interest-free, suspending the first monthly payment for a year."

Relief flooded through him. "Thank you," he said gratefully. "Seriously, I can't tell you what this means to me."

The older man held up a hand. "In lieu of interest, however, we will be requesting commercial air time on your show—"

"No problem!"

"—at a time or times to be determined. Basically, we will just have our spokesperson record a promotional message informing your listeners of the services offered by The First People's Bank."

"Sure." Chet had never felt more appreciative in his life. "Whatever you want."

The other man stood, offering a hand across the desk. Still holding his hat, Chet extended his other hand and shook.

"Let's get this done, then. I'll introduce you to Ms. Coppick, our newest loan adviser, and she'll get you started."

The two of them walked out of the office and over to one of the desks opposite the teller windows.

He did not even know the banker's name, Chet realized. The man had not told him, and he had not asked.

Did it matter?

He put his MAGA hat back on.

No, he thought. It didn't.

NINE

1

WHEN DURL MEADOWS walked into Brave New World shortly before noon, Kyle almost didn't recognize him. Ordinarily jaunty and good-humored, the old man seemed not merely downcast but beaten. He silently carried in a box of books, put it on the counter, then went out to his car for another load. All total, he had five boxes he wanted to trade in, and he insisted that he needed money not store credit.

"What's going on?" Kyle asked, concerned.

"The bank's taking my house."

"What?"

Durl nodded. "Got the notice yesterday. Seems my loan was sold off to this First People's Bank, and for some reason they decided to change my terms, which I guess they can do because they're in charge now. So instead of paying seven hundred a month like I been doing, they want the whole amount all at once."

"That can't be legal."

"I didn't think so, either. But I been looking into it, and it may very well be. The original loan was from Lincoln Savings. When they went under, it was sold to some holding company and then to someone else. I kept writing checks for the same amount, just to different companies.

Now, somehow, your next door neighbor bought it up, and even though the contract was between me and the S and L, it's changed hands so much that I guess that no longer applies. To me, a contract's a contract, and both parties have to agree to any changes, but maybe there was a hidden clause in there or maybe regulations have been relaxed so much that they don't need my approval." Durl's usual anti-government rhetoric was nowhere in evidence. "Banks shouldn't be allowed to do that to people. Someone needs to crack down on this shit."

"There must be someone who can help you, someone who knows about this stuff."

"I'm open to suggestions. Because right now I'm just trying to scrounge up whatever I can and hope if I offer them enough, they'll put it off another month."

"But what'll you do then?"

Durl shook his head, and the look on his face was one of utter dejection. "God knows."

That was the day's first notice that things were going off the rails.

The second came mid-afternoon when Rollie Brown came into the shop to announce that *he* was going to be opening up a used bookstore. At first, Kyle assumed he was joking. "Is it because you can get more for those Michael Connolly books than I gave you?" he asked. But Rollie didn't smile, and it became quickly clear that he was serious. He told Kyle where his store was going to be and what type of books he planned to sell. There seemed to be some sort of chip on his shoulder, and beneath his matter-of-fact statements, Kyle sensed an undercurrent of hostility.

Where was that coming from?

They parted awkwardly, and shortly afterward, Trixie popped into the store. She sometimes dropped by when business at the consignment store was slow, but it had been a week or two since he'd seen her. "Hey, Kyle."

"How's Trix?" It was his standard greeting.

"Weird," she said. "I see Gary every morning, walking by my front window on his way to work. It's not only that he's dressed in a suit and doesn't even glance at my store, just keeps straight on, it's the fact that he works at that *bank* that gnaws at me." She said the word "bank" as though it were a synonym for excrement. "You even talk to Gary anymore?"

"I've been cut off," Kyle admitted.

"We all have." She shook her head. "So how's business?"

"It was up for awhile with the new foot traffic, but now it's settled back down to its usual crappy self. Oh, and one of my customers is going to open up a rival book store." He smiled brightly. "How are things with you?"

Trixie sighed. "Remarkably similar." She nodded toward the window. "I didn't even bother to lock the store when I came over. No one's going in there this afternoon. Not even to steal anything."

Kyle frowned. "Why's that? I would think people who've just cashed a check or withdrawn some money might want to spend it."

"Are they spending it here?" She raised a Spock eyebrow.

"Good point," he conceded.

"And now the bank's actively working against us. I assume they're financing your new rival?"

"They are," he admitted.

"They're also supporting a new consignment store over on Manzanita, which, of course, is closer to Wal-Mart and Safeway and all the new stores that are draining us dry. I mean, I'm barely making it as it is. How am I supposed to fight that?" She looked at him across the counter. "So what do you think the goal is? Put the stores to either side of them out of business so they can expand?"

The thought hadn't even occurred to him, and he was disappointed with himself for being so slow on the uptake. Of course that was the plan. Brave New World and It's New to You would close, and the bank would tear down the walls that separated First People's from the two businesses, tripling its size. Or, who knew, maybe the two stores would be torn down and the extra space would be used for parking. The bank could definitely use a parking lot.

"I think we should speak again at the next council meeting," Trixie said. "In fact, I'm thinking we should form a more formal downtown business association to protect our interests."

"Count me in," Kyle told her.

She smiled gratefully. "I was hoping you'd say that. I talked to Fred about it this morning, and he's supposed to spread the word on that side of the street, but I thought you could help me recruit Nancy to the cause." She smiled ruefully. "We're not exactly on the best of terms."

"Sure," Kyle said. Nancy Hall owned the florist's up the block. Last year, Trixie had accepted Nancy's jilted daughter's unused wedding dress on consignment and had made the mistake of showcasing it in her window. Nancy interpreted that as a humiliating slap in the face—she'd wanted it hidden in the store and sold on the QT—and she'd pulled the dress from the consignment store and stopped speaking to Trixie. Kyle and Nancy were still on good terms, though, as far as he knew, and he had no doubt that she'd be willing to side with her longtime neighbors against the interloper.

A red Nissan pulled into the empty parking space in front of Brave New World, and Trixie saw it through the window. "One of mine," she said, and bade him goodbye, the bell above the door tinkling as she opened it and walked outside. Kyle saw her greet a tall thin woman and a shorter equally thin woman who got out of the car, walking next door with them.

Sighing, Kyle picked up the Andrew Vachss book he'd been working his way through. The days were a lot lonelier with Gary gone. And at times like this, with no one else in the store, even cranking up the music couldn't make the place seem less empty.

And, periodically, he still heard that directionless tapping on the other side of the wall he shared with the bank.

The bell above the door rang again.

Kyle looked up. "Nick!" It was a surprise to see his son, who ordinarily stayed as far away from the store as possible. Embarrassment, he assumed. Teenagers were always ashamed of their parents. "Did I punish you and forget about it?" he joked. "Are you here to work?"

Nick smiled feebly, but there was no humor in it, and the fact that his son was willing to indulge in a sympathy smile meant that something was *really* bothering him; he hadn't extended his parents that sort of courtesy since he was thirteen.

"What is it?" Kyle asked.

He wasn't expecting a direct answer, was prepared to conversationally fish for the real response, but Nick just came out with it: "I think there might be something wrong with Victor."

I always thought there was something wrong with Victor, Kyle was tempted to joke, but restrained himself.

"Not that," Nick said, obviously attuned to what he was thinking. "He hasn't been at school all week, he's not answering his phone, and I can't even contact his parents. I even went over to their house, but no one was home." There was an odd look on his son's face, one he couldn't read, and something about that left Kyle feeling unsettled.

"It could be a coincidence. You called at the wrong time. Or maybe his mom or dad had a family emergency. One of his grandparents could have had a stroke or died, and the whole family had to—"

"I think they might be missing."

He could tell from the look on Nick's face that it sounded shocking even to him when spoken aloud, but he could tell as well that his son believed it, and that conviction set off alarm bells in his own head. "Do you want me to call the sheriff?"

Nick shifted uncomfortably on his feet. "I don't know. I mean there's no..." He took a deep breath. "I was thinking maybe you could come over to their house with me and...see what you think. I mean, maybe they're there," he added quickly, "and I'm just overreacting. But maybe...if you think..."

"We call the sheriff?"

Nick nodded unhappily.

Kyle walked around the counter and touched his son's shoulder. "Come on," he said kindly. "Let's check it out."

He locked up the store, flipped the sign from Open to Closed, and the two of them exited out the back, where Kyle had parked his truck. "You didn't ride your bike?" he asked Nick.

"Walked."

"Long walk."

Nick shrugged.

They got in the pickup's cab, and, following his son's directions, Kyle drove to the Clarks' house.

He had a bad feeling as he pulled into the driveway. The family's Explorer was parked in front of the garage, and Nick informed him soberly that the vehicle had been in the same spot, unmoving, for nearly a week. Getting out, the entire neighborhood seemed quiet and abandoned. Granted, it was the middle of the afternoon, and most people were probably at work, but there were not even any dogs barking. The two of them walked up the steps of the front porch, Kyle intending to ring the bell or knock on the door to see if anyone was home.

His cell phone rang.

"Don't answer it!" Nick said quickly. There was an edge of panic in his voice, and when Kyle looked over at his son, the boy's face was ashen.

"What is it?"

"Don't answer the phone!" Nick looked quickly around. "You know what? Maybe we should get out of here."

The phone stopped ringing, going to voicemail. "Hold on, bud. Why are you panicking about a phone call?"

Nick shook his head. "Nothing. It's nothing. Let's just see if they're home, and if they're not, let's call the sheriff."

It wasn't nothing. Kyle could not recall ever seeing his son so frightened, but this wasn't the time to push it. He'd always found it easier to talk to the boy while driving in the car, and he figured the two of them would have a heart-to-heart—or the closest the two of them could get to that—once they were on their way back. For now, he pushed the doorbell, hearing its muffled chime inside the house, and stood there, waiting to see if anyone answered.

Once again, he had the sense that things here were a little too quiet.

"Hello!" he called. "Anyone home?"

No answer.

"Maybe we should talk to the neighbors," he suggested. "See if they know anything. Like I said, maybe they were called away and had to go somewhere, and asked one of the neighbors to keep an eye on the place."

"Their car's here," Nick pointed out.

"But Victor's isn't."

It was a longshot, and seemed highly unlikely even to Kyle, but he was starting to absorb his son's panic and was trying to keep both of them grounded. He glanced to his right, toward the house next door—

—and saw, out of the corner of his eye, that the Clarks' small garage door was open.

How could he have not noticed that before? Their Explorer was parked in front of the closed big door, but on the side of the garage, the small door was wide open.

Nick must have seen where his eyes were looking. "I think that was closed the last time I was here." There was a nervous tremor in his son's voice.

"Let's check it out." Kyle led the way off the porch and up the driveway. Inside, the garage was dark, daylight barely penetrating past the open doorway. He stepped over the raised sill, reaching for a light switch on the wall to his right. His fingers found one, and he flipped it on. Light from a bare bulb in a porcelain socket attached to an open beam suffused the garage in a yellowish glow. There were the usual boxes and bikes, a toolbench and freezer, lawnmower and edger, and, in the center of the cement floor, two bodies, butchered.

Victor's parents.

"Jesus!" he exclaimed, instinctively pushing Nick out of the garage.

He was unaware that he'd been holding his breath until he exhaled explosively once in the open air. The bodies had no smell. He wasn't sure how that was possible. If they'd been in the garage for more than a day—and he suspected they had—the stench of death should have been unbearable, but there'd been no advance warning about what was in the garage. His phone was in his hand and he was dialing 911 even as Nick was asking why he'd been pushed out and what was in there. Somehow, the boy hadn't seen the bodies, and for that Kyle was grateful, because it was a sight he would never forget as long as he lived.

A dispatcher answered. "Nine one one. What is your emergency?"

"Dead bodies," he said. "Murdered. They're all cut up." He'd planned to be more clear and articulate, but those were the words that came out.

"Murdered?" Nick shouted. "Victor?"

"What is your location," the dispatcher said at the same time.

He shook his head. "No," he told Nick. "His parents, I think."

"Location?" the dispatcher repeated.

Kyle ran into the front yard, looked at the black metal numbers nailed vertically to a porch post. "Six eleven Pinyon Drive," he said. He closed his eyes, saw in his mind the bodies, the blood, the organs. "And hurry."

2

"SHOULD we move the car so the M.E.'s wagon can get in the driveway? Sheriff? Sheriff?"

Brad nodded absently at Hank, waving him toward the street. His head was pounding like a mother, and he tried to remember if he had a bottle of aspirin in the car. It hurt badly enough that he was even tempted to see if the Clarks had any in their medicine cabinet, but he knew that was unprofessional. This was a crime scene, for Christ's sake.

There'd been too damn many crime scenes lately, and he was pretty sure that the stress from dealing with so much violence and death was what had caused his headache. This was the worst one yet, even more sickening than what had happened to the bank manager. That had looked like the work of a crazed killer, someone completely out of control. Even now, he could see that caved-in face, recall the putrid stench of decaying flesh. But this was *methodical*, and that made it seem all the more evil. The Clarks hadn't been stabbed in a frenzy, their heads crushed in a rage. They had been killed somehow and then sliced open, their organs removed from their bodies and piled up on the cement next to them. Blood was everywhere, but even through the wash of red, it had been easy to see that the bodies had been laid out like specimens, as though the killer had dissected them and taken them apart to study how they worked.

He stood, watching, as Hank backed the car out of the driveway, parking on the street. Seconds later, the M.E.'s van arrived, pulling into the just-vacated spot.

He should probably be the one to show the M.E. the bodies, but his head was hammering, and he really didn't want to see *that* again. Mitch and Issac were still there, Issac shooting pictures, and when Hank walked up, Brad told him to take the M.E. and his assistant into the garage.

Vern and Norris were in the house right now, going over the place with a fine-toothed comb, and Brad clomped up the porch steps and went in to check on their progress. According to the Decker kid, the Clarks had a son. There was no sign of him anywhere on the property, he was not answering his phone, and he'd apparently been MIA for the past few days. In Brad's book, that made him not just a person of interest but their prime suspect. Nine times out of ten, in situations like this, it was the missing family member who ended up being the one who'd done it. At least that had been his experience, although, admittedly, on a much lesser scale.

He wished now that he'd asked the Deckers a few more questions. He'd briefly interviewed the boy and his dad before allowing them to leave, advising them to come by the station later to give a full statement. They'd both been pretty shaken up—hell, *he* was shaken up—and since they weren't witnesses, just civilians who'd happened upon the scene, he'd thought it best to send them home. Having a little more background on the family, though, might help steer the search in the proper direction, since, according to Norris and Vern, they'd turned up nothing yet.

"Skip the front of the house here," Brad told his men. "I want you to look in the kid's bedroom. If we're going to find anything, it'll probably be there. Right now, he's our only suspect."

"Really?" Norris said. "You think their son killed them? And did *that*?"

Brad shrugged. "It's happened before."

"Maybe the kid was kidnapped," Vern suggested. "Someone kills the parents, kidnaps the kid…"

"What for?"

"Well, it can't be ransom, 'cause there's no one left to pay it, so maybe…I don't know, sex stuff?"

"Unlikely," Brad told him. But the idea of kidnapping, especially in such close conjunction with the brutal slayings in the garage, made him think about the girls, and, excusing himself, he ducked into the laundry room to give Patty a quick call.

She answered on the second ring. He tried to make things seem casual, but she could tell that he was checking up on them and immediately asked, "What's wrong?"

"Nothing's wrong," he said. "I was just—"

"Where are you? Is someone else dead?" There was a catch in her voice. "Is it a child?"

Sighing, he broke down and told her. Patty had been making plans to pick up Sue, Jillian and Shannon from school and then drop them off at Shannon's house for an hour or so while she met with new clients, but when she learned what had happened, she told him that she and the girls would be going straight home after school. "I'm not letting them out of my sight," she said.

Good, he thought.

There was a pause. "What's going on?" Patty asked finally. Her voice was low, hushed, frightened. "All these people are…*dying*. Here. In Montgomery. I mean, I've *never* heard of anything like this before anywhere, not even on the news. Never! That mass murder or suicide or whatever it was with the people from the bank? That's Ripley's Believe It or Not stuff. It just doesn't happen. Not just here. Anywhere!"

"You're right," he agreed.

Her voice dropped again. "I want you to be careful."

"I will. I always am."

"But more than usual. This isn't normal. Things like this don't happen."

He was touched by her concern. "I will," he promised. Norris stepped into the laundry room doorway, motioning for Brad to come with him. "I have to go. I'll be home as soon as I can."

"Call me if you're going to be late."

"I will."

"Love you."

"You too. Bye." Clicking off, he met his deputy's eyes. "What is it?"

"You've got to see this."

"You found something?" They were already walking.

"In the kid's room, like you said."

Brad followed him through the middle doorway of the hall, where Vern was standing next to a twin bed. On the floor in front of him was something Brad could not have imagined.

He stared at it, eyes widening.

"Jesus."

3

WHEN Nick awoke in the morning and heard the TV in the living room, heard his parents' voices in the kitchen, saw sunlight streaming into his room from between the slats of his windowshades, he could almost believe that none of it had happened, that he had dreamed it all and this was just a normal Saturday. But when he checked his phone and saw that he had twenty messages, he knew that it had not been just a figment of his imagination. He scrolled through the messages, searching for one that was from a genuine friend and not just a curious acquaintance. Sent less than ten minutes ago was a text from Aaron, three simple words: *Is it true?*

He texted back *Yes*, then shut off his phone. He'd call Aaron later and tell him the whole story, but right now he just wanted to have breakfast and not think about any of it. Thankfully, his parents must have felt the same way, because they kept the conversation light and off-topic, talking as they ate about TV shows they were binge watching and staying far away from what had happened at Victor's.

It was mid-morning and he was in his room playing *Halo* online, trying to distract himself from yesterday's horror, when the doorbell rang. To his surprise, his mom called out, "Nick! It's for you!"

Who could it be? He hurried down the hall and out to the living room, surprised to see Aaron at the door. He and Aaron were friends, but they were school friends, and he didn't think either of them had been to the other's house until now.

His mom faded discreetly away, retreating back into another room, and Nick stepped onto the porch, the screen slamming behind him. "What's up?"

Aaron's voice was low. "I think I know where Victor is."

Nick glanced quickly back into the house to make sure his mom wasn't within earshot, then led Aaron onto the lawn. His voice, when he spoke, was low as well. He didn't want his mother to hear. "Where?"

"I overheard Gina and Catherine talking at the Circle K, and Gina said that Holly said that Sue Rumsey saw him working at the new bank."

"*Working?*" The idea seemed unbelievable.

"Sue went in to check on her college saver account, and she says Victor was working there as a teller but he pretended not to know her."

Nick's voice was barely above a whisper. "You know they think he killed his parents, right? They found a whole bunch of weird shit in his room, cult shit."

"So what do we do? Tell our parents? Call the law? Tell our parents, right? And have *them* call the law?"

"I don't know. Maybe we should check it out ourselves first, make sure he's really there. Because if he is, don't you think the sheriff would've already caught him? And if that story's true, where's he sleeping at night? He's obviously not going home." Nick shook his head. "I'm not sure I believe it. You know what a liar Gina is."

"Okay, then. Let's check it out."

"Is the bank even open on Saturday?"

"We'll see."

"Let me tell my mom and get my bike."

Ten minutes later, the two of them were coasting down Main into the old downtown. They hid their bikes by the overgrown gulch at the beginning of the business district and walked up the cracked sidewalk to the bank.

"What do we do if we find him?" Aaron asked.

Nick opened the glass door and walked inside the bank. "Ask him what's going on."

They spotted Victor almost immediately. He was one of only two tellers at adjacent open windows in the center of a long line on the right side of the room. He looked odd in his white shirt and tie, with his hair neatly combed, but as they reached his section of counter, Nick saw that it was not only his clothing and hairstyle that made him look odd.

There was something off about his eyes...

Aaron figured it out immediately. "Dude! What happened to your eyelashes?"

He was right. Their friend's lashes were gone.

"I had to pull them out," Victor said calmly.

Nick looked at his nametag. "And how come you're calling yourself V.J.?"

A weird look came over their friend's face. "I've always been V.J."

Nick and Aaron looked at each other, mentally drawing straws. Nick understood instantly that he'd picked the short one, that if anyone was going to bring up what they were really here to talk about, it would have to be him. He gathered his courage. "Your parents are dead," he blurted out. "My dad and I found them in your garage. We were looking for you."

He expected some sort of reaction. But there was none. Victor— or V.J.—simply stared blankly from underneath his lashless lids.

"You've been absent for, like a week."

"I work here now."

"Your parents were *murdered*," Nick said. "The cops think you did it."

"Your mother was getting boned by the gardener. She's such a fucking slut."

Nick felt the anger rise within him. "Did you kill them?"

"I saw it online." Victor grinned. "Your mom was lying on her stomach, grunting like a pig, while the gardener was shoving it all the way up her ass."

Nick reached for him through the window opening, but Victor—

V.J.

—moved back and easily avoided contact. His face darkened. "That's going to cost you," he said. "Your account's going to be deducted ten dollars."

"I don't give a shit."

"His mom really was being buttfucked by the gardener," Victor tried to tell Aaron.

But Aaron wasn't listening. His phone was out, and he was calling 911. Behind him, appearing as if from nowhere, was a tall man Nick recognized from the assembly as Mr. Worthington.

His heart started pounding. He shouldn't have come here with just Aaron. He should have contacted his dad. How could he be so stupid? If Victor—V.J.—*had* killed his parents, Mr. Worthington knew all about it and was covering for him. Nick had no idea what the connection between the two might be, or why there would be any connection at all, but Mr. Worthington had hired Victor for a job *and* had tried to keep Nick away from the Clarks' house.

Get off Victor Clark's porch, leave his yard, stay off his property and stop snooping. Do I make myself clear?

The man put a hand on Aaron's shoulder. "Are you sure you want to be doing that, son?"

The phone to his ear, Aaron pulled away and started walking toward the door. "Yes," he replied. "And I'm not your son."

"This is Aaron Mund," he said into the phone. "I'm at The First People's Bank, and I found Victor Clark." There was a pause. "Yes." Pause. "I'm here right now. With my friend Nick Decker."

"Bad move," Mr. Worthington said quietly. Presumably, he was talking to Aaron, but he was looking directly at Nick, and the coldness in those eyes made Nick want to immediately run outside and get as far away from the bank as possible.

Aaron still had the phone to his ear, and he looked through the teller window. "The sheriff's on his way," he told Victor. "Yes," he said into the phone. "I'm still here."

Victor—V.J.—backed up. The area behind him seemed darker than it had been, darker than it should be. Another bank employee, an older woman, passed in front of him, as did another man holding a sheaf of papers, and suddenly their friend was nowhere to be seen. Nick squinted into the gloom—well aware that there should not have *been* any gloom—but Victor was gone.

So was Mr. Worthington. He was no longer behind Aaron, and looking around the bank, Nick saw no sign of him anywhere. Other employees were staring at them—a middle-aged man behind a desk, a young woman coming out of the vault, an older man by the water cooler—and none of them seemed friendly. Gary, his dad's old coworker and friend, stepped up to the teller window that had been occupied by Victor and looked out expressionlessly. "May I help you?" he asked in a peculiar British accent. There was no indication that Gary even recognized who he was.

"Let's get out of here," Nick said under his breath.

"I just called the sheriff."

"We'll wait for them outside."

The atmosphere was tense, but no one stopped them as they made their way back toward the front door. Once on the sidewalk, Nick led his friend next door to the book shop, where his dad was just opening up. They went inside, and he explained to his father what had happened.

"You went in there by yourself?" he could hear the anger in his dad's voice. "Why didn't you come and get me?"

"We thought we could handle it."

Aaron nodded. "That place is freaky, Mr. Decker. It's why I called the law."

Two sheriff's vehicles were pulling up just at that second, and the three of them walked out. Aaron identified himself as the one who'd dialed 911, and he and Nick told the sheriff the whole story, leaving nothing out.

"Do you think he's still in there?" Sheriff Neth asked them.

Nick and Aaron looked at each other, then shrugged. "He might have slipped out the back door," Nick said. "But I'm pretty sure he didn't go out the front. We would've seen him."

"Unless they have, like, a basement or something," Aaron suggested. "Because he was...gone. We didn't see him. And Mr. Worthington definitely seemed like he was threatening us. For sure *he* would hide him."

"We'll see about that," the sheriff said grimly. He nodded at the three deputies next to him. "Stay here," he told Nick and Aaron. "We'll come and get you if we need you."

Nick, his dad and Aaron stood on the sidewalk, trying to watch what was happening through the bank's tinted windows but able to glimpse only an occasional indistinct movement from within. As four minutes became seven, became ten, became fifteen, the three of them retreated back to the bookstore, where his dad got them bottled waters out of the small fridge and they stared out at the sidewalk, waiting for the sheriff and his men to re-emerge. They did so soon after, appearing angry and frustrated. Nick and Aaron followed his dad outside to see what had happened, and they were informed that, according to Mr. Worthington, no Victor or V.J. Clark worked for or had ever worked for The First People's Bank.

"We saw him!" Nick and Aaron cried almost in unison. "He was there!"

"I believe you," the sheriff said. "But there's no way to prove it. We searched every inch of that place, and everyone swears that they don't know anyone named Clark and they've never seen anyone matching his description."

"Even Gary?" his dad asked softly.

The sheriff nodded. "Even Gary. Now as far as I'm concerned, they're all lying through their teeth. And if we catch them at it, there's going to be hell to pay. Obstruction of justice, interfering with an investigation, all of that. But until we can prove otherwise, we're out of luck." He looked at Aaron and Nick. "Now, do you two want to come down and give a statement? Make it official?"

Nick glanced over at his dad, who nodded.

"Sure."

The sheriff smiled. "All right, then. This'll help," he assured them.

"I'm coming with you," his dad said, and Nick felt a gigantic sense of relief. This was all adult stuff, and he was way out of his depth. It felt hugely reassuring to know his dad would be by his side. "We'll call Mom, tell her to meet us there. And Aaron? Maybe you should call your parents. Have them come along, too."

Aaron nodded.

"Let me close up shop. Aaron you can call your parents, then you two get your bikes, put them in the store, and we'll head down." He looked over at the sheriff and his deputies. "Meet you at the station in fifteen minutes?"

"See you there," the sheriff said.

AT home, after an hour at the sheriff's office, Nick sat in the high-backed chair he used to like to pretend was a throne and faced his parents, who were seated on the couch. None of them seemed to know what to say.

His mom shook her head. "Victor killed his parents? I can't believe it."

"I can't either," Nick admitted. He stared down at the carpet, filled with an almost overwhelming sense of loss.

"I can," his dad said. "Did you hear what they found in his room?"

Nick looked up. "Not exactly. Cult stuff, I think."

"When you were giving your statement I was talking to Deputy Dillman, and he said Victor's room was filled with bugs and animals that he'd killed and taken apart in some kind of ritual."

"My God," his mom breathed. She turned toward Nick. "Did you suspect any of this? Was there any indication...?"

He was as shocked as she was. "No. Nothing."

"So the bank," his dad said, giving voice to what they were all thinking. "It's turned Gary into some kind of Stepford teller. First it hired Victor, now it's hiding him. What's going on there?"

No one replied because no one had an answer.

"I want you to stay away from there," his dad told him. "You, too," he said, turning to his mom. "There's something wrong with that place, with those people, and until things are sorted out, we all need to keep away."

"But you're right next door," Nick pointed out.

"And there's a wall."

"Do you think they're going to find Victor?" he asked

"They will eventually," his mom said. "They always do."

"What about the people at the bank? You think they'll go to jail? You think they'll close the bank?"

His parents looked at each other.

"I don't know," his dad admitted. "I honestly don't know."

But Nick knew that he hoped so.

They all did.

TEN

1

"THERE'S SOMEONE OUT there, Mommy!"

Darlene, seated in the saggy center of the low couch, looked up from her phone. Tiffany was standing next to the kitchenette in her pajamas, clutching her blue Dory pillow. The short hallway behind her was dark.

Darlene put her phone down on the seat next to her and stood. This happened at least three nights a week, and there was never anyone there, but it was her duty as a mom to check in order to make her daughter feel more secure. She walked the three steps to Tiffany, took the little girl's hand, and brought her to the window, pulling back the curtains.

"Look," she started to say. "There's no—"

A man was standing outside the trailer.

Darlene let the curtain fall and instinctively backed away. She'd seen the man for a brief second, illuminated by the light above the door that shone onto the yard, and he'd looked big. And threatening. His clothes were dark, and he stood in an aggressive stance, facing the trailer, legs slightly spread, arms out at his sides, like a wrestler facing his opponent.

"Stay here," she whispered to Tiffany. "Don't move."

There was a knock at the door.

The sound made both of them jump.

There's only one door, she thought, panicked. *We can't escape. We're trapped.*

Her trembling finger attempted to press 911 even as she shouted, "Go away! You're trespassing on private property!"

"Ms. Altman?" said the man on the other side of the door. He had a British accent, and his voice was unexpectedly calm and soothing. "My name's Gary Dawes. I'm here from the bank, and I would like to talk to you about the unique financial opportunity we're willing to offer you."

Her finger hesitated over the last 1. Was it possible? Could he really be just a solicitor? It was dark outside, but when she glanced at the clock, she saw that it was only seven-thirty, not that late.

She didn't finish dialing the emergency number. "What do you want?" she called out.

"I told you. I'm from the bank. Would it be all right if I came in?"

"You can stay right there," she told him.

"Very well. As I said, my name is Gary Dawes, and I'm here representing The First People's Bank. We're new in town, and as a gesture of good will, we're providing special opportunities to selected individuals. I believe you were sent an email—"

"I don't have email!" she said. "I don't have a computer! Can't afford it!"

"Well, that explains the mixup. You see, I'm here to answer any questions you might have about our offer and to walk you through the application process. Although, if you don't have internet access, we will have to fill out the application at the bank itself rather than online."

Giving Tiffany's hand a small squeeze, Darlene edged a little closer to the door. "Application for what?"

"Why a home loan, of course. Wouldn't you rather live in a house?"

"I can't afford that."

"With the bank's help you can."

Darlene thought for a moment. Slowly, carefully, she unlocked the door and opened it a crack. She'd braced herself, prepared to slam the door shut if he tried to rush in, but, standing before her, the man seemed neither as big as before nor as threatening. He looked perfectly ordinary, in fact, although perhaps a bit rougher than his refined accent would indicate.

Cautiously, she opened the door wider. "What exactly are you offering me?"

"Zero percent interest," he promised. "You go out, find a house, we finance it for you, and you pay no interest on the loan whatsoever."

"I still wouldn't have enough for the monthly payments." She gestured behind her toward the trailer's interior. "This is all I can afford."

"What if you got a raise? An extra two hundred a month?"

She laughed harshly. "That's never going to happen."

His eyes met hers, and the laughter died in her throat. "Let the bank take care of that."

She felt the way she had when she'd first seen him standing in the darkness outside the trailer. Goosebumps arose on her arms. She glanced protectively toward Tiffany.

"Ed won't give me—" she began.

"He will," the man promised, holding her gaze. There was a significant pause. "Are you in?"

"I can't—"

"*Are you in?*" There was an insistence in his voice that made her feel frightened.

Darlene nodded meekly.

The man backed down the rickety wooden steps. "Then come into the bank tomorrow and sign the paperwork." He made a pistol of his thumb and forefinger, pointing it at Tiffany, hiding behind her. "You, little girl, are soon going to have your very own room in your very own house. Aren't you lucky?" He smiled at her.

Tiffany didn't reply but retreated further into the trailer, holding the Dory pillow in front of her face.

Darlene closed the door.

2

KIRK Halpin pulled into the Burger King drive-thru behind a Dodge Ram pickup so wide that it barely fit in the narrow lane, and from his shirt pocket withdrew the folded scrap of paper on which he'd written everyone's order. Jean, he remembered, wanted a salad, but the others' preferences were a jumble of hamburgers with or without various condiments that he couldn't have possibly committed to memory. He himself wanted a chicken sandwich, but he wasn't sure which one, which was why he'd volunteered for the lunch run today. It would give him time to peruse the menu and make a decision.

The man in the pickup finished ordering and pulled away, but before Kirk could drive up to the speaker, his door was yanked open. Strong hands grabbed his head and jerked him out of the car. His left elbow hit the armrest on the door; his right arm twisted painfully as it was pressed between his body and the seat. There was a ferocious smell of sweat and something even more unsavory, and then he was dumped hard on the cement. With the car still in gear and his foot no longer on the brake, the Nissan rolled forward, gaining a little bit of speed on the slight incline and drifting to the right until it smacked into two of the cement-filled metal poles that separated the drive-thru from the parking lot.

The man who had pulled him from the car helped him to his feet. In contrast to his overpowering body odor, the man was dressed professionally in black slacks, white shirt and blue tie. There was something off about him, though. The untamed roughness of the tanned, lined face did not match the civilized veneer of the clothes.

"You're going to need a new car," the man said. "Did you know that The First People's Bank is offering auto loans at zero percent financing?" He smiled, revealing several missing teeth.

Kirk pulled away from him. "It's just a dent." The car's engine was still running—he could hear it—which meant that the minor collision had not caused any major damage. He started walking toward the vehicle, taking his phone out as he did so, intending to take a picture of the lunatic who'd accosted him so he could share it with the police.

Suddenly, the man ran past him, hopped into the car, slammed the driver's door shut and sped backward, burning rubber and nearly knocking Kirk over. The back bumper slammed into another pole, and then the Nissan was speeding forward, past the speaker, around the corner of the Burger King.

"Stop!" Kirk yelled, running after him.

But the man did not go far. He made a U-turn in the street, steering into the parking lot on the other side of the drive-thru lane, accelerating as he headed straight toward the cinderblock wall that separated the Burger King from the transmission shop behind it.

Kirk slipped between two of the poles and ran into the parking lot, waving his arms and screaming for the man to stop.

His car hit the wall head-on with an ear-splitting crash that completely collapsed the front of the vehicle and sent metal parts skittering across the asphalt. Smoke billowed upward from the engine beneath the crumpled hood, and orange flames were visible from within the smoke.

Somehow, miraculously, the man emerged from the wreckage unscathed, exiting the open driver's door and straightening his tie as he walked toward Kirk.

"I'm calling the sheriff!"

"Why?"

"*Why?* You destroyed my car!"

"No."

"What do you mean *no?*" Kirk looked around for witnesses, but though there were three cars parked in the lot, they were empty. Back in the drive-thru line, the Ram pickup was gone, and apparently there'd been no other vehicles behind his own.

"You think anyone's going to believe that an officer of the bank hijacked your car and crashed it into a wall for no reason?"

Oh, there's a reason, Kirk thought. *You were trying to get me to sign up for a loan. And when they see you, when they see that you look like a toothless fucking convict, they're definitely going to believe me.*

But he said nothing. He'd *heard* things about this new bank. Nothing specific, exactly, but there seemed to be a general uneasiness on the part of people, and the other day both Joey Accordia and Beto Gonzalez had expressed regret about switching their accounts over to First People's. When he'd asked why they didn't just switch back, neither had answered and both had seemed strangely unsettled. He'd thought nothing of it at the time, but now that reaction seemed entirely understandable.

The man stopped in front of him. "Look. A crazy person assaulted you, stole your car and totaled it. Not your fault. The insurance company will give you some money, and you can supplement it with a loan from the bank and get yourself a better car."

"I don't want a better car!" Kirk pointed. "I want *that* car!"

The man chuckled harshly. "Good luck with that."

Kirk used his phone to snap a quick picture.

With one swift movement, a rough hand reached out, grabbed the phone from his hand and threw it hard on the ground, smashing it. Just to make sure, the man stomped on its corpse with a heavy scuffed shoe.

"You can use some of that loan money to get you a new phone, too," he said.

Laughing raucously, he walked back toward Burger King, as, with an audible *woosh*, the Nissan was engulfed in flames.

3

ALFRED Murdoch took his usual break at the eighth hole, after hitting two under par for the first time this afternoon. This was the section of the course that abutted the park, and there was a shared restroom at the border of the two that he liked to use because it was clean and always empty, unlike the dirty overcrowded men's room by the pro shop.

Telling Bruce to wait and watch his clubs, Alfred trekked across the green to the restroom. There was no door, just a privacy wall, and he walked around it, through the open entrance. He'd never encountered anyone else here before, but when he stepped inside, he heard a noise from the stall. Stepping up to the first of the two urinals, he began unzipping his pants—

And spotted a figure in his peripheral vision with gray hair and pale skin passing from left to right, from the stall to the doorway.

Glancing over his shoulder, he saw a naked old lady standing barefoot in the center of the dirty cement floor, hands on her hips in a Peter Pan pose. Unnerved, he turned toward her.

"You want me to suck it?" she asked. She nodded at his open fly.

"No!" he said, automatically zipping up.

"Want to stick it in my pussy?" She turned around, wiggled. "Or see if it fits in my ass?"

"No! Jesus, what's wrong with you?" He no longer had to go to the bathroom, and he tried to think of a way to get past the old bat and out the door without forcibly pushing her aside. The last thing he needed was to face some trumped-up assault charge from a crazy woman.

"I don't think your wife would like it if I blew you," she said. "Your kids, either."

So that was it. She was going to try and blackmail him. Well, it wouldn't work. "Get out," he said through gritted teeth.

"Help!" she screamed. The sound echoed off the empty walls.

"Quiet down!" Alfred hissed. He stepped forward, waving his hand to shush her, and she backed up, her eyes widening in mock fear.

"Don't hurt me!" she pleaded, a little too loudly.

"What do you want?" he demanded.

"You're not getting the full return from your investments that you should be," she said, and the contrast between her suddenly reasonable tone and her naked wrinkled body was jarring. "We've been looking at your portfolio and have noted that the funds in which you are invested have underperformed by nine point six percent."

"Who is 'we'?" he asked.

"Oh, I'm sorry. The First People's Bank. I understand that you have a checking account with your credit union—and that's fine— but your investment portfolio, your very *large* investment portfolio, is being managed by a New York firm who are not doing right by you, primarily because they can't possibly tailor their approach to your specific needs here in Montgomery, Arizona. Which is why we think it would be advantageous for you to allow First People's to manage your financial assets. Thanks to deregulation, banks are back in the game, and as investors ourselves, our ears are much closer to the ground than any outside manager."

It made no sense. This naked old lady was here to convince him to let the new bank take over his investments?

"Why would I do that?" he asked.

"Would it help if I sucked you off?"

The sudden shift startled him, caused him to step back.

"Not back there!" she yelled, her voice echoing. "I don't like it back there!"

"Shut up!" he hissed.

She smiled. "All we're asking is that you give us a chance. Let us go over your portfolio with you and show you how we can better manage your financial investments."

He took a step forward and to the left, intending to walk around her, but she slid to the side, blocking him. She pinched the nipple on her sagging right breast, ran her tongue over her lips.

"What do you want?"

"I told you. Come to the bank so we can discuss strategies for minimizing your risks and getting you better returns. Your finances are being mismanaged and rely too heavily on ventures and speculations completely at odds with both your long- and short-term needs. The First People's Bank is ready to offer a plan tailored specifically to you. All you need to do is meet with one of our investment specialists and hear us out."

After a short discussion, Alfred agreed to show up at the bank tomorrow with all of his paperwork and go over possible investment approaches. The woman finally let him pass, and he strode back across the green to where Bruce was waiting. Of course, there was no way in hell he was going to do any such thing. The fact that an institution would hire that old hag to try and sexually blackmail him guaranteed that it would not receive his business. Hell, it shouldn't even *be* in business, and the first thing he was going to do after finishing this round with Bruce was report The First People's Bank to the Better Business Bureau, the state attorney general and whatever government entity oversaw banking operations.

They didn't realize who they were fucking with.

He reached Bruce, still watching over his golf bag, and from behind heard a loud shrill whistle.

The old lady, still naked, took two fingers from her mouth and waved at him from the front of the restroom. "Thanks for letting me get you off!" she called.

Alfred turned away, simultaneously angry and revolted.

"So," Bruce asked calmly, picking up a nine iron, "are you switching over to First People's?"

4

TESS smelled smoke.

She mentioned it to Deke, but the Cowboys were in the middle of a play, and he nodded absently, not taking his eyes off the flat screen, although a few minutes later, during a commercial, even he detected the odor. It was definitely a fire rather than a barbecue, and both of them sniffed the air in an effort to determine its origin. It seemed to be coming from outside, and they walked into the front yard to discover that their roof was burning.

"Call 911!" he ordered, rushing over to the hose and turning it on.

"My phone's inside!"

"Go to Suzie's!" Water was gushing from the hose, and he put his finger over the opening to make it spray, aiming up at the flames on the roof.

Tess ran next door to Suzie's house, yelling, "Fire! Fire!" But even as she did so, she wondered if she should have run inside to get her cell phone instead. The blaze was not yet out of control, and she could have grabbed some family photographs at the same time, or the punchbowl her mom had given her as a wedding present, or something else with sentimental value that could not be replaced.

Suzie's door was unlocked as usual, and Tess ran into her friend's house, still shouting "Fire!" From the living room end table, she grabbed the cordless phone out of its cradle and pressed 911.

Suzie ran out from the hall, still buttoning her pants, the sound of a toilet flushing behind her. "What's going on?"

But Tess was already screaming into the phone, telling the dispatcher that their house was on fire and repeating the address over and over again so the fire department would know where it was. Even before she hung up, she could hear sirens starting from far away, and she dashed back outside, past Suzie, horrified to see that Deke had not been able to stem the spread of the flames and that the entire house seemed to be burning.

It was that shake roof. They'd known it was a fire hazard, but they hadn't had the money to get it replaced.

The firemen arrived remarkably quickly, but not quickly enough to save their home. They saved part of it, and the garage, but almost the entire roof was gone, as well as the two bedrooms, the bathroom and the kitchen. Basically, the entire back of the house was destroyed, and the firemen were cleaning up, and Tess was crying into Deke's shoulder, when a cleancut man in a gray business suit walked up, clearing his throat to get their attention. Curious neighbors, even Suzie, were being kept off the property behind yellow caution tape, but somehow this man had gotten through, and he smiled insincerely as Tess looked up at him.

"A tragedy," he said, shaking his head. "A tragedy."

His sympathy was as insincere as his smile, and Deke frowned at him. "Who are you?"

"I work for The First People's Bank."

"So?"

"So you're going to need to buy a new house," the man said. "Our bank can offer you—"

Deke looked at him belligerently. "We have insurance. We'll rebuild."

"You don't think it would be more prudent to buy a new house in a less fire-prone neighborhood?"

"No."

"And if your house burns down again?"

Was that a threat? Tess examined the man. How much did he know about *this* fire? Because there hadn't been a storm or lightning, and she was pretty sure there'd been no problems with the home's wiring. How exactly *did* the fire start?

And how and why had he gotten here so quickly?

"Go away," Deke said. "Come on," he told Tess. "Let's find out what's what." And he started walking toward the fire captain in charge of the scene.

Before she could follow him, the man from the bank inserted himself in front of her. "He didn't smell the smoke in time, did he? And your house didn't have any working detectors."

"We won't make that mistake again," she assured him.

He leaned in. "The thing is, he could have easily died in his sleep if the fire had occurred at a different hour." His voice was barely above a whisper. "And he still could." The man smiled. "Why don't you talk to him about moving. I think a new house would be...*safer.*"

She met his eyes for a second, then looked away, frightened.

"Besides, that lack of smoke detectors? Insurance company's not going to like it. They use minor details like that to try and deny coverage. This house is going to sit here like this until all the i's are crossed and t's are dotted. Could be six months, could be a year, could be two." He smiled again. "Talk to your hubby. We'll finance a *new* house no problem."

"Tess!" Deke called, noticing that she wasn't behind him. He frowned at the man from the bank.

Tess hurried over to where he was asking the fire captain about a timetable for going back in to assess the damage.

She glanced behind her.

The man was gone.

ELEVEN

1

WHEN COY ARRIVED at the bank Wednesday morning, Ben Shanley was waiting for him, and before Coy could even get to his desk and put down his briefcase, the manager was calling him over in the overly hearty voice he used when dealing with hesitant customers. This couldn't be good, and for a brief moment Coy thought he was going to be fired. But then Shanley closed the office door behind them and sat down heavily in the chair behind his desk. There was a moment of silence. "We're in big trouble," the manager said finally. "And I need your help."

Coy was not invited to sit down, so he remained standing awkwardly. "O...kay," he said hesitantly, not sure where this was headed.

"It's that new bank. First People's. They're not only scooping up B of A's old customers, but they're stealing some of ours as well. And somehow they're signing up people who've *never* had bank accounts before. That untapped base is our Holy Grail, and banks and credit unions've all been trying to stimulate that segment for years to no avail. But these guys've done it."

He wasn't sure what this had to do with him or how he could help, but he nodded his understanding and agreement.

"We're hurting," Shanley said simply. "In fact, we're not just hurting, we're going down. There've been some…inauspicious ventures, some poor investments over the past few years, and we find ourselves a trifle over extended." He glanced quickly toward the closed door. "If there were ever to be a run on the bank…" He shook his head. "The big banks, the national banks, the *multi*-national banks, the ones with politicians in their pockets, if they were in our shoes, they'd get a bailout because they're too big to fail, and their collapse would jolt the entire economy. Unfortunately, we're *not* too big to fail. There's not a politician alive who would lift a pinky finger to save us. Which means we're on our own here. And that's why I need you to meet with a representative of First People's."

"Me?"

"Yes. You."

Coy was confused. "You're the manager. Shouldn't you or someone from the board—"

"We wouldn't come off well," Shanley said curtly. "Not for something like this. We'd take the blame for the bad decisions; we'd take the heat. They'd want to punish us. What we need is someone encouraging, someone who can put a positive spin on our situation, someone not involved in any decision-making, someone who can't be blamed for anything we might have done or might not have done. A go-between. We need a go-between."

"But…what would I say? I wouldn't even know where to start or—"

The manager waved a hand dismissively. "I'll tell you what to say."

Coy reminded him of Florine's midnight visit, of her declaration that Evergreen Title was now working exclusively with First People's. "Should we address that, too?" he asked.

"We'll address everything. We're fighting for our lives here. It all has to be out in the open."

Coy didn't want to go. He thought about his previous spy mission, where he'd been unceremoniously ejected and tossed out on the sidewalk, but Shanley told him that the meeting had already been arranged and was scheduled for ten o'clock this morning. "So we'd better get busy. There's a lot to go over."

He read through a series of emails sent between the management of the two banks, the gist of them being that Montgomery Community was willing to enter into some sort of ill-defined "arrangement" with First People's, although whether that meant designating certain areas of town as non-competitive, agreeing not to poach each others' customers or...something else, the emails did not make clear and Shanley did not know. The initial idea for some type of "arrangement" had been suggested by Julius Pickering of The First People's Bank, and Coy's job was to hear him out, learn the proposed terms, and report back. Not having any authority, he would not be able to agree to anything or enter into a deal, but would only be authorized as a messenger. Representing Montgomery Community, he was to make the bank appear strong, successful and magnanimous in its willingness to entertain such a notion, all without offending his hosts.

"I can do it," he promised, and for the next half-hour, the manager coached him.

Giving himself ten minutes to cross town, twice what he needed, Coy drove down the highway onto Main, finding a parking spot across the street from the bank. From this angle, it had the appearance of some quaint cinematic financial institution like the Bailey Savings and Loan or the bank in *Our Town*. It looked reliable, trustworthy, almost homey.

But he didn't like First People's, and he couldn't understand how they were able to do as well as they did with the business model they were following. Once past all the bells and whistles of their big grand opening, they still didn't seem to be integrating well with the community. Rumor had it that the bank had turned down Dennis Whittaker for a home-improvement loan, even though, as high school principal for the past decade, he held a stable steady job, while that ne'er do well Bob White had been given money interest-free to put up a shack on that trash-strewn scrap of land he called his property.

So why was it that customers were deserting Montgomery Community for *this* bank? To him, it seemed destined for failure.

Maybe Shanley was right, maybe they'd made a few missteps here and there, but Montgomery Community *knew* this town. These interlopers were just bribing people with false promises.

As much as he might believe in the merits of his own workplace, however, Coy knew he was in no position to act superior. He was here on a mercy mission, and if First People's didn't show them some love, they might very well end up shutting their doors.

He walked across the street and inside, past the two security guards who had thrown him out the last time he'd been here. Involuntarily, his heart rate accelerated, but he ignored the fear and pressed on, asking a thuggish-looking man at the desk nearest the door where he might find Mr. Pickering.

Suddenly someone was standing next to Coy, although how that had happened without his noticing was a mystery. "I'm Mr. Pickering. You must be Mr. Stinson."

Coy nodded cautiously. Pickering seemed familiar to him, although he had never met the man before. He was like a perfect amalgam of every banker Coy had seen in movies or on television.

Only...

There was something slightly off-putting about him, something unnatural and fundamentally aberrant in his otherwise bland and benign deportment that Coy recognized but could not pin down.

"Let us step into my office."

Coy followed him between desks until they walked through an open doorway in the side wall. The room in which he found himself was large, functional yet designed to impress and possibly intimidate visitors. How could there even *be* an office here? Coy wondered. With stores to either side of the bank, there was no space in the building for *any* other rooms, let alone one of this size.

Nevertheless here it was: wood-paneled walls on which hung framed prints of famous landscape paintings, a bookcase filled with leatherbound volumes, a massive oak desk. Its contents itemized in such a manner, the office would seem to be perfectly normal. Yet there was something hideous about it. Just as with its occupant's appearance, no single element was particularly unusual or out of place, but the overall effect remained one of profound unpleasantness. And there was something both strange and terrible about the shadows that lurked in the corners, shadows not tied to any specific object but seemingly manifested out of nothing.

Pickering walked around to the other side of the desk and sat down. Coy was invited to sit as well, and he did so in a comfortable ergonomically designed office chair opposite the bank...manager?... president? He realized for the first time that he did not know Pickering's position. Shanley had not told him.

There was a standing eight-by-ten frame on the desk between a computer monitor and a stack of folders, facing Pickering, and the man turned it around so Coy could see the photo within. It was a full color photograph of a naked woman, a very familiar woman, her legs spread wide to display her completely bald and extremely pink genitalia.

Coy's heart sank.

Florine.

"That's my wife," the banker said. He grinned. "Some beaver, eh?"

His *wife*? How could that be? Coy stared at the familiar curvy body in the picture, his head spinning. Had Florine married Pickering within the past week? Or had she been married all along, even when the two of them had been dating? Had their relationship been part of some elaborate long-range plot to feed information about Montgomery Community to First People's? None of the possibilities made any rational sense, but they were all equally awful, and he sat there, feeling like a chump, wondering how much the man in front of him knew, wondering if the banker had been behind the whole thing.

"So..." Pickering said. "To what do I owe this visit?"

Dully, Coy said what Shanley had told him to say, describing how the two banks could help each other, offering to share Montgomery Community's local contacts and knowledge of the town with its upstart rival. It was a merger they were proposing, though Shanley had made clear that he was not to call it that. "Let them decide how to refer to it," he'd told Coy. "It'll make them feel like it's their idea."

He would have been more confident if there were a visual component, if he had graphs or charts, or a brochure to hand out, but it was evident that this entreaty was a last-minute operation, and when he'd said his piece, he sat silently awaiting a response.

Pickering didn't react right away. He stared at a spot over Coy's head, almost as though he were frozen, and for a second Coy was afraid he would have to repeat the whole spiel because the man hadn't been listening. But then Pickering turned the framed photo around to face him and told Coy, "You've given me something to think about. Let us mull things over. Talk amongst ourselves. We'll let you know our decision by the end of the week."

Coy nodded.

He hazarded one last glance at the back of the frame, saw in his mind the photo of a spreadeagled Florine.

"Is there something else I can help you with?"

A touch of annoyance had crept into Pickering's voice, and Coy quickly shook his head. He didn't want to queer the deal because he'd overstayed his welcome. "No," he said. "Thank you for seeing me."

Pickering's eyes bored into his. "Good. Now get the fuck out of here before I have my guards toss you out on your ass again."

2

GIRLS' night out.

Anita could not remember the last time she'd hung with her friends for an evening. In fact, it had been so long that until all four of them had arrived at The North Fork, she wasn't even sure they *were* still friends. Acquaintances, yes—they kept up on Facebook, sent each other birthday emails—but these days, aside from Jen, she saw no other women on a daily, weekly or even monthly basis.

That's what marriage, motherhood and middle-age could do to you.

Such a sense of social isolation was probably what had led to the situation with Steven. That, in turn, had prompted her to get the old gang together again. She did feel a little guilty about leaving Kyle and

Nick home alone tonight, especially after recent events, but the two of them had been through it together—she'd been little more than a bystander—and it was probably good for them to have some time to themselves. She was well aware that this was nothing more than an after-the-fact rationalization, but the truth was that Kyle had always been more self-sufficient than she was. He was perfectly happy to be left alone, but she needed more, and while they had both grown up in Montgomery, she had always been a part of things and he had just been...apart. That difference had been an ingredient in their appeal to each other, an element of their mutual attraction, and in a very real way, it was what had made their marriage work.

Until it didn't.

The fact was, while their family had cut her off from her social life, it had given Kyle one. Left to his own devices, he would have been content reading a book or binge-watching television. It was she, and to a greater extent Nick, who were responsible for whatever engagement he had with people outside the store.

Now, drinking and hanging out with Ellen, Sharon, Patty and Gabrielle, she realized how much she missed being with her friends. Patty had gotten a new job since the last time they'd spoken. She'd quit working for that handsy Wade Portis at the Ford dealership and had been hired to work in the office at the junior college. Sharon was planning to break up with Chuck but didn't know how to do it without causing him to freak out. So much had happened. Everyone's life was so dynamic. In comparison with hers, which was completely static.

Another reason she'd almost gotten into that mess with—

Steven.

Her breath caught in her throat. There he was. At the bar, leaning in and sitting too close as he chatted up a topheavy bim. Anita could see him clearly between the shoulders of two cowboy-hatted men sitting across from their wives at a tall narrow table. She quickly looked away, praying she hadn't been spotted, and crouched down a little behind Ellen in an effort to avoid being seen.

A moment later, she hazarded another glance in that direction.

And their eyes met.

"Shit," she said.

He left the bar and started toward her.

"Oh, shit."

"What is it?" Ellen asked.

Anita nodded toward Steven. "I've been trying to avoid him but he spotted me."

Sharon squinted. "Is that the guy from the nursery?

"Yeah."

"He always seemed alright to me. In fact, I thought he was kind of cute."

Anita didn't respond as she watched him approach. There was a smirk on his face and a swagger in his walk. She remembered the last time she'd seen him, in the greenhouse with his pants open and his erection out, and when she brought the bottle to her lips to take a fortifying sip of her beer, her hand was shaking.

"Hey there, ladies." He nodded. "Anita."

She ignored him, turning to Ellen and trying to come up with something to say in order to make it seem as though they were in the middle of a conversation, but her mind was blank.

"I haven't seen you for a couple of days," he told her. "What're you up to?"

"Nothing," she said, still not looking at him. She kept her hands on the table to keep them from shaking.

"Well, I'm expanding my business," he bragged. "Getting into home security."

She gathered up her courage. "A nursery and home security," she said drily, letting the idiotic incongruity speak for itself.

What had she ever seen in him?

"That's right. Got some major backing from that new bank. They believe in me." That last was accusatory since it was clear even to him that she did not.

Good.

Something was needling her, a subtle nagging in the back of her mind, and it took her a few seconds to realize what it was.

Got some major backing from that new bank.

That was it.

The bank.

Just thinking about the place made her shiver, and she recalled with guilt and horror her initial—

sensual

—reaction upon meeting Mr. Worthington, her guilty feelings amplified by the fact that the banker had shielded Victor from the police after Victor had slaughtered his parents.

What in the world was happening in this town?

Steven was describing the alarm and surveillance systems he could install in houses, apartments and trailers. It was an attempt to make himself sound professional and successful, and while it was ostensibly for the benefit of everyone at the table, Anita knew his pitch was really aimed at her.

When he finished talking and there was an awkward silence as none of them asked any followup questions or exhibited any interest in him or what he had to say, Steven got the hint. Excusing himself, he walked back to the bar, and Anita breathed a sigh of relief, finishing off the rest of her drink.

Her friends were silent for a moment, looking at each other with raised eyebrows and stifled smiles. It was Patty, of course, who broke the ice. "What was *that* about?"

Anita shook her head. "Nothing."

Ellen bumped her shoulder. "Don't do that. Share."

She hadn't come clean with Jen, not even after Jen had apparently deduced what was going on, but she unburdened herself now, and it felt freeing to be able to speak openly about things she had only thought privately.

"He exposed himself?" Sharon said, grimacing with distaste. "What a creep."

Ellen nodded. "That's just icky."

"Do men actually think that works?" Gabrielle wondered. "Do they really think that if we see it we'll get so excited that we'll do whatever they want?"

"It's my fault," Anita said softly. "I shouldn't have let it go that far."

"It's not your fault," Patty said. "At least, not all your fault."

"Marriages are tough," Gabrielle offered. "Sometimes you have to work at them. I know we've had our ups and downs."

"I had an affair," Ellen admitted, taking a sip of her drink.

They stared at her, shocked.

"It's true," she said quietly.

"What happened?" Anita asked.

"We went through kind of a rough patch early on, before the boys were born, when I was still an aide at the high school. We weren't really talking...or doing much of anything else. I stayed after work a few too many times, got a little closer than I should have, and ended up doing something I shouldn't have. Everything straightened itself out eventually, but...there was a lapse."

"So who was it?" Patty.

"I'm not going to say."

"Come on!" Everyone.

"Okay. Fine." There was a long pause.

"Who?" they prodded.

"Dennis."

Eyes widened all around. "Dennis Whittaker?" Sharon said.

Ellen nodded, embarrassed. "I know you used to go out with him," she said, turning to Anita.

Anita raised her hands. "Tenth grade. And nothing happened."

Patty cackled. "Well, it happened with Ellen."

"Gross," Gabrielle said.

"It actually was," Ellen confided. "Gross, I mean. Sort of." She fanned a hand in front of her. "I'm not getting into it."

"Dennis," Sharon said wonderingly.

"Yeah, well, it was a mistake. One I regret." She turned toward Anita. "One you were smart to avoid."

"I still think he's cute," Sharon reaffirmed. "But you definitely dodged a bullet there."

"So did your husband ever find out?" Gabrielle asked.

Ellen shrugged. "I don't know. I think he might have. But we never talked about it, and we've been back on track ever since."

They were silent for a moment, letting it all sink in.

"Anybody have anything else?" Patty asked. "Any of you used to be a man?"

They laughed and decided to order one more round before calling it a night.

"This was fun," Anita said as they prepared to leave. "We should do it more often."

"We should," they all agreed, but they were each so busy now that she knew it couldn't be a regular thing. It would probably be awhile before they could make time to meet like this again. The thought made her sad.

She cast a furtive glance toward the bar. She didn't see Steven, but the bim he'd been hitting on was still in place, talking to someone else. She imagined him waiting for her behind one of the cars in the dark parking lot, taking his penis out and stroking it so that it would be hard when she saw him.

"Anyone need a ride?" she asked as they got up and headed for the door.

"No."

"Nope."

"I'm fine."

"I'm good."

"Well, could one of you walk with me to my car? Just in case..." She left the sentence unfinished.

"One for all and all for one," Patty told her. She hefted her purse. "My pepper spray's ready to go."

Once in the open air, they all grew a little tense. The night was dark, and The North Fork was not only set back from the highway but ringed by an intimidating line of ponderosas that effectively blocked any lights from the street behind it. There were still quite a few vehicles in the parking lot, and each time they walked past one, Anita tensed up, half expecting to see a dark figure leap out at her.

Ahead was her own car, and she breathed a sigh of relief when she saw it.

Then she noticed the vehicle parked next to her Kia.

Steven's truck from the nursery.

She audibly sucked in her breath, but Ellen immediately grabbed her hand in support, and Patty walked in front of them both, pepper spray at the ready.

He must have still been inside the bar, because there was no sign of him out here. There was no one in or around the truck, and Anita quickly said her goodbyes, got in the car, then watched and waited as her friends got into their own vehicles. They drove in a caravan onto the highway, staying together until they reached their own neighborhoods and honked their final farewells before branching off onto different streets.

3

"CAN'T you sleep?"

Patty rolled over in bed to face him, and Brad sighed, shaking his head. He *couldn't* sleep. He'd been in bed since nine, trying to catch up on all the shuteye he'd missed over the past week, and for the first hour or so he'd actually dozed, but some random household noise had roused him from slumber after that, and he'd been wide awake ever since. The only reason he hadn't gotten out of bed to watch TV in the living room was because he hadn't wanted to wake his wife.

Now that Patty was up, though, he kicked off the covers and swung his legs out of bed. He sat there for a moment staring down at his bare feet, fatigued but not sleepy, frustrated by the unwillingness of his brain and body to rest when they were supposed to.

But how could he shut down and relax with everything that was going on?

He saw in his mind the B of A manager slaughtered in the ditch by the control road; all those dead bodies laid out in the field; the Clarks butchered in their own garage; Carl Yates shooting himself in the head, brains and bone and blood bursting out the other side.

More than anything else, though, it was the new bank that was keeping him awake.

He could not forget the odd feeling he'd experienced inside the bank, a space that to him seemed far too large for the building it was in. And he could not shake the sense that something was wrong with the employees he and his men had questioned, many of whom had seemed vaguely familiar, like people he had once arrested.

More pertinently, the bank seemed to be at the swirling center of everything bad that was happening in Montgomery. It was the bank's rivals from B of A who had been found dead in the forest. The bank had hired that Victor kid who had killed his parents (although everyone at the bank denied it. Denials he flat-out disbelieved). Even Carl had killed himself because a bank was foreclosing on his place, although, granted, it had been a different bank.

It was all probably just a bizarre coincidence, but, as a sheriff, he found coincidences automatically suspect, and Brad could not help thinking that there was a picture here he wasn't seeing simply because he could not connect the dots.

Yet.

Patty had scooted over to his side of the bed, and she sat next to him on the edge. She smiled. "Should we turn on the radio? Listen to Chet's show?"

"While he tells all his dimwitted insomniacs that they should kill me? I don't think so."

Patty frowned. "Has he really been saying that?"

Brad nodded tiredly.

"Throw his ass in jail," she said fiercely. "Threatening a police officer."

"I would if I could," Brad confessed.

Patty was silent for a moment. She turned toward him. "Do you think one of them might actually—"

"They're kooks," he declared. "All bark and no bite. Just like Chet. They're not going to do anything."

"Carl did something," she said softly. "And Chet blames you for it. I'm not sure he's as toothless as you think he is."

Brad put a hand on her bare knee. "I always take precautions, and I don't take anything for granted," he assured her. "But, honestly, I'm not worried about Chet and his dingbats."

"Then what are you worried about? Because there's some reason you're wide awake at two in the morning."

He sighed again. "Everything. All of it. Do you know how many people have died here in the past month? And I'm not talking old age. I'm talking murder and mysterious circumstances. It's overwhelming. We're just a little podunk force here, and we're way out of our depth. *I'm* out of my depth."

"Can't you call...I don't know, the state or something? The FBI?"

"Yeah. And we have. We are. And maybe they'll send someone, but I'm pointman on this. This is my town, my jurisdiction, and me and my guys need to get our asses in gear and show some results." He shook his head. "Then there's that damn bank."

"What bank?"

"The new one. The First People's Bank. They're hip deep in something, and I need to prove that, too."

Patty straightened. "That bank's been a godsend for real estate."

"Seriously?"

"Well, maybe not in the long run, because their loan requirements are really lax, but—"

"Isn't that what led to the housing crisis?"

"Realtors have to use good judgment. I'm not selling to just any Elmer off the street. If I think someone doesn't qualify, I'll steer him in another direction. But there are people who are borderline, who don't look that good on paper but who I know are good for it—I've been in this business many years; I can spot them—and the new bank is giving them an opportunity."

"Are you talking about your new clients?"

"Oh, no. I told you, they're buying by the golf course. They'd qualify anywhere."

"Now that you brought them up—"

"*You* brought them up."

"—you do seem to be spending a lot of time with these people," he said. "Maybe a little too much time."

"I suppose so," she mused. "But, believe me, it's going to pay off."

"Still, the girls."

"I know."

"And with all this going on, I'm having to put in extra hours, and work right now is not exactly...kid-friendly."

"I understand. And I'll try to schedule my outside meetings during school hours, so I can be there for them when they get out."

"That's all I'm asking." He shifted position and his hand slipped from her knee, accidentally sliding up her thigh, where his fingers touched wetness.

He looked at her, eyebrow raised. "Really?"

She nodded, smiling.

Leaning back on the bed, she spread her legs, and he got on top of her. They did it wordlessly, silently, and when he sensed that it was about to happen and she was going to make some noise, he put his mouth over hers to muffle it, so the girls wouldn't be awakened.

Afterward, they both used the bathroom, then both went back to bed.

Where they both fell asleep.

WHEN he awoke in the morning, Patty was gone.

The girls were still in bed, and a note on the kitchen counter told him to make them breakfast. He was angry that, even after her promise last night to spend more time with the kids, she'd left him here without telling him where she was going, while he was supposed to get them ready and take them to school.

Only it wasn't a school day, he remembered. It was Saturday. With so much going on, he was losing track of time.

So who was going to watch the girls? He still needed to be in the office by eight, and he grew even angrier as he realized that he was also going to have to arrange for daycare.

What could Patty have been thinking?

"Time to wake up!" he called out.

Judging by the screams and laughter that greeted his words, Sue and Jillian were already awake. Brad was not much of a cook, and the only breakfast foods he knew how to prepare were cinnamon toast or Cheerios, but he offered them their choice of either, and they both voted for cinnamon toast with hot chocolate.

He drank some coffee and checked his phone while Sue and Jillian ate their breakfast, hoping Patty had arranged for someone to watch the girls. There were no messages, but Patty called right at that moment, apologizing profusely. An emergency had come up, she told him.

"Emergency?" he said. "I'm the goddamn sheriff. I deal with real emergencies."

Jillian's eyes grew wide. "Daddy said a bad word!"

"Keep eating," he told her. He took the phone down the hall to the bedroom. "It wasn't a real emergency," he told Patty. "It was a real estate emergency. There's a big difference. You should have woken me up and told me. Now I have to get to work *and* find someone to watch the kids."

"Just drop them by my office on your way," she said. "I'll be there before you will. And you're right. I should have woken you up. I'm sorry. Forgive me?"

He couldn't stay mad at her when she used that voice, and he apologized for getting angry, and she apologized again for not waking him, and they hung up on good terms.

He walked back to the kitchen. For some reason, his tackle box was out, moved from the rec closet to the floor in front of the dryer, and he wondered if Patty had needed something from it. What could that be, though? The mystery gnawed at him as the girls finished eating and then went off to brush their teeth, and though he thought about calling her back, he decided to wait and ask her in person.

Patty was indeed waiting for them at the real estate office, and Brad gratefully dropped off Sue and Jillian. He'd had the scanner on low, so the girls couldn't hear it while they chattered away in the back seat, but there'd been a robbery and assault overnight, and he needed to get to the office as quickly as possible. The amount of crime in Montgomery was getting ridiculous. Their little town was turning into a miniature Chicago.

He kissed Sue and Jillian, gave each of them a hug, then handed them off to their Mommy.

It was not until he was driving away that he realized he'd forgotten to ask Patty about the tackle box.

That's okay, he thought. He'd ask her later.

4

JEN awoke at six to the sound of tapping.

At first she thought someone on the street was having some remodeling done and that construction was starting. Then she thought it might be the woodpecker she'd seen yesterday on the telephone pole behind their house. But she quickly realized that the tapping was not coming from outside.

It was coming from The Room.

A chill passed through her, and Jen instinctively reached for Lane, but his side of the mattress was empty. He was already up and in the bathroom, and as the tapping continued, she got out of bed and stepped into the hallway. The noise was louder here, and she could definitely tell that it was coming from behind the closed locked door of The Room.

The wave of cold that passed over her could have merely been her own physical fear response, or it could have actually come from beneath the doorway to The Room. Either way, it rooted her in place, and in a small trembling voice she called, "Lane?"

"Be out in a minute!" came his reply from the bathroom, and for a moment, the tapping paused.

Then it started again.

She stared at the closed door of The Room. What was in there and how had it gotten into the house in the first place?

It.

She was already thinking of it as "it."

The tapping continued.

Was something knocking on the door itself, or was there an object within the room that was being struck? It was impossible to tell, but either way, it sounded like wood rather than metal. Definitely not plastic or glass.

Was there a pattern to it? She couldn't detect any. The taps came in even intervals, and there were no differences in their length or volume. The sound was metronomic in its constancy, and the fact that she couldn't readily identify its source contributed to Jen's unease.

What was in there?

Gathering her courage, she knocked on the door, a light polite rap.

The noise on the other side stopped, replaced by a less mechanical, more biological sound that almost reminded her of a laugh.

It sounded once, then all was silent. But that once was enough. She ran back into the bedroom, slamming shut the door and screaming as she leaped on the bed and hid her head under the covers like a child.

She heard the toilet flush, its sound muffled by the blanket, and seconds later, Lane burst into the room. "What is it? What's going on?"

She threw off the blanket and practically jumped into his arms.

He seemed confused. "What's wrong?"

"I can't live like this!" She was practically sobbing.

"Like what? What are you talking about?"

"That noise!" She pointed to the wall that separated them from The Room. "Didn't you hear it?"

He nodded. "I admit, it's annoying..."

"*Annoying*? What the hell *is* it? There's a room in our house that we can't go in, and something's *living* in there! Something that knocks on the wall or the floor or the ceiling or whatever furniture is in there with it." She pulled away from him, looking frantically into his eyes. "I knocked on the door, and the sound stopped, and something laughed! *Laughed*!" She shivered. "We can't live like this! *I* can't live like this!"

"What do you want to do?" he asked her. "Give up our home? Because that's the only other choice."

"I could. Easily. Because it's *not* my home. It's not *our* home. We haven't settled in here. We haven't even finished unpacking! Most of our boxes are still in the garage."

"What are you saying?"

"We sell it. We put it on the market, recoup our loss and look for someplace else."

"That's crazy. We haven't even made our first payment yet."

She looked at him levelly. "I'm not living in a house where I can't go into one of my own rooms, a room that has some sort of *thing* in it. I mean, Jesus, there could be a...a mental patient tied up in there, or a wild animal, or—"

"A monster?"

"See? You're thinking it, too!" She put her arms around him, felt the tension in his muscles. "This isn't normal, this isn't right, and I'm not living like this, afraid of my own house."

"All right, okay, it's freaky. It creeps me out, too. But...I'm not sure there's anything we can really do about it. I mean, we did sign the agreement—"

"And whose fault was that?"

"Fine. Blame me all you want, but I'm pretty sure we're locked in."

"I'm pretty sure we're not. Because people sell houses all the time. People *flip* houses. There are shows about it!" She looked up at him. "And that's all we'd be doing. We bought a house, now we try to sell it for more than we paid and make a profit."

"What if we can't sell it?"

"We walk away. People do it all the time. The bank'll take it, and then it'll be their problem."

Lane shook his head. "Our credit would be ruined. We'd never be able to buy a house again. And you know how much you wanted a house. How much *we* wanted a house." He thought for a moment. "Although..." he said slowly.

"Although what?"

"We could rent it out. Our monthly payments are low, pretty much what rent for a place like this would be. We could rent it out to a couple or a family and use the money to make payments while we tried to sell it. It'd give us the chance to wait for a decent price."

Jen immediately felt brighter. "Yes! Let's do it!"

"I'll have to find out how," he mused. "Although I think Stapely, at work, has a rental unit. I could ask him. Even if he doesn't know, he'll know someone who will."

She smiled. "Then we can get a real house, one that's all ours. A home."

He smiled back at her. "That's all I've ever wanted."

"Me, too."

They hugged.

And from inside The Room, the tapping started again.

TWELVE

1

AFTER BEING SUMMONED, Coy walked cautiously into Ben Shanley's office. The manager looked different today, he thought. Younger? Tanner? Something. He couldn't quite put his finger on it, but the change was visible and extended to the office itself. The furnishings appeared to be the same but now they looked fresher, hipper, more stylish. Even the light seemed brighter, as though the windows had been dusty before and had been washed to let in more light.

Shanley was certainly in a good mood. Not usually one for displays of emotion, he came bounding around the desk, a huge grin plastered on his face. "You did it!" He said gratefully. He pumped Coy's hand. "Thank God, man! You saved us."

Coy was guarded. "I just told them what you told me."

"Well, they bought it. Hook, line and sinker. And now we're back in business!" He threw an arm around Coy's shoulder, a gesture as unusual as it was awkward. "Come on out with me. Let's tell the staff."

Coy had just stepped into the office, but he walked back out again, this time with the manager's hand on his shoulder as though they were best buddies.

"Gather round!" Shanley announced. "I have some news!"

After the recent rumors about the bank's future, everyone was noticeably wary. Maggie and Cal stood close together, shoulders touching. Everett was frowning.

"I'm sure you've all heard the rumors about Montgomery Community's financial health and future," the manager began. "We're all aware of the impact First People's has had on us. B of A is gone, and we should have rightfully inherited their customers, but obviously that hasn't been working out the way we'd hoped. Now, however, I'd like to formally announce that we will be entering into an agreement with The First People's Bank, a mutually beneficial agreement that will allow both of our institutions to thrive."

"A merger?" Maggie asked.

"Not precisely, no. We'll be more like...partners. We're still independent, allowed to run our business the way we see fit, but from now on, we're required to give First People's a cut."

"A *cut*?" Cal snorted. "What are they, loansharks?"

The manager looked around nervously, as if worried that the walls might hear. "Now, now. We'll have none of that talk. The First People's Bank was gracious enough to assist us in our hour of need, and we should be grateful for the help."

"And what exactly is that help?" Cal asked.

The manager held up a hand.

"I know you have questions, but I don't have all the answers. Not yet. The board is currently negotiating the details. As I learn more, I will let you know, but, rest assured, Montgomery Community is in it for the long haul." He grinned, raising a fist. "We're back, baby! We're back in black!"

Glances were exchanged over Shanley's atypical and over-the-top enthusiasm. The whole thing was weird, and Coy felt it, too, but at the manager's signal, Coy stepped back with him into his office.

"That went well," Shanley said. He smiled with satisfaction. "I'm meeting with the board this afternoon, and I can't tell you how much we appreciate you making that visit. None of us could have done it, and you pulled it off perfectly. You'll never know how close we were to..." He trailed off, shook his head. "Anyway, you pulled our wieners out of the campfire just in time, and we're grateful. *I'm* grateful." He pointed at Coy. "There's a promotion in your future, son. Bet on it."

Coy shifted his feet uncomfortably. "So...we're partners, but we have to give them a cut? That's the deal?"

"And we had to give something up."

"What's that?"

"Jimmy."

Coy glanced through the open doorway toward the teller windows, noticing for the first time that Jimmy was not there. He frowned. "That makes no sense."

The manager's expression was unreadable.

"So you fired him? They wanted him fired?"

"They wanted him."

"He's working there now?" Coy was confused. "Is that supposed to give them an advantage? I mean, Jimmy's a good guy and all, but he's our newest teller. Seems like it would have been smarter to take someone more experienced, someone the customers know and already have a relationship with."

The manager's voice was low. "Drop it."

"But—"

"I said drop it." There was an implied threat in the tone of voice that made Coy back up a step, but Shanley immediately brightened. The abrupt change was startling. "So we're in business!" The manager's hand was on his shoulder again. "Now get out there and get to work!"

Eager to leave the office, Coy walked back out to his desk.

"Bizarre," Cal whispered as he passed by.

"At least we're still employed," Coy replied in a voice just as low.

"Yay!" Maggie said quietly.

Immediately upon sitting down, his phone rang, and he picked it up. "Montgomery Community Bank, Coy Stinson speaking."

"Coy?"

It was Florine.

Heart pounding, he glanced instinctively at the *Pirates of the Caribbean* coffee cup she had given him and that he had not yet removed from his desktop. "Yes?" he said carefully.

"I heard the news. Congratulations."

He didn't know what to say, so he didn't say anything.

Florine seemed not to notice.

"This is really a courtesy call. You know that auditor I told you about? The one who was looking into escrow accounts connected to Montgomery Community? He died! He was sucking on a bag of dicks, and he choked and keeled over, dead!"

What? Coy frowned. A bag of dicks? What the hell did that mean? She was making no sense, and a feeling of uneasiness crept over him.

"Dead as a doornail! Which means, if I'm reading my cards right, all inquiries into Montgomery Community are null and void. I thought you'd want to know that if there are any home loans ready to be issued, you're good to go."

Before he could ask for clarification or respond in any way, the line went dead, Florine's uncharacteristically excitable voice succeeded by a dial tone. He replaced the handset in its cradle and turned on his computer. He actually didn't have any pending loans. It had been a slow week, and that was one of many reasons he and the other bank employees had been worried. He was still worried—an alliance with another bank might be good in theory, but there was no guarantee it would lead to increased business—and he forced himself to push aside all thoughts of Shanley's irrational exuberance and Florine's crazy phone call, and start the workday the way he always did, sending out cold emails to potential clients in a fishing expedition, hoping someone would bite.

THE day turned out to be not half bad. Patty Neth from Gold Star Realty referred an aspiring homeowner to him, and after jumping through all the hoops, it looked like the guy and his wife were good loan candidates. Cal had been anticipating a foreclosure on another couple after three missed payments, but something happened and the couple came through with the cash, plus the late fees and interest, saving the bank from having to inherit the debt.

Maybe Shanley was right. Maybe things really were turning around.

He drove home feeling good.

He stopped feeling good when he saw Florine's car in his driveway.

Dread spread outward from the knot in his stomach. He did not want to see her, and all he could think about was the explicit photo on Pickering's desk.

That's my wife. Some beaver, eh?

Was she really his wife? She almost had to be; how else would he have gotten that picture? But Coy had known Florine for years, even before they'd started dating, and she'd never seemed anything other than single, never given any indication that concurrent involvement with another man was even a remote possibility.

More than anything else, more than anything at work, anything having to do with the banks, it was Florine that had been keeping him off balance. From her unprovoked attack at First People's to her deranged appearance with excrement-encrusted papers at his house—

I want you to move to another state or die.

—to the graphic photo of her in Pickering's office to her bizarrely exuberant phone call—

He was sucking on a bag of dicks.

—her behavior and the events swirling around her had left him feeling hurt and angry, confused and frightened. Now she was here again, and he had no idea what she wanted or why she had come over.

Or where she was.

He'd been hoping to find her waiting for him in her car, but when he peered into the driver's side window, he saw that it was empty. His eye went to the backyard gate, but it was closed. Could she be inside the house? As far as he knew, she still had her key to the place, and he moved forward slowly, approaching the front door with trepidation.

His own housekey was out and in his hand, but he didn't need it. The door was unlocked, and he opened it and walked inside.

She was waiting for him on the couch, in the dark. He flipped on the living room light as he walked in, and immediately noticed that something was wrong with her. Her skin was pasty, and there was a strange bulge beneath her right eye. When she opened her mouth, he could see that she had somehow lost a front tooth. "Hi," she said. "It's nice to see you again."

Her appearance made it easier for him not to be sucked in or won over. "What are you doing here?" he asked. "You made it pretty clear that you wanted nothing to do with me anymore. In fact, you said you wanted me to die."

"I—"

"Does your husband know that you're here?"

She looked genuinely puzzled. "My...husband? What are you talking about?"

"Julius Pickering?"

"Mr. Pickering?" She let out a small incredulous laugh, and he saw that one of her bottom teeth was missing as well.

Was it possible that he'd been the victim of some prank? Had Pickering made up that story and put a fake photo on his desk in order to throw him off his game and gain a psychological advantage? It was not outside the realm of possibility. You could do a lot with Photoshop these days.

He pushed those thoughts aside. They were beside the point. "What do you want?" he said tiredly. "Why did you break into my house?"

"I didn't—"

"What do you want?" He walked around the edge of the counter that separated the living room from the kitchen and turned on the kitchen light, getting himself a cold water bottle from the refrigerator. He did not offer one to Florine. She still had not answered his question, and when he turned back to look at her, her demeanor had altered. There was a sly grin on her face, a change in expression that made her countenance seem even more disturbing.

"Remember my coworker Ling? Remember I told you she used to try and steal my accounts? Well, she died this morning." Florine's grin widened, and Coy could see that her gums were a dark grayish blue. "We've both had a lucky day."

"Get out," he told her. He didn't like what was happening here, was afraid of where it was headed, and whatever feelings he had once had for her were definitely gone. He was frightened of this woman, and he wanted her out of his house.

"Things are changing," she said. She coughed, and the sound was horrific, a deep phlegmy hack that made him think of TB and lung cancer and respiratory disease.

"Get out," he repeated. He did not want to hear her talk about how things were changing, and definitely did not want her to tell him *why* she thought things were changing. He'd had the same sense all day, ever since Shanley had called him in to congratulate him, and though Coy hadn't been able to articulate his percolating concern, Florine had done it for him.

Things are changing.

Maybe it would have been better if Montgomery Community had gone under and he and his fellow employees had had to look for jobs elsewhere. He didn't like this agreement with The First People's Bank, this...collusion. It felt wrong to him. Everything about that bank felt wrong to him, and he didn't want to be a part of it.

Florine stood. On the seat of the couch where she'd been sitting was a large wet spot.

Grimacing, Coy put down his water bottle and strode over to the front door. He held it open. "Leave."

She walked over to him, looked up coquettishly. "Are you sure you don't want me to spend the night?"

This close, he could see a thin sheen of sweat on her pasty skin. The bulge beneath her right eye made it look as though that eye was partially closed. What had happened to her? How could she have deteriorated so quickly?

Things are changing.

"Go," he said.

She kicked his shin, and the pain was searing. "Fuck you, then!" she yelled. "Fuck you!" Running out to her car, she got in and backed up crazily, not bothering to turn on her headlights though it was getting dark. With a screech of tires and roar of engine, she sped down the street and was gone.

He closed the door, feeling numb. Montgomery Community was now in league with The First People's Bank, Bank of America having closed, all of its former employees dead. Over at First People's, Julius Pickering had a nude photo of Florine on his desk and claimed she was his wife. She said she wasn't, and had suddenly become so physically degenerated that she looked as though she'd contracted a fatal disease. She also said that the auditor who had been investigating Montgomery Community was dead, as was her rival at the title company.

His head was pounding. It was all too crazy, and he looked over at the wet spot on the couch and ran into the kitchen, barely making it to the sink before throwing up.

2

"DON'T put wet towels in the hamper!" Anita called out. "I told you a thousand times!"

"Sorry, Mom!" Nick shouted from his bedroom. "I forgot!"

"Well, don't forget!" She finished emptying the hamper and separating clothes into piles on the bathroom floor. Throwing the whites into a laundry basket, she carried them out to the washing machine.

After starting the first load, she returned to clean the bathroom, a chore she'd been putting off for nearly two weeks now. If she and Kyle were more responsible parents, they'd make Nick do it, but he had a big history report due on Monday and needed to spend almost all of his weekend working on that. Maybe next time.

As always, she decided to start by cleaning the toilet. Spraying Lime-A-Way and using the white-bristled scrub brush, Anita scoured the inside of the bowl, using the brush to get under the rim—

—where a small black square attached to a short black wire popped out and into the water.

What was that?

She frowned. Leaning forward and looking closer, she saw what looked like a small circular lens in the center of the square.

Her stomach heaved. Had someone somehow installed a miniature camera in the toilet? Had it been filming her as she...?

Anita felt sick.

Who could have done such a thing? She knew it wasn't Kyle or Nick, but who else had access to their house? The answer was no one. They didn't employ a maid, no one had repaired anything recently, none of their friends had been over in the past week or two.

And, access aside, who would even have any incentive to—

Steven.

I'm expanding my business. Getting into home security.

A shiver ran down her spine as she stared at the small black object bobbing in the cloudy blue water. It had to be him. But when could he have done this? And how? She straightened, glanced around. Were there other cameras in the house? Had he snuck in while the three of them were out one day and hidden surveillance equipment in all of the rooms?

Her eyes darted to the corners of the bathroom, to the light in the ceiling, to the wall above the mirror, but she didn't see anything. She opened the fogged glass door and poked her head in the shower stall. There, in the upper right corner, she saw another small black square with a tiny lens in its center, aimed directly at the spot where her breasts would be if she were showering.

Kyle was at the shop, and even though Nick was home, she wasn't yet ready to bring this up with him, so she made her own way through the house, looking for additional evidence that she and her family were being spied upon.

She found it.

There were small cameras placed at chest level on one of the bookcases, at crotch level underneath the computer desk, on the floor of the kitchen in two spots, angled upward. Now that she was looking for them, they were easy to find, but had she not been aware of their existence, she would probably never have noticed.

In the bedroom, there was a tiny camera attached to the ceiling fan above their bed. The last time she and Kyle had done it, she realized, she had been on top. The camera would not just have seen her bare butt, it would have caught Kyle with his hand deep in her crack, working it.

She was more certain than ever that it was Steven, and she felt not only embarrassed but violated, knowing that her most private and intimate moments had been watched by that pervert. Before all this started, they'd been casual friends, and she wondered if they had left it there, if she had not allowed herself to get closer to him, whether this would still be going on. He was a sicko, no doubt about it, but maybe he would have turned his attention to someone else if she hadn't encouraged him.

No. That was victimspeak. And if there was one thing Anita was not willing to be, it was a victim. She immediately called the sheriff. A woman answered the phone, and for that she was grateful, because it made it a little easier to describe what she'd found than it would have been if she'd been speaking to a man. The woman promised to send someone out to the house as soon as possible, and after hanging up, Anita called Kyle at the store to tell him what she'd found, although she danced around the reasons why she thought it might be Steven. That would probably come out, she figured, but she wanted to give herself time to come up with a story close to the truth that didn't make her look like an adulterous slut.

Before the sheriff's men arrived, she needed to tell Nick what was going on, and she went to his room, where he was actually at his desk reading a book about Reconstruction and making notes. She didn't want to frighten him, but she didn't want to downplay what was happening either, and she took the middle road, describing what she'd found without voicing any of her suspicions.

"Someone snuck into our house and set up cameras?" he said, incredulous.

"Looks that way."

"You think it's the bank?"

"What?" she said. "No."

"I mean, after that whole Victor thing, maybe they're looking for ways to discredit us."

She was still pretty sure it was Steven, but she was impressed with his reasoning. "I don't think so, but we'll let the sheriff figure it out. And, speaking of Victor, after all this, if you're home alone, don't let anyone in. Not even your friends."

"I never do," he told her.

"Good."

There was the sound of a vehicle pulling to a stop in front of their house, and she looked out Nick's bedroom window to see a sheriff's car. "They're here," she said. "Why don't you just stay in your room while I talk to them."

"What if there are cameras hidden in here? You haven't looked yet."

"I'll tell the sheriff. They'll probably want to search the whole house. Meanwhile, see if you can find anything."

She closed the door behind her and walked out to meet the sheriff's men, who were halfway up the lawn as she stepped onto the porch.

"Mrs. Decker?" The uniformed man in the lead held out a hand as he walked up the steps. "I'm Deputy Dillman." He motioned to the man behind him. "This is Deputy Fredericks. We understand that you have discovered surveillance equipment that has been installed in your house."

She nodded.

"Why don't you show us what you found?"

Anita walked them around the house, pointing out the cameras she had located. After their first stop, the kitchen, the two deputies excused themselves and went back to their car. When they returned, Deputy Dillman was carrying a camera, and Deputy Fredericks some sort of electronic tablet as well as a stack of plastic bags. Both were wearing rubber gloves. As she led them through the house, they photographed the cameras before removing them and placing each in a separate bag.

"Those are only the ones I found," Anita pointed out after the deputies had bagged the cameras from the final room, the bathroom.

"There might be more. I don't know. Is there a way for you to search the house and see if you can find any others? Can you...sweep each room somehow? Electronically?"

The deputies looked at each other.

"We can search the house, sure," Deputy Dillman said. "And we will. Every room. As for sweeping, I'm not sure. We'll have to talk to our tech guy and see how that works."

"So we might have to live here while there are still cameras spying on us?"

"We'll go over this place with a fine-toothed comb. If there's anything here, we'll find it."

He was trying to reassure her, but it wasn't working, and she found herself wondering how small cameras could get. Maybe there were ones that were pin-sized. She glanced around the room. Maybe they were being spied upon right now.

Perhaps sensing her concerns, the deputy was suddenly very officious. "So do you have any idea who might have done something like this?"

"I have a very good idea," she told him. "Steven Hollister."

"The guy from the nursery?"

Anita nodded.

"What makes you think he might have something to do with this?"

"Well, he exposed himself to me in the greenhouse the last time I went to his nursery. And the other night, he came up to me and my friends at The North Fork and behaved in a very creepy way. I was so freaked out seeing him there that I had to have someone walk me to my car. That's when he told me that he was expanding his business and getting into home security."

"Did you report any of this?"

She shook her head. "I thought I could handle it. And I didn't think 'expanding into home security' meant putting surveillance equipment in my bedroom and bathroom."

"We'll talk to him," Deputy Dillman promised. "Are there any other possibilities?"

"Not to my knowledge."

"I'm going to go out to the car then and call this in, ask for a team to come out and search your house for any more devices. It may take the rest of the day. Once the team arrives, Deputy Fredericks and I will go talk to Mr. Hollister and see what he can tell us. One way or another, we'll get to the bottom of this. Keep in mind that the person who did this will face criminal penalties, but you also have grounds for a civil suit, should you choose to proceed in that direction."

Anita nodded.

The two deputies walked back outside. While she waited, she went down the hall to tell Nick what was going on. He didn't even look up from his desk as she opened the door. "I heard it all," he said.

"They're going to be searching the house for more devices. I don't know if you want to be here for that. You could go to the shop if you want, hang out with your dad."

"I need to work on this paper."

"You could go to the library. It's going to be pretty hard to get anything done with guys searching the house for cameras and listening devices."

He sighed, closed his book. "Fine. I'll go to the bookstore."

She couldn't help smiling. "Hate the library that much, do you?"

"Ha ha," he said flatly as he gathered up his materials and put them in his backpack. "Tell them it could be the bank, too," he told her before he left. "I'm serious. You weren't there. That place is wrong."

She saw him out, then closed the door behind him. The two deputies remained outside, one in the driver's seat of the car, the other leaning into the open window of the passenger side.

Nick's mention of the bank had given her an idea, and Anita searched through her purse until she found the business card she'd been given at the grand opening. She dialed the number, and felt her face heat up as she heard the banker's firm clear voice. "The First People's Bank. Mr. Worthington speaking."

Tongue-tied at first, Anita hesitantly introduced herself, then attempted to describe what was going on, explaining that she had found cameras hidden in her home and that she suspected they had been put there by Steven Hollister, whose foray into home security had been bankrolled by First People's.

"Yes?" the banker said. His tone of voice wasn't defensive or dismissive; it merely sounded as though he was curious about why she had called to tell him this.

"I think it might be appropriate for you to cancel his loan. Especially if it's found that he's using that money to commit crimes."

She expected a lot of questions, but there was only one: "If we cancelled his loan, what would you do for us?"

That seemed like a strange thing to ask. "What do you mean?"

"Well, he has to pay interest on his loan, which means the bank makes money. If we cancel the loan, we don't get any of that money. To make it worth our while, you would need to offer some sort of compensation, something that would even things out."

"You want me to pay you?"

"Not necessarily." His voice was smooth. "Anita, do you remember when we met during the grand opening? I'm sure you do. I certainly do. In fact, I recall you being a very attractive woman."

Anita's stomach sank.

"I was thinking that instead of money, you could provide the bank—the bank meaning *me*—with a more personal form of recompense. If you could come by later today, maybe you could..." He didn't finish the sentence.

It seemed suddenly hard to breathe, but she kept her voice as even as possible. "What are you talking about?"

He chuckled. "Well, this penis isn't going to suck itself."

She clicked off, trembling.

Seconds later, her cell phone rang with the arrival of a text, and she looked down to see an ad from The First People's Bank: *BJs for Cash?* the headline read.

She deleted it instantly and turned off the phone.

The house phone rang.

Afraid to answer, Anita hurried outside. She did not want to be alone, and she stood near the deputies while they waited for the arrival of the team that was going to search her house for electronic devices.

3

"WHO found him?" Brad asked as he and Issac walked out the rear of the sheriff's office and across the asphalt to the closest car.

"Tessa James. Her husband, Clem, was one of the Bank of America workers."

"Oh." In his mind, Brad saw the meadow with its weeds and wildflowers and dead bodies.

"I think she was leaving flowers. The real spot's pretty far out of the way, so families have taken to making a little shrine by the bank entrance, where people can see it."

"And she found *that*? Jesus."

They reached the car. "Who's driving?" Issac asked.

Brad tossed him the keys. "It's all yours."

Five minutes later, they were pulling in front of the Bank of America building, using the siren and loudspeaker to shoo away a silver pickup that was trying to take the spot they wanted. A crowd had gathered on the sidewalk but remained a respectful distance from the bank's doorway. An older man Brad didn't know had put himself in charge and was standing guard, making sure no one got too close.

Brad may have known ahead of time what he would see, but an idea could never compare to reality, and the sight was still shocking.

Lashed to the double doors of the bank was the body of a young man. On the cement at his feet were roses and other flowers left for the makeshift memorial. A series of ropes crisscrossed his shoulders, chest and legs, anchoring him to the rectangular metal handles that dug into his back. He was wearing business attire, but his white shirt and black slacks were shredded and ragged, his red tie wrapped several times around his neck. It was his face that was truly alarming, however. Like Glen Taggart, the Bank of America manager, his face had been caved in, and within the dark hole bordered by rent skin and broken skull could be seen teeth, eyes and a nose, all of them jumbled together in a messy pulpy mass.

Even without a face, Brad recognized the victim. Jimmy Collins. The new teller at Montgomery Community.

Why was everything these days connected to a bank?

"Call the M.E.," he told Issac. "And cordon off the area."

"Move back!" he told the gathered spectators. "A hundred yards." He made a point of thanking the old man who'd been voluntarily controlling the small crowd, and asked if he wouldn't mind maintaining the perimeter until it was sealed off. Happy to be of use, the man grabbed his little bit of sanctioned authority and ran with it.

Brad walked slowly around the building. His gun wasn't out, but his holster was unbuckled should he need to draw his weapon. He doubted that would be necessary, however. His best guess was that the murder had occurred sometime between midnight and dawn, although how no one had noticed Jimmy Collins' body until the widow had come to leave her flowers he had no idea. It seemed to him that someone should have spotted it earlier. He glanced around, saw, cattycorner, the Exxon station. Killing the young man, or at least tying his body to the door, would have taken awhile. Hadn't someone from the gas station seen something?

He'd have to talk to the employees, take a look at any security camera footage they might have.

Around the back of the bank, on the curb of the sidewalk between the building and the parking lot, he found a pair of black-handled scissors. Even without bending down to look, he could see that the blades looked rusty, and he would be willing to bet that that rust color was blood. He glanced up at the side of the building and found what he was looking for: a security camera. Was it still working or had it been disabled after the branch closed? He wasn't sure, but it was worth checking into, and he used his radio to call Issac and tell him to bring gloves, a camera and an evidence bag back here.

Brad continued his perimeter search, finding nothing else of interest. He returned to the rear of the building, helping Issac with the scissors.

"Think we'll be able to get a partial print?" the deputy asked.

Brad shook his head. "Doubtful. People don't leave prints on scissors. The handle's too narrow. We might find something, though. And if that's Jimmy's blood, we can prove it's the murder weapon."

"I don't think that's what caved his face in."

"Well, we can prove it was used in the assault, okay? Is that specific enough for you? Jesus, don't be so technical."

They walked back to the front of the bank, Issac cowed and Brad annoyed. He wasn't angry at his deputy exactly; he was angry at the situation, and he felt bad about jumping down Issac's throat, but he wasn't about to apologize.

Most of the crowd had drifted away, but a few new people had come up, and the elderly gentleman was still in place, keeping the space near the police tape clear. One of the new onlookers was Mr. Worthington, from First People's Bank. Brad frowned. Why was he here? His own bank was on the other side of town. Had he somehow been alerted that the murdered body of his rival's employee had been left at the doorstep of another shuttered bank? Even if he had, why would Mr. Worthington come by to see it.

Mr. Worthington.

Brad realized that he didn't know the man's first name. Even though he had questioned the banker about the Clark kid. How was that possible? How could he have not gotten a first name?

Mr. Worthington.

Their eyes met for a second, and Worthington looked again at Jimmy Collins' body. He shook his head mournfully. "Sometimes the god of money demands terrible sacrifices."

What the hell did that mean?

Brad didn't get the chance to ask, because the banker was already walking away, just as the M.E. wagon was pulling up.

The next hour was a nightmare as the medical examiner and his assistant studied the body and then, once all of the photos were taken, took Jimmy down. It was a convoluted process, and two more men had to be called in. The ropes were cut, and the extra helpers, wearing coveralls over their clothes because of the blood, had to hold up the body so it wouldn't collapse once the restraints were gone. Both Brad and Issac had to look away several times.

As the body was loaded into the wagon, the sheriff turned to his deputy. "This is getting way out of hand," he said. "I'm calling in the FBI."

"Do you really think they'd take a case like this?"

"I saw them on the news the other night helping to find a missing kid in Georgia. We have bodies galore here. They'll help us."

Leaving Issac at the bank and calling for Vern and Norris to meet there with a forensics kit, Brad drove back to the station, where he told Carol to contact the FBI and let them know the sheriff's department needed help.

"I don't…I mean…Who do I ask for? Is there a specific person or department you want me to call?"

"Figure it out," he told her. "When you get to someone who can make a decision, patch him through."

Brad went into his office and shut the door behind him. His head was pounding, and he took the bottle of generic aspirin out of his lower right drawer, popping two pills in his mouth and swallowing them without water. A lingering bitterness on his tongue caused him to grab the half-empty water bottle on the edge of his desk and quickly down its contents.

He couldn't get the sight of Jimmy Collins out of his mind. That wasn't just a murder, it was a *ritualistic* murder. It almost reminded him of what had been done to Keen and Bedelia Clark, and he wondered if Victor Clark had anything to do with this. The little psycho was still out there somewhere—thanks to Worthington—and after what they'd found in the kid's room, Brad had no trouble believing he might strike again.

Could that have been why Worthington had shown up to see the body?

Had the Clark kid called him and told him about what he'd done?

Everything that was happening here was so far beyond him that he felt completely overwhelmed. They were making progress on none of it, and if the FBI didn't step in, he was going to have to…

What? Give up on trying to find the killers? Quit his job?

He didn't know, but he would have to do something, because this was way out of his league.

He was online, attempting to look up Jimmy Collins' next of kin—it wouldn't do to have his parents hear about their son's death from a gossipy neighbor before they had been officially informed—when Carol buzzed him on the intercom. "Sheriff? Can you come out here?"

He left the screen as is and walked out to the receptionist's desk. "What is it?"

"I got through to the FBI, and it looks like you have to fill out a form first." She pointed to an online form displayed on her computer.

Brad was annoyed. "I can't just talk to someone?"

"It doesn't look like it."

"This is bullshit. You know what? I'm calling our congressman, whatever his name is. He should be able to get the attention of the FBI. I hope. Find his number and get him on the line for me," he told Carol. "We need to get this done."

He went back to his office, located the contact information for Jimmy Collins, and made the difficult condolence call to Jimmy's parents. The uncomfortable conversation lasted longer than he wanted it to, and immediately after hanging up, Carol told him that she had Congressman Thurmond waiting.

Brad spent the next twenty minutes going over the details of the hellish last month in order to make clear to the congressman why the department was requesting the FBI's assistance.

Promising to do what he could, Thurmond said he would call back within the hour.

The sheriff fielded calls from his deputies out in the field, directing them in their efforts, before dialing Montgomery Community Bank to let Jimmy Collins' employer and his workplace associates know what had happened, although, as it turned out, they'd already heard.

Much later, after far more than an hour had passed, the congressman called back, and Carol put him through immediately.

"What's the news?" Brad asked.

"Well, the news isn't so good."

The sheriff felt his hopes dissipate. "What does that mean?"

"I called Mark Norman at the FBI—I've had contact with him before—and asked him to cut through the red tape for me. He got back to me pretty quickly, but it was a hard no, though he wasn't sure why. So I contacted both of our senators, explained the situation, asked them to weigh in, but no luck there, either. Word got back to me through the grapevine that I should lay off, so I had my staff do a little digging. Turns out The First People's Bank has contributed rather heavily to all of the senators on the finance committee, including one of our own. That probably wouldn't make that much difference ordinarily, but they were also big contributors to the president's election campaign, and the president, as you know, controls the FBI. I'm not alleging some big conspiracy—we're too disordered here in Washington to pull off any big conspiracies—but the bank bought themselves some friends who have apparently not only freed them from regulations but freed them from investigations." Brad could almost hear his shrug over the phone. "Sometimes the god of money demands sacrifices."

It was the second time today he'd heard a version of that phrase, and he didn't like it. "Apparently that sacrifice is justice," he said and hung up on the congressman.

The god of money.

The phrase stayed with him the rest of the day, through one false start after another, and though he had a difficult time falling asleep that night, eventually he nodded off, and he dreamed of a god who was a legless armless rectangle, like a dollar bill, and whose face in an oval opening in the center of its body had to be fed with the sacrificed corpses of the poor.

4

SITTING on the low wall by the band room, Nick and Aaron ate their lunches in silence. They'd told no one about what had happened with Victor—

V.J.

—but that Saturday was with them, even when they didn't talk about it, and the encounter at the bank weighed heavily on them both.

At least Aaron had not seen Victor's parents. Well, technically Nick hadn't either, but he'd been there when their bodies had been discovered, and he'd heard enough of his dad's and the sheriff's conversation to be able to conjure details of the scene in his mind. Aaron had been lucky enough to have been spared that.

Where was Victor? he wondered. Had Mr. Worthington helped him escape to another city, state or country, or was the banker hiding him somewhere? It had to be one of the two, and either way, Mr. Worthington had to be involved. Nick had no doubt about the man's complicity, and the idea that an official from a bank, a bank located right next to his dad's store, was involved in protecting a murderer made him feel nervous and anxious. Mr. Worthington knew who he and Aaron were and knew that they had called the law.

And he didn't seem the type to forgive and forget.

"What are you losers doing?"

Nick looked up from his sandwich at the sound of the familiar voice and saw Victor—

V.J.

—standing in front of them. Where he had come from and why they hadn't noticed his approach was a mystery. He looked terrible. His skin was pale and his eyes were puffy. There was an expression of tremendous rage on his face, and Nick's first thought was that he had come to kill them. He glanced over at Aaron, who appeared to be just as shocked and just as frightened as he was.

"Where's Stacey?" Victor asked, and his voice sounded tired. "I came to see Stacey."

Nick had no idea where Stacey Wilder ate lunch. With the other cheerleaders, he assumed. Certainly not here by the band room. Besides, as much as Nick disliked the cheerleader, he would not tell Victor her whereabouts even if he did know. He looked into those angry eyes and attempted to convey a sense of normalcy, as though they were still two best friends just hanging out and talking. "How would I know where she is? You know she has nothing to do with us."

"Yeah," Aaron said.

Victor—no, V.J. He was definitely more V.J. than Victor now—looked from Nick to Aaron and back again. "You guys called the pigs on me."

Nick found courage and some semblance of their old relationship within him. "And you deducted ten dollars from my college account. Call it even."

Victor would have laughed at that, but V.J. just gave him a blank stare.

Nick looked away. The stare made him uneasy, and he wondered if Victor had had the same expression on his face when he'd dismembered his parents.

From the corner of his eye, Nick saw that Aaron was surreptitiously dialing his phone—911, no doubt—and he wanted to somehow let his friend know that he should not be doing that. They were dealing with a wild animal here, and they did not want to set it off. If Victor knew that Aaron was calling for help, the results might be disastrous. But he knew of no way to warn Aaron without drawing Victor's attention to what he was doing.

"I'm going to find Stacey," Victor said, and without another word turned on his heels and walked off, heading for the lunch tables in front of the cafeteria.

Picking up the phone in his lap, Aaron quickly finished dialing and apparently got through to someone. "Victor Clark is here at Montgomery High. He just showed up, and he's looking for Stacey Wilder. I don't know what he plans to do to her, but he looks angry." There was a short pause. "Aaron Mund." Another pause. "I just saw him! Me and Nick Decker!" A very short pause. "Just tell the sheriff! Now!" He ended the call. "That operator just wanted to talk. I thought 911 was supposed to be an emergency line."

"The principal needs to know," Nick said.

They immediately hurried over to the office, telling Ms. Sanchez, the registrar, that they needed to talk to Principal Whittaker, it was an emergency. When she started to ask why, they walked around the counter and moved past her, rushing into the principal's office. Mr. Whittaker was on the phone, but Nick didn't let that slow him down. "Victor Clark killed his parents and he's wanted by the sheriff," he said quickly, not sure how much of this was public knowledge. "Aaron and I just saw him by the band room, and he's headed over to the lunch tables looking for Stacey Wilder."

Startled and seemingly a little confused, the principal told the person on the phone he would call back, then made Nick repeat what he'd said.

"I called 911," Aaron added after Nick finished, "so the sheriff's probably on his way."

Principal Whittaker did not seem to know what to do. He picked up his phone, then put it down, finally standing up. "Thanks," he said. "I'll take care of it."

He left them sitting in his office, looking at each other, and they heard him talk briefly with Mr. Bollinger, the vice principal, and then to the secretaries out front. There seemed to be a lot of commotion, and Aaron said, "Do we wait here or are we supposed to go?"

"I don't know," Nick admitted.

Seconds later, Ms. Sanchez's voice came over the intercom. They could hear it echoing from loudspeakers all around the campus. "All students: please proceed to your fourth period classes. Lunch is over. If you have not finished eating, please bring your lunch with you. You will have time to finish it in the classroom. I repeat: lunch is over. Please proceed immediately to your fourth period classes."

"I guess we're supposed to go," Aaron said, standing up.

The two of them walked out of the office. The announcement had been calmly delivered and seemingly noncommittal, but even though it had only been a few minutes, word had obviously gotten out, as it always did, and, outside, students were rushing to their classes in a panic, as though a bomb were about to go off.

"Do you think he found her?" Nick asked quietly. "Do you think he did something?"

Aaron shook his head. "I don't know."

Two sheriff's deputies hurried by, already on campus, and jogged past them, hands on their weapons.

Ms. Sanchez repeated her announcement, and without another word, Nick and Aaron parted, walking through the quickly emptying atrium to their separate classes in different buildings.

THEY captured him in the gym.

Before making the announcement that lunch was over and every-one should go to their classes, neither the principal nor anyone else in the office had thought about where Victor might be headed. The cheerleaders were practicing at lunchtime in the gym, a fact known to the administration. Having been told of Victor's intent, they should have been prepared for him to make his way there, but they weren't, and all of the kids who had P.E. fourth period ended up in the gym, finishing their lunches on the bleachers.

Where they had a perfect view of the takedown.

Nick heard about it in fifth period. Josh Burns, who'd been there, filled them all in on the specifics. He and his friends had taken seats near the top of the bleachers and had been there for several minutes, with other students still coming in, when they saw Victor.

"He was walking in with a couple of freshmen, and you could tell right away something was wrong," Josh said. "He looked like a zombie, for one thing. Even from up where we were, his skin looked all weird and white, and he had his hands around the freshmen's necks, leading them in. Like Michonne when she first showed up on *The Walking Dead*. Coach Phelps was by the door, and he saw it and started to say something, but Victor went wild and started running through the gym. I was glad we were up there at the top, because he was knocking people over right and left. It was like he was looking for someone. Everyone was screaming, and Coach Phelps and a couple of jocks blocked his way, and then the law showed up, and they grabbed Victor and put handcuffs on him and took him away. The whole thing? Three minutes, tops."

Nick wanted to know what happened after that, but no one at school had any idea. At least none of the kids did, and if the adults knew, they weren't talking. He assumed that Victor had been arrested, and was being held either at the jail or at the hospital, chained to his bed, with one of those guards outside his door. Because he definitely looked sick.

He wondered if Victor would be tried as a juvenile or an adult.

Was anything going to happen to Mr. Worthington? Nick certainly hoped so. They should definitely be able to get him on something. Obstruction of justice? Maybe. Although, according to what he saw on the news, a lot of people didn't even seem to consider that a crime anymore.

He wondered if he or his dad would be called to testify. They had been the ones to find Victor's parents. And he and Aaron had found Victor at the bank and had spotted him today at school. Probably all three of them would have to testify.

Nick was called to the counselor's office during sixth period. He could not recall ever being called into Mrs. Lee's office before and had only spoken to the counselor in private one time, when he'd wanted to transfer out of a math class. The call slip said nothing about a reason, and he assumed that it had something to do with Victor, so it was a complete surprise when he sat down in the small office and the counselor said, "Congratulations, Nicholas. Mrs. Nelson has nominated you for a fifteen-hundred dollar writing scholarship."

It took a moment for his mind to shift gears. "A scholarship?"

She nodded.

"Me?" he asked incredulously. He could not believe it. That witch hated him.

"Yes." Mrs. Lee smiled. "Apparently, Mrs. Nelson is very impressed with your writing ability." The counselor handed him a printout. "Now this is a new scholarship, offered this year for the first time. It's sponsored by The First People's Bank..."

He heard nothing she said after that. It was as though his body had been dunked in ice water. He was cold all over, and the counselor's voice became a low drone in the background of his much louder thoughts. The fact that the teacher who'd gotten him suspended was teaming up with the bank seemed very suspect to him. She had turned him in to the principal because of his writing, and now she said she was a fan of his work and thought well enough of it to recommend him for a scholarship? Was this a freaky coincidence or was Mrs. Nelson working in collusion with the bank? Who had approached whom? Had his teacher heard about the scholarship and known about his problems with the bank, and recommended him for that reason? Or had Mr. Worthington found out about his problems with Mrs. Nelson and recruited her to recruit him?

Nothing about this added up, and it was only when he realized that Mrs. Lee had stopped speaking that he once again paid attention to the counselor. She was looking at him expectantly, as though she'd asked a question and was waiting for an answer, and Nick was embarrassed to have to say, "Excuse me?"

"I said, you've been given a real opportunity. It's not a sure thing, but from the way Mrs. Nelson talked, it's pretty close."

"Thanks," he said, folding up the printout as he stood. "I'll think about it."

"Don't think about it, do it!"

He nodded and backed out of her office, into the hall. There was no way he was going to involve himself with anything that had to do with the bank. Another thought occurred to him: maybe there was no scholarship. Maybe Mr. Worthington just wanted him to fill out the application so the bank could obtain personal information about him.

Walking across the atrium on his way back to class, he crumpled up the paper and tossed it in a trash can.

HIS parents had decided that it was not safe for him to walk or ride his bike around town right now with everything that was going on, so after school, Nick waited by the parking lot for his dad to pick him up. Aaron was supposed to meet him here and get a ride, too, but he didn't show up, and when Nick saw his dad's truck pull into the parking lot, he tried calling Aaron to tell him they were leaving, but got his friend's voicemail.

He left a message—"*Call me*"—and sent a text, but there was no response to either by the time they got home. Not wanting to worry his dad, he said nothing about it, telling him instead about

Victor's capture, but after his father dropped him off and drove back to the bookstore, Nick called Aaron's home phone, only to hear it ring and ring until an operator's recorded voice said that the person he was calling was not answering, and suggested that he call again at another time.

He was getting the same feeling he'd had when Victor stopped coming to school, and he called Aaron's cell again, with no luck, before texting him and sending him an email.

It was midafternoon and still light outside, but he turned on the TV and the lights in the living room, and stayed in the front of the house until his mom arrived home.

Later that evening, after dinner, when both of his parents were home, they had what his mom called a "family meeting." It was the first and only, but she pretended for some reason that it was a common occurrence, that their house was a democracy and this sort of *Brady Bunch* practice was perfectly normal. She did it, he supposed, to soften the edges of what they'd gathered to talk about, and she began the conversation, telling them that the sheriff had caught the man who'd hidden cameras in their house and that he was in jail. It was Steven Hollister, the man who owned the nursery out on the highway.

Your mom's getting boned by the gardener.

He remembered seeing his mom's Kia parked there, and he tried to read her face as she spoke. He knew he shouldn't put stock in anything Victor said, but he couldn't help wondering, and he was grateful now that the only expressions he saw on his mom's face were ones of fear and relief.

His dad was frowning. "Why would the guy from the nursery put cameras in our house? It doesn't make any sense."

"He's starting a new security business. I guess he had the equipment and..." She threw up her hands. "How would I know? He's crazy."

His dad shook his head. "Well, at least it's over."

They both quizzed Nick in more detail about what had happened with Victor at school, but he didn't have any more to add than what he'd already told them, so he basically retold the story over again. He paused for a moment, deciding whether or not to go further, then told them that he hadn't been able to get ahold of Aaron all afternoon.

"Do you think something happened to him?" He could hear the worry in his dad's voice.

Nick shrugged.

"Nicholas?" His mom prodded.

"What's your gut tell you?" his dad asked.

He looked from one to the other. "It reminds me of when Victor didn't show up at school."

"Okay," his dad said. "I'm dropping you off and picking you up at school every day until...well, for the whole year, maybe. We'll see. And when you're at school, stay on campus and try to stay around teachers or adults..."

Nick hadn't told them about the bank scholarship Mrs. Nelson had nominated him for, and he decided not to do so. He didn't want to worry them even more.

"...All of us, if we see something, say something. Got that?"

"What about you?" his mom asked. "The bank's right next door to the store. You're on the front lines."

"All quiet on the western front."

"So far," she said.

"So far," his dad agreed.

Nick worked on his homework until nine, finishing everything that was due tomorrow, before deciding to quit. It had been a long day, and he was tired. Ordinarily, he would have masturbated in the bathroom while changing into his pajamas, ejaculating into the toilet. But today he waited until he was in his bedroom, taking a wad of Kleenex with him and doing it under cover of the blanket.

Just in case there were still some cameras in the house that had not been found.

THIRTEEN

1

THE ELECTRICITY WAS off when Kyle opened the back door to Brave New World. It had obviously been off for some time, maybe all night, since, in addition to the lights not turning on, the interior of his little refrigerator was warm, and the small carton of coffee cream he kept in there was spoiled. The whole block might be having a blackout, and he put his sack lunch on top of the refrigerator and was about to check with Trixie to find out if the consignment shop still had electricity, when he heard a noise from somewhere in the front of the store. It was the sound of something moving around, something too big to be a rat or even a cat.

Something that almost had to be a person.

He remained in place, unmoving, listening.

The sound came again.

With the electricity out, the store's alarm was off, and he realized that someone might have used that as an opportunity to sneak in.

Or had cut the electricity in *order* to sneak in.

"Who's there?" he demanded.

Silence.

Kyle looked around the storage space for some kind of weapon but found only a boxcutter on the middle shelf. Picking up the metal rectangle, he pushed out the blade. "Who's there?" he called again.

Slowly, he walked toward the front of the store, blade extended.

He had almost reached the cash register when, in his peripheral vision, he saw movement off to the left. It looked like a shadow, the shadow of a boy, and, facing it full on, he watched it duck behind a bookcase, merge into the wall and disappear.

Not sure he'd actually seen what he thought he'd seen, Kyle walked over. The store was silent, and there was no one in it but him. The shadow, if shadow it had been, had disappeared. He ran his fingers over the bricks in the wall. There was nothing to prove that anything had happened, and he was ready to put the experience down to an overactive imagination, when he realized that this was exactly the same spot where he and Nick had first heard that weird tapping.

The bookstore suddenly seemed darker. Morning light was coming in through the glass front door and the big display window, but it was as if a cloud had passed over the sun. The shop was gloomier than it should have been, and though he was embarrassed to admit it, there were goosebumps on his arms, and he wished the lights were on.

Turning, he noticed for the first time that the center bookshelf opposite the wall, smack dab in the center of the Theater/TV/Film section, was completely empty.

Someone had stolen an entire shelf full of books.

How had he not seen that immediately? Too distracted by the shadow, apparently. He touched nothing, in case there were fingerprints, but he moved forward and looked more closely at the empty bookshelf, trying to recall the titles that had been there. Who could it have been? he wondered. Gary? Did Gary still have a key? Kyle wasn't sure, but he decided that later this morning he was going to go next door to the bank and demand that Gary turn over everything he had.

Maybe it had been Rollie Brown, stealing stock for his own bookstore. Or maybe Gary, working for the bank that had given Rollie his loan, had done it to help Kyle's rival.

The Art of Alfred Hitchcock. The title suddenly came to him, and in his mind's eye, he could see its gray spine on the shelf. A gray spine with the word "Hitchcock" spelled out in red. Next to that had been the oversized book *The Lost Encyclopedia* about the TV show *Lost*. He remembered that the cover photo had wrapped around the spine, the title spelled out in white letters against a blue sky.

He needed to write down everything he remembered. The sheriff's department would want to know.

Kyle walked to the front counter and took out a pad of paper and a pen, writing down the titles of the two books, and another one he suddenly remembered: W.C. *Fields, His Follies and Fortunes.*

He looked out the window. What had always been a cute old-fashioned downtown now seemed to him to have an air of menace. It was definitely more crowded than it had been in a long time, but there was something unsavory about much of the foot traffic. The people using the sidewalk these days were not the elderly couples or young women pushing strollers whom he might have seen in the past. A man walked by, a man with a shaved head, wearing a muscle shirt that showed off his tattooed arms, who looked as though he might have just been released from prison.

A lot of them looked like *him.*

And it was all because of the bank.

The truth was that the air of menace he felt here on Main had spread outward to the entire town. Montgomery was no longer the safe happy community in which he'd grown up, the one where he'd married his high school sweetheart and raised his son. There was about it now an anxious uneasy vibe, a feeling that things were going wrong. Some of it, to be fair, might be unconnected to the bank. But it all coincided with the bank's appearance, so the timing linked everything together.

The lights in the store came on. He heard the *beep beep beep* of the alarm and hurried over to disarm it before it went off. Whatever the problem was, it had been fixed and—

The lights went off again.

Instead of calling Trixie to find out if she was having problems too, he called the electric company directly and was told that the entire downtown had suffered an overnight blackout because of an unexpected and unexplained power drain.

The bank.

He knew it was true even before any facts could be confirmed. He had no idea *why* the bank had used so much power, but there was not a doubt in his mind that it had done so.

"We haven't located the source yet, but we're working on it," the woman on the other end of the line told him. "Everything should be up and running within the next twenty minutes."

Immediately after he got off the phone, the lights came on again and the alarm started beeping. He hurried over to the keypad to punch in the code. The power went off again, but moments later the electricity came on and this time it stayed on.

He called 911 to report a break-in, and an hour later, after he'd opened, a sheriff's deputy came by and took a report. The deputy didn't bother to dust for fingerprints, and when Kyle suggested he do so, he said that they were responding to a lot of calls this morning and that someone would be by later to follow up.

Kyle was still waiting for that to happen when his first customer of the day came in shortly before eleven. It was Durl Meadows. Kyle had blocked off the last aisle to preserve whatever evidence might be found there, but access to those books made no difference to Durl. He wasn't shopping but was continuing his efforts to raise money to stave off foreclosure. While clearing out his closets, he had found more books to sell back, and he lifted a box onto the counter. "What can I get for these?" he asked. "I need every cent I can find."

Kyle brought the box down, putting it on the floor behind the counter. He picked up the top two titles. One was an anti-government screed published by a far-right press that would appeal to almost no one, and the other was a common paperback romance worth almost nothing. Looking down into the carton, he saw more of the same.

"I'd like to help you," he said. "But I'm not exactly flush myself and can't offer you much." He thought for a moment. "You know what, though? I have an idea. I don't know if it's true or not, but someone told me that Rollie Brown's buying books to boost the stock in his new store."

"I don't think it's even open, yet."

"Maybe not, but he's accumulating stock, and what I heard is that he's trying to hurt my business by outbidding me. Word is that he's trying to corner the market in Montgomery by offering twice what I'll pay." Kyle grinned. "By my estimate, you have about five bucks worth of books here. That's what I'd offer you. But I'm going to give you a written estimate of fifty. You can take that to Rollie, see if he'll fork over a hundred."

Durl chuckled. "You think he'll fall for that?"

"With his extensive knowledge of the book business?" Kyle's grin widened. "I think he will."

"If he doesn't?"

"He'll probably at least give you more than five bucks."

"Well, it's worth a shot." Durl's spirits sank as quickly as they'd risen. "I assume you saw the paper today?"

Kyle shook his head. "Paperboy didn't deliver my copy this morning. I called to complain, and they said one would be delivered, but it still hadn't been by the time I left. Why?"

Durl held out a copy of the *Montgomery Gazette*. "Read it."

Kyle took the paper, scanning the front page. The top headline was once again about Victor Clark, who had apparently been transferred to the county's main jail in Globe. "What am I looking for?"

"The full-page ad. Page three."

Kyle opened the newspaper.

It was an ad in the form of a letter, one of those pretentious media buys big corporations made when they were caught doing something illegal and forced to apologize to their customers. This was no mea culpa, though. It was more of a triumphant announcement. With simple letters in bold Lucida Sans type, centered in the middle of the page, printed 26 point against a flat white background, the ad read:

Dear Montgomery Community Bank,

We sincerely thank you for your kindness and generosity, and for welcoming us to your town with open arms. Now that we have entered into a mutual agreement to share our resources and talents, both of our institutions will remain well positioned to meet the complex financial needs of our customers and effectively serve all of the people in Montgomery.

Sincerely,

The First People's Bank

"What the hell?" Kyle said.

"They're consolidating power." Durl glumly took back his newspaper. "Now I can't even try to refinance with Montgomery Community. They're all working together as one big happy family."

"This isn't right."

"I'm not even sure it's legal. Aren't there anti-trust laws and things?" Durl's hatred of government regulation seemed to have disappeared entirely. "I'm not sure how chummy they're actually getting, but this needs to be investigated. I'm going down to the paper after this and tell them to look into it."

Kyle couldn't resist. "You mean those enemies of the people?" he asked with a slight smile.

"Sure. Kick a man when he's down."

"Sorry," Kyle said. "You're right."

"Can dish it out but can't take it, huh? Man up. I'm just joking. But we do need another bank here. People can't be driving all the way to Globe or Randall if they want to go to a different bank."

"There's the credit union."

"If you're a federal employee and you belong."

"What about those online lenders? Have you thought about looking into that?"

Durl sighed. "Even if I qualified, which I don't, I can't afford their kind of interest. Face it, I'm screwed no matter which way I turn."

Kyle was about to say something in response, when there was a muffled boom from somewhere across town. Seconds later, the windows rattled gently, as though there'd been a minor earthquake. Above the roofs of the buildings across the street, from what looked to be someplace near the highway, a cloud of smoke began billowing upward.

"What was *that*...?"

Durl's phone was already out. "Gotta make sure my wife's all right."

Neither Anita's work nor Nick's school were in that direction, so Kyle didn't have that concern, and instead, he quickly called the sheriff's office, hoping to get through and find out what happened before other calls started flooding in.

He did get through.

And he found out what happened.

The Federal Employees Credit Union had been firebombed.

2

JEN looked as terrible as Anita felt.

Both of them had had a hellish week, and Anita found herself coming to work earlier each day, partly to get out of that house (her suspicion that there were still undiscovered cameras had not gone away and had led to her behaving like an automaton in her own home), but also to commiserate with Jen, whose own house troubles were just as creepy and unnerving. Anita had never heard of anything like what was happening to her friend, and when Jen had taken her over to the house one lunch hour to show her The Room, she had experienced its eeriness herself. There definitely had been something in that room, and the mere fact that she considered it a some*thing* rather than a some*one* told her all she needed to know about the house.

At least Steven was a flesh-and-blood person.

She had helped Jen carry a few pre-packed boxes out to the car, and the two of them had taken the boxes back to the old apartment where Jen and Lane were once again living. Anita had jokingly suggested that her friend call *Ghost Pursuers* or one of those other paranormal shows to investigate what was going on, but her feeble attempt at humor had fallen flat because there *did* seem to be something supernatural in the house. And what made it even more disconcerting was that it was not some random phantom that exhibited itself at midnight but an unseen tenant in a locked room that had been concretely specified in a contract with the bank.

The bank.

She, Kyle and Nick were no longer the only ones who were suspicious of First People's. All week, in the office, she had talked to patients who were having financial troubles related to the bank. And not just ordinary financial troubles but convoluted machinations that had led to a nursery school expulsion, firing from a job, a broken leg, a repossessed car, overdue bills and, the one that affected them, loss of health and vision insurance. With this morning's bombing of the credit union making First People's Bank and its BFF Montgomery Community the only financial institutions in town, the anti-bank mood seemed to have only increased. The atmosphere in the waiting room was grim, and there only seemed to be one topic of conversation.

Dr. Wilson had not been himself lately, either, acting even ruder and more unpleasant than normal. Anita and Jen both avoided him during downtimes, and when there was a mid-morning lull and Jen went to use the restroom, Anita got on the computer so she wouldn't have to interact with the optometrist.

Checking her email, she encountered a bunch of spam…and what appeared to be a financial statement from The First People's Bank.

What the hell?

She clicked on the email and, sure enough, a bank statement was displayed. How was this possible? She read through the displayed text and columns of numbers carefully. It appeared as though a fake checking account had been created in her name. Not only that, but out of that account a series of checks had been written to various companies and individuals—the amounts subtracted from a starting balance of zero.

Which, according to the statement, meant that she was currently in debt to the tune of $3,249.

This was not only a major mistake on someone's part, but it had the potential to completely screw up her credit rating. And she didn't like the fact that the statement was sent to her work email. Such lax cybersecurity could lead to identity theft and God knew what else.

Only maybe it wasn't a mistake. Maybe all of it was intentional.

This penis isn't going to suck itself.

Was the bank, or, more specifically, Mr. Worthington, making a purposeful effort to sabotage her? Anita couldn't rule it out, and she picked up the phone next to the computer and dialed the 800 number listed on the statement. She didn't get through to a person but had to listen to the options on a recorded menu before requesting to talk to "a customer service representative."

Worthington came on the line.

Neither of them mentioned their last exchange, and the banker was polite and solicitous after she'd explained her problem, cancelling the fake account, removing all charges associated with her name and apologizing to her for the "misunderstanding." She was left with no place to go, the situation having ostensibly been resolved. She was still angry, but there was no longer anything for her to be angry about, and she hung up before she said something that made things worse. She had the distinct feeling that this was merely the first skirmish in a much longer war, and for the rest of the morning she was out of sorts, using each spare moment to check her email and make sure the bank had not involved her in anything else.

"Hey," Jen said when Dr. Wilson closed the office for an hour shortly before twelve. "Do you have any plans for lunch?"

"Not really."

"Want to go out? My treat."

"Sure. But I'm paying my own way. You're not exactly swimming in money right now."

Jen smiled. "You're right. And thanks."

"Do you want to go to Juan Wang's?"

"I was thinking B.B.'s. I'm in need of some comfort food."

"Sounds good. I'll drive," Anita offered.

On the way, they drove past the credit union to check it out, both of them shocked by the extent of the damage. They'd expected blown-out windows and maybe a little fire damage, but the entire place was gutted, blackened by what had to have been an extensive blaze, and even a significant segment of the adjoining Wal-Mart's brown wall had been partially destroyed. Both businesses as well as the parking lot were closed off.

"That was a major bomb," Jen said quietly.

"Yeah. It makes me kind of nervous. What if they planted other ones around town?"

Significantly, neither of them speculated as to who "they" might be. They both had a pretty good idea.

"I'm sure there are bomb-sniffing dogs checking everyplace. They've probably called in the FBI or some federal agency. I mean, wouldn't this be considered terrorism?"

"It is in my book."

They continued on toward B.B.'s, more subdued than they had been before seeing the blast site. The traffic was much lighter than at a normal lunch hour, and near the corner of Pine Street and First, they passed an abandoned car with its doors wide open and no one in sight. The vehicle's presence was unnerving, and neither of them spoke as they put it in the rearview mirror.

When they reached the diner, the south side of the small parking lot was blocked off. The B.B.'s sign was down and two men were standing on the bed of a pickup parked at the base of the pole, apparently getting ready to put up a new one. There'd been wind last night, but not enough to do that much damage, and Anita wondered if maybe kids had vandalized it.

They walked inside, a sullen waitress behind the counter telling them to sit wherever they wanted, and Jen chose a booth near the last window. All of the waitresses seemed unfriendly, Anita thought. And young. It had been awhile since she'd come to the diner, and she wondered what had happened to the older waitresses she remembered. Jen must have noticed, too, because she asked the dour woman who brought them their menus where Rose was. The woman dropped the menus on the table. "You want Rose? Fine."

The waitress left, walking the length of the counter and striding through the swinging door into the kitchen. They heard her yell "Rose!" above the sound of pots and pans and clattering dishes, and a moment later, a waitress Anita *did* recognize came over to their table.

She smiled. "Hi, Jen." She nodded pleasantly to Anita.

Jen spoke quietly. "What's going on? I don't recognize anyone. Did the new owner bring in his own staff?"

Rose leaned closer, taking out her pad and pen to make it seem as though she was writing down their orders. "The new owner's not the owner anymore. He defaulted on his loan and the bank took it over." She tapped the top of Jen's menu with her pen.

Anita looked at her own menu and saw the name printed at the top: The First People's Diner.

No.

She glanced out the window. The two men in the pickup truck were lifting the replacement sign they were going to mount on the top of the pole, and she could see the new name displayed in black letters against a yellow background. She looked toward Jen. Her friend's face was ashen.

Rose's voice was still low. "Oh, yeah." She shook her head. "Big changes afoot. Half of the gals were fired the first day. Jeani quit. I'm looking for another job, but I can't afford to leave until I find one."

Anita had been looking at the menu. "This can't be right," she said, pointing. "Twenty bucks for a hamburger?"

"That's the Montgomery Burger."

"Nine dollars for a side order of fries?"

"*Pomme frites*, yes."

"How much for a cup of coffee?" Jen asked.

"Our special blend? Six dollars a cup, no refills."

Jen looked from Anita to Rose. "We can't afford to eat here."

The waitress nodded. "I know. No one can. Rafael, one of the cooks, thinks the bank's trying to drive the diner out of business."

"But why?" Jen asked. "They own the place now. If they wanted to close it, they could just close it."

Rose's voice dropped even lower. "I don't know. But if I were you, I'd leave and never come back."

Nodding, the two of them handed her their menus and scooted to the edge of the booth, standing.

"If you hear of any openings anywhere, let me know," the waitress whispered. "I gotta get out of here, too."

"I will," Jen promised.

Walking out, they were aware that the other waitresses were watching them with hostile eyes. Anita hadn't paid attention on their way in, but she saw now that there were no other customers.

She wasn't aware that she'd been holding her breath until they were in the open air and she was able to breathe freely. "What… was…*that*?"

"I don't know," Jen said, looking up at the workers installing the new sign. "But let's get out of here."

"Juan Wang's?"

"Juan Wang's."

3

THE bank sprang up overnight.

Such a thing was impossible, but there it was, gleaming windows set in new white walls, standing in what had been the vacant lot next to Derrick Montoya's law office. The mayor spotted it the second he turned onto Manzanita Street, and for a second he thought he was still asleep and dreaming. Because there was no way an entire building could be built in one night. Even if a hundred workers had somehow shown up after he went home at six, cement could not have dried in time, nor could paint, nor could the macadam of the brand new parking lot. Not to mention the installation of plumbing and electrical wiring. The entire thing was a complete impossibility.

Yet there it was.

An unfamiliar shiver traversed the length of his spine.

Fear.

According to a backlighted sign affixed to the wall above the double doors, this was another branch of The First People's Bank, although Derrick had no idea how that could be. The Planning Commission had not signed off on it, and the council had definitely not approved its construction.

Or had they?

There was a nagging sense in the back of his mind that in their last meeting they *had* voted to allow an expansion of the bank, but the memory was hazy and there were no specifics attached to it. How could that be? He tried concentrating, going through in his mind everything that had happened at the meeting as though he were confirming the minutes, but he could remember nothing they'd discussed or voted on that had in any way involved the bank.

Still...

He drove into what was now the expanded parking lot he shared with the bank. One thing he *did* know for sure: a council meeting was scheduled for tonight, and there was no way this wasn't going to come up. Local businesses had been up in arms about the *first* bank. The appearance of another branch was going to really set them on the warpath.

Derrick had never been in the downtown branch, but now that there was one right next to his office, he decided that he ought to check it out. To his surprise, he saw that it was already open for business, and he glanced down at the clock in the dashboard. Eight-eleven. He had never heard of a bank opening so early, and instead of pulling up in front of his office, he parked by the bank.

The icy shiver that had been tickling his spine had spread out in a cold wave through his entire body. He wished he could pretend not to know the source of his fear, to put it all down to some vague general feeling, but the reason for it was very specific.

This place should not be here.

The bank was fully staffed, and everyone ignored him when he stepped inside. None of the grim-looking employees bothered to glance up, and when he approached the person at the closest desk, he recognized one of his former clients, a man who'd been convicted of aggravated assault against his neighbor and sentenced to three years. Looking around the room, he saw several faces he recognized. All of them had been involved as defendants in criminal cases. Was the bank hiring convicted felons to staff this branch? It seemed that way. And while giving people a second chance was laudable, maybe having them work around large sums of money on a daily basis wasn't the smartest idea.

The place was silent, and as yet no one had even glanced in his direction. He looked up at the ceiling. Were all of the lights on? The room seemed darker and gloomier than it should have been. In fact, the overall atmosphere of the bank felt unpleasant and vaguely threatening.

Derrick bypassed the desk of his old client, searching for someone in charge, a manager or supervisor, an administrator. He was still looking when a tap on the shoulder made him jump and swivel around.

Standing before him was a squat, powerfully built man who looked like a wrestler crammed into a suit that was almost comically too small for him. The man scowled at him. "What do you want?"

Thrown off by the harsh bluntness of the demand, Derrick said, "I was looking for the manager."

"You don't have an account here," the man said belligerently.

"No," Derrick conceded, "but—"

"Then get the hell out."

Offended, he drew himself up to his full height. "Excuse me, but do you know who I am?"

"I don't give a shit. Get out." The squat man's hands were balled into fists.

Derrick scanned the room to see if anyone else was paying attention, hoping someone in charge might inform this thug about the proper way to treat customers. Everyone was watching, but no one made any attempt to correct the man's behavior. Indeed, their faces wore the anticipatory expressions of people waiting on a fight.

Turning silently and walking away before things escalated, Derrick vowed to use whatever power he had as mayor to shut this place down. No matter how the building had been manifested, its construction had never been approved and it was in violation of multiple rules and regulations. He moved his car in front of his own office, unlocked his doors and spent the rest of the morning poring over state and local statutes.

WHEN he'd first been elected to the council ten years ago, Montgomery Town Hall had been little more than a doublewide trailer with pre-fab additions to the front and back. Although it had since moved to a real building adjacent to the library, it was still pretty bare bones, even for a rural municipal building, and the mayor's office was little bigger than a walk-in closet, its only furnishings a dented metal filing cabinet and a beat-up metal desk. On the wall to the right of the desk was an *Arizona Highways* calendar with the dates of council meetings circled in red.

Derrick usually came in here with his laptop an hour or so before each meeting to look over items on the agenda and do whatever research might be required. He was often the only person in the building, but tonight, although he'd arrived even earlier than usual, Roy Freeman was already there, waiting for him.

Uh oh, he thought. Roy never arrived early.

"What's up?" he asked, opening the door to his office.

The other councilman held up his phone. "Did you see the new email from Vince?"

Derrick shook his head.

"You'd better read it."

Derrick switched on the lights and put his laptop on the desk, opening it and turning it on. "What's the gist of it?"

"Read it."

He didn't want to. Montgomery had been operating under a deficit ever since the start of the last recession, and though revenue had ticked up as the economy improved, they were currently in such a deep hole that it would be nearly a decade until they were once again solvent. And that was *if* good economic times continued. The finance director had always been the voice of doom and gloom, and his emails inevitably involved bad news accompanied by dire predictions. Derrick would have preferred to ignore the man, but he was usually right, and Roy's early presence told him this was probably a curveball he was not going to like.

He found the email, clicked on it.

No.

Although there'd been no prior announcement of the fact, Vince's email informed them that the town's public debt was now being held by The First People's Bank. In an effort to lower interest payments, the finance director had transferred the debt, through a complex series of transactions and arrangements, to the bank, which, according to Vince's email, gave First People's a say in the town's budgeting process, specifically veto power over expenditures that might adversely affect the payment schedule.

"What do you think that means?" Roy asked when Derrick looked up from the laptop. "Sounds to me like we won't be able to do our job."

"First of all," Derrick said, "I'm not sure Vince is right about any of this. Just because we're making payments to a bank, it doesn't give that bank the right to tell us what to do. *We're* the elected officials. We decide how the town's money is spent. And, for the record, the finance director works for *us*. Vince doesn't tell us what to do, we tell *him* what to do."

"That's right." Roy nodded, considerably relieved. "That's right."

"We still have to be frugal, we still have to be careful, but we also have to do what's best for the people of Montgomery. The fact is, revenues are up, and after all of the cuts we've made in the past few years, I'll be damned if I'll shortchange this town in order to feed the coffers of a damn bank." He did his best Dana Carvey George Bush. "Not gonna do it."

Roy smiled. "I'm with you." He started typing on his phone as he backed into the hall. "See you on the field."

Once again, the council chambers were filled with irate townspeople, all of them apparently here to protest The First People's Bank. They waited not so patiently as the council approved the minutes of the last meeting and ran through old business, lining up to speak even before the floor was opened to public comments. Derrick glanced over at his fellow councilmembers. He'd spoken with none of them before the meeting other than Roy (and probably shouldn't have even done that per open meeting laws), but he hoped they'd received the finance director's email and had taken from it the same lesson he and Roy had. Lacy and Shelley could most likely be counted on, but Al was always a question mark.

Derrick announced the opening of public comments. Fred Winters, the barber, was first up, and if Derrick remembered right, he'd been one of the most militant speakers at the last meeting.

Why didn't we just let Fred expand The Hair Force? He wouldn't be here if we had.

The mayor shifted uneasily in his seat. Where had *that* come from? He was hoping to build public sentiment *against* First People's, not defend the bank. Which meant that it was a good thing that Fred and the other business owners were riled up. If the finance director was right and the bank would be able to determine spending priorities and subvert the democratically elected council on a technicality, they'd need allies.

"I don't know if anyone else has noticed, but there's a new branch of The First People's Bank on Manzanita, next to the mayor's law office. It just opened today. It was just *built* last night!" He shook his head. "How that's even possible, I'll let someone else figure out. But my question to you—" He pointed at the council. "—is how can you *let* them open another one? The first one wasn't even legal!"

Men and women in line behind him nodded in agreement and there were more than a few declarations of "Yeah!" and "That's right!"

"The council may not be doing its due diligence," Fred continued, "but I've been talking to people around town and doing my own research. Did you know that First People's charges different people different overdraft fees and different monthly service fees? When my friend Tully's son tried to open a savings account, they told him there was a required minimum balance of two hundred dollars. They told his daughter she had to have a minimum balance of three dollars. Three!"

There were shocked exclamations from the gathered townspeople.

"Different people are also getting different interest rates on their accounts. This cannot be legal. And yet here you guys are letting them open up a second branch!"

"Time," Lacy declared.

Derrick raised a hand to quiet the crowd. "Fred, that's not our purview. We're the Montgomery town council. We have no say over federal banking regulations."

Derrick blinked.

Did he really just say that? He thought of his experience in the bank this morning. Why was he defending those bastards?

He didn't know, but he was, and he couldn't seem to stop himself.

"Maybe you can't control what First People's does in a business sense," Fred said. "But you can control whether they're allowed to flout our building codes, or whether they're allowed to have multiple branches in a town as small as ours. That *is* your purview. In fact, that's exactly what you were elected to do."

A chorus of voices shouted in agreement.

Derrick banged his gavel.

"Time!" Lacy repeated.

All of the speakers made essentially the same points, that approval should not have been given to open The First People's Bank in Montgomery, that the building of the mysterious second branch was flat out illegal. Many of them were former Bank of America customers or people belonging to the credit union who ascribed blame for the closing and firebombing of their respective financial institutions to the new bank. But as the evening wore on, Derrick found himself growing more and more defensive of First People's. His original intention to disentangle the town's finances from the clutches of a rapacious lender whose employees had threateningly expelled him this morning from their building was forgotten as he dug in with his support. He had no idea where this was coming from, but he could sense its incongruity even as it was happening. He wanted to side with the protesting townspeople—but for some reason he didn't.

Comments were cut off after an hour. There were still several people to go, and Derrick made a motion to carry over the discussion to the next meeting, which was seconded and approved. The remaining agenda items were addressed, and the meeting ended with no one happy.

Afterward, walking alone to his car, his phone buzzed as he received a text. Who could it be at this hour? Derrick wondered. He stopped to read it: *Good job tonight! –Worthington.*

How could Worthington have known what went on tonight? Had someone from the bank been observing the meeting? Derrick didn't think so. He read the text again. It was definitely unnerving, but, at the same time...he *had* done a good job tonight.

Feeling uneasy and off balance, he shut off his phone and hurried through the darkness to his car.

4

"HELLO, caller. You're on the air." Chet pushed the button on his console next to line one.

"Hello, Chet? How you doing? My name's Teague, and I want to talk about sasquatch scat I found when I was hunting along Blue Ridge last weekend."

Chet cut him off. "Sorry, Teague. Tonight's topic is the sheriff department's gestapo tactics. Let's stick with that." He saw a blinking light on line two and pressed the button beside it. "Next caller."

"Long time, first time. How you doing?"

"The same as I've been doing all night. Get to your point."

"Well, I've been a loyal member of your army since day one, and I think it's about time we rose up against this fascist."

"Now you're talking," Chet encouraged him.

"Montgomery is turning into a damn police state! We're supposed to have open carry laws, but I was at the Safeway gettin' gas, wearing my double holster, and I was arguin' with this snowflake from the Valley had one of those Darwin fish on his little hybrid car, and a cop on the other side of the pump started starin' at me real suspicious like."

"Sheriff's deputy," Chet corrected him. "They're not cops."

"Whatever. This *pig* started eyein' me, and I knew he wanted to take my guns. I mean, what'd he think I was gonna do? Shoot the guy? What kind of country is this?"

"You make a good point. Law enforcement is supposed to pro-tect *us*. But in Montgomery, we need to be protected from *them*."

"That's how the Revolutionary War started, Chet."

"Thank you, caller. You make a lot of sense." He dumped line two and reached for the paper on which he'd typed the copy for his first commercial, wishing the station had a more up-to-date comput-erized system. "We'll be back right after these words."

A hand pulled the copy from his hands and Chet jumped. He hadn't heard anyone come in and thought he'd been alone in the stu-dio. He swiveled around to see the man from the bank, who handed him a new piece of paper.

There'd already been several seconds of dead air. Remembering the terms of his loan, and not wanting the silence to extend for so long that listeners tuned out, he read what he'd been given. "The system is rigged. But if you listen to this show, you know that already. The question is: what are you going to do about it? Vote? Yes, of course. Exercise your Second Amendment right to arm and defend yourself? Certainly. But what else can you do? Well, for one thing, you can make sure that your money is not invested in ways that run counter to your beliefs as an American. That is why I am asking all of my listeners to trust The First People's Bank with all of your financial needs. The First People's Bank. The bank that knows what is right."

Chet pressed a button on his console. "Caller? What's on your mind?"

He pressed another button to take himself off the air, and, quickly, while the caller made his statement, turned to the banker. He still had no idea how the man had gotten in the studio, especially without him seeing or hearing it, but there wasn't enough time to go into that. "Is that all you need?" he asked.

The banker shook his head. "No." He handed Chet a paper-clipped set of pages. "We want you to skip your other commercials and read the rest of these during your remaining breaks."

Chet looked over the first page: *Things are changing in this coun-try. And when America is no longer the America we know, and these great states are no longer united, you need to be able to protect yourself, your family and your community...*

He flipped to the next page: *When they come for your guns, are you going to be able to fight back?...*

"Fine," he said, and came back on air. He had no idea what the man had been talking about, so he dumped the call. "Sorry. We seem to have lost you there." He put on the next call. "What's up?"

LEAVING the station after his show, Chet was surprised to see a group of four men waiting for him in the parking lot behind the building. They were middle-aged white guys dressed in camouflage, so they were obviously his people, but he still felt a twinge of apprehension as he walked toward his Jeep.

"Chet!" one of them called out. He had a huge gray-black *Duck Dynasty* beard.

He waved, kept walking.

"Chet!"

All four men were walking toward him, and he saw no way to avoid them. Their pickup was parked right next to his Jeep, the only two vehicles on the lot save for Gil Consatino's van, and since Gil worked the shift after his, it would be morning before he came out of the station. He was stuck.

"Hey, guys," he said as they approached.

In addition to the man with the giant beard, there was a short beefy dude with a shaved head, and two tall skinny guys who had to be twins.

"Good to meet you!" "Great to meet you!" "Glad to finally meet you!" They were shaking his hand, clapping arms around his shoulders, patting him on the back.

"So why are you gentlemen out so late?" he asked. He considered their clothes. "In from a hunt?"

Duck Dynasty shook his head. "Nah. We were just out partying."

"And listenin' to your show," the guy with the shaved head chimed in.

"Well, I'm glad of that. Always happy to meet a fan." He had continued walking, hoping to reach his Jeep before getting bogged down in a conversation. Ahead, he heard a noise, a rustling in the bushes behind the vehicles. He looked toward the source of the sound, just outside the scope of the building's lights, and shivered involuntarily, the night suddenly seeming a little bit darker.

The bushes shook.

"You through in there?" Duck Dynasty called.

An elderly woman emerged from the foliage, straightening out a too-tight skirt. "I'm done. We gonna keep partying?"

One of the tall twins grinned. "Want a free BJ? This old broad's givin' 'em like they're goin' out of style."

"Going by my wife, they are," Duck Dynasty said. All three of his friends laughed.

Chet eyed the old woman. She looked familiar, somehow, and while he couldn't be sure, he thought he'd seen her in the bank when he went in to apply for his loan.

"She can suck the chrome off a trailer hitch," Shaved Head promised.

The woman smiled proudly.

"No, no. I'm good," Chet assured them. There was a short pause in the conversation, and he jumped in. "Well, I'd better get going. It's been a long night." He took out his key, moved toward the Jeep.

"Reason we're here," Duck Dynasty said (he seemed to be the leader), "is cuz we're members of your army."

"Excellent," Chet replied.

"And we were thinking that maybe it's about time we became a *real* army."

Chet stopped. *A real army.* He had to admit that the idea was appealing.

"Hell yeah!" Shaved Head declared.

An actual armed force? It wasn't unheard of. There were citizen militia groups who patrolled the border. He didn't see any reason why they couldn't have such a group patrolling Montgomery, doing the job that worthless sheriff *should* be doing. It might even make the sheriff toe the line a little.

Duck Dynasty seemed to be reading his mind. "There's a lot of bad hombres out there, and that pussy sheriff ain't doin' shit about it. Instead, he's killin' innocent people like your brother, lettin' people be crucified in the middle of town. What kinda lawman's that?"

"A worthless one," the twin on the left said.

"We all have guns. Ain't no reason we couldn't be out there pro-tectin' the town."

Chet looked at the old lady. Had *she* somehow put this idea in their minds? He wasn't sure where that notion had come from or what had made him think it, but these four weren't the brightest bulbs in the box, and the knowing expression on her wrinkled face made him think it could be the case.

Had the bank put her up to it?

That was a definite possibility. Technically, in lieu of interest on his loan, all he had to do was provide the bank with free air time for commercials—which he had already done tonight. That quid pro quo was the only agreement stipulated in writing. But implicit in the banker's approval of this arrangement was the idea that he might be called upon to provide extra favors.

How was this a favor to the bank, though?

"I don't see that fuckin' sheriff crackin' down on illegals," Shaved Head offered. "Half my kid's class is brown. When I was growin' up, there was none of that shit. Where did they all come from? *That's* somethin' a private army could do somethin' about."

"You're right," Chet told him. This idea was sounding better by the minute. "And we could use my show as real time tip line. See something, say something. Anyone in town spots something not right, they can call in, and you guys would be out there ready to respond."

"First responders!" Shaved Head pumped his fist in the air. "Hell yeah!"

Chet was thinking out loud. "We get the rest of my army in on it, too. Let them know how things are evolving. Maybe I don't spell everything out on the show, where the sheriff and everyone can hear. But we set up a meeting, set some ground rules, make some plans."

Duck Dynasty's smile could be seen in the center of his beard. "Now you're talkin'."

"Maybe I will take that BJ," Chet said. He was already half hard, and even though the old lady was gross and disgusting, he could close his eyes and pretend she was a babe. She'd have to do it in his Jeep, though. He wasn't whipping it out in front of these guys.

He looked around for the woman, but she seemed to have disappeared.

"Hey, where'd that broad go?" one of the twins asked, swiveling around.

"Guess she left," the other twin said.

"Shit."

"Where did you guys find her?" Chet wondered.

The four men looked from one to the other. "I don't know," Shaved Head admitted.

"We were in the Wal-Mart parking lot, drinkin' and listenin' to your show, and she just kinda showed up," Duck Dynasty recalled.

Both twins were grinning. "And said she'd blow us," the one on the right said.

The bearded man was frowning. "In fact, I think she was the one who suggested we come and see you. Said your show was ending, and if we went to the station we could meet you."

Chet nodded, not surprised. He remembered her now. She *had* been at the bank. She was the teller who'd made him a copy of the loan forms once they'd been signed.

Maybe the bank *had* sent her out.

It didn't matter. A good idea was a good idea no matter where it came from.

"So," he said. "What kind of firepower do you men have?"

FOURTEEN

1

B RAD WAS IN his office, eating a late lunch of Fritos and canned Coke, when Jasper Brooks walked up to the front desk and confessed to the murder of Jimmy Collins.

Paul and Vern immediately ordered him not to move. Brad heard the commotion and was hurrying out even before Carol had a chance to alert him, seeing Paul already slapping on the cuffs. *Jasper?* Brad was shocked. He had been the one to discover Glen Taggart's body, so there was kind of, sort of, almost a semi-Bank of America connection. But what could Jasper possibly have against the new teller at Montgomery Community? Even if he had wanted to kill the young man, why had he done so in such an outlandishly gruesome and public way? It made no sense. If Jasper had killed Jimmy Collins and lashed him to the door of the closed bank, why had there been no evidence of it on scene? And why had he waited until now to turn himself in? Nothing about this rang true.

Then Vern unfolded the oil-stained towel Jasper had brought in with him, revealing the murder weapon: a length of metal pipe, covered in dried brown blood.

As with the evidence against Leroy Fritz in the murder of Glen Taggart, that pretty much clinched it, at least from a legal standpoint, and Brad forced himself to put aside the doubts he had been enumerating in his head.

"Bag 'em," he ordered. "And by the book. We can't afford any contamination."

Paul herded Jasper to the interrogation room, while Vern walked down the hall to the supply cabinet for a pair of gloves, an evidence bag and a camera.

Maybe they wouldn't need the FBI's help after all, Brad thought.

Immediately after the bombing, he had called the Bureau, and this time they'd jumped to. A bombing implied terrorism, and in the current political climate, any perceived hesitation would read as incompetence or worse. Within hours, men from the Phoenix office had helicoptered in, followed shortly by a team on the ground. They'd swarmed over the credit union all day and night, leaving no speck of dust unexamined. Everything was now being analyzed at "The Lab," wherever that might be, and though the feds had shared nothing with his people, Brad had been assured that "incidents" such as this were usually resolved quickly. Based on, from what he could tell, nothing whatsoever, he was given a capture estimate of two days.

Frustratingly, even though the Bureau had left two men in town, they had steadfastly refused to help with any other case.

Now, apparently, one of those cases had solved itself.

He felt a little less confident after an hour with Jasper in the interrogation room. The self-identified Vietnam vet prided himself on being a stoic asshole, and he had not dropped that role here. Despite the fact that he'd confessed, Jasper refused to elaborate or go into any detail. Brad wanted to know the how and the why of it— everyone in the department did, everyone in *town* did—but Jasper said only, "I did it. Charge me and I'll take my punishment." After that, he was silent.

Brad left the booking and paperwork to Paul and Vern while he, Hank and three other deputies descended on Jasper's cabin, looking for evidence. Two hours later, they'd come up with nothing—no evidence of any communication with Jimmy Collins on the primitive and obviously seldom-used computer, no bloody clothes or gloves, no sign of blood anywhere—and Brad gave the order to expand their search to the surrounding property. While there was nothing connecting Jasper to the young teller, they did find in the bedroom a blue tote bag from The First People's Bank's grand opening, an item that probably meant nothing but that Brad found troubling nonetheless.

He was scheduled for a five o'clock meeting with Agent Yamato from the Bureau, to talk about the bombing, and Brad left Hank in charge as he drove back to the office. The FBI guys had maintained a strict barrier between their case and everything else, but he thought he might ask for some advice about getting information out of Jasper—as much as it pained him to ask those arrogant agents for anything.

Unfortunately, the barrier still held, the FBI still didn't give a shit about their local murders, and there was no new information on the bombing, so the meeting lasted mere minutes.

"What about all of the dead bank employees we found in the meadow?" Brad pressed. "Can't you classify that as an X-file or call in the Fringe division or something?"

Yamato did not even bother to respond.

Angry that he had been called away from his investigation to be told non-information that could have and should have been texted to him, Brad was about to visit Jasper's cell and take another crack at the old man, when his cellphone rang. It was Jillian, and his heart skipped a beat when he heard her voice. The girls never called him at work. "Hey, honey," he said. "What is it?"

"It's getting dark, and Mommy's not back yet. She said she'd just be gone for a little while, but it's been too long." Jillian sounded almost ready to cry. "I tried to call her, but she didn't answer. She told us not to call you, but it's getting dark!"

"Where is she? Do you want me to call her?"

"We want you to come home!" Now she was crying.

"I'll be right there, sweetie. You're both at home?"

A sniffle. "Yes."

"Turn on all the lights and keep the doors locked. I'll be there in a few minutes."

"Okay." Sniffle.

"Love you," he said.

"I love you, too. But hurry up, Daddy! It's getting dark!"

Jasper could wait. He wasn't going anywhere. "Call Hank," Brad told Carol. "Tell him I have a family thing, but I'll be back out there as soon as I can. I'll keep my radio on in case something comes up."

The receptionist nodded.

"No one else goes home unless they clear it through me. Everyone gets overtime."

"Me, too?"

"Unless you can convince Issac to take over for you."

"No, that's okay. I can use the extra money, and I don't have any plans for this evening anyway."

"I'll be back." Brad hurried outside. He was fuming as he sprinted toward his car.

Damn it! Patty had promised she wouldn't leave the girls alone. She'd sworn it wouldn't happen again. How could she be so irresponsible? He speed dialed her cell, but it went directly to voicemail, and he angrily threw his phone on the seat next to him.

Driving through town, he put his roof lights on, though he left the siren off. He wanted other drivers to get out of his way so he could get home as quickly as possible, but he didn't want the girls to hear his siren and panic.

Jillian was right. It *was* getting dark out. The day had flown by so quickly, particularly the afternoon, that he hadn't realized how late it had gotten. How could Patty have left the girls alone when the sun was almost down?

It was conceivable that something had happened to his wife, and he wondered why that had not been the first possibility that had occurred to him, particularly with everything that had been going on. He supposed it was because Jillian had told him Mommy had purposely left her and Sue alone. That and his sheriff's sense that, because there'd been no accidents called in or anything unusual reported around town, she was probably okay.

He shut off the lights as he approached the house and slowed down before pulling into the driveway. Immediately after unlocking and opening the front door, both girls rushed forward to hug him. "It's all right," he told them. "I'm here."

"I was scared!" Sue said. "Jillian tried to scare me!"

"I did not! I was scared, too!"

Sue screamed with fright. "See?" she said. "She's doing it again!"

"Calm down," Brad told them. "It's all right. There's nothing scary." He noticed that the drapes were all open. With the lights turned on throughout the house, it made the world outside the windows appear even darker. "You should have closed the drapes," he said, doing so himself. Two little girls alone in a house watching TV with the lights on and the curtains open? If he saw this on the job, he'd question the parents about their negligence.

"How long ago did Mommy leave?" he asked.

Jillian shook her head. "I don't know."

"A long time ago!" Sue said.

"I'm sorry," he told them. "We talked about this after the last time, and Mommy promised she wasn't going to do this again."

The girls looked at each other.

Brad's stomach sank. "What?"

Another look.

"She *has* done this before today?"

"She—" Sue began.

"We'll get in trouble!" Jillian told her.

"No you won't," he promised. "Tell me."

Jillian looked at the floor. "She does it every day."

Every day? The realization shocked him, and he was cut to the quick by a sharp sense of betrayal. That was not something he had expected, not after their discussions. He looked at the girls and thought of Patty leaving them to their own devices, suddenly aware that he did not know his wife the way he thought he did.

Not wanting to frighten the girls, but needing to know what had been going on in his home behind his back, he questioned them calmly, almost casually, without pressure, letting them know that he was just trying to find out where Mommy was so they could get her back. He learned that, each day this week, she had picked them up at school, then dropped them off at the house to do their homework, telling them she had to "go back to work," and asking them not to tell Daddy. Before today, she had always returned within an hour or so, well before the sun started to go down.

Brad nodded, not letting them see how angry he actually was. Once again, he attempted to call his wife's cell, doing it from the house phone, hoping she would see the number and think the girls were calling her, but, as before, it went directly to voicemail.

Where could she be? If his men hadn't all been busy with real work, he would have been tempted to send a few out to find her. That would have scared her. And shamed her.

Although the best way to shame her would be to take the girls with him and hunt her down himself.

Where could she be? he wondered again. She was always talking about those new rich clients. Where had they bought their house? Hadn't she said it was the big one by the golf course?

"Come on, girls," he said. "We're going for a ride."

"Where?" Jillian asked suspiciously.

"To get Mommy."

"Yay!" They both cheered, excitedly running out of the house in front of him.

"The police car!" Sue shouted. "We get to ride in the police car!"

"Daddy's a sheriff," Jillian reminded her.

Brad closed and locked the door of the house. "You sit up front with me," he told them. "There are no seatbelts in the back."

Sue's eyes widened. "We get to sit in the front?"

"Yep."

They cheered again, opening the car door and scrambling in.

He got behind the wheel. Maybe he should have left a note, in case Patty returned before they could find her, but he figured it would serve her right if she came home and found the girls gone. Might scare some sense into her.

The sky was purple in the east, although rose-colored in the west, and the buildings they passed by, when not illuminated by interior or exterior lights, were black silhouettes. He drove as a civilian, without lights or siren, but still it took only slightly more than five minutes until they reached the golf course. Condos were on the near side, near the clubhouse, but the failed development they wanted was on the opposite edge of the green. He could see the single home that had been built even from here, a lonely McMansion standing sentry over empty acre lots. The lights were on, and he felt his anger rising as he imagined Patty sitting in there, sipping wine with her yuppie clients, while her children cowered in fear in their own home, calling him at work to come and save them.

He found the turnoff to the winding single-lane road that led around the golf course and took it. The house remained in sight the entire way, a man-made edifice on the border between the flat grass of the green in front and the dark wildness of forest behind. It was well-lit. Even the driveway was lined with landscaping lights, and Brad pulled up in front of the house, parking next to Patty's Acura. The building itself was oddly designed, with seemingly more windows than walls, and while he couldn't immediately determine where the front door was situated, he could clearly see into several rooms.

"There's Mommy!" Sue called out, pointing through the windshield.

Brad couldn't tell exactly where her finger was pointing, but he scanned the various windows until movement caught his eye. There she was, her back to them, gesturing with her hands as she spoke to someone.

"Come on," he said, unbuckling his seatbelt. He opened his door and got out, walking around to the passenger side. He opened the door, helped Jillian help Sue take off her shoulder harness, and, holding each of their hands, walked with them up to the house.

The location of the door quickly became clear, and they strode up a winding path to the entrance, Brad pushing the button for the bell and then, after a second's hesitation, knocking. They waited, but there was no response, so he did it again. Another moment or two passed, and he was about to try a third time, when the door opened.

"Mommy!" Jillian and Sue cried together.

The expression on Patty's face was not just one of surprise but one of fear. The fear turned instantly to anger, and she glared at Brad. "Why did you bring them here?"

Sue started crying.

"*Them*?" Brad said pointedly. "You mean your daughters? I brought them here because Jillian called me at the station, where Jasper Brooks had just confessed to murder, because it was getting dark and you'd left the girls alone and they were scared."

Jillian was crying, too. "I'm sorry, Mommy! I'm sorry!"

"I think you'd better come home." Brad kept his voice quiet, though he wanted to yell.

Patty glanced behind her.

"Tell them you have a family you have to take care of. You've spent more than enough time babysitting this couple."

"I—" she began.

Brad frowned. Patty was standing in a Mexican-tiled foyer, and behind her was the room in which they'd seen her through the window. She'd glanced back there a few seconds ago, and he had, too, and while he'd thought nothing of it, he realized now that there was something in the scene did not seem quite right. He peered over her shoulder and saw a person seated on a couch in the other room.

Only...

The person had not moved this entire time. And his or her head was slumped forward at an extremely unnatural angle.

Was the person dead?

Could Patty have—?

"Stay here, girls," he said, letting go of their hands. "Don't move." He strode past Patty, who was caught off guard by his action and slow to react.

The figure was a dummy. He could see that even before he reached the other room, but when he did reach it and walked around to the front of the couch, he discovered that it was wearing his clothes: a pair of his jeans, one of his weekend yardwork shirts, his old shoes. The head was nothing more than a plastic bag stuffed with crumpled newspaper, on which a rudimentary face had been drawn. It was topped with a cheap thrift store wig.

Next to the male figure on the couch were two smaller females made out of Jillian's and Sue's clothes that had been filled with assorted rags. Creepily undersized doll heads were balanced atop the stuffed clothing. Brad seemed to recall Sue complaining a week or so ago that her sister had stolen some of her dolls. Apparently, it had been her mother who'd taken them.

All three of the figures were facing a television, which was playing an old VHS recording of *Ghost*, one of Patty's favorite movies. The walls of the otherwise empty room were decorated with the generic framed artwork that she sometimes used to spruce up ugly houses that she was trying to sell.

Patty had run up behind him. "It's not what you think."

He didn't know what he thought. This was so crazy that he was unable to form a quick opinion. He did think that the girls needed to be kept as far away from this as possible, and he was grateful to see that at least Patty had had enough sense to keep them in the foyer by the front door and out of this room.

But there was no way he could trust her with Sue and Jillian anymore. Those days were over. Beyond that, however, he didn't know what he was going to do. He certainly couldn't watch the girls all the time, not with everything that was going on, and a sense of panic welled within him as he considered his very limited options. Could he farm them out to friends' families? Once in a while, perhaps, but obviously not every day. Patty's parents lived in Texas, so they were out of the question, but his parents had retired to the outskirts of Sedona, and while his dad probably wouldn't come, he was sure he could get his mom over to stay with them and take care of the girls for a few weeks until he could figure out a more permanent solution.

But what about Patty? What was he going to do with her? Her problems went far beyond anything he could handle. She obviously needed professional help, although what that might turn out to be, he had no idea. He felt overwhelmed, and as he looked toward the window, he realized that when he and the girls had seen her, she'd been talking to the figures on the couch.

How many times over the past few weeks had she been late for something or other because she had to meet with the buyers of this house? How many times had she talked about them or described her contacts with them? Lies. They had all been lies.

"Did anyone actually buy this house?" he asked her.

She shook her head, wouldn't meet his eyes.

"Daddy?" Jillian called from the foyer.

"I'll be right there! Just wait a minute!" He turned back toward Patty, gestured around the room. "What would even make you *think* of something like this?"

She was struggling to hold back tears. "There *was* a couple that wanted to buy it, but when we went to the bank to discuss financing, they decided to back out. I ended up talking to the loan officer about it, hoping to interest him, I guess, or hoping he knew someone who might be in the market for such a big ticket property." She shook her head, confusedly. "I don't know how it happened, but he made me realize that since it was unsold and I had access to it and it had been for sale for so long, I could...use it, sort of, and maybe pretend that I lived here and..." Now she did start crying. "It all just got out of hand, and I don't even know how it happened!"

He put his arms around her and held her, looking over her shoulder at the girls, who were talking nervously amongst themselves.

"It's all right!" he called out to them. "Don't worry!"

Brad pulled slightly away, holding Patty's shoulders and looking into her face. "I'm taking the girls, and we're going to go home now," he said. "You close up here and meet us back at the house. You need to clean all this up and get rid of it, but don't do that now. Wait until tomorrow. I was called away from duty and I'm supposed to go back to work, but I'm going to call Hank and tell him to take over for me tonight. The girls and I will stop off and get a pizza for dinner. We'll put them to bed early, but then we need to talk. Do you understand?"

Patty sniffled, nodding.

"Good. We'll see you at home."

His stomach churning and his mind racing, he put a reassuring smile on his face and walked back over to where Jillian and Sue were standing. They looked worried, but when he took their hands and told them they were going to get pizza and meet Mommy back at home, they relaxed a little.

"We're not in trouble?" Jillian asked.

"Of course not!" he told her, and though her eyes were still red from crying, she smiled up at him.

"Come on."

They walked outside, down the winding path, back to the car. As the girls were getting in and he held open the passenger door for them, he glanced up at the window and saw Patty on her phone.

Who could she be talking to?

Frowning, he closed the car door and walked around to the driver's side, getting in. Looking through the windshield, he saw that she was standing in the same place she'd been in when they arrived. She was no longer on her phone, but she was once again talking to the fake family on the couch. He saw her begin to pace agitatedly, and she raised her right arm as though to emphasize a point.

Feeling cold, Brad turned the car around and headed back down the driveway to the street.

2

ANOTHER branch of The First People's Bank appeared overnight.

It showed up on the west side of the highway near the nursery. No one had known it was coming, and its construction had not been approved, but it was there in the morning, a dark brooding structure that, while only a single story, looked as though it were crouched and waiting to rise to its full height. There were no cars parked in the newly paved lot in front of it, but the bank was clearly staffed. Through the glass doors, in the dimness of the interior, individuals could be seen moving about, performing their duties, and of the few people who slowed down on the highway and tried to peek curiously to see what was what, none stopped by and none went in.

3

HIS gut had been right. Aaron had been absent from school all week, and had not responded to any texts, voicemails or emails. Nick had not been brave enough to go by his friend's house, but he told his mom and dad about it this time, and they had contacted the sheriff. He wasn't sure what had happened after that, but there'd been nothing on the morning announcements and no one from the sheriff's office had called his parents back, so he assumed Aaron and his family were still alive.

Somewhere.

The truth was, there'd been absences in most of his classes this week, and while there might have been some kind of bug going around, Nick didn't think so. Ever since Victor's capture in the gym, the school had had a weird vibe, and he was sure he wasn't the only one to have noticed it. The entire town, in fact, seemed to be under some kind of spell. No one talked about it, no one acknowledged it, but everyone was aware, and when he'd gone with his parents to the grocery store, several of the shelves and refrigerated cases were either empty or nearly so, as though shipments had not arrived or people in town had stocked up in preparation for some disaster. Throughout Montgomery, a lot of homes appeared to be for sale, and the streets, while never really filled with traffic, seemed nearly deserted.

Now he was here, eating lunch alone, looking out at a quad that was curiously underpopulated.

Greg Holloway walked by, but no fellow jocks were with him, and he didn't make the effort to utter even a token threat.

Nick finished his sandwich and glanced toward the office. They'd been told the other day in their homerooms that the school now had a student financial adviser to help kids manage their college saver accounts. It was part of a new public-private partnership between the school and The First People's Bank. All sorts of services were supposedly offered, and the adviser was available any time. Students were even allowed to get out of class to meet with him, but Nick didn't think any of them had done so. He assumed the financial adviser had been given a room in the office, and he found himself wondering where that was. In his mind, he saw Mr. Worthington seated in Principal Whittaker's office, waiting patiently behind that big desk like a spider for a fly, while the principal was demoted to a smaller space somewhere else in the building.

He was certainly never going to visit any financial adviser.

The only thing left in his lunch sack was a banana his mom had packed for him, and there was no way he was going to put anything with that shape in his mouth on school grounds, so he threw the sack away just as his phone buzzed, alerting him that he'd received a text.

Aaron? he thought hopefully.

He checked his phone. No.

It appeared to be from either Mrs. Nelson or his counselor. There was no name attached to the text, only the school's tag, but it asked him to stop by the library before the end of lunch period in order to discuss the writing scholarship. He had not applied for it and had no intention of applying for it, but he had not told that to anyone at the school, and they were no doubt wondering when he was going to turn in his application.

Lunch still had fifteen minutes to go, and he had nothing to do, so he wandered over to the library. Quite a few kids usually came in here during lunch, but today the building appeared to be empty. There was not even anyone at the front desk, and that was definitely unusual because Ms. Swanson was paranoid about students smuggling in food or smuggling out books, and she kept a sharp eye out for troublemakers. He was about to turn and leave, when he heard his name spoken from between the stacks: "Nicholas Decker."

He recognized that voice.

Mr. Worthington.

The text had not been from his teacher or the counselor. It had been from the banker.

"Nicholas."

Heart pounding, he immediately turned to leave, but on the door through which he'd just come was imprinted a shadow.

The shadow.

It had left his house, and that was frightening enough, but its connection to the bank was what really sent a chill through his bones. Because once again, something about the shadow reminded him of that figure he'd seen through the window of the empty storefront that had become First People's. And while he'd never thought it through or fully articulated it in his mind until now, there seemed something *demonic* about the shape, with its three arms, its too-long neck, its overlarge head with the spiky top. What's more, it still had that strange quivering quality, as though it was actually alive, and Nick slowly began to back away from it.

"Oh, Nick!" Mr. Worthington called.

He needed to escape the library. The shadow was wavering against the door, so he definitely wasn't going out that way, but he didn't know if there was any other exit.

Where was Ms. Swanson? Where were the other students who were usually in here?

He turned, moving a little to the left, and thought he saw a tall figure standing halfway down one of the aisles between bookcases.

"Nicholas!"

He could hide in the bathroom, Nick thought, but he might get trapped in there. He could feel himself starting to panic. The impulse to flee was almost overpoweringly strong, and he willed himself to fight it. That was the mistake people made in movies when trapped in an enclosed area—running. It allowed them to be chased and, eventually, caught. He was close to the door right now; anything he did would move him further away from it.

Maybe he could lure the shadow away from the door.

He had no idea how he would do that and was afraid to even try. As much as he wanted to avert his gaze, he kept glancing at it, and each time it seemed to him darker and more *there*.

What if he tried calling 911? Or called the office and told them to send someone over because he was trapped here in the library?

"Nicholas!"

He glanced down the aisle and saw that the figure was closer. It was *definitely* Mr. Worthington. Nick could see him now, though he was mostly still in shadow, and the banker was grinning widely, teeth unnaturally white in his semi-shaded face.

There was no time to call anybody.

The banker was closing in.

He might be terrified of the shadow, but it was, after all, just a flat silhouette. Mr. Worthington was real, and before he had time to analyze or think through his action, Nick sprinted forward, arms outstretched, shoving open the door and running outside. His hand touched the shadow, and his fingertips experienced a cold tingling, but it might have been his imagination. Then he was outside and dashing through the quad. Students were dispersing, heading to classrooms, and while he hadn't heard the bell ring, he realized it must have.

Breathing heavily, heart pounding, he forced himself to stop running as he made his way over to his locker to take out his books for fourth period.

He did not look back at the library.

WHEN his dad picked him up after school, Nick told him about the text he'd received and about seeing Mr. Worthington in the library. He half-expected to get a lecture because he hadn't reported it to the principal or vice principal or anyone in authority, but his father must have understood the situation better than expected because he said nothing. Nick *didn't* tell him about the shadow, but that was the reason he didn't want to be home alone, and he surprised his dad by saying that he wanted to go back to the bookstore with him instead of heading to the house.

It felt weird being this close to the bank. Just a wall separated them, and beyond that who knew what was happening? Logically, he understood that customers were probably just withdrawing cash or making deposits, workers calculating totals. But in his mind, the bank had become mysterious and horrific, and no matter what rationality suggested, he could not help thinking that bad things were going on in there.

The bookstore had no customers, and there was no real work to do. On the checkout counter was a facedown paperback that his dad had obviously been reading. Nick had homework—some problems in math, and reading for English and social studies—but he wasn't in the mood right now, and he stepped behind the counter and sat down in the chair that used to be Gary's.

"Did they ever find out who broke in?" he asked, although he knew his dad would have told him if someone had been caught.

His father shook his head. "No prints, no clues, nothing."

"Do you think it might have been Gary?"

"Maybe," he admitted. There was a short pause.

"What?" Nick asked.

"Even if it wasn't Gary, I bet the bank had something to do with it."

They were both silent for a moment.

"There's another First People's Bank in town now," Nick said finally. "I didn't say anything, but I saw it when you were driving me to school this morning."

His dad sighed. "I saw it, too. That makes three."

"*Three?*"

"They opened one up by the mayor's law office last week."

Nick's pulse quickened. "I thought they just built a new one so they could have a parking lot." He pointed at the wall. "I thought they were going to close this one."

His dad shook his head grimly. "It doesn't look like it. I think they're just expanding."

"But how many banks can Montgomery have?"

"I guess we'll find out."

They were both silent again. Outside the window, people were on the sidewalk striding past. The majority seemed to be either leaving or heading toward the bank. He saw no one going into any of the other businesses. Almost all of them looked worried, concerned or just generally not happy.

It was like living in a horror movie, Nick thought. Except in a horror movie, the hero would fight the monster or solve the mystery and everything would go back to normal. He had a hard time imagining things going back to normal. A bank was not something that could be vanquished. And with three of them now, even if one closed there would be two left. As far as he could tell, his family and everyone else was just stuck here in town until...

Until what?

He had no idea, and that, he realized, was the scariest thing of all.

4

AFTER the service on Sunday, Dennis Whittaker attempted to leave church by the side door rather than the front, hoping to catch Claire Osocampo before she made it out to her car. She was the only reason he attended services at all, and over the past few weeks, he'd made a purposeful effort to sit in a new pew every Sunday. Like kids in a classroom, most parishioners usually sat in the same seats each time. The behavior was territorial as much as habitual, but he was attempting to show that he didn't consider such things, indeed, didn't notice them at all, but randomly sat down at whatever spot was most convenient.

His goal was to eventually sit by Claire.

It had to happen naturally. Years before he'd become principal, when he'd just been a teacher, she'd been one of his students. She was twenty-eight now, but pursuing her still seemed, well...wrong, so instead of being seen as making an effort to talk to her, he had to make running into her after the service appear casual and unplanned, just as it would when he finally sat down on the pew next to her.

Pastor Peters caught him before he could exit the church.

If Dennis had had more time, he would have asked the preacher why he was still inside rather than out front schmoozing parishioners the way he should have been, but he needed to get outside quickly, and he merely nodded politely when Peters called his name. "Good sermon," he said and pushed open the door.

The pastor closed it.

Those few seconds had cost him his chance. Claire was probably halfway to her car by now, and the only way he could run into her was if he actually ran. He slumped in defeat, resigning himself to trying again next Sunday.

"Just the person I was looking for," the preacher said. "What are the odds?"

Dennis forced himself to smile.

"I would've bet two to one," the pastor added, and laughed nervously. "Maybe three to one at the outside."

Always a little creepy, Pastor Peters had, of late, been acting even stranger than usual. And his constant shilling for the bank was downright bizarre. Dennis didn't know what was behind it, but he didn't really want to know. His experience with First People's had not been a good one, and the preacher's association with the bank definitely did not count as a point in his favor.

"What is it?" Dennis asked politely.

"I've been tasked by a representative of The First People's Bank to let you know that you will need to find a ride home from church."

"What?"

"They're taking your car."

What the hell? Dennis pushed past the pastor and ran out the side door. On the street, two men in white shirts and ties were circling his Camry, as though looking for a way to get in. Thank God he always locked his vehicle. "Hey you!" he called, hurrying over. "That's my car! Stay away from there!"

His way was blocked by a man dressed in business attire. The man looked familiar, but Dennis could not immediately place him. Then he said, "Halt," and Dennis recognized the voice. It was the bank officer he'd dealt with while trying to secure a home improvement loan. "Those employees are only doing their duty."

"That's my car!"

"That *was* your car. I thought the minister explained that to you."

Dennis was so mad he was shaking. "If any of you so much as *touches* my car, I'm calling the sheriff!"

There was a loud slap. And another, and another, and another, as the two men circling the Camry smacked their hands down on the vehicle's hood and trunk.

"Touch!" one of them said.

"Touch!" the other repeated.

The loan officer was still blocking his way, and the man's voice when he spoke was flat and deadly serious; a cop reading the riot act to a criminal. "Before applying for a loan which we both know you did not receive, you opened a checking account at The First People's Bank in order to qualify as a customer. You did not opt for overdraft protection."

"So?"

"So your account has a current balance of negative three dollars."

"That's impossible!"

"You withdrew a hundred dollars from our ATM two days ago. At the time, your account had a balance of one hundred."

"First of all, I had *two* hundred in there—"

"No," the man said firmly. "You did not. You had two hundred the week prior, but that was before fees and surcharges were tallied at the end of the month."

"A *hundred dollars* worth?"

"That is correct. So at the time of your withdrawal, there was one hundred in your account."

"Really? Then why did the ATM let me take the money?"

"Oh, you had enough to make the withdrawal, but taking it all left nothing in your account. An ATM cannot close out an account, so a three-dollar service fee was charged automatically. Since you did not have overdraft protection, this left you three dollars in arrears. And, as per policy, any negative balance can be collected by the bank in the manner it deems most appropriate."

"Three bucks?" Dennis took out his wallet. "Here you go."

The loan officer chuckled. "That's not how it works, Mr. Whittaker. You know that. I just told you, as set forth in your terms and conditions, which you apparently did not take the time to read, the bank has the legal right to recover the amount it is owed by what it determines is the most efficacious means. In this instance, that means confiscating your vehicle, selling it at auction, collecting the three smackeroos, plus a reasonable processing and transfer fee, and then recompensing the remainder to you."

"You can't do that!" he yelled.

"Oh, but we can."

A crowd had gathered by this time, curious about the ruckus, and Dennis was humiliated to see that Claire was among those in the front. There was nothing he could do that wouldn't make him look weak or foolish. He could try to fight and get bogged down in an endless shouting match—probably one in which he would be the only person yelling—or he could give up, and either start walking home or beg for a ride from a fellow parishioner.

A hand touched his shoulder, and he jumped, startled. It was Pastor Peters. "I'm sorry," he said. "I don't like being a part of this—"

Dennis turned on him. "Then why are you? You come up to me after church and tell me that someone from the bank told you to tell me that they were stealing my car? What is that? And when did they tell you? Before church started?" He pulled away. "You could've given me a heads up instead of just acting like their lackey and humiliating me in front of your whole congregation."

The loan officer moved next to Pastor Peters. Dennis saw the preacher flinch as the other man flanked him. It was the banker who spoke first. "You know, pastor," he said. "I'm not a religious man, but there's always been something I wondered about."

"Yes?" the preacher said warily.

"How did the world get populated? There was Adam and Eve, right? And they had two boys."

"Cain and Abel."

"Right, right. Well, either the brothers fucked their mom, or Adam and Eve had daughters and the brothers fucked their sisters. I mean, there's no other way it could have worked, am I right?"

The pastor did not reply.

"Then, to expand the population, the brothers probably fucked their own daughters, or Adam fucked their daughters, or..."

"That's enough!"

The loan officer looked taken aback. "I'm sorry. I thought it was a legitimate theological observation."

"First of all, as everyone knows, Cain killed Abel—"

"Oh, so just *Cain* fucked his mom."

"If I wasn't a man of God..." He pulled hard away and strode purposefully back toward the church.

"Ten to one odds our man of God returns right now and watches us repossess your car!" the loan officer said loudly to Dennis. "After all, there is a very big game this afternoon! A lot of wagering going on!"

Pastor Peters stopped, turned around and stood silently and shamefacedly next to the banker.

"Much better," the loan officer said. He turned to Dennis. "So, do you need a ride home?"

DENNIS did get a ride, but instead of leaving with a man from the bank, he accepted an offer from Jack Thorne, one of his teachers who was also a member of the congregation. He rode in the front seat with Jack, while the teacher's wife sat in back with their son. Rather than go home, he had Jack drop him off at the school, where he intended to decompress by doing a little work in his office. He needed time to think, and tending to school business after hours relaxed him and helped clear his mind. At home, he would only stress out about the car, come up with zero ideas to solve the problem and grow ever more frustrated.

Already, walking from the parking lot to the administration building, he was thinking about the lawsuit he would bring against the bank and wondering whether his car insurance would cover such an expense or whether he might even be able to get the school district involved. Striding around the side of the building to the quad, where the entrance was located, Dennis was confronted with large block letters spraypainted in black over the rows of lockers that lined the 100 and 200 buildings:

NO IMIGRANTS
MEXIKINS GO HOME
WHITE POWER

Swiveling his head to survey the school's central courtyard, looking for more vandalism, he discovered other spraypainted messages in less obvious locations. On the wall by the band room: IF IT AINT WHITE IT AINT RITE. Upstairs on the wall of the 300 building between English classes: IF YUR BROWN YUR GOING DOWN. On the cement in the center of the quad: REPELL ALL INVADERS.

The graffiti shocked him, not just for the racist sentiments expressed, but for the fact that it was there at all. Montgomery High was not immune to petty vandalism. Declarations of love, drawings of penises, and vulgar epithets aimed at teachers were all over the locker rooms and bathroom walls. But they were invariably scrawled in Sharpie and individually inscribed. He'd never encountered such a large scale defacing of school property.

The grammatical mistakes were perhaps the only things that were not surprising. It was about what he'd expect from a student holding such views.

Although…he wasn't entirely convinced it *was* a student. Or even a group of students. It was more likely, he thought, that an adult, maybe one of Chet Yates' listeners, had been pissed off by some imagined offense—his daughter dating someone Hispanic or his boy beaten out for varsity football by someone with brown skin—and had drunkenly stopped by the school last night and spraypainted his hate all over the campus.

Luckily, it was the weekend. It might be Sunday, but he could still call 911, let the law see what had happened, then call Raul the custodian and have it all cleaned up and painted over before school started tomorrow.

Dennis walked down the two steps from the walkway to the entrance of the administration building. Taking out his key, he unlocked and opened the door, quickly tapped the code for the alarm on the pad mounted on the wall to his right, and was about to switch on the lights, when he saw a yellow beam slashing across the floor in the center of the darkened hallway ahead.

The light, he noted instantly, was coming from open doorway of the new financial adviser's office, and staring through the darkness at that illuminated beam made the hairs on Dennis' arms prickle.

"Hello?" he called.

"In here!"

He hadn't expected a reply, but he wasn't surprised when he got one. Although he'd been hoping someone had just forgotten to turn off the light in the office, a part of him had known the adviser would be there.

How was that possible, though? The alarm had been on. Movement would have set it off. Had the man been sitting completely still at his desk since…Friday?

The goosebumps intensified.

Dennis could easily imagine that scenario, and he quickly flipped on the set of lights that illuminated the open area behind the front counter where the secretaries and registrar had their desks, before walking slowly toward the hallway.

"Didn't know you'd be working on the weekend," he called ahead, trying to retain some sense of normalcy.

There was no answer.

He reached the hallway, turned on the lights in the corridor. "Did you see all that vandalism out there? I'm calling the sheriff. We need to catch whoever did it."

No response.

He was the principal, in charge of this school and, technically, the financial adviser's superior. But since the first day the adviser had appeared on campus, that had not been the dynamic of their interpersonal interactions. The man had blatantly ignored the few rules Dennis had laid down and had exhibited nothing but disrespect toward him personally. For his part, Dennis was intimidated by the adviser's aggressive self-assurance.

He didn't like the idea of the two of them being alone in here without the vice principal, counselors, secretaries and student aides who were usually around during school hours, and the silence was definitely starting to creep him out, but before continuing on to his own office at the end of the hall to call 911 about the vandalism, he made an obligatory stop to see the financial adviser.

Where three black spray cans were sitting atop the man's desk.

Anger coursed through him. He stepped forward, into the small room, confronting the adviser. "Did you graffiti my walls?"

"What are you talking about? I found these at the scene and picked them up." The adviser met his gaze. "Why would I vandalize the school?"

"Did you call the sheriff?"

"I was about to call you."

"Oh, so you just found them?"

The financial adviser smirked. "Look, I was just trying to help. But if you don't want my help..." He shrugged. "Here, take them. They're all yours." He waved a hand in the direction of the spray cans.

And Dennis saw a black spot of smeared paint on his index finger. He *had* done it.

Their eyes locked. The other man knew that he knew, but he knew as well that Dennis did not dare confront him any further. He'd *wanted* him to know. The adviser smiled. "I have a lot of savings accounts to go over here. Do you think you could get out of my office and find something else to do?"

Dennis left without speaking. He had something else to do, all right. He was going to call the sheriff, show him those cans and have that creep arrested. He strode into his office, flipped on the light, picked up his phone and dialed 911.

The financial adviser popped his head in the doorway. "You know what, boss? I'm calling it a day. See you tomorrow." He lifted a hand in farewell. Hanging from the hand was a brown plastic grocery bag, and from within the bag Dennis heard the clanking of spray cans.

He should have ordered the man to stop right there, but he didn't, and just at that second, a dispatcher answered his call on the second ring. "Nine-one-one. What's your emergency?"

Chuckling, the financial adviser walked up the hallway toward the front door of the building as Dennis responded, "This is Principal Whittaker at Montgomery High School..."

FIFTEEN

1

"**H**OW ARE THINGS?**" Carol asked sympathetically.

Brad shrugged. He felt like shit and knew he looked like it, too.

"Don't worry. The girls'll be fine. My Jeremy's in daycare, and he loves it."

"It's not even really daycare anyway," Hank said to the sheriff, overhearing. "It's just an afterschool program."

Brad nodded. He didn't want to talk about it and wished people wouldn't keep bringing it up. "Where are we on the Jasper Brooks thing?" he asked, changing the subject.

"Still nothing but the weapon and his confession," Hank said. "But that should be more than enough. His prints are all over that thing, and the M.E. says it's a match. I don't think we have to worry."

Brad wasn't worried about any future trial. He was worried about finding the truth. And the lack of corroborating evidence did not sit well with him. In the back of his mind was the same fear he had about Leroy Fritz, that both men were patsies, that they had been set up to take the fall for murders they had not committed. The only arrest he was sure they'd gotten right was the Clark kid. That little psycho had definitely killed his parents. There was no doubt in his mind about that.

Thank God the judge in Globe had denied Victor Clark bail, because The First People's Bank, for some reason, was paying for his defense. Clark had been only a part-time employee, and had been working for the bank for only a week or so. It was a mystery why they would offer to fund his defense.

Of course, why had Worthington tried to shield the boy in the first place?

Brad was still trying to work out a way to charge the banker as an accessory, although both times he'd discussed it with the deputies who'd been on scene, they'd been unable to point to a statement or action that would qualify under statute as unlawful. The bastard had been careful, and he obviously knew his stuff. Any attempt to collar him without cause would be considered harassment. Brad had no doubt that the bank would have high-priced lawyers come after the department full throttle if they didn't have an airtight case.

He suddenly wondered whether First People's would be footing the bill for Jasper's and Leroy Fritz's defense teams, too.

It didn't seem out of the realm of possibility.

Carol handed him a stack of printouts. "Foreclosure evictions," she said softly. "Twelve new ones."

"Put 'em in the pile," he told her.

"You're still not going to enforce them?"

He shook his head.

Carol and Hank exchanged a look.

"What is it now?" Brad asked tiredly.

"Chet Yates is riling up his army. I heard him last night, and he said that you singled out his brother. Carl's the only one you enforced, and you did it to get rid of him."

Brad turned to his deputy. "Why do you listen to that shit?"

Hank shrugged his bony shoulders. "Nothing else on."

"Goddamn it."

"All I'm saying is, we should keep our eyes open. There's a mood out there."

Brad nodded. "Heard."

Hank and Carol exchanged another look.

"Okay, spit it out. I'm not playing Twenty Questions with you two."

"Bill G. didn't show up for his shift this morning." Carol's voice was unusually subdued.

Brad frowned. "Maybe he's sick."

"He didn't call in."

"Could be a family emergency."

Hank cleared his throat. "I heard him talking to Norris the other day, complaining about his shift schedule, the way he always does. Only this time he said that he was thinking about applying for a job at the bank, said they were offering him service credit for his years here and would start him at the same salary with the same benefits."

Brad's jaw tightened. "Get him on the phone," he ordered Carol.

"I've been trying to reach him for the past half-hour."

"Where's Norris?"

"He's off, but I could call him."

"Call him." Before she could pick up the receiver, he asked. "Is everyone else in? I haven't had time to look at the assignment board yet."

"So far as I know."

"I'll check," Hank offered, hurrying off.

Behind them, the front door of the station opened, and a pleasant-looking man in a dark blue suit strode confidently toward the front counter. Brad did not recognize him, but he had the air of a banker, and that made Brad immediately suspicious. He stepped forward. "Can I help you?"

The man smiled. "Are you asking if you *can* help me or if you *may* help me? Do you want to know whether you have the *ability* to offer me assistance, or whether I am giving you *permission* to assist me?"

"Either one," Brad said shortly.

The man chuckled. "I'm just *funnin'* with you." The slang term sounded sarcastic and condescending coming from his mouth, particularly with the intentionally dropped *g*. "My name's Julius Pickering, and I'm with The First People's Bank. I'm here as part of a community outreach program the bank has instituted. We don't want to be merely a depository for people's savings or a lender to which individuals are beholden; our goal is to integrate ourselves with the citizens of Montgomery and truly become a part of the town. To this end, we are sponsoring a Pop Warner football team and a Little League baseball team. We are providing defibrillators to the fire department and are prepared to generously offer you here at the sheriff's department a bulletproof vest for every officer." He favored them with a smug smile and stood as though waiting to be thanked.

The last thing Brad wanted was to accept anything from the bank, but the truth was that bulletproof vests would be very welcome. "We work for the county," he said. "You would have to contact county government in Globe about any donations to the department."

"Then that we will do." The banker tipped an imaginary hat, then turned to leave.

"And I would appreciate it if you told your bosses to stop trying to poach my men," Brad said.

The man stopped, looked back. "The First People's Bank has done no such thing. We merely offer opportunity to people, and those who are dissatisfied with their current circumstances often take advantage of that opportunity." Smiling, he nodded and walked out the door.

"Prick," Brad muttered.

"They could never hire me away." Carol shivered. "That place scares me."

"Yet after everything that's gone on, Bill G. defects?"

"Maybe," Carol reminded him. "We don't know for sure yet."

"We know."

The phone at Carol's desk rang, and she picked it up. "Montgomery Sheriff's Department, Sheriff Neth's office." There was a pause. "Just a minute." She put the caller on hold. "It's Nash Weems," she told Brad. "He wants to talk to you. He sounds angry."

Brad sighed. "Who isn't these days? I'll take it in my office." He walked back to his desk and picked up the phone. "Nash?"

"What the hell, Brad?"

Conversations with the gun shop owner almost always started out this way. "What can I do for you, Nash?"

"You can tell me how the town approved three more gun shops—*three*!—all of a sudden, without any notice, when it took me months to get an approval, and I had to do everything but sign over my first-born. Remember, I had that one location but the town said it was too close to the high school, so I had to move halfway across town? Guess what? One of these new guys is right there in my old spot by the high school. I mean, what the hell?"

"I have nothing to do with business licenses. You know that. I don't even work for the town. I'm county."

"But you work *with* the town, and I assume they keep you up on what's going on, right?"

"I know nothing about this, Nash. Your call is the first I've heard about it. But it is a free country. I understand that you're not happy with the competition, but—"

"They're selling military assault weapons."

That brought him up short. Certainly there were people in town who owned assault rifles and military grade weapons. But, if so, they'd purchased them elsewhere. Nash might have a bigger selection than Wal-Mart or the average sporting goods store, but he still stocked primarily handguns and hunting rifles, ordinary guns for ordinary people. Brad did not like the idea that more serious weaponry might now be easily available in Montgomery.

"Can I also assume," Nash said, "that you're not aware of the new bullet factory out by the airport?"

"No," Brad said. "I'm not."

"Well, then. I was approached the other day by a guy I'd never seen before trying to sell me local made bullets. Said he was new in town and set up shop in that old quonset hut on the south side of the airport. I guess it's not really a factory; I think it's just him and a bullet-making machine. Anyway, I told him I only sell from reputable manufacturers, but there's no guarantee he won't sell to those new stores. Or directly to individuals, people supposed to be my customers. And there's no guarantee that his bullets won't explode or not work or...who knows what. It's not as if there's quality control inspections."

Brad was frowning. "Let me look into it," he said.

"That's all I'm asking."

"I can't promise anything. This could all be on the up and up."

"I understand."

"But I'll see what I can find."

"You know, if the town's giving them preferential treatment when I had to stick to the letter of the law, I'm going to sue."

"That's between you and the town, Nash. I work for the county. I told you."

"Yeah, well…"

Brad told Nash goodbye and hung up. Looking out his window onto the parking lot, he wondered why, all of a sudden, three new gun shops and a bullet manufacturer were coming to Montgomery. That was an awful lot for a town this size, and he had a hard time believing the community could support so many. And while he had absolutely no basis for thinking so, he couldn't help wondering if this had anything to do with The First People's Bank.

Suddenly the offer for bulletproof vests didn't seem so benignly altruistic.

It seemed more like a warning of things to come.

Brad pushed the thought aside. He was just being paranoid, he told himself.

And he tried to believe it.

THE afterschool program only held kids until six, and Brad was there to pick up his daughters at five fifty-five. They were quiet and subdued, as they had been since Patty had moved in with her fake family.

That had been unexpected. As crazy as the situation had been, his assumption had been that it would be resolved in a normal way. Which meant that she would throw away those dummies, stop going to that house and act like a responsible adult. They would talk things out. Maybe she would start seeing a psychiatrist or get medication, maybe they would separate as they worked through issues, but those details would be determined in a rational manner.

Instead, she had come home, taken some clothes and her laptop, told him privately that she'd decided to live with her "new family" and had left him to explain it to the girls. In the days since, he had called her sister and parents in Texas, but she'd made no effort to contact them, and they were even more in the dark than he was. As far as he could tell from his not-so-subtle efforts to keep track of her, she was still showing up at the real estate office, still doing her job, and though she never answered her phone when he called, he had a feeling that was simply because she chose not to pick up when she saw his number. He'd confided in no one else other than her family, had given the people at work only the barest outlines of what was going on, and was keeping the girls in a cocoon spun from half-truths and omissions.

Jillian and Sue got in the front seat of the car.

"So what should we have for dinner tonight?" he asked, feigning a positivity he did not feel.

"Is Mommy coming home?" Sue inquired.

"Probably not," he told her. "But I'll try to call her and find out."

The girls suddenly perked up.

"Can we talk to her?" Jillian asked.

"Sure, if she's not too busy."

Jillian slumped back down in her seat. "That's a no."

He didn't know how to respond to that. She was right, but he wanted both of them to maintain as much of their optimism as possible. They were going to need it.

He looked over at his daughters. "What did you do in school today?"

"We had an active shooter drill," Jillian said.

"*What?*"

"We had to sit quietly in our classroom under our desks while the teacher locked the door."

He had heard nothing about this. While he supposed the school had the right to conduct its own drills, with something so potentially frightening to kids, the administration should have given parents a heads up so they could talk to their children about it.

More importantly, as the town's chief law enforcement officer, he should have been informed, because in any real world scenario, he would be calling the shots during the response, and if he and his team were to operate effectively, they would need to know the school's protocols.

"It only lasted about five minutes."

He nodded, not wanting them to see how upset he was. Tomorrow, he was going to have to have a little talk with the school's principal and straighten her out. To put the fear of God in her, he'd fill her in on Nash Weems' news that gun shops and bullet companies were popping up all over town and let her know that the prospect of an active shooter probably wasn't as remote as the district might think it was.

"So what else did you do?" He addressed Sue. "Did you go over that math homework in class?"

"Yes. And a man from the bank came and talked about saving money."

The bank.

Brad felt cold.

"Really?" he said, keeping his voice calm and composed.

"Yes! And he used me as an example!"

His interior alarm went off. "An example?"

"Uh huh. He said if I kept putting pennies and nickels in my piggy bank, like I have been, I could bring it to the bank when it was full, and they'd keep my money there, and I could take it out whenever I wanted or even put more in!"

"How did he know you had a piggy bank?"

"He remembered me from when Shannon's mom took me over there and got it for me."

"He remembered you?"

"Yeah!"

Brad didn't like that, and he was about to warn both girls that he wanted them to stay as far away from the bank or anyone associated with the bank as possible, when Jillian suddenly said, "Macaroni and cheese!"

He frowned, confused. "Macaroni and cheese?"

"For dinner. You asked us what we wanted for dinner. Macaroni and cheese! Mommy made extra last time and put it in the freezer."

"Yeah!" Sue seconded. "And then Mommy'll have to make some more because it's all gone!"

"Mac-a-roe-nee!" they chanted in unison. "Mac-a-roe-nee! Mac-a-roe-nee! And cheese!"

"Okay," he agreed. "Macaroni and cheese it is."

They cheered.

"When you call Mommy, tell her we're all out," Jillian said.

"I will," he promised, and, turning onto their street, decided to talk to them about the bank some other time.

2

COY was eating breakfast when someone rang the bell and then knocked at his front door. Leaving the spoon in his bowl of Cheerios, he went out to see who it was. He couldn't think of anyone who would be dropping by to see him this early. The only possibility he could come up with was Florine, and after their previous encounter, the last thing he wanted was her turning up and making a scene in front of neighbors who might be leaving for work.

The knock came again, and he opened the door to see a kid standing on his porch.

The boy was wearing a dirty t-shirt with no sweater or jacket, though the weather was chilly. His hair was short and spiky, and there was a bratty look on his face. In his hand, he held an old-fashioned receipt book. "You owe me twenty dollars," he said.

Coy blinked. "What?"

"I'm your paperboy. I'm here to collect."

"I don't subscribe to the newspaper," Coy told him. "I just read a copy at work."

"I deliver it to you."

"I've never seen it."

"You still owe me twenty bucks."

"Look," Coy said, "I'll call the newspaper office and get this straightened out."

"You'll pay me the money you owe me."

"I don't owe you any money."

"Fine. Then we'll just deduct it from your salary." The kid closed his receipt book and smirked, saluting sarcastically. "Have a nice day, *sir.*"

Coy stood in place as the boy moved on to his next door neighbors, the Steinbergs. It was impolite, but instead of closing the door and going back to his breakfast, Coy stepped onto the porch to watch.

When the boy reached the Steinbergs' stoop, he kicked their front door as hard as he could several times. There was no waiting for a response; Frank Steinberg opened the door and yelled, "What do you think you're doing?"

The Steinbergs' house and his own were not *right* next to each other—there was half a yard and a driveway between them—but Coy could clearly see what was going on, and the morning was quiet enough that he had no trouble hearing.

The boy stared at Frank belligerently. "You owe me twenty bucks, bitch."

"What the—?"

"I deliver your newspaper. You owe me twenty bucks."

"I don't even *get* the newspaper!"

"You do now."

Frank slammed the door on him.

The kid went crazy, kicking on the door and pounding it with his fists, but Frank did not open it again. Coy smiled. The boy turned to him, clearly aware that he'd been watching. "Don't worry," the boy said. "We'll get him." And moved on to the next house.

Coy's smile faded. He went back inside.

His cereal in the bowl was soggy, but he finished it anyway, along with his cold cup of coffee. *We'll deduct it from your salary?* Where had the little urchin gotten a line like that? Obviously, he'd been coached, instructed to use that threat if someone refused to pay, which indicated to Coy that this extortion tour had been sanctioned.

By the paper? He found that hard to believe, but he looked up the phone number for the newspaper and called it.

"The First People's Montgomery Gazette," answered a pleasant-voiced woman.

The First People's...?

"What did you say?" He wasn't sure that he'd heard correctly.

The woman laughed lightly. "I know it doesn't exactly roll off the tongue."

"Did The First People's Bank—"

"Yes, they did, Mr. Stinson."

He frowned. How did she know who he was? He hadn't given his name. Even if she was looking at Caller ID, it would only show his number.

"We understand that you did not pay your paperboy the amount owed."

"That's why I'm calling. Because I don't owe anything. I don't subscribe to the Gazette."

"Everyone subscribes to the Gazette," she told him. "When The First People's Bank took over, they provided everyone in town with a subscription."

"A free subscription?"

"No, naturally, readers have to pay to receive the paper. It is a product, like everything else, and it does cost money to produce. But supporting print journalism in these troubled times is well worth the small subscription cost."

"Cancel my subscription," Coy said. "And I'm not paying money for a newspaper I never asked for in the first place and never even got."

The woman's voice hardened. "Then we will be forced to garnish your wages."

"Try it."

"As part of the extended First People's family, I'm sure you realize that we—"

He hung up on her.

Looking out the front window, he saw that the paperboy had moved to the other side of the street. The little punk was attacking the Wallaces' door, and Coy smiled, knowing that the couple was on vacation in California for a week. Served the brat right.

He went into the bedroom to get ready for work.

At the bank, the mood was somber. As it had been since Jimmy's death. The teller's murder had hit all of them hard. Ben was the only one who seemed unaffected, and try as he might, Coy could not forget the conversation he'd had with the manager immediately after First People's Bank had agreed to work with them.

"We had to give something up."

"What's that?"

"Jimmy."

The words seemed ominous now, and try as he might, he could come up with no interpretation other than the obvious one: Ben had known what was going to happen. For there was no doubt in Coy's mind that First People's was behind Jimmy's death, no matter what anyone might say.

"They wanted him."

The manager was not here today. It was a scheduled absence, a meeting of some sort, but each time the phone rang, a small part of Coy could not help thinking that it was the sheriff calling to tell them that *Ben's* body had been discovered crucified on the Bank of America building.

He spent the first hour of the day going over the paperwork of two loan applicants he had met with yesterday. Only one of them actually qualified for the loan he was seeking, but Montgomery Community's policy had shifted since its affiliation with The First People's Bank, and under the new formulations, the applicant who qualified was scheduled to be turned down, while the one who was almost guaranteed to default within the next six months was to emerge from the process with flying colors. This was a dangerous road, Coy knew. He had no idea how Ben and the board could go along with this, and if Montgomery Community had been in trouble before, it was doubly in jeopardy now. First People's might be backing them up, but there was no way the bank could remain anywhere close to solvent if it continued on this way.

His phone rang, and Coy picked it up.

It was Ben.

"I need you to do something for me," the manager said without preamble. "Go into my office and see if you can find a…" There was a muffled exchange, as though he'd put his hand over the phone and was talking to someone else. "…See if there's a book, a ledger, anywhere on my desk. It'll be old looking, maybe beat up, I don't know. But see if it's there or not and call me back." He gave Coy a number then immediately hung up.

That was weird.

Exiting the screen he was on, Coy stood and walked past Cal and Maggie's desks, past the lone customer at the middle teller window, and into Ben's office. He had not been inside here since the day the agreement with First People's had been announced.

"We had to give something up."

There'd been a change in the office that day. It had seemed newer, cleaner, brighter. But there'd been another change since. The room Coy entered now was not the freshly refurbished space he'd seen last but a dark, oppressive chamber more appropriate to a deteriorating mansion than a bank. The lights, tied to a motion detector, had turned on automatically when he entered, but the recessed bars gave off a sickly yellowish glow rather than the clean white fluorescence found in the rest of the building.

He walked toward the manager's desk, which had seemed sleekly modern the last time he'd been in the room but now looked heavy, old and far too bulky. On top of the desk, facing outward, was a framed photo of a naked Florine, her legs spread wide. It was a different picture than the one in Pickering's office, and it complemented the rest of the room, because the Florine depicted was not the one he had dated but the woman he'd last seen: sickly, pale, blotchy. She was smiling, showing several missing teeth.

The sight of her depressed him.

And frightened him.

Coy didn't want to be in here any longer than necessary, and he quickly walked around to the other side of Ben's desk. He expected to have to search for the book the manager had asked him to locate, maybe dig through some drawers or look under papers, but there it was in the center of the desk, a dusty leatherbound ledger that resembled a register of accounts that might have been found in Ebenezer Scrooge's office. Opening it, he saw on the first page, in faded calligraphic script: *The First People's Bank.* Flipping to a page at random, he saw "1936" underlined at the top. Columns below that were headlined "Men," "Women," and "Children," with numbers in each column that varied by months noted on the left side of the sheet. He turned to another page, and another, and saw exactly the same thing.

1941...1945...1953...

Coy picked up the phone on the manager's desk and dialed the number he had been given. Ben answered, but it sounded as though he were on speakerphone. "Hello?"

"I found it," Coy said.

The manager cried out in pain. His voice when he spoke was higher and more stressed. He was speaking quickly. "It can't be there! Are you sure?"

"It's right on your desk."

"You lied to us," someone said in the background. The accent sounded British.

"I told you." Coy recognized Pickering's voice.

"That's impossible," Ben shouted. "I didn't—" He screamed in agony, and the connection was cut. There was only a loud dial tone.

Startled and alarmed, Coy put down the phone. Before he could pick it up again to dial 911, it rang. Answering, he heard Pickering's threatening voice. "Don't even think about it."

Again, the connection was severed.

He stood there stupidly, phone in hand. Would he be putting Ben in even greater jeopardy if he called the sheriff? There was no doubt in his mind that that was exactly what Pickering was implying would happen, but Coy wasn't sure he could live with himself if something actually happened to the manager—

if he was killed

—because he did nothing.

Coy looked down at the ledger. What *was* that thing? And what was its significance? It seemed to be the impetus for whatever was going on at the other end of that telephone line, and his first impulse was to take it immediately over to the sheriff's office and describe exactly what he'd heard. But then he thought about Pickering's warning—

Don't even think about it

—and what had happened to Jimmy, and realized that he was way out of his depth.

He put the phone down. Whatever had happened to Ben had happened. If it turned out that he was dead, or if he didn't come back by tomorrow, Coy would go to the sheriff with what he knew. If it turned out to be something less, he would confront Ben and demand that the manager tell him what was going on. Either way, he was pretty sure he was through here. He couldn't see himself continuing to work in this bank, in this environment. Not with everything that had happened.

He thought for a moment, then left the ledger in place and walked out of the manager's office, over to Cal and Maggie's adjoining desks. "We need to talk," he said.

3

WHEN Jen awoke, she was back in the house.

She and Lane had gone to bed early after what had been a long day for both of them, falling asleep to a rerun of *The Office* on the bedroom TV. That had been in their apartment. But when she woke up, it was still night, and she was lying on the floor of the empty bedroom in the house they had bought and abandoned.

There was a low insistent tapping on the other side of the wall.

She bolted upright. Moonlight shone through the sheer curtains. Lane was nowhere to be seen, and her first impulse was to call out his name, but the tapping in The Room and the silence in the rest of the house motivated her to remain quiet.

How had she gotten here?

She had no idea, but she was terrified and wanted only to escape. Some sort of supernatural force had brought her back, though for what reason she could not conceive. On the wall in front of her, where the tapping came from, she saw a shadow, a shadow that undulated as though it were underwater. She stared, trying to make sense of it, but its shape confused her. There were three arms, and a giraffe-like neck topped by a giant head with jagged crown, all emerging from an ordinary man's body. To her mind, it resembled some sort of primitive deity with its amalgamation of human and animal characteristics, but, again, it was a shadow, and she glanced around the darkened room trying to locate a figure that it could be the shadow *of*.

Nothing.

It corresponded to nothing that she could see, almost as though it were its own separate entity, and that made its undulating movement seem suddenly more sinister.

She needed to get out of here. She wanted nothing to do with the house, especially not The Room, and she jumped to her feet and dashed out of the bedroom before whoever—*whatever*—had brought her here discovered that she was awake. She was in her pajamas, but she didn't care, and she ran down the hall, through the living room and out the front door.

Outside, all of the houses on the street were for sale, and identical signs posted in each yard, visible by moonlight and streetlamp, were for The First People's Bank Realty. In the driveway, her Accord was in the process of being towed, and painted on the side of the tow truck in blue letters was: *The First People's Bank Repossession Company*. Through the cab window of the truck, Jen saw a driver with a very long neck whose spiky-topped head seemed far too big for his undersized body.

Then she really woke up, it was morning, and she was in her bed in her apartment and Lane was snoring next to her. Heart still pounding from the events in the dream, Jen awoke with a huge sense of relief, but the uneasiness engendered by the nightmare stayed with her as she got out of bed and went to the bathroom. Usually, she could tell she was dreaming even when she was in the dream—a byproduct of dealing with night terrors as a child—but this had seemed utterly real, and she could still feel the coolness of air on her face from running outside to get away from the house.

The house.

Jen was pretty sure she knew why she'd dreamt about it. Although they'd found people to rent the home, the tenants had told them yesterday that they were out at the end of the month. After only a week. It wasn't that the rent was too high, they'd been assured when they tried to bargain with the tenants.

It was The Room.

She and Lane had said nothing, but they'd understood completely. It was why they themselves had left.

What was *in* that room?

She wished she'd never laid eyes on the place, wished Evangeline had never shown it to them. She still resented the way the real estate agent and the banker had bulldozed her and Lane into buying the house, and she resented the way Lane had made that initial decision for both of them. She had never felt comfortable about the sale, had wanted, had *needed*, more time to think, and she couldn't help focusing on how things would have turned out differently if she had put her foot down.

Jen finished in the bathroom, then woke Lane up before going into the kitchen to make breakfast. Through the thin kitchen wall, she could hear the rush of water in their neighbor's shower next door, but experiencing ordinary sounds this way was reassuring, and she thought for the first time that maybe she preferred to live in an apartment rather than a house after all.

There was a thump against the front door, and Jen popped out to pick up the newspaper that had been thrown. It was being delivered each morning, though they were not subscribers, and she supposed that she should call the newspaper office and let them know, but the truth was that she'd been putting off informing them because she enjoyed reading the paper with her breakfast. Rolling off the rubber band and opening it up, she was surprised to see that the name of the newspaper had changed. Surprised and disconcerted.

The First People's Montgomery Gazette

After the nightmare she'd had, the bold masthead seemed to purposely challenge her, and she folded the paper back up and put it down on Lane's side of the breakfast table. She *would* call and let the *Gazette* office know that the newspaper was being wrongly delivered to their apartment when they weren't subscribers.

Lane came out, poured himself some coffee, sat down and unfolded the newspaper, glancing at the top headline. He frowned. "Did you see this?" he asked her.

"What?"

"It says home foreclosures in Montgomery are at a record high, that according to the county assessor, more houses were foreclosed on in Montgomery over the past month than in all of the rest of the county combined." He threw the paper down. "I guess we're in our own mini-recession. Which means we can kiss the thought of getting out from under this goodbye."

Jen thought of her dream.

"Our choices seem to be: walk away and probably permanently destroy our credit; sell at a loss and keep paying the rest of the loan for a house we don't have, or try to find new renters and wait it out until things turn around."

"So we wait it out," Jen said.

He nodded wearily.

She hadn't been by the house since they'd moved out, and it was not exactly on her way to work, but she couldn't get the image of all of those neighborhood For Sale signs out of her mind, and she decided to drive by on her way to the optometrist's office.

Three of the houses *were* for sale, it turned out, but what shocked her was the condition of some of the others. In the few weeks since she'd been here, what had been a nice street lined with modest but well-maintained homes had deteriorated into a slum. In that short amount of time, somehow, weeds had overgrown yards, broken cars and motorcycles had proliferated, and there was even a house with a boarded-up front window. The entire tenor of the neighborhood had changed, and she realized that, irrespective of the town's foreclosure rate, they were going to have to lower the rent if they hoped to lure any new tenants.

Their house was one of the nicer ones on the block, but she still shivered as she passed by. Although their renters had paid through the end of the month, and she and Lane had assumed they would stay until then, it appeared that the family had already moved out.

Which meant that whatever was in The Room was all alone.

There was no one around to hear it tapping on the walls.

Jen accelerated, grateful when she finally passed the end of the block. Slowing the car, she became aware that she'd been gripping the steering wheel far too tightly. Relaxing a little, she glanced in her rearview mirror to see an overweight man run across the street from one yard to another wearing only his underwear.

Had he run into *their* yard?

The placement seemed about right, but Jen wasn't about to backtrack and find out. She wasn't going anywhere near that neighborhood again without Lane by her side, and she sped up until she reached the highway and was able to merge with the light morning work traffic.

Anita was sitting in her car when Jen arrived, and she got out and stood waiting while Jen parked in the space next to her. Jen assumed at first that her friend had delayed going in because it was still early and she didn't want to be alone with Dr. Wilson, who was not the most approachable person even under the best of circumstances. But neither the optometrist's Mercedes nor the rental car he'd been driving for the past few weeks were in the small lot on the side of the office, and when Jen got out of her Accord, Anita said to her, "He's not here yet."

She closed the car door and locked it. "Didn't you bring your key?"

"Of course. And I tried to get in, but he changed the lock."

That was a surprise. "When did this happen?"

"I have no idea. He doesn't tell me anything. When's the last time you used your key?"

"It's been awhile," Jen admitted.

"So do you want to call him or do you want to flip for it? Because I sure don't want to."

"I don't either."

"We flip, then."

Jen opened her purse, looking for a coin, but Anita pulled out a quarter before she could find anything. "Call it in the air."

She tossed the coin, and Jen called out, "Heads!"

"Damn," Anita said, picking her quarter off the ground. "Okay. I'll call him."

Jen was pretty sure neither of them had ever tried calling the optometrist anywhere except the office, but they both had his cell number in case of emergency. Anita put her phone on speaker so they could both hear, and after five rings it went to an automated voicemail. She looked like she was about to leave a message, but at the last second, she ended the call instead. "I didn't know what to say," she admitted.

"I wouldn't either. 'Where are you?' 'Why are you late?' I don't think he'd respond well to anything like that."

"Should we go to his house? Maybe he overslept."

"Either that, or we could wait here in the parking lot."

"You're right. Maybe we *should* wait," Anita said. "Because if he shows up and we aren't here..." She didn't have to finish the sentence.

They were both dancing around the real worry. Because the truth was that Dr. Wilson had *never* been this late. And he had been acting strange lately.

Jen broached the subject. "Maybe we should call the sheriff..." She paused. "In case something happened to him."

These days, that was not a suggestion out of left field.

"Let's just wait. Give it..." Anita looked at her watch. "Ten minutes. After that, we'll see."

Jen nodded.

"Maybe you should try your key," she suggested. "Just in case."

If they could get in, it would be better than sitting in their cars or just standing outside, so Jen walked up to the side entrance to try her key. It didn't fit...but the door opened anyway. She was leaning her shoulder on it as she attempted to work the key into the hole, and apparently it had not been properly latched, because it moved inward, causing her to jump back.

She and Anita looked at each other.

"Not a good sign," Anita said softly.

Inside, some lights were on while others were off, their status seemingly chosen at random. The waiting room was dark, while their work area behind the counter was well-lit. The wall display of various frame styles was not illuminated, but lights were on in both exam rooms. Dr. Wilson's office was dark.

"Hello!" Anita called out.

There was no response. All was silent.

The two of them looked at each other. "What do you think we should do?" Jen asked. "Do you think someone broke in? Should we call the sheriff?"

"I don't know. Is anyone here?" Anita shouted.

Again, no response.

Anita walked forward.

"I'm not sure we should do this," Jen said, following. "Someone could be hiding out there in the waiting room or—"

They reached the first exam room. Inside, on the chair, Dr. Wilson was leaning back. His eyes had been gouged out, and his face, clothes and the chair were covered with blood. In a crimson puddle on the floor beneath his dangling right arm was a metal instrument resembling an ice pick, and, next to that, what had been one of his eyes, with muscles, veins and ganglia still attached. The other eye was nowhere to be seen, although there was a butchered mass of tissue lying atop the optometrist's slanted chest.

Jen cried out the second she saw the gruesome sight. Anita gagged loudly but immediately had the presence of mind to rush over to the counter and pick up the phone. Jen, too, hurried away from the scene and caught her breath, trying to decide whether she thought Dr. Wilson had been murdered or had committed suicide.

Was he even dead?

She didn't know. Neither of them had bothered to check. While he looked dead, it was possible that he was still alive, barely clinging to life, and though she didn't want to, she moved back toward the exam room. Anita was talking on the phone to a dispatcher or paramedics, and it was reassuring to hear her friend's voice as she re-entered the room.

Dr. Wilson was unmoving, and all of the visible blood appeared to have coagulated. *Didn't that mean he was dead?* She saw no spurting, no fresh flowing, and when she tried to focus on his face, neck and hands—the areas with visible skin—she saw no sign of muscle movement. She'd intended to check for a pulse, but realized that she wasn't brave enough to hold his wrist or place her hand on his neck.

He *had* to be dead.

Besides, what could she do if he wasn't? Her minimal CPR skills were rusty, and his injuries might be so extensive that it could do more harm than good if she moved him.

In her mind, Jen saw him suddenly jerking upright, the way a seemingly lifeless body would in a movie, and the thought made her hurry out of the exam room and back to where Anita was just getting off the phone.

"Someone'll be here in a minute," Anita said.

They exited the building the way they'd entered, opting to wait outside for the emergency responders.

"Why do you think he did it?" Anita asked.

"*Do* you think he did it?" Jen responded.

They were both speaking quietly, even though they were outside.

Anita nodded. "It doesn't look like foul play to me. It looks... self-inflicted. Besides, they say that financial problems are the leading cause of suicide. I mean, he didn't say anything, but that situation with the car? It seems to me like he was having money troubles."

Jen shook her head. "I don't know. He didn't seem like the kind of guy who'd do something like that."

"Too arrogant?"

"Well...yeah."

"You never can tell," Anita said.

They were both silent after that, waiting.

4

KYLE rifled through the stack of records in the box before him. There was a lot of good stuff in there. He flipped past a complete collection of Joni Mitchell, idly reflecting on the weird vanity of her 1970s album covers, where she'd posed as a sort of buck-toothed sex symbol—naked on *For the Roses*, in a bikini on *The Hissing of Summer Lawns*, faux Faye Dunaway chic on *Hejira*.

"I'm sorry," he said, looking up. "I'd like to buy these, but Brave New World only sells books. Originally, I thought about selling music too, but I don't really have the space for it, and to be honest I'm not sure there's that much of a market for records and CDs in Montgomery."

The man pulled his box back. "That's okay. Rollie Brown over at Amazing Stories said he'd buy them. I just stopped in to see if you'd give me more." He lifted the box off the counter. "I guess not."

"Rollie's store's already open?"

"Yep."

"And he's calling it Amazing Stories?"

"Your store's named after a science fiction book. His is named after a science fiction magazine. What's the dif?" The man started for the door.

"I just thought he might be more original. Especially since his taste is mostly suspense and thrillers."

"Yeah? Well, at least he pays." The man walked out.

Kyle watched him leave, once again wondering how long he'd be able to stay in business. The outlook had been bleak even *without* competition. Rollie's opening probably sounded his death knell.

Maybe they should leave Montgomery. The thought had never occurred to him before—this was their home—but perhaps the time had come to consider it. They had no other family here. Anita was going to be unemployed, and unless Wal-Mart's optometry department suddenly needed an extra assistant, it was going to be difficult for her to find a job. Nick was in the middle of high school, but he had no girlfriend, his best friend was in jail and his other friend was missing, so it wouldn't be much of a hardship for him to relocate.

The idea of getting a fresh start someplace else was definitely appealing. He knew this town, he liked the people in it (for the most part), he loved this area, but things had changed since the bank had moved in next door. And he wasn't sure they would ever return to the way they had been.

An actual customer walked in, an older gentleman with an anachronistic handlebar mustache. Kyle had never seen him before, but the man seemed to know what he wanted, and after a quick look around the shop to orient himself, he walked over to the nonfiction section, pulling several books off the shelves and bringing them over to the front counter. They were all art books and all somewhat pricey. It was Kyle's first sale in three days, and while it was definitely nice to have money coming in, it brought home to him even more how unsustainable his financial situation was.

Soon after, Trixie stopped by. "Hey," he said. "How's Trix?"

"I saw a customer walk past my window. With books in hand!"

Kyle chuckled. "Yes. An honest-to-God customer. It's been awhile since I've had one of those."

"Tell me about it."

"So what's that?" he asked, pointing. In her hand, she was holding a clipboard.

She placed it on the counter in front of him. "A petition. Our downtown association—which you are a part of, even if you didn't show for our meeting," she chided. "—was hoping you'd sign it."

"What's it for?" He picked up the clipboard, reading the text at the top of the attached page. His would be only the second signature after her own.

"It's a protest against The First People's Bank. It requests that the town council approve the establishment of a municipal bank."

"A municipal bank?"

"Oh, yeah. Take them straight on."

"What exactly is a municipal bank?"

"It's like a publicly owned utility, except it's a publicly owned bank. Instead of some big private company being in charge, it's a municipality. A state, county, city, whatever."

"So Montgomery would open its own bank to compete with First People's?"

"And, ideally, retroactively withdraw its approval for The First People's Bank. All three of them."

"Who's this Coy Stinson?" Kyle asked, still going over the text.

"He works at Montgomery Community. He's helping us with this." She shook her head. "What am I saying? Helping us? He thought of it. We're going to have him present it to the council in case they ask any technical questions."

Kyle picked up a pen from the counter. "Well, I'm in," he said, signing. "You want me to hit up Nancy, for you?"

"Oh, we're best buddies now. You missed a lot by not showing up."

He laughed. "I get the hint."

"Seriously," she said. "We could've used you. Everyone's united against the bank, but there are a lot of...personalities, let's say. You could definitely help keep things on track when we get together."

"I would've been there, but that was the day Dr. Wilson—"

"I know," she said, "and I understand completely. I'm just saying that, going forward, we need you."

"I'm there," he promised.

Trixie brightened. "Good!" She took back her clipboard and petition. "I'm off to get more signatures."

"Good luck."

There were no more customers for the rest of the morning, although a parade of lowlifes passed by his window on their way to the bank, many of them eyeing him disdainfully. He ate his lunch at the counter, alone and in silence.

At three o'clock, he picked up Nick from school. There weren't as many parents as usual waiting in the lot. There weren't quite as many kids exiting the school, either. Nick walked by himself through a sparse crowd up to the truck. He was subdued as they drove away, and when Kyle asked what was wrong, his son just shook his head.

"What is it?" Kyle prodded.

"I don't know. Nothing."

"It's not nothing."

"Just a feeling, I guess."

"What kind of feeling?"

"I don't know. Like something's off, I guess. Or something's wrong. Or something might...happen."

"Happen?" Kyle said. "Like what?"

Nick shrugged.

Back at the bookstore, things were not quiet. As soon as he opened the door and walked in, Kyle heard the tapping. His son heard it, too, and the two of them looked at each other.

"What do you think it is?" Nick asked.

Kyle shook his head. "I have no idea. I've never been able to figure it out." He walked over to the spot from which the noise seemed to originate, and it was the same as before. Only this time, one of the bricks in the wall seemed to be protruding slightly more than the others. He tried to recall what in the bank was directly on the other side of the wall from where they were standing, but couldn't quite remember.

Hadn't it been an empty section of wall? Between a water cooler and an unoccupied desk?

On impulse, he walked out the front of the store and peeked in the window of the bank. It was hard to see with the late afternoon sun reflecting off the glass, so he cupped his hands on the sides of his eyes and pressed his face against the window. Desk...desk...potted plant...water cooler...cabinet.

Cabinet?

He didn't remember that.

It was square and vaguely European. Antique looking. Like something a wealthy collector would have in his house. Above it was a framed photograph of...someone. He was pretty sure neither had been in place the last time he'd visited.

"Hey, you! Get away from there!"

He pulled away to see a security guard waving at him from in front of the bank's door.

"It's a public sidewalk," Kyle told him.

"And that window's private property."

"And my store is right here. And you're an asshole. So I guess we've covered just about everything." Kyle turned away and walked back into Brave New World. Why would a bank have a cabinet like that? he wondered. Just for decoration, probably. But the fact that it was located in the exact spot where the tapping seemed to originate caused him to think. It was definitely big enough to hide a person inside. That made no sense, though. Would someone sit all day in a box just to periodically knock on the wall?

Nothing about this tracked, and he conceded to himself that he was wasting time trying to find a logical explanation where none existed.

At home that night, he brought up the idea of moving to another city. Nick was immediately receptive, and Kyle couldn't remember the last time he'd seen his son grin so broadly. "Yes!" he said. "I vote for New York or L.A."

"We don't have the money for that. We may not have enough money to move at all. But if we did, it would probably be Mesa or Tempe, maybe Glendale or Peoria. Somewhere in the Phoenix area."

Anita was already shaking her head. "We can't afford to move. I don't think I even have a job anymore after...what happened."

"All the more reason," Kyle said. "It'll be a lot easier to find a job in a metropolitan area than it will here in Montgomery."

"This," Nick told them, "is rational behavior. You know how, in horror movies, someone's house is haunted, and they stay? Even though all they'd have to do to stop everything is just move out? That's what we need to do here. Dad's right."

"Who said anything about horror movies?" Kyle asked.

"Come on, Dad. We all know what we're talking about. And you're exactly right. We need to get out before the bank ends up killing *us*."

Kyle couldn't argue, because it was the thought in the back of all of their minds.

How is this possible? he wondered. *How could it have come to this?*

None of them had much to say after that, the three of them lost in their own private thoughts. But they stayed together in the living room for the rest of the night, something that hadn't happened since Nick hit puberty. And all three of them watched the same program on TV without complaining, an HBO movie, a comedic look at financial deregulation and how it had led to the great recession.

SIXTEEN

1

THEY WERE WAITING outside his house when he awoke shortly after noon. Chet had never given out his address over the airwaves, but he shouldn't have been surprised that his army had been able to track him down. It was impossible to remain completely anonymous in a town as small as Montgomery. And nothing was really private in this internet age.

His army.

They actually looked like an army, albeit a rather ragtag version. There were ten of them, dressed in fatigues, and though he had his doubts that any of them had actually served, all of the men standing in his driveway were armed with rifles and handguns. Seeing them through the window, he tried to recall if he had talked about anything on the show last night that would inspire this call to arms, but honestly couldn't remember.

Quickly, Chet dressed and walked outside.

The guy with the *Duck Dynasty* beard seemed to be the ringleader—Chet had since found out that his name was Melvin—and the man saluted, checking around to make sure the others were doing the same. "Reporting for duty!" he declared.

What duty that might be, Chet still did not know, but he nodded in approval.

Melvin stepped forward, taking out his phone. "We have a report here of a gang of illegals hanging out at the Lottaburger. Or what *used* to be the Lottaburger. Now it's that wetback chink place."

"Juan Wang's?"

"Yeah. We're heading over there to show 'em what's what, let 'em know this ain't no place for their kind. Maybe round 'em up if they don't have papers and drop'm off at the sheriff's station, show them how *real* law enforcement's supposed to work. After that, we're gonna patrol the town. Thought you might want to come along."

He'd actually been thinking about going to Juan Wang's to eat, but he wasn't about to let *that* be known, and he nodded. "Just give me a few minutes, and then we'll head out."

Melvin saluted. "Yes, sir!"

Chet closed the door behind him. He opened the entryway closet and put a Levi jacket over the Jose Cuervo t-shirt he'd pulled on. He went back into the bedroom and shoved his keys in his right front pocket, his wallet in the left rear. He considered bringing along a weapon, but immediately decided against it. He had no faith in his "army" out there, and if things went sideways, he needed to stay above the fray, claim plausible deniability.

Although if one of them took out Sheriff Neth, he wouldn't be shedding any tears.

He grabbed a can of Mountain Dew from the fridge and went back outside.

"Let's roll," he said.

THERE was no one at Juan Wang's when they arrived save a skittish elderly couple who quickly left, but they came across two tree-trimmers further down the street who were sitting on the ground in the shade of their panel truck, eating lunch.

The army pulled in back of the truck.

They were traveling in three vehicles: two pickups and Melvin's Cherokee. Chet was riding at the front of the caravan with Melvin, and they were the first out. Melvin's gun was holstered, but he knew it was there if he needed it, and that confidence showed in his demeanor. He walked right up to the tree trimmers, his boots touching the closer one's jeans. "Taking a siesta, eh, *muchachos?*"

They ignored him, kept eating their sandwiches.

Melvin kicked the man. "I'm talking to you, beaner!"

Both men stood. They were clearly able to take care of themselves, but when they saw how many people they were up against, they began backing away. The one who'd been kicked held up his hands to show he was no threat. "We don't want no trouble."

"Then why're you in our town?" someone demanded.

The man gestured toward a sign on the side of the panel truck. "We work for Mr. Armstrong."

"That don't mean shit to me," Melvin said.

The tree trimmers looked at each other, not sure where to go from here.

Melvin leaned forward. "We want you out of this town." He glanced over at Chet, flashed him a quick grin. "By sundown." He patted the weapon at his side.

Shouts of support and encouragement greeted his threat. "Yeah!" "Get out of our town!" "Go back to Mexico!"

Melvin pointed. "Sundown."

The members of the army returned to their vehicles. What they had just done was illegal, Chet knew, but damn if it didn't feel good to do it. It felt *right*, and they drove off, looking for other wrongs to rectify, other places where they could focus their collective energy on problems that needed solving.

On the side of the highway, a short-haired overweight woman wearing masculine clothes was crouched by the side of an old Pontiac trying to change a tire. Melvin honked at her. "Get right with God, dyke!"

"Butch bitch!" someone yelled from the back seat.

The woman looked up at them, confused.

Melvin sped away, kicking up dust and gravel that no doubt spattered her, the pickups behind them following suit.

They were all laughing, and Chet thought that he hadn't had this much fun in years.

Tonight on the show, he decided, he was going to issue a real call to arms, tell his listeners about the adventures the army had had today and proclaim a state of emergency, order them to meet up with Melvin and his men so they could set this town right.

"Hey, let's stop by the bank for a minute," one of the men in the back seat suggested. "I'd like to pick up my hunting knife."

Chet frowned. *The bank?*

"He works there," Melvin explained. "In fact this little excursion today was his idea."

A warning bell sounded at the back of Chet's mind. He turned in his seat to look at the man, and realized that he was the person who'd actually taken down Chet's account information when he'd applied for his loan. Chet hadn't recognized him in camouflage gear.

The apprehension he'd felt upon hearing about the involvement of the bank was superseded by an embarrassment that this man knew about his financial troubles.

The man smiled at him. "Proud to be here, sir. I'm a listener and a fan and a patriot." He leaned forward in his seat. "Not to toot my own horn, but I helped write some of your commercials."

"Good job," Chet said before facing frontward again. "Thank you."

They stopped by the First People's branch that was next to the mayor's law office. "You don't have to get out," the man from the bank said. "This'll just take a minute. But *you* have to get out," he told the man to his left, since he was sandwiched in the middle of the back seat.

"Let him out, Del," Melvin ordered.

Del opened the rear passenger door and got out. The other man hurried into the bank, emerging moments later with a large knife.

Where in the bank do they store knives? Chet wondered.

Melvin was looking at his phone as the two men got back in the Cherokee. "Looks like there's a cockroach convention in the park. They're tryin' to play soccer on the baseball diamond. American kids won't be able to use the field my tax dollars paid for."

"I think kids are at school right now," Del pointed out.

"Shut the fuck up, Del. No one asked you." He looked over at Chet. "Ready to fight for truth, justice and the American way?"

Chet grinned. "Ready."

And off they went.

2

WALTER had cancelled his Wednesday morning Bible study class at the bank's request, and was glad to have done so. He was alone in the empty church, and rather than attempt to explain the meaning of obvious parables to over-interested and under-informed parishioners like Norma Crenshaw, he was free to look up information about this weekend's upcoming games and check out the spreads. FreshBets had also added a new feature to their site, a single-dollar game where you could wager on the outcome of an electronically flipped cartoon quarter. It was an addicting little diversion, one that he could easily spend an hour playing without losing too much money.

But when he turned on his computer and went to the site, a message appeared in the center of his screen: ACCESS DENIED. He signed out, shut down and tried again with the same result. He sat there, frowning, wondering what was wrong. He owed money, sure, but not much, and he was guaranteed to get it back over the next several days, so he couldn't be locked out because of that. Had he broken some sort of rule? He had no idea. He half-expected the lights to flicker and Pickering to appear in his doorway, but when that didn't happen, he thought that perhaps *he* should contact the bank to find out what was what.

He'd been given no email address or phone number for Pickering or the bank, so he attempted to Google it. Apparently, First People's had no website. Not only that, but all references to it seemed to have been scrubbed. His search attempt got no hits, something that had never happened to him before, and the only note on the otherwise empty screen were the words *"0 of 0 Search Results."*

He tried to go on FreshBets again and once more was denied access. Shutting off his computer, he decided to go to the bank and talk to Pickering directly. Sunday's sermon was already written, and without today's class, there wasn't much to do…

And he really wanted to play that quarter-flip game.

He left the door to the chapel open—there was always the chance Norma or one of her biddy buddies might come in to pray—and walked behind the church to his dusty Toyota. He'd never actually been to the bank, but he knew from talking to parishioners that there were now three branches open. One was in the old downtown, one was somewhere else, but the only one he'd seen himself was off the highway near the nursery, and that was where he drove.

His was the only car in the parking lot as he pulled in. The bank building itself was a hulking single-story structure, its glass doors and windows so dark that it was hard to tell whether anyone was inside. The impression he had was that of a spider waiting for a fly, and for a second the image was so strong that he considered leaving and going to one of the other branches.

But he wanted to get this problem solved, and there was no telling at which location Pickering might be. Maybe he wouldn't even need to speak to Pickering but could get help from someone else.

Or maybe Pickering would just appear.

Pushing that thought aside, he got out of the car, walked up to the door of the building, pushed it open and walked in.

The interior of the bank was black.

It was not dimly lighted. Its walls were not darkly paneled. It was *black*. As though a worker with a grudge against the company had maliciously coated walls, floors and ceiling with paint the color of pitch. The people working here, as well, were dressed in somber attire, and Walter scanned their faces, looking for someone he recognized. The pastor knew a lot of people in town, but none of these individuals were familiar to him.

He approached a hard-looking man with close cropped hair and a prominent scar across his left cheek who was seated behind a black desk. He intended to ask where he might find Mr. Pickering, but before he could even open his mouth, the man was out of his chair and walking around the desk. "Hail Satan!" he declared.

Walter's eyes widened in shock.

The scarred man grinned crookedly. "Just kidding, Rev." He punched Walter's arm, *hard*, in what was supposed to be a gesture of camaraderie. "What can I do you for?"

Rev? The man obviously knew who he was, and Walter tried to remember if he'd seen him before, but his mind was still drawing a blank. "I'm looking for Mr. Pickering," he said.

"This is about your gambling site, isn't it?" The scarred man shook his head. "Sorry, rev. You've been cut off."

Walter noticed that all business in the bank had stopped. Although he hadn't seen anyone move, the other employees seemed nearer than they had been, as though they were closing in on him. He suddenly felt nervous. "That's all right," he said. "I'll talk to him later."

"You don't understand. You won't be talking to him at all. He has no more use for you."

They *were* closer.

Walter glanced behind him toward the door and saw that it was blocked. A huge bald man with blue lines tattooed across his face stood next to a short monkeylike woman, both of them positioned in front of the doorway.

Deliver me from evil, he silently prayed.

"Why don't you pull down your pants, rev," the scarred man said. "Show Hester here your penis." He drew out the word with a mocking drawl: *peee-nis*.

There were rough chuckles all around. Walter suddenly noticed that the teller closest to him was not writing something down with a pen, as he'd originally thought, but was carving something unseen on the counter with a scalpel. And he saw that a woman seated behind a nearby desk had no teeth in her beaklike mouth. In the darkness of a far corner, a tall man with his pants undone was squatting down and appeared to be defecating.

Lord give me strength.

Walter turned and made a beeline for the door. He strode briskly, staring straight ahead. His pulse was pounding, and he fully expected to be stopped by the bald behemoth or the monkey woman, but he kept his eye on the prize, pretending they weren't there, and when he reached the pair, they parted to let him pass.

"Y'all come back now! Hear?" someone called out behind him, followed again by that rough laughter.

Sweating profusely, his heart thumping so loudly he could hear it in his ears, Walter pushed open the glass door and walked out of the gloom into welcoming sunlight. Maybe this was a sign that it was time for him to give up gambling. It had been stupid of him to come here. He knew that there was something off about Pickering and the bank—and he hated what they had done to his church—but his addiction had so clouded his mind and commandeered his focus, that coming here to get access to a website reinstated had seemed like the only logical action under the circumstances.

That delusion had been scared out of him.

He was going back to his office to do what he should have been doing all along, crafting the best sermon he could for this Sunday and making himself available for parishioners in need of spiritual guidance. He had learned his lesson. He was not going to allow himself to even check FreshBets to see if he had again been granted access. He was through with gambling.

He'd give two to one odds on that.

3

ROLLIE Brown decided to take a short detour and drive through the old downtown on his way to work. He snickered as he passed Brave New World, wondering how long it would be before Kyle gave up the ghost and admitted defeat.

He wasn't exactly sure when, why or how he had become so competitive. He had always liked Kyle, and until recently, Brave New World had been his favorite store in town. Now, however, nothing would do but to crush his rival. Mercilessly.

He'd even fantasized about throwing a Molotov cocktail through the store's front window and burning the whole fucking place to the ground.

The thought made him smile.

Bypassing the highway, Rollie pulled off Main onto Pinyon and took the winding street all the way to Granite, where his store was located next to the Goodwill, across from Jake Simmons' used car lot. The library was only two blocks away, so book lovers did frequent this area, but he had to admit that the location didn't seem to be as prime as he'd originally thought it would be. Business was definitely slower than expected.

Still, Amazing Stories was doing better than Brave New World.

Part of that was because he was investing in his business while Kyle was stagnating. The loan he'd gotten allowed him to outbid his rival at every turn, and his stock was increasing exponentially. At the moment, more money might be going out than coming in, but that's how investment worked, and pretty soon that trend would reverse itself.

Rollie parked in front of his store, took out his key, unlocked the door and walked inside. Trying to see the bookshop the way a customer would, he had to admit that he could use some better bookcases. Kyle did have him beat in that department. But he was proud of his music section, something Brave New World did not have. In an alcove at the rear of the store, boxes of records were sorted by musical style atop a table, while shelves on the side walls housed CDs. It looked pretty impressive even from here, and he wondered if he should amend the sign painted on the front window to "Amazing Stories Books and Music" from "Amazing Stories Books," which was what it said now.

He turned on the lights, unlocked the cash register and clicked on the radio. It only received the local Montgomery station, which played country music exclusively, but that was what he liked anyway, and as Merle Haggard's "Big City" issued through the mounted speakers, Rollie thought to himself that if he didn't own this store, he would shop here.

The door opened, and three men walked in. He recognized one of them as the loan officer from The First People's Bank who'd gotten him the money for his store. The other two he didn't know.

"Welcome," he said. "Let me know if you need any help—"

The expression on the loan officer's face told him that they weren't here to buy books.

"Mr. Brown," the man said.

Rollie nodded. The other two men, he saw now, looked like thugs. "Can I help you?"

"We don't need your help, Mr. Brown. We are here because, well, to put it bluntly, you and your shop are not performing up to expectations."

Something in the man's tone caused a shiver of fear to pass through him, but Rollie pushed that feeling down and met the loan officer's gaze. "What do you mean by that?"

"I mean that the bank issued you a loan with the under-standing that you would be able to make a go of this business. Unfortunately, according to our calculations, you have squandered your opportunity."

"But it's the first month! I'm just starting out!"

"Nevertheless."

"But..."

"The bill is due, my friend." He made a motion, and through the door stepped Evangeline Evans, the Realtor who'd leased him this space.

"What are you doing here?" He could hear the fear in his own voice.

"Oh, she's a little behind on *her* payments, but we're letting her work it off."

Evangeline, he noticed for the first time, was holding a hammer. On her face was a thin cold smile.

Fear flooded through him. He looked from the hammer to the loan officer's face and back to the hammer. "Let *me* work it off!" he said. "I'll do whatever you need me to do!"

"What we need you to do is be an example."

"I'm talking about doing some work for you." He nodded at Evangeline. "I could go over to Brave New World and teach Kyle a lesson, if you wanted. Break his arms, cut off a finger—"

"Unfortunately, Mr. Decker is not part of The First People's family. He's out of our jurisdiction. You on the other hand…"

"But if we took him out, I'd have more business!"

"Hold him," the loan officer said.

The two thugs grabbed Rollie's arms and pulled him taut between them. Evangeline stepped forward, hammer raised.

"People need to know that if they do not live up to their obligations, there are consequences," the loan officer said.

"But I haven't done anything!" Rollie screamed. "I haven't missed a payment!"

"Gag him."

The thug on the left was holding Rollie with one hand. He used the other to stuff a slimy snot-covered handkerchief in his mouth.

Rollie forced himself not to throw up, afraid he might choke to death on his own vomit.

But he was going to die anyway.

They'd be caught if he did die. None of them were wearing gloves. Their fingerprints were everywhere, and once the sheriff found his body—

"Oh, we're going to Keshoggi your body," the loan officer said calmly, as though reading his thoughts. "There'll be nothing to find."

The first blow hit him on the right side of the head, just above his ear. He felt the rounded metal end of the hammer smash the bone of his skull and embed itself within the flesh and shattered fragments. The pain was overwhelming, a searing white-hot agony that so dwarfed anything he had ever experienced there was no basis for comparison. Blood gushed out of his head, over his ear and down his body. Were he able to reason, he might have thought he'd feel nothing after that, so overloaded were his senses, but when the hammer pulled out and Evangeline swung it at his shoulder, crushing the clavicle beneath, pain flashed anew, and his body sagged beneath the weight of the trauma, held up only by the strong hands of First People's goons.

And the blows kept coming, one to his chest, cracking his sternum, one to his crotch, mashing his testicles. He felt nothing but pain, thought no thoughts except acknowledgment of that pain, and then another strike in the center of his face made even those thoughts disappear.

The last sounds he heard, though he was unable to recognize them as words, were spoken by the loan officer.

"Good job," the banker told Evangeline. "But you still have to make your payments."

SEVENTEEN

1

"*ALL UNITS. ACTIVE shooter at Montgomery High School.*"

They were the last words Brad had ever thought he would hear, ones he'd hoped never to hear. The call came over their radios as he and Hank sat in the diner—

The First People's Diner

—waiting for their food. He practically knocked over the table getting up, and had his radio out, responding as the two of them sprinted out the door. "Heard! We're on our way!"

There were already sirens wailing, and theirs joined the chorus as they skidded over the gravel of the small parking lot, bottoming out as they bumped onto the street. His heart was pounding, and his overactive imagination was already visualizing a bloody massacre, but a small secret part of him was relieved that the high school was the target and not his girls' elementary school.

It was one of those situations where kids must have called or texted their parents the moment the assault started, because in addition to the three deputies who had arrived before them, a growing group of civilians was in the parking lot, on the sidewalk and grass, teary faces pleading with Issac, the lone deputy handling crowd control. Brad and Hank quickly exited the cruiser, and Brad waved at Issac to thank him for keeping people back before rushing over to where Vern and Mitch were arming up and preparing to go in. Both had already strapped on vests.

"What do we know?" Brad demanded.

"Two shooters," Mitch said. "Identities unknown. Calls are still coming in, I think, from students and teachers, but what we heard so far is that two kids, both males, armed with assault rifles, went into the administration building about ten minutes ago and started firing. No word on who was in there at the time, or if anyone's killed or injured. The boys' current whereabouts are unknown. The rest of the school's on lockdown."

"Okay," Brad said. "We'll enter from the front, then spread out in pairs over the campus. Hank and I will take the administration building. Carol," he said over the radio, "let us know if anyone calls in or texts a location. Those teachers and kids are on their phones, and you may hear it before we see it."

"*Gotcha.*"

"You, too, Issac. If you hear anything from the parents."

"*Roger.*"

Norris, Paul and Bill F. arrived, hurrying up. "What's our move?" Paul asked.

Brad explained as they strapped on their vests. Hildy and Clint pulled up a moment later, already armed and suited. Brad quickly ran through the plan once again. They were a man extra, and he stationed Bill F. at the front of the school near Issac in case something went wrong and one or both of the shooters made it out.

"Keep your radios on," he ordered. "Stay in contact."

They moved quickly. There'd been no sound of gunfire, and that was definitely a good sign, but he didn't trust it, and the silence of the school put him even more on edge. He and Hank peeled off to the left, alert for any noise or sign of movement. The door to the administration building office was not only wide open, but the glass had been shot out.

"This is the sheriff!" Brad hollered, rifle aimed at the doorway.

He heard whimpering, and a small crying voice called out, "Help!"

"Are you all right in there?" he shouted. "Is anyone with you?"

"They're gone!"

He could see movement now, a high school girl staggering through the office toward the door. Her hands, held in front of her, were coated with blood.

"Cover me," he ordered Hank, and rushed forward to escort the girl to safety.

"They're all dead in there," she cried. She wiped the tears from her cheeks, leaving a smear of crimson across her face. "They're all dead. They're all dead."

"Who killed them?"

"Dave Reynolds and Jim Hardy. They had...*guns*."

Brad recognized the names and was shocked. Reynolds was the football team's star quarterback. Hardy was the baseball team's undefeated pitcher two years straight.

"Are you sure?"

She nodded emphatically.

Brad relayed the information over his radio. He asked the girl if she knew where they'd gone, and she shook her head vigorously back and forth.

"All right," he told her. "Hank," he said, "take her out front and meet me back here." He nodded toward the office. "I'm going in."

"Are you—"

"Yes. I'll be fine. Take her out and hurry back."

Hank and the girl rushed off, and he stepped inside the building. He moved slowly and carefully. He believed the student when she said that the shooters were gone, but it paid to be careful.

The first thing that hit him was the smell. Shit and piss and the coppery odor of blood. They must have shot off a lot of rounds because the scent of carbon was in the dusty air as well. Behind a counter whose top was chipped and shattered by bullets lay two women, one on top of another, both covered in an alarming amount of blood. Further on, down a short hallway, three more bodies lay bleeding onto the floor. Brad recognized one of them as Dennis Whittaker, the principal.

"*Building one's clear,*" Mitch said over the radio. "*Should we tell everyone to stay on lockdown?*"

"Until it's over," Brad said.

"*Then we're heading toward the gym.*"

Hank returned, stunned at the extent of the carnage.

"*No one in the band room,*" Paul announced. "*Moving on to the theater.*"

"*I'm in the library—*" Clint began. His voice was broken off by the sound of automatic rifle fire, its staccato bursts immediately audible both over the radio and live from outside.

The shooters were in the library.

"Go! Go!" Brad ordered.

He and Hank ran out of the office, weapons ready. He realized that he didn't know exactly where the library was, but when he spotted Vern and Mitch sprinting across the school's interior courtyard toward a building at the far end, he followed their lead, Hank keeping abreast of him. All four of them arrived at the same time, Norris and Paul only seconds behind.

They'd prepared for these sorts of tactical maneuvers during training sessions, but the most recent one had been awhile back, and Brad prayed that rustiness would not end up getting one of them killed.

The gunfire had stopped for several seconds, but it started up again, and Brad motioned for Vern to open the door. Indicating that the others were to follow him, he entered the building defensively, leading with his weapon, crouching low. They crossed the first hurdle and weren't mowed down, but there was a uniformed body lying unmoving on the floor to their right. He couldn't tell if it was Hildy or Clint. Paul quickly checked for a pulse, then shook his head. Another burst of gunfire erupted. It was too loud to determine the source, but nothing was splintering around them, so they obviously hadn't been seen.

The deafening noise exploded once again, accompanied by a strobe like flashing at the end of the aisles ahead. Brad caught the eye of each of the others, verified that they were all on the same page, and took the center aisle, moving low and quick. In his peripheral vision, between the books, he saw Hank keeping pace in the aisle to his left, Mitch on the aisle to his right. He hoped to Christ they'd be able to take down these kids without taking them out. He didn't want to kill a teenager. His brain ran through all the possible scenarios, and he decided that he would show himself, order the shooters to put down their weapons. If they didn't comply immediately, if either of their weapons started to swing toward him or his men, he would shoot. He would aim first for the arm attached to the trigger finger, then the legs, but if neither of those stopped the movement, he would shoot to kill. It would be a split-second decision, one that he had only a single chance of getting right—

Then he was there.

The bookcases came to an end, and he was in an open area that had probably been a computer lab but was now a debris field of overturned chairs, splintered tables, shattered monitors and broken keyboards. If the other member of Hildy and Clint's team was here, Brad didn't see him, but he did see the shooters. They were directly in front of him, and close, but luckily facing away. Even with only a partial rear view, he could see that they had military assault rifles.

He stood straight, legs apart in a shooting stance, gun held two-handed and steady. "Drop your weapons!"

They didn't, and tried to turn, and he fired off a round into the shoulder of the one closest to him. His deputies must have come up with the same plan, since the boy's knee was shattered by a bullet, and the kid next to him dropped to the floor, legs buckling and arm gushing blood.

Then they were on the students, kicking the weapons away, and Hildy emerged from behind one of the overturned tables, holding a wounded forearm.

Clint, Brad thought with a sickened realization. *They killed Clint*.

The boys lay on the floor, bleeding into the flat carpeting, screaming in agony. Brad picked up his radio and called for an ambulance, but, amazingly, paramedics were already outside the building and waiting, and as soon as he made the call, they burst into the library.

"How many in here?" one of them shouted.

"One dead, three wounded!" Brad called out.

"Two wounded," Hildy said. "I'm okay."

"Three wounded," Brad stated flatly.

Stretchers were rolled in.

"Preserve the prints on those weapons," he reminded Hank. "We have more than we need, but let's not get sloppy."

It felt like an hour had passed, but it had not been more than a few minutes since they'd first entered the library.

Wanting to give the paramedics space to work and feeling suddenly claustrophobic, Brad made his way down the aisle to the front of the library, moving outside and taking a deep breath of fresh air. He felt as though he were going to vomit. He hadn't given the official word that it was all clear—they still needed to search the school to make sure there were no other shooters—but someone must have, or the word had simply gotten out, because there was a crowd in the courtyard. Primarily parents, he assumed.

"Jesus," Mitch said, stepping next to him and wiping the sweat off his forehead with the back of his hand. "Where'd they get that kind of firepower?"

Brad shook his head tiredly. "I don't know."

"I know."

The sheriff turned to see Mr. Worthington standing right behind him. Neither he nor Mitch had previously noticed the bank manager.

"Yeah?" Mitch said. "So where'd they get it?"

"The Gun Barrel, over on Ponderosa."

"How do you know that?" Brad asked.

"We financed it."

"The store?"

"The store, sure. But the shooting as well."

Brad's blood ran cold. "*What?*"

"Oh, we didn't know it was going to happen," he said cheerfully. "I'm not saying that. But for our customers who might be a little short on cash, we have programs to help them finance purchases. Cars, couches, guns, what have you. So, indirectly…"

Mitch stepped forward threateningly. "You mean to tell me that you gave a loan to *kids* to buy *assault* weapons?"

Worthington shrugged, still smiling. "They're customers. We opened a college saver account for each student in the school, which meant that they were eligible. We can't discriminate, you know. Illegal."

Classes were emerging from their lockdown locations, though Brad had not announced that it was safe to do so, teachers leading students out in double lines, as though they were kindergarteners. Parents rushed to their children immediately upon seeing them.

Worthington surveyed the campus in a self-satisfied manner. "Yes, every cloud has a silver lining, as they say. Someone was going to make money from this. Why shouldn't it be us?"

"Have you no shame?" Brad said, his voice low.

"Don't worry." The banker grinned. "People will send their thoughts and prayers. That always solves the problem."

He started to walk off, then turned back around. "By the way, we're thinking of offering a free Glock to everyone who opens a new account with a minimum hundred dollar deposit." He held up a hand. "But only if they're of legal age." His smile broadened.

Brad pointed a finger at the man. "I don't know if what you've done is illegal, but believe me, I am going to look into it. I am going to do everything I can to make sure you can't pull anything like this ever again."

"Yeah," Mitch seconded.

Worthington laughed. "Good luck with that." And he sauntered off in a jaunty manner that made Brad want to tackle him.

"I hate that motherfucker," Mitch said under his breath.

"You and me both," Brad said.

It might have been only a formality at this point, but they searched the rest of the school, fortunately finding nothing. FBI agents and TV news crews arrived within the next couple of hours, and the sky was filled with the unfamiliar sound of multiple choppers. Brad had no idea how the FBI picked and chose which cases to handle, but he was grateful for the assistance and gladly handed over the reins to this nightmare.

As annoying as he sometimes found his chief deputy, Hank had really stepped up lately, and Brad put him in charge at the scene, thinking that if he ever left this job, the department would be in good hands.

Why had that even occurred to him?

He knew why.

Clint

It was up to him to call Clint's wife and tell her the news. This was the first time the department had ever lost a man, and the possibility that such a thing would happen in his lifetime had been so remote until now that he had not even considered how he would approach such a duty. A cowardly part of him wished that she'd hear it from someone else and then call him for confirmation, so he wouldn't have to be the one to break it to her, but no call had come by the time he reached the station, and he knew that if he put off the notification any longer, it could turn into a problem.

How could she not have heard yet? he wondered. Maybe she had heard but had simply felt no need to call the station. Maybe she was with her husband now at the hospital or the morgue or wherever they had taken him.

None of that mattered, though. It was still his job to call her.

"Update from the hospital," Carol said when he walked in. "Hildy's going to be fine. They had to put a pin in his elbow and it'll be two months before he can use that arm. So...desk duty, I'm assuming. But he's lucky because a quarter of an inch to the left and it would've hit an artery."

He nodded tiredly. "Thanks."

"Are you—"

"I have a phone call to make," he said, and closed his office door.

HANK was still on scene, "overseeing the feds," as Mitch put it, but the rest of his deputies had returned, giving Brad the rundown before writing up their reports. Issac hung back after the others had left his office. "What is it?" Brad asked, knowing from the expression on his deputy's face that he wasn't going to like the answer.

Issac leaned forward conspiratorially. "News," he said.

"Yeah?" Brad prompted.

"Word on the street is that this isn't the end of it. The bank's arming different factions in town. They want to start a war."

"Word on what street? And what factions are we talking about?" Brad shook his head dismissively. "Jesus shit. This isn't fucking Chicago. We don't have *gangs* here."

"All I know is—"

"You can't believe every random rumor."

"But what if there is a shootout?"

"It's not the OK Corral, either."

Issac nodded but remained in place.

Brad sighed wearily. "Fine. Go ahead and chase it down. Who knows? Things are so crazy now that it might be true. And if it turns out that we sat on our asses when we could've done something…"

"Right on it," the deputy said.

"Make sure you tell the FBI what you told me. Let them get in on the fun."

"Will do."

Brad followed him out of the office, walking past Carol's desk to the bullpen, where Vern, Mitch and Bill F. were typing on computers. Paul and Norris were standing in the door of the break room, awaiting their turns. A pall hung over the station. Clint was not supposed to have been in today, but his absence still filled the building, a black hole of emptiness at the heart of the department.

"Norris!" Brad raised his hand, calling the man over.

The deputy made his way across the room. "What's up?"

"You and Bill G. are pretty tight, right?"

Norris shifted his feet uncomfortably. "Yeah, but… I mean, I didn't know he was planning to quit or—"

Brad held up a hand. "I don't care about that. I just want you to have a talk with him, see if he knows anything about the bank financing the shooting, maybe find out what else he knows, see where his loyalties lie."

Norris nodded soberly. "I'm on it...And, honestly, I didn't know anything about—"

"I'm not blaming you for anything. I'm not even blaming Bill. I just need you to find out what he knows, and if he can help us."

"Done." Norris headed over to the unused desk in the corner, which had no computer but did have a phone.

Brad got himself some coffee, then wandered back toward his office, thinking he needed to stop by the hospital on his way home and check in on Hildy.

"Who's on duty tonight?" he asked Carol.

"Who do you want?"

He shook his head. "Let's ask for volunteers. I'm not going to make anyone do anything, not after what we went through today."

By the time five o'clock rolled around, they'd pretty much done all they could for the day, and Brad left Vern and Bill F. in charge overnight since they'd both volunteered. They'd also gotten more sleep than anyone else the night before.

He needed to pick up the girls, who'd gone to their friend Shannon's house after school, but he wanted to stop by the hospital and see Hildy, so he said a quick goodbye and drove over to Montgomery General. Hildy was pretty doped up, which was just as well, because Brad didn't really feel like talking, especially about the subject they would end up talking about. They spoke briefly, but Hildy kept fading in and out, and after a few minutes, Brad left, telling the deputy that he'd stop by again tomorrow.

He hadn't stayed long, ten minutes maximum. Still, it was dark by the time he picked up the girls, and he was grateful to learn that Mrs. Carrell had fed them dinner. He apologized profusely for being so late.

"Don't give it a thought," she said. "We heard what happened. It's just awful! But you caught the boys, right?"

"Yes we did, ma'am."

"Thank goodness for that."

"Well, thank you again. I can't tell you how much we appreciate all your help. You're a godsend."

"Anytime." She waved to Jillian and Sue as he herded them out to the car. "Glad you could come by!"

"Thank you, Mrs. Carrell!"

"Thank you, Mrs. Carrell!"

They were only driving down the block, but Brad made sure they were buckled in. His parents were supposed to drive up tomorrow to help out with the kids, and tomorrow couldn't come too soon, as far as he was concerned. He had no idea how single parents did it, especially the poor ones holding down two jobs. It really did take a village.

Seconds later, they were home. The lights were on behind the pulled curtains of the living room, and he frowned, trying to remember if he'd forgotten to turn them off this morning. The three of them got out of the car. Taking his key out, he opened the door and walked inside.

Where Patty was lecturing two dummies that had been placed on the couch and made up to look like Jillian and Sue.

A dummy dressed in one of his extra uniforms was lying on the floor with a knife stuck in its chest.

Patty turned to look at him.

And the girls screamed in terror.

HE felt bad about committing Patty, but he hadn't really had a choice, and thinking about what had happened to her made Brad feel more depressed than he'd ever been in his life. Her appearance when they'd come home last night had been truly shocking, and for a brief fraction of a second, he'd thought that it wasn't her. But that fantasy had died instantly, and he'd rushed the girls out of the house and back into the car before returning to call Vern at the station. He kept his eye on Patty to make sure she didn't try to leave as he described to Vern what had happened, asking the deputy to hurry over, explaining that he was going to leave with the girls once Vern arrived. He didn't want them to see their mother cuffed and taken away.

Patty was still talking to the dummies made up to look like their children. The slashes that covered her face—made no doubt with the knife embedded in his effigy—were superficial enough that they had stopped bleeding, but the dried streaks and crisscrossing cuts were so dense and overwhelming that they made her look like a completely different person.

A monster.

How had it come to this? What had happened to her? Had she always been unstable and he just hadn't noticed or had something—

the bank

—occurred that had pushed her over the edge and *caused* her to unravel?

She kissed the top of the Sue dummy.

Vern arrived quickly, and Brad reiterated the plan, telling the deputy to remain in the house with Patty until he and the girls were gone. He'd call as soon as he could.

They spent the night at the town's only motel, the rundown Montgomery Motor Inn. He'd had enough sense to bring extra clothing for all of them, but he'd forgotten some of the small things like toothbrushes, and after they checked in, he drove them over to Wal-Mart, calling Vern while the girls were distracted to make sure Patty was safely at the hospital where she couldn't harm herself. He told Vern that he would call the hospital later and look in on her in the morning but his priority right now was his kids.

After a nearly sleepless night on one of the most uncomfortable beds he'd ever lain on, he took Jillian and Sue out for breakfast at Burger King. None of them had mentioned what they'd seen last night, but before she exited the car, Sue asked, "Can we sleep at home tonight? I like home better."

Tellingly, she did not mention her mother, and, his heart aching for both girls, he said, "I have something better planned," although her question made him realize he was going to have to clean up that horrific tableaux in the living room.

The "something better" was Grandma and Grandpa, and his parents arrived at the Burger King before they'd finished their meal, having left Sedona before dawn. His dad, as usual, greeted him with a complaint. "I still don't understand why we had to come so early."

Sue got out of her seat to give him a hug. "Hi, Grandpa!"

He smiled down at her. "Hi, sweetie."

"We're going to be staying with you," his mom told Jillian, beaming happily.

"Not exactly," Brad said.

She frowned. "What do you mean, 'not exactly'?"

"I want you to take them with you," he told his mom. "They can stay at your house, and I'll pick them up on the weekend."

"But what about school?"

"Yeah," Jillian said. "Aren't we going to school?"

"Not today," he told her, and turned back to his parents. "They can afford to miss a week. I'll get whatever homework they have and email it to you."

His dad looked concerned. "What's going on, Bradley?"

"A lot. I can't explain it all right now, but I will. The most important thing, though, is to get Jillian and Sue away from here."

"We heard about the shooting on the news…"

"That's part of it, but there's more. A lot more. And I'd feel better if I knew the girls were safe."

"And did Patty really—" his mom started to say.

He shot a look at the girls, who were finishing off their orange juices. "Little pitchers," he said.

She nodded. "Okay. Tell me later."

He left his parents and the girls at Burger King, went back to the motel, then made a quick trip home, packing everything he thought they might need in two suitcases. He wasn't sure what his mom and dad had talked to them about, but both Jillian and Sue seemed more worried when he returned than when he'd left. He took them both aside, told them everything was going to be okay. They were just going to stay at Grandma and Grandpa's for awhile, but he would call them every morning and every night. He smiled. "It's their house, so you'll have to do what they say, but you know Grandma and Grandpa are a little bit wacky, right?"

Both girls giggled.

He gave them each a hug in turn and kissed their cheeks. "Don't worry. You'll be fine."

It was Sue who mentioned the elephant in the room. "Will Mommy be fine, too?"

He put a hand around the back of her neck, touched his forehead to hers. "I hope so. I think so. But I'll let you know."

He stood in the parking lot next to his dad's Explorer and waved as the SUV backed up. The vehicle paused, and a window rolled down. "You have to call school and tell them we're absent or we'll get in trouble!" Jillian called.

"I will," he promised.

He stood there, still waving, as they drove onto the highway and headed north.

The day was spent mostly in meetings. With the FBI overseeing the school shooting investigation, Agent Yamato was in charge, and he and Brad videoconferenced with a higher-up at the Bureau, met with the coroner for an autopsy report, met with the other FBI agents for an update and met with Brad's deputies to go over what they'd learned.

If this was what being a big time FBI agent was like, Brad was glad he was just a small town sheriff.

He had managed to convince Yamato that Worthington needed to be interviewed, and was gratified to learn that two agents had been dispatched to the downtown branch of the bank. He was less thrilled to find out later that no evidence of wrongdoing was found. Not sure what Worthington had told the agents, Brad described his encounter on the school grounds, but Yamato dismissed his concerns with an indifferent "it's not illegal to brag."

"To brag that they were financing school shootings?" he prodded, but Yamato would not bite.

It was a load off his back that Sue and Jillian were with his parents. Several times, he checked on Patty in her room at the hospital, asking her if she had anything she'd like him to tell the girls, hoping to tap into a maternal vein and somehow break through the wall she'd erected, but she steadfastly refused to engage with him. They were waiting for a full psych evaluation, but someone from the county had to come up and do it, and the soonest the doctor could get here was tomorrow. In the meantime, she was restrained and probably doped up.

In a way he was happy for all the work. It kept him from having to focus on how quickly and completely his life had gone to shit.

He took off early to clean up the house, leaving Hank in charge and telling him to call if Yamato or any of the feds started causing problems. Vern had taken photos of the dummies last night on the off chance that there were any charges to be filed, and though there was no way Brad would allow that to happen, he used his phone to take some photos of his own before stripping the mannequins of their clothes and breaking down the figures until the pieces were small enough to shove into the oversized construction-strength Hefty bags that he kept in the garage for major yard work. Tomorrow, he'd toss everything in the dumpster behind the station, but for tonight, he just threw the trash bags on the cement of the driveway.

He knew his parents ate dinner around five o'clock, so he waited until six before calling to talk to the girls. They seemed in a surprisingly positive mood—his mom's doing, no doubt; he knew his dad had nothing to do with it—and for that he was grateful. Apparently, his parents had gotten another cat since their last visit, a very playful kitten, and the girls were gushing about it. He realized as he talked to them that not only had he forgotten to get their homework for the week from their respective teachers, but he'd also forgotten to call the school about their absence. He made a note to do both on the Post-It pad next to the phone.

He hated to let them go, and when he finally hung up, the house seemed depressingly silent. Brad turned on the television, not caring what was on, just wanting to hear voices, and made himself some Pasta Roni for dinner. Not bothering with a bowl or plate, he ate out of the small square casserole dish he used to microwave his food.

He went to bed early, tired more from stress than actual work.

And was awakened by a gunshot and the shattering of glass.

He was instantly alert, noticing immediately that a bullet had broken his bedroom window then splintered Patty's dresser against the opposite wall.

He rolled out of bed, grabbing his service revolver from the drawer in his nightstand and ducking low as he sped out of the bedroom, down the hall and to the front door. Peeking through the peephole, he saw a wide-angle vision of men in army fatigues with guns pointed at his house. Another bullet shattered the front window of the living room.

Brad ran around to the back door, hurrying outside and peeking around the corner of the house. None of the men were looking in this direction, so he approached through the side yard, staying close to the wall. He heard drunken laughter and a shouted taunt.

"Not so brave now, are you, Sheriff?"

He could see now that one of the men was Chet Yates. Seeing the others surrounding him in their surplus olive uniforms, he thought of what Hank had said about Chet's "army" and the radio host's on-air exhortations to shoot the sheriff.

There were a couple of ways to play this, and the most prudent one would be to hide until they left, then call for backup, but Brad was not in the mood for prudence today. He swung into a shooter's stance and yelled, "Drop the weapons! Hands on your head!"

Chet's face twisted with hate.

"Don't do it, Chet! I don't want to shoot you, but I will!"

"Just like you did to my brother, motherfucker!" Chet swung his weapon around.

And Brad put a bullet in his chest.

That made it real. He ducked behind the edge of the house, expecting an onslaught after that, but the gathered men were stunned into inaction, weapons dangling at their sides as they stared at the limp bleeding body of the radio host crumpled on the ground.

"Drop 'em!" he ordered, moving out and aiming at the bearded bald man who appeared to be the ringleader of those remaining.

Brad was heavily outnumbered, but his position as sheriff and his willingness to use deadly force had apparently sobered up the invaders and put the fear of God into them, because as one they placed their weapons on the ground.

Seconds later, two sheriff's vehicles were blocking off any escape route for the intruders' pickups. Someone in the neighborhood must have dialed 911, and for that Brad was grateful. He had the advantage of shock and awe, but there was no telling how quickly those assholes might shake off their stupor and go on the attack again.

Mitch hurried up, rifle trained on the gathered men.

Brad bent down, checked Chet for a pulse. "He's still alive. Call for an ambulance." The sheriff applied pressure to the wound, felt the unconscious Chet flinch involuntarily beneath him, a good sign. "Who else is here?" he asked Mitch.

"Issac and Paul."

"Arrest everyone. Charge them all. We'll let the DA sort things out once the weaker ones start cracking and we find out what's what."

He was still pressing down on the wound, the squishiness beneath his palm feeling a little less warm and a little less wet than it had a moment earlier.

He felt bad about shooting Chet, but not that bad. If he hadn't acted, *he* would probably be the one lying on the ground, and he doubted that anyone in the "army" would be calling an ambulance for him.

Thank God the girls weren't here, he thought.

The idea that Jillian and Sue *could* have been here and that a stray shot could have killed one of them filled him with fear and rage, and though he knew it was wrong, he pressed down harder on the wound, gratified to feel Chet Yates squirm in pain beneath him.

2

COY met with Cal and Maggie before the town council meeting. They were the only people from the bank in whom he had confided, and they'd helped him draft the proposal he was going to present. Neither of them were brave enough to continue on—"We need our jobs,"

Cal said simply—but they were behind him, and if everything went the way he hoped and a municipal bank was established, they were definitely the first people he would hire.

Ben had never returned after that baffling and disturbing phone call. It had been nearly a week now that the manager had been absent, and everyone had simply continued to show up for work and do their jobs, making sure the bank ran the way it was supposed to. There were a lot of questions, a lot of speculation, but no one actually knew what had happened. A stack of authorizations continued to pile up on Ben's desk, waiting to be signed, and the first time Coy had put them there, he'd noticed that the mysterious old ledger was nowhere to be seen. Someone had taken it.

1941...1945...1953...

Several times over the past six days, he'd considered reporting the manager's absence—but to whom? The board? They answered to The First People's Bank now. First People's? It was more than possible that they were behind Ben's disappearance. The sheriff? Coy wasn't sure he had standing to do so. He realized for the first time that he didn't know if the manager had any family.

"We had to give something up."

Ben's admission about the cost of the merger (or whatever they were calling it), had never been far from his mind, and now he was starting to think that Montgomery Community had had to give up not only Jimmy but Ben.

Could he be next?

Coy did not want to find out.

There was an overflow crowd in the council chambers. Word had obviously gotten around, and supporters had turned out in force. The business owners who had signed the petition were here, of course, but there were many others as well. He recognized some of Montgomery Community Bank's customers, along with various people he either knew or had frequently seen around town. Even the sheriff had come, along with two deputies flanking the door, and that gave Coy confidence.

Coy sat down in an aisle seat next to Trixie Johnson, who had saved a spot for him. The meeting was called to order, various bits of old business were attended to, three votes were taken, an item of new business on the consent calendar involving the timing of the stoplight in front of Wal-Mart was discussed, and then Coy was allowed to present his proposal.

He stood up before the council. He was nervous, and it showed, but he was also resolute, and he cleared his throat. "You should all have before you a copy of a draft proposal drawn up by myself and supported by the four hundred and eighty-six Montgomery citizens who signed the attached petition.

"I don't know if you've had time to look over the materials yet, but basically what we are proposing is a municipal bank, a bank owned by the town of Montgomery. A *true* Montgomery Community Bank. Although," he added with a slight smile, "one with a different name, since that one's already taken."

There were a few token chuckles.

He started describing how a municipal bank was structured, delineating a way in which the town could finance one and set it up, but realized he was getting into the weeds when he heard restless stirring from the crowd behind him, and saw two of the councilmembers talking to each other on the dais. Adjusting, he cut the technical part of his presentation short, and returned to making the case that the town not only could take such action but that it should.

"The upside?" he asked rhetorically. "This could put a stop to predatory lending practices, avoid risky financial investments, give us a chance to refinance public debt at lower rates, and generate profits that could be reinvested in the community. On a micro level, it could also do away with usurious banking fees and unfair surcharges. The downside? Well, there is an element of economic risk should citizens not support the bank—" He gestured around the packed room. "—but as you can see, and as our petition proves, the idea does have quite a bit of community backing. And, having worked in the banking business for the past two decades, I can safely say that further customer growth is virtually assured if these initial supporters are satisfied. Success breeds success."

"Let me interrupt you," the mayor said, leaning forward.

Coy nodded. "Certainly, sir. What is your concern?"

"My concern is that a *town* can't own a commercial enterprise. We can't run our own *bank*."

"Tell that to the Bank of North Dakota," Coy said. "It's been a publicly owned bank for a hundred years, and has weathered countless recessions and market downturns." He glanced down at his cheat sheet. "Or the Territorial Bank of American Samoa, which is also publicly owned and was started because commercial banks weren't doing business in the territory."

The mayor looked skeptical.

"There's a track record of success. All we have to do is follow that blueprint." He looked at Trixie, who smiled her encouragement. "Which brings me to the reason we're all here today, the reason we're proposing this bank in the first place: First People's."

"Yes!" someone exclaimed.

"I'm not going to beat around the bush. We all know the terrible effects that bank has had on our town in a remarkably short period of time. You've all seen the foreclosures, heard about worthy people who were denied loans which were then given to unreliable individuals and criminal operations. Not to mention the downright *weird* things that have been happening around town. Murders. Deaths. Bombings."

There were murmurs of assent.

"The First People's Bank is now the only bank in town, aside from Montgomery Community, with which it has inexplicably entered into a partnership. We have here a monopoly. And somehow, under all of our noses, two new branches have popped up. Not to mention the fact that they purchased the newspaper, B.B.'s Diner and have their eye on who knows what other businesses."

"It is a legal enterprise," the mayor said. He somehow seemed surprised by his own defense of the bank.

"Maybe it is, and maybe it isn't. But you gentlemen—and ladies— have allowed it to do business here, and I'm hoping by now you have come to regret that decision. Although, even if you have, there may be no legal way to undo what you have done. Even if that's the case, however, we can fight fire with fire and offer up some competition. Let the people decide."

He was on a roll. "You see, we don't know what private banks are doing. Not really. Yes, there are federal regulations, but how are they enforced? Wells Fargo created millions of unauthorized accounts and was only caught because of a whistleblower. God knows what's going on at First People's."

There were shouts of support and agreement.

"I've spent my entire career in the banking business, and I know how loopholes can be exploited, how misdeeds can be covered up. And that's the point of this: transparency. If we had our own bank, a *real* community bank, we the people would *know* what was going on. We would be the ones in charge. We would control it."

The crowd grew silent, and from the rear of the chambers came the sound of a single person clapping slowly. Coy turned to see who it was.

Pickering.

"Excellent speech," he said, walking forward, still clapping. "Complete bullshit, but excellent nevertheless."

The banker's eyes were boring into his own, and Coy was forced to look away. But he did not stop talking. "If we had our own bank, we could not be intimidated or threatened by those who had control of our finances. This man here would have no power over anyone if people simply banked with another institution. Like the one we are proposing."

"You arrogant little nobody." Beneath his calm voice, Pickering was genuinely angry. "You think you can compete with *us*? You're not even playing the same game. The big boys wouldn't even allow you on the field. *We* control this town."

He was booed and shouted down, and Coy felt a surge of elation at the audience's fiery and passionate response. He was surprised and glad, but more than anything, he was proud of his fellow townspeople for having the guts to defy the bank. Pickering had obviously not expected such a reaction either, and as he scanned the crowd, Coy could not help thinking that he was memorizing faces, mentally taking down names.

Begone, he thought, *before somebody drops a house on you.*

"I think..." The mayor shook his head as though awakening from a stupor. "I think this is an idea worth pursuing." He banged his gavel for no apparent reason. "We will read over the information you have provided us, and vote on whether Montgomery will establish a municipal bank at our next session."

There was a spontaneous standing ovation. The assembled townspeople stood as one, clapping, whooping and cheering. Coy was excited and far more encouraged than he had expected to be. He had not thought things would move so quickly. After hearing Trixie and the other business owners talk about the council's refusal to cross First People's, he'd assumed that gradual, incremental change would be the best they could hope for, and that only after many meetings and countless emotional arguments. This was better than anything he had imagined, and the crowd's response told him that they had struck a nerve. Looking around, he saw that Pickering was no longer here. He had slunk away in the commotion, and it was that, more than anything, that gave him cause for hope. He was not unaware that there was probably danger ahead—he thought of Jimmy, crucified on the door of the old Bank of America; Ben, calling him in panic from some undisclosed location—but there was strength in numbers, and the numbers were definitely on their side.

The meeting adjourned, he walked outside with Trixie and several other downtown business owners, all of them patting each others' backs and high-fiving, thrilled with the way the evening had gone and optimistic that change was in the air. The sheriff was there, too, and he went out of his way to shake Coy's hand, telling him that the municipal bank idea was not only brilliant but necessary.

Others stayed behind as well, instead of going home, including the mayor, and as they talked, as people began to gradually open up and trust each other enough to say what they *really* thought, the stories started to come out.

The owner of the bookstore—Coy had already forgotten his name—was the first to break the ice, describing how First People's had poached and indoctrinated his sole employee, how from the beginning there had been odd sounds from behind their shared wall, and how the bank, among other things, had financed the nursery owner's foray into home security, which had resulted in their home being unlawfully surveyed. The man put his arm around his son, standing next to him, and, nodding at the sheriff, said that the boy's friend had slaughtered his family and had been hired by the bank, which had tried to cover for him.

That broke the dam, and, one by one, the gathered men and women shared horror stories of their encounters with the bank. For the first time, everyone seemed to understand the scope of what they were facing. It was daunting, that was for sure, and well nigh unbelievable, but once they'd gotten over those mental hurdles, they all seemed to come to the same realization he had, that there *was* strength in numbers, and when the sheriff signed on, too, telling them about his wife, Coy began to believe that they really did have an opportunity to reverse whatever it was that The First People's Bank had set in motion.

It was the bookstore owner's wife who contributed the most intriguing and possibly most significant information to the discussion. She had a friend who had received a home loan from First People's, and in order to obtain the loan, the bank had stipulated that she and her husband had to keep one room of the house free. But free for what? The bank's purposes, certainly, although that turned out to be a locked room which seemed to contain some sort of prisoner and from which mysterious sounds emanated. They'd left the house, but the kicker was that she'd continued to dream about the room, and her dreams appeared to have some vaguely premonitory power.

Coy had always been a rational man, but logic and rationality had flown out the window long ago, and neither he nor anyone else had any trouble believing that that restricted room held some sort of secret that First People's did not want revealed.

The council meeting had ended at nine, but it was after eleven before they finally broke up and went their separate ways, with what amounted to an assurance from the mayor that he would do what he could to make a town-owned municipal bank a reality. With everything he'd heard, Coy found himself becoming increasingly paranoid driving home, and he kept checking the rearview mirror to make sure he wasn't being followed. He had to pass the newest branch of First People's on the way to his street, and though the parking lot was empty, he could see what looked like a lone candle, or perhaps a dull flashlight, moving slowly behind the building's tinted windows. Shivering, he sped past.

Arriving at his house, he half-expected a toothless feral Florine to jump out of the bushes and attack him, but he made it to the front door unmolested and, once inside, he locked the door behind him and went room to room, making sure he was alone. The phone rang, but he ignored it and got ready for bed. He was still planning to go to work in the morning, although he had no idea how that was going to play out. Would he still have a job? Would The First People's Bank invoke some sort of hidden clause in the two banks' participation agreement and fire him?

Would he be killed or made to disappear?

Anything was possible, but he was so tired that even those thoughts were not enough to keep him awake, and he fell asleep moments after his head hit the pillow.

In his dream, he discovered a secret room in his house, and from behind the locked red door that was its entrance, he heard the eerie sound of Julius Pickering chuckling softly.

3

THE council meeting last night had been an eye opener, and for the first time in a long while, Kyle saw a ray of hope.

A municipal bank.

The upside, as Coy Stinson would put it, was that it seemed like a legitimate, doable plan. The downside was that it would take time to implement. He knew nothing at all about the details of how to start a community bank, but he knew that there were rules and regulations that would have to be followed, not to mention the fact that a physical location would have to be found, a building equipped with the necessary materials and machinery to do business. Money would have to be obtained as well, *actual* money, a lot of it, coins and bills, money that people would be able to withdraw.

That ray of hope started to fade.

The phone rang, and Anita called out, "I'll get it!" A moment later, she came into the room, still holding the phone. She put her hand over the mouthpiece. "It's Jen," she whispered. "The sheriff called her about the house. He wants to see it, and Lane's at work and can't get off, and she wants us to go with her."

"Sure," he said.

Nick was in his room playing a game on his computer—the high school was still closed, and no one seemed sure when classes would resume, especially with both the principal and vice principal dead—so Kyle asked him if he wanted to come along, and Nick immediately said yes. "We're leaving in five," Kyle said, and smiled to himself. The one positive that had resulted from all this was that their family seemed to have drawn closer together. Two months ago, Nick would never have agreed to go anywhere with them.

"Jen wants us to pick her up," Anita said. "I texted her last night when we came home, so she sort of had a heads up, but I think she wants more details before she meets the sheriff."

"Is she mad?"

"No. More like relieved, I think."

Nick sat up front with Kyle, so Jen could sit in the backseat and talk with Anita when they picked her up. She seemed nervous and uncertain when she first got into the car, but as both he and Anita explained in more detail what had happened at the council meeting and afterward, Jen's apprehension faded. The idea that they were bringing the fight to the bank seemed to give her energy.

The sheriff was waiting for them when they arrived, sitting in a patrol car with one of his deputies. Both men got out when Kyle pulled up.

Introductions were made all around.

"Now tell me about this room," the sheriff said. "I heard her version of it—" He nodded toward Anita. "—but I'd like to hear it from you."

Jen took a deep breath. She described how the bank manager had ordered them to set aside one of the bedrooms for a purpose to be determined at a later date; how they had arrived to find the door to the room already closed and locked; how they'd *heard* things in there; how they'd rented out the house and their tenants had heard things in there, too; how she'd dreamed multiple times about returning.

"I want to see this room," the sheriff told Jen. "First of all, contract or no contract, I'm not sure it's legal for the bank to keep you from using a part of your own house. I'd consult a lawyer about that. Secondly, if you're right, and there's someone or something *in* there, that falls under my purview."

"I told you, you can't get in there. It's locked."

"There's no key to the door?"

Jen shook her head.

"Do I have your permission to break it open? I promise that the department will reimburse you for any damage that needs repair."

"Do it."

The sheriff and his deputy went to the trunk of their car and took out a large heavy tool that looked like a black log with two handles on top of it. Jen opened the house, and the rest of them walked in behind her. The air inside was stale, and with the shades drawn, the partially furnished front room was dark. Kyle felt uncomfortable, and glancing over at Nick and Anita, he could tell that they did, too.

Jen led them directly into the hallway, flipping on an orangey overhead light that somehow made it seem creepier than the darkness had. She pointed at a closed door. "There."

The sheriff nodded. "Step aside," he told them. He tried the knob to make sure it would not turn, then motioned for his deputy to break down the door. Kyle noticed that the sheriff kept his right hand close to his open holster, a move that did not exactly inspire confidence.

Holding the overhead handles, the deputy swung the log-shaped implement against the door directly below the brass knob. There was a loud splintering noise, and the door flew open. The sheriff and the deputy moved in carefully. Kyle followed behind them.

The room was smaller than expected and dark, like a vampire's lair. The lone thick drape was pulled tightly shut, and when Jen, next to him, flipped the light switch, nothing came on. There was something big and bulky in the center of the floor, the only object in the room, but it was difficult to tell what it was until the sheriff took out and turned on his flashlight. The beam played over a wooden crate about four-foot square.

A knock sounded from inside the crate, followed by a strange noise that could have been a laugh, could have been a grunt.

Kyle shivered, a chill passing through him.

The deputy had made his way over to the drape, pulling it open. There was suddenly more light in the room.

"What's in there?" Nick asked.

Kyle shook his head.

The sheriff's flashlight was still trained on the crate. He walked around the square wooden object, no doubt looking for a way to open it. "Hello!" he said. "Is anyone in there?"

Another knock.

"Do you have any tools in the house?" he asked Jen. "A hammer, screwdriver, something?"

"I don't think so. Unless the renters left something. I could check."

"I have a lug wrench in the trunk," Kyle offered. "One end's like a crowbar."

"Perfect. Can you get it?"

Kyle rushed out and returned moments later, handing the item over.

"Maybe you should all wait in the hall," the sheriff said. "Me and Hank can handle it." But no one moved as he looked for a spot to insert the crowbar end of the tool, finally choosing a position on the opposite side near the upper left corner. Grunting, he applied pressure, and the lid moved upward a small but perceptible amount. He did the same thing only a little to the right, then continued along the entire edge, moving around the first corner and then the second before the top was raised enough that, with Hank's and Kyle's help, it was able to be pried all the way off.

"Jesus," Kyle said.

For inside, crouched in the middle of the crate, was a small child, a boy dressed in raggedy old-fashioned clothes. He stood when the lid came off. He could not have been more than five or six, a malnourished five or six, but he managed to leap up and out of the box, landing on the floor in front of Jen, Anita and Nick.

Jen gasped, backing away.

Anita instinctively grabbed Nick's hand.

He was just a boy, but his skin was wrinkled and wizened, and as small as he was, he appeared frighteningly old. He looked from one of them to another with rheumy eyes.

"Holy fuck," Hank said.

"*Sometimes the god of money demands terrible sacrifices,*" the sheriff whispered.

"What's that?" Kyle asked.

Brad shook his head. "Something I heard recently."

They all stood staring at the child, and it was Anita who spoke first, letting go of Nick's hand and approaching cautiously. "What is your name?" she asked kindly.

"Theo."

His voice was little more than a sandpapery whisper, and he cleared his throat before and after saying his name, as though he had not spoken in a long while, which, Kyle supposed, he hadn't.

"How long have you been in that box, Theo?" the sheriff asked, taking over.

"A long time." His eyes became slightly sharper. "Where is my bank? What street is it on?"

They all exchanged glances.

"Are Mr. Pickering and Mr. Worthington there?"

"The First People's Bank?" the sheriff said.

"It is *my* bank," the boy told them. "They stole it from me."

None of them seemed to know what to say. There were so many questions, Kyle thought. How *old* was this kid? How could First People's be *his* bank? Why had he been shoved in a box and kept here in this locked room? And how was he even alive? He said he had been in that box a long time, which Kyle took to mean a *long* time, and that meant that he had somehow survived without food or water.

What was he?

That was the big question, and Kyle wondered if they would be able to get an answer to that.

The boy cleared his throat. "How many banks?" he asked. "How many banks are there?"

It was disconcerting enough just to hear that rough whispery voice, but to have it emerge from the mouth of an archaically garbed child with an old man's head was truly disturbing, and Kyle saw Nick moving reflexively back toward the doorway.

"There are three branches in town," the sheriff said. He was treating the boy as an equal, and that seemed to be an effective approach, since it kept him talking.

"Where is the first bank?"

"Next to my bookstore," Kyle offered.

The boy—*Theo*—looked directly at him for the first time. He saw no evidence of anything childlike in those eyes, only great age and the knowledge of something terrible. "Will you take me there?"

"Do you want to press charges?" Hank asked. "Kidnapping?"

The deputy was operating on a different, more prosaic wavelength, but his boss knew that what was happening here was so far out of the ordinary that the only way to get to the bottom of it was to follow this thread to the end. "We'll take you there," he said. His eyes met Kyle's but he was speaking to all of them. "There's no need for you to come. You can go home."

"I'm coming," Kyle said.

Anita and Jen were nodding. Only Nick seemed unsure, but before Kyle could ask what he wanted to do, his son said, "Let's go."

Theo was remarkably spry. Just as he had leapt from the crate, he now bounded down the hallway in front of the sheriff. The rest of them, more than a little uneasy, remained further behind. Outside, the boy blinked in the sunlight. He seemed surprised to find himself where he was.

"Over here," the sheriff said.

He and Hank got into the patrol car with Theo, while the rest of them got into the Optima. The sheriff put on his siren, Kyle following through town in his wake. Both vehicles double parked in front of the bank.

Brad must have called for help on the way over, because, from the opposite end of the street, two more sheriff's cars came speeding up, parking across the street and blocking Main to through traffic as Kyle, Anita, Nick and Jen stepped out of the car.

Kyle had no idea what, if anything, the child had said on the trip downtown, but Theo and the sheriff walked two abreast to the front door of the bank. The sheriff held the door open, letting the boy go in first. Hank followed, the rest of them close behind. The newly arrived deputies hurried to catch up.

With so many law enforcement officers coming through the door, it must have looked like a raid, and Kyle noticed the surprised and worried looks on the faces of several customers. The employees gave no indication that anything unusual was happening.

At first.

But then, from one of the desks, Mr. Worthington stood, staring at them in shock. "Julius!" he yelled. There was a tinge of panic in his voice.

Pickering emerged from his office, hurrying over. He visibly blanched when he saw the boy. "Mr. Gianopuolos."

"I thought we were still in Georgia."

Worthington and Pickering looked at each other. Kyle saw with not a small degree of satisfaction that they were both frightened.

"How long ago was Georgia?" the boy asked. "How many banks ago?"

He did not wait for an answer but strode toward the wall on the left side of the room that the bank shared with Brave New World. With his authoritative air and the deference he was shown, Theo might have been an adult, a little person, but it was clear that he was not. He was a child. That knowledge had never been in question, and for the first time Kyle wondered why.

Theo was striding directly over to the antique European-looking cabinet against the wall, the one that corresponded to the site where Kyle had heard tapping. And whispering. The framed photograph on the wall above the cabinet, he noticed now, looked a little bit like Theo. It wasn't him, but it could have been a relative. His father, perhaps. They both had similarly swarthy skin and slightly foreign features.

"Kyle."

Above the ambient bank noise, he heard the familiar whisper, his name spoken far more loudly than usual, and he could tell from the look on everyone else's face that they'd heard it, too. But when the whisper came again, and he saw his son's expression, he had a sudden intuition and asked, "What did that voice say?"

Nick was pale. "My name."

They'd all heard their own names.

The boy had reached the cabinet, and without preamble, he opened it, pulling off its single shelf a small primitive statuette the approximate size of a half-gallon milk carton. It was a hideous figure, a homemade object constructed from animal fur, moldy cloth and household debris. The head, perched atop a spindly neck, was far too large for the body and was crowned with jagged triangular pieces of metal. There were two legs and three arms, all of them rubbery and wiggly. The form was instinctually abhorrent to him, and next to him Jen stammered fearfully, "That's what I dreamed about."

Nick looked haunted. "It's the shadow," he breathed. "The one in our house. I saw it in the library at school, too."

What can that mean? Kyle wondered.

Holding it aloft, Theo turned to face them.

"No!" Mr. Worthington sprang forward as if to grab the figure out of the boy's hands, but Hank blocked the man, shoving him roughly to the side.

"Don't even think about it," the deputy warned.

"What is that thing?" the sheriff asked. His voice was unexpectedly subdued.

The aged child spoke in his unnerving sandpapery voice, talking to all of them, to no one, to himself. Kyle noticed for the first time that he had a trace of an accent. "He would not give my father the money, the fat banker. He had plenty but we were immigrants. He put us out on the street, and I prayed. I prayed for help, I prayed for revenge. I *prayed*. And the god appeared to me, and I made a statue of it, and I kept praying, and it granted my wish. I wanted to help people like my father. *They* wanted to…" He trailed off, turned toward Worthington and Pickering, an expression of hatred on his face.

"We only—" Pickering began.

The wizened boy lifted the idol and smashed it on the ground. There was a…*flash*, only it was neither a light nor a sound, more a feeling that shot through the building and everything in it, as though the destruction of the object had released some sort of unseen energy. To Kyle, it felt as though he'd been jolted awake from a sound sleep.

Then it was gone.

In order to make sure the object was completely obliterated, Theo apparently intended to stomp on the remnants of the statue, but he collapsed just as he was raising his leg, falling to the floor at the foot of the cabinet.

Screams were erupting all around. Desks were on fire. Customers were fleeing, but many of the employees were rooted in place, engulfed in flame. Pickering and Worthington no longer existed. Where they had been there were only outlines of bone dust, and though Kyle had not seen it happen, he knew that that *flash* had obliterated them.

"Everybody out!" the sheriff ordered. He picked up Theo's unmoving body. "Issac!" he yelled. "Radio the fire department! Hank! You and the others help the injured out of here! Now!"

If the bank burned, the whole block would probably burn. Or, at the very least, his store and Trixie's would. There was no way the fire department could arrive in time to save their businesses, not at the rate the blaze was spreading.

But the fire did not actually spread. In fact, Kyle was not sure it was even a fire. Because he felt no heat, and as the cold flames engulfed individuals or objects or areas of the bank, those people, places and things disappeared, replaced by emptiness. Grabbing Anita, who was holding tight to Jen's hand, and pushing Nick in front of him, Kyle fled the building. Outside, the flow of refugees was pushing off the sidewalk out into the street. Sheriff's deputies were helping men and women escape. He saw one of them dragging Gary out, the flesh of his former employee's face half burned away. Gary looked stunned, confused.

Sirens and flashing red lights meant that the fire trucks had arrived, but the street was blocked by sheriff's vehicles, and deputies started scrambling to move their cars out of the way. Kyle glanced fearfully toward Brave New World, but there was no sign of any conflagration encroaching on it. Indeed, there seemed to be few flames left within the darkening windows of the bank. To his left, the sheriff was still holding Theo, the limp form in its archaic clothes looking like little more than an oversized rag doll. Kyle met Brad's eyes, not even needing to speak, and the sheriff shook his head.

The boy was dead.

The street was becoming ever more crowded. Commotion always attracted an audience, and the sirens had led onlookers onto Main. Among the newcomers, Kyle saw Coy Stinson, and he hailed the banker over.

"What the hell happened?" Coy asked.

Kyle was not exactly sure. He described the crate in the locked room and the discovery of the aged boy in the antique clothes who had demanded to be taken to *his* bank, where Pickering and Worthington had called him "Mr. Gianopuolos."

Would it ever be possible to piece together what had really occurred? He thought of the sheriff's quote: "*Sometimes the god of money demands terrible sacrifices.*" From what Kyle could gather, the child had prayed to some sort of god that had enabled him to open a bank, intending to help poor people like his family. Pickering and Worthington had somehow imprisoned him and then used him to open up new banks as they travelled across the country. He tried explaining this to Coy the best he could but realized even as he was talking that it sounded completely ridiculous and made no logical sense.

What the hell did these days?

Still, Coy did not disbelieve.

There were questions Kyle had as well, practical questions about the bank's dissolution, and he asked Coy what was going to happen to all of the people who had accounts with First People's.

"Well, if you continued to bank with Montgomery Community, everything's safe. We might have had a connection to First People's, but we're FDIC insured, and no one's going to lose a dime. I'm not so sure First People's followed all the rules and regulations, but there's no way to know until we get some auditors out. Maybe our business relationship will mean that we're on the hook for some of it, maybe the government will be left holding the bag, maybe those people will be shit out of luck. Hard to say at this point."

"So they could go broke? What happens, then? Will we have our own mini-recession here in Montgomery?"

Coy shrugged. "Uncharted waters."

Lane arrived, pushing his way through the crowd, and Jen ran over to him.

"Do you think we still need a municipal bank?" Anita asked Coy.

"I don't know," he admitted, "but people would probably like a little more transparency and control after all this." He glanced around. "Where is this mysterious boy?" he asked Kyle. "I'd like to see him before something happens and...I can't."

"Better move fast." Kyle pointed to where the sheriff was carrying Theo's body toward a newly arrived ambulance. Thanking him, Coy hurried off.

Through the crowd, Kyle saw Trixie, who waved at him before entering her store. He turned his attention back to the bank. It's front door was open, and everyone was out. He saw no sign of any fire. The bank looked once again like the empty storefront it had been before First People's arrival.

"Come on," he told Anita and Nick. The three of them made their way through the growing throng to Brave New World. Kyle got out his key, opened the door and hurried to turn off the alarm. Nick, to his surprise, took the initiative and flipped on the lights. Through the window, they watched the chaotic scene outside.

"So what happens now?" Nick asked as the fire engine pulled out and the crowd began to disperse. "Are we still going to move?"

"Do you want to move?"

He shifted his feet. "I don't know."

"I'm still unemployed," Anita pointed out. "I'm not even sure I *will* be able to find a job in town. And the bookstore's not exactly thriving."

"But it's still open."

"So...what?" she said. "We stay here until you go out of business?"

"For now, I guess. We'll see what happens."

"We just keep on?" Nick asked. "Like we are?"

"Yes, we do." Kyle smiled at him. "That's life," he said.

EPILOGUE

THEY HAD ENTERED the bank with high hopes. His daddy had filled out all of the paperwork and for the past week had been practicing his pitch in front of the mirror, in front of Rayshon and in front of his buddies at work. He'd tried to practice in front of Momma, but she just said he was being foolish and to knock it off. No bank was going to give his black ass a dime.

"That just shows how much she knows," Daddy said, winking and elbowing Rayshon.

But immediately after entering the bank, Rayshon decided that Momma was probably right. He saw it in the looks they got from the well-dressed women behind the teller windows and the business-suited men at the desks. Daddy had not even put on a tie— did he *own* a tie?—and Rayshon was embarrassed by his father's shabby dress.

And his own.

He was not the one asking for a loan, but he was part of the presentation, and he should have worn nicer clothes as well. Instead, he had on his regular torn jeans and faded Bulls t-shirt. But maybe that was part of Daddy's plan. Maybe he wanted them to look like they *needed* the money.

Inside a gleaming modern office with windows that went all the way up to the ceiling, they met with an old white man who shook their hands while wearing an expression that said he was going to wash his hands as soon as they were out of sight. Reading over the papers Daddy had filled out, and glancing periodically at the computer monitor on the desk in front of him, he said, "I believe we have everything we need here. Is there anything else you think I should know?"

It was time for the pitch, and Daddy was ready. "What our community needs," he told the banker, "is a place where kids, kids like my son here, can spend time safe and supervised, where they can do their homework or socialize without fear."

The white man looked bored. "There are plenty of afterschool programs. Schools have them, churches have them, the Boys and Girls Clubs have them. And they're not exactly moneymakers."

"But our neighborhood *doesn't* have one," his dad emphasized. "And making money isn't the point. Kids need—"

The man laughed. A sick, sickening sound that reminded Rayshon of a smoker's cough. "Making money isn't the point? It's *exactly* the point! We're a bank, not a charity." His mouth was smiling but his eyes were not. "Look, Mr. Washington, you seem like a nice guy, but you're just not a businessman, and our institution only provides loans to *businesses*. Now I thank you for coming in, but I don't have any more time to waste on this—"

"*Waste?*" Daddy said, and Rayshon knew at that moment that if there had ever been a chance to get funding for the afterschool program from the bank, that chance was gone.

The white man stood. "Good day, sir." He nodded at someone behind them, and a security guard Rayshon had not realized was there stepped forward, ready to escort them out.

Anger and humiliation were battling within his daddy, and Rayshon would not know which one won until they were alone. They were walked back through the bank like criminals, and though the door was opened for them, it was not a sign of respect. It was to let them know they did not belong here.

When he grew up, Rayshon decided, he would run his own bank. He would never let a thing like this happen. He would help people, not hurt them, and if there was a good idea, he would give money for it no matter where the idea came from.

And a small voice in his head, a voice that was not his own, told him to pray for that.